TAMERA ALEXANDER

→ FOUNTAIN CREEK CHRONICLES | BOOK ONE ←

REKINDLED

DOUBLEDAY LARGE PRINT HOME LIBRARY EDITION

BETHANY HOUSE PUBLISHERS

Minneapolis, Minnesota

This Large Print Edition, prepared especially for Doubleday Large Print Home Library, contains the complete, unabridged text of the original Publisher's Edition.

Rekindled
Copyright © 2006
Tamera Alexander

Cover design by studiogearbox.com

Published by Bethany House Publishers
11400 Hampshire Avenue South
Bloomington, Minnesota 55438

Bethany House Publishers is a division of
Baker Publishing Group, Grand Rapids, Michigan.

Printed in the United States of America

ISBN-13: 978-0-7394-7024-4
ISBN-10: 0-7394-7024-8

This Large Print Book carries the
Seal of Approval of N.A.V.H.

DEDICATION

To my parents, Doug and June Gattis
Growing up beneath the shelter of your love
shaped me for eternity, and I'm forever grateful.
That love spilled over into me and gave me wings.
It still does. Thank you for continually pointing
me to the Cross and for being "Jesus with skin"
in my life.

To my mother-in-law, Claudette Harris Alexander
You first started me on this writing journey by
sharing with me just how *softly His love comes.*
I trust you can now see where your gift has led
me. We miss you every day. Scout out the best
hiking trails. We'll be Home soon.

Do not consider his appearance or his height,
for I have rejected him.
The Lord does not look at the things man looks at.
Man looks at the outward appearance,
but the Lord looks at the heart.

1 SAMUEL 16:7 NIV

Colorado Territory, 1868
In the shadow of Pikes Peak

Larson Jennings had lived this moment a thousand times over, and it still sent a chill through him. Shifting in the saddle, he stared ahead at the winding trail of dirt and rock that had been the haunt and haven of his dreams, both waking and sleeping, for the past five months. Along with his anticipation at returning home, there mingled a foreboding that crowded out any sense of festivity.

He carefully tugged off the leather gloves and looked at his misshapen hands. Gently flexing his fingers, he winced at the unpleasant sensation shooting up his right arm. The skin was nearly healed but was

stretched taut over the back of
much like it was over half of h
Scenes from that fateful night flashed
in his mind. Blinding white light, unbear
heat.

He closed his eyes. His breath quick
ened, his flesh tingled, remembering. He
may have denied death its victory, but death
had certainly claimed a bit of him in the
struggle.

What would Kathryn's reaction be at seeing him like this? And what had the past
months been like for her, not knowing where
he was? To think she might have already
given him up for dead touched on a wound
so deep inside him, Larson couldn't bear to
give the thought further lead. Kathryn would
be there. . . . *She would.*

Maybe if he'd been a better husband to
her, a better provider, or perhaps if he had
been able to give her what she truly wanted,
he'd feel differently about coming back. But
their inability to have a child had carved a
canyon between them years ago, and the
truth of their marriage was as undeniable to
him as the scars marring his body. And the
fault of it rested mostly with him—he knew
that now.

He rode on past the grove of aspen that skirted the north boundary of their property, then crossed at a shallow point in Fountain Creek. Distant memories, happier memories, tugged at the edge of his misgivings, and Larson welcomed them. Kathryn had been twenty years old when he'd first brought her to this territory. Their journey from Boston had been hard, but she'd never complained. Not once. He'd sensed her silent fear expanding with each distancing mile. He remembered a particular night they'd spent together inside the wagon during a storm. Wind and rain had slashed across the prairie in torrents, and though a quiver had layered her voice, Kathryn swore to be enjoying the adventure. As they lay together through the night, he'd loved her and sworn to protect and care for her. And he still intended to keep that promise—however modest their reality might have turned out in comparison to his dreams.

Kathryn meant more to him than anything now. She was more than his wife, his lover. She completed him, in areas he'd never known he was lacking. He regretted that it had taken an intimate brush with death for him to see the truth. Now if he could only help her see past the outside, to the man he'd become.

His pulse picked up a notch when he rounded the bend and the familiar scene came into view. Nestled in stands of newly leafed aspen and willow trees, crouched in the shadow of the rugged mountains that would always be his home, the scenery around their cabin still took his breath away.

Larson's stomach clenched tight as he watched for movement from the homestead. As he rode closer, a breeze swept down from the mountain, whistling through the branches overhead. The door to the cabin creaked open. His eyes shot up. A rush of adrenaline caused every nerve to tingle.

"Kathryn?" he rasped, his voice resembling a music box whose innards had been scraped and charred.

He eased off his horse and glanced back at the barn. Eerily quiet.

It took him a minute to gain his balance and get the feeling back in his limbs. His right leg ached, and he was tempted to reach for his staff tied to his saddle, but he resisted, not wanting Kathryn's first imag of him to be that of a cripple. Vulnerability flooded his heart, erasing all pleas but one.

God, let her still want me.

He gently pushed open the cabin door and stepped inside. "Kathryn?"

He scanned the room. Deserted. The door to their bedroom was closed, and he crossed the room and jerked the latch free. The room was empty but for the bed they'd shared. Scenes flashed in his mind of being here with Kathryn that last night. Disbelief and concern churned his gut.

He searched the barn, calling her name, but his voice was lost in the wind stirring among the trees. Chest heaving, he ignored the pain and swung back up on his mount.

Later that afternoon, exhausted from the hard ride back to Willow Springs, Larson urged his horse down a less crowded side street, wishing now that he'd chosen to search for Kathryn here first. But he'd held out such hope that she'd been able to keep the ranch. He gave his horse the lead and searched the places he thought Kathryn might be. Nearing the edge of town, he reined in his thoughts as his gaze went to a small gathering beside the church.

Two men worked together to lower a coffin suspended by ropes into a hole in the ground. Three other people looked on in silence—a woman dressed all in black and two men beside her. Watching the sparse gathering as he passed, Larson suddenly felt sorry for the departed soul and wondered what kind of life the person had led that would draw so few well-wishers. Then the woman turned her head to speak to one of the men beside her. It couldn't be . . .

A stab of pain in his chest sucked Larson's breath away.

Kathryn.

He dismounted and started to go to her, but something held him back.

Kathryn walked to the pile of loose dirt and scooped up a handful. She stepped forward and, hesitating for a moment, finally let it sift through her fingers. Larson was close enough to hear the hollow sound of dirt and pebbles striking the coffin below. He was certain he saw her shudder. Her movements were slow and deliberate.

She looked different to him somehow, but still, he drank her in. He felt the scattered pieces of his life coming back together.

His thoughts raced to imagine who could be inside that coffin. He swiftly settled on one. Bradley Duncan. He remembered the afternoon he'd found the young man at the cabin visiting Kathryn. Despite past months of pleading with God to quell his jealous nature and for the chance to make things right with his wife, a bitter spark rekindled deep inside him.

Larson bowed his head. Would he ever possess the strength to put aside his old nature? At that moment, Kathryn turned toward him, and he knew the answer was no.

He didn't want to believe it. He knew his wife's body as well as his own, from vivid memory as well as from his dreams, and the gentle bulge beneath her skirts left little question in his mind. Larson's legs felt like they might buckle beneath him.

Matthew Taylor, his foreman and supposed friend, stood close beside Kathryn. Taylor slipped an arm around her shoulders and drew her close. Liquid fire shot through Larson's veins. He'd trusted Matthew Taylor with the two most important things in the world to him—his ranch and his wife. It would seem that Taylor had failed him on both counts. And in the process, had given Kathryn what Larson never could.

With Taylor's hand beneath her arm, Kathryn turned away from the grave. He whispered something to her. She smiled back, and Larson's heart turned to stone. They walked past him as though he weren't there. He suddenly felt invisible, and for the first time in his life, he wasn't bothered by the complete lack of recognition. Defeat and fury warred inside him as he watched Kathryn and Taylor walk back toward town.

When the preacher had returned to the church and the cemetery workers finished their task and left, Larson walked to the edge of the grave. He took in the makeshift headstone, then felt the air squeeze from his lungs. Reading the name carved into the splintered piece of old wood sent him to his knees. His world shifted full tilt.

Just below the dates 1828–1868 was the name—

LARSON ROBERT JENNINGS

CHAPTER ONE

Five months earlier
December 24, 1867

Larson Jennings peered inside the frosted window of the snow-drifted cabin. Sleet and snow pelted his face, but he was oblivious to winter's biting chill. A slow-burning heat started in his belly and his hot breath fogged the icy pane as he watched the two of them together.

His wife's smile, her laughter, wholly focused on another man, ignited a painful memory and acted like a knife to his heart. It was all he could do not to break down the door when he entered the cabin.

Kathryn stood immediately, stark surprise shadowing her brown eyes. "Larson, I'm so glad you're home." But her look conveyed something altogether different. down her cup and moved away fr seat next to Bradley Duncan at the kr table. "Bradley's home from university dropped by . . . unexpectedly." Lowerir. her gaze, she added more softly, "To talk. . . ."

Bradley Duncan came to his feet, nearly knocking over his cup. Larson turned and glared down at the smooth-faced, educated boy, not really a man yet, even at twenty-three. Not in Larson's estimation anyway. Larson stood at least a half-foot taller and held a sixty-pound, lean-muscled advantage. He despised weakness, and Duncan exuded it. Having learned from a young age to use his stature to intimidate, Larson was tempted now to simply break this kid in two.

He turned to examine Kathryn's face for a hint of deceit. Her guarded expression didn't lessen his anger. Trusting had never been easy for him, and when it came to his wife and other men, he found it especially hard. He'd seen the way men openly admired her and could well imagine the thoughts lingering beneath the surface.

"Mr. J-Jennings." Duncan's eyes darted to Kathryn and then back again. "I just ped by to share these books with thryn. I purchased them in Boston."

Larson didn't like the sound of his wife's name on this boy's lips.

"I thought she might enjoy reading them. She loves to read, you know," Duncan added, as though Larson didn't know his wife of ten years. "Books don't come cheaply. And with your ranch not faring too well these days, I thought . . ."

Almost imperceptibly, Kathryn's expression changed. Duncan fell silent. Larson felt a silent warning pass from his wife to the boy now shifting from foot to foot before him.

The rage inside him exploded. A solid blow to Duncan's jaw sent the boy reeling backward.

Kathryn gasped, her face drained of color. "Larson—"

His look silenced her. He hauled Duncan up by his starched collar and silk vest and dragged him to his fancy mount tied outside. Once Duncan was astride, Larson smacked the Thoroughbred on the rump nd it took off.

Kathryn waited at the door, her shawl hed about her shoulders, her eyes dark with disapproval. "Larson, you had no right to act in such a manner. Bradley Duncan is a boy, and an honorable one at that."

Larson slammed the door behind him. "I saw the way he looked at you."

She gave a disbelieving laugh. "Bradley thinks of me as an older sister."

Larson moved to within inches of her and stared down hard. She stiffened, but to her credit she didn't draw back. She never had. "I don't have siblings, Kathryn, but take it from me, that's not the way a man looks at his sister."

Kathryn sighed, and a knowing look softened her expression. "Larson, I have never looked at another man since I met you. Ever," she whispered, slowly lifting a hand to his cheek. Her eyes shimmered. "The life I chose is still the life I want. What other men think is of no concern to me. I want you, only you. When will you take that to heart?"

He wanted to brush away her hand, but the feelings she stirred inside him were more powerful than his need to be in control. He pulled her against him and kissed her, wanting to believe her when she

she didn't ever want for another man, another life.

"I love you," she whispered against his mouth.

He drew back and looked into her eyes, wishing he could answer. But he couldn't. Something deep inside him was locked tight. He didn't even know what it was, really, but he'd learned young that it was safer to keep it hidden, tucked away.

A smile touched Kathryn's lips, as though she were able to read his thoughts.

Larson pulled her to him and kissed her again, more gently this time, and a soft sigh rose from her throat. Kathryn possessed a hold over him that frightened him at times. He wondered if she even knew. She deserved so much more than what he'd given her. He should be the one buying her books and things—not some half-smitten youth. He wanted to surround Kathryn with wealth that equaled that of her Boston upbringing and to see pride in her eyes when she looked at him.

A look he hadn't seen in a long, long time.

The familiar taste of failure suddenly tinged his wife's sweetness, and Larson loosened his embrace. He carefully unbraided his fingers from her thick blond hair. Her eyes were still closed, her breathing staggered. Her cheeks were flushed.

He gently traced her lips with his thumb. Despite ten years spent carving out a life in this rugged territory, her beauty had only deepened. No wonder he caught ranch hands staring.

She slowly opened her eyes, and he searched their depths.

Kathryn said she'd never wanted another man, that she was satisfied with their meager life. And the way she responded to him and looked at him now almost made him believe his suspicions were unfounded. But there was one thing that Kathryn wanted with all her heart, something he hadn't been able to give her. No matter how he'd tried and prayed, his efforts to satisfy her desire for a child had proven fruitless.

In that moment something inside him, a presence dark and familiar, goaded his feelings of inadequacy. He heeded the inaudible voice, and flints of doubt ignited within him. It wouldn't be the first time Kathryn had lied.

He set her back from him and turned.

"I've got work to do in the barn. I'll be back in a while."

Preferring the familiar bite of Colorado Territory's December to the wounded disappointment he saw in his wife's eyes, Larson slammed the door behind him.

Kathryn Jennings stared at the door, its jarring shudder reverberating in her chest. It was a sound she was used to hearing from her husband, in so many ways. Though Larson's emotional withdrawal never took her by surprise anymore, it always took a tiny piece of her heart. She pressed a hand to her mouth, thinking of his kiss.

Shutting her eyes briefly, she wished—not for the first time—that Larson would desire *her*—the whole of who she was—as much as he desired her affection. Would there ever come a time when he would let her inside? When he would fully share whatever tormented him, the demons he wrestled with in his sleep?

She looked down at her hands clasped tightly at her waist. Many a night she'd held him as he was half asleep, half crazed. As he moaned in guttural whispers about his mother long dead and buried.

But not forgotten, nor forgiven.

Knowing he would be back soon and anticipating his mood, Kathryn set about finishing dinner. She added a dollop of butter to the potatoes, basted the ham, and let the pages of her memory flutter back to happier days—to the first day she saw Larson. Even then, she'd sensed a part of him that was hidden, locked away. Being young and idealistic, though, she considered his brooding sullenness an intrigue and felt certain she held the key to unlocking its mysteries. Time had eroded that certainty.

She drew two china plates from the dining hutch, ones she used only on the most special occasions. Though their cabin lay draped in winter at the foot of the Rocky Mountains, miles from their nearest neighbors and half a day's ride to the town of Willow Springs, she managed to keep track of the holidays. And this was the most special.

A half hour later, they sat across from one another at the table, hardly touching the carefully prepared meal, and with not a hint of the festive mood Kathryn had hoped for that morning.

"What did you tell Duncan this afternoon?" Larson broke the silence, his voice oddly quiet.

Kathryn looked up, her frown an unspoken question.

He studied her for a moment, then turned his attention back to his plate. "Did you tell him about the ranch?"

She shook her head and swallowed, only then gaining his meaning. "No, I didn't," she said softly, knowing her answer would hurt him. No doubt Duncan had heard from others, which meant things must be worse than she thought.

Larson pushed his chair back from the table and stood. An unseen weight pressed down on his broad shoulders, giving him an older appearance. "I'll sell some of the horses in order to see us through. And if we make it to market this spring, if winter holds steady, we should make it another year."

Kathryn nodded and looked away, sobered by the news. Feeling her husband's eyes on her, she looked back and smiled, hoping it appeared genuine. "I know we'll be fine."

Larson walked to the door and shrugged into his coat. Hand on the latch, he didn't look back when he spoke. "Dinner was good tonight, Kathryn. Real good." He sighed. "I've got some work to do. You go on to bed."

She cleared the table and washed the dishes. Drying off the china plates, she ran a finger around the gold-rimmed edge. A present from her mother four years back. Only two had arrived unbroken. But they were the last gift Elizabeth Cummings had given her before she died, and knowing her mother had touched this very dish made Kathryn feel a bit closer to her somehow. Her mind went to the two letters she'd written her father since her mother's passing. Though the letters hadn't been returned unopened, neither had William Cummings answered. His apparent disinterest in her life—though not new to Kathryn—still tore at old wounds.

Refusing to dwell on what she couldn't change, Kathryn slipped the plates back into the hutch. Her hand hit against a small wooden crate wedged carefully in the back, and a muffled chime sounded from within, followed by another single stuttered tone. Glancing over her shoulder to the door, she pulled the small box from its hiding place.

Kathryn opened the lid and, thinking of

what lay within, a warm reminiscence shivered up her spine. A smile curved her mouth despite the caution edging her anticipation. It had been months since she'd allowed herself to take it out, though she'd thought about it countless times in recent weeks. Especially with the harsh winter they were having. What would happen if the rest of the winter was equally cruel?

A lone wrapped item lay nestled within the box. She carefully began unfolding the crumpled edges of a *Boston Herald* social page dated December 24, 1857. The irony of the date on the newspaper made her smile again. Exactly ten years had blurred past since she'd fled the confines of her youth for a new, more promising life with the man who'd captured her heart.

And who held it still, despite how different life was from how she'd imagined.

She lifted the music box from the paper and ran her fingers over the smooth lacquered finish. It was the last birthday music box she'd received from her parents and her favorite. The one commemorating her seventeenth birthday. Each had been diminutive in size and exquisite in design and melody. Six years ago she'd parted with all of them, save this one.

She glanced behind her to the frost-crusted window half obscured by snow, then back to the box in her hands. Sometimes she missed the sheltered world of affluence. Not that she would trade her life with Larson. She only wished their ranch had been more successful. For his sake as well as hers.

Gently turning the key on the bottom, she took care not to overwind it. Lifting the lid, her breath caught at the familiar melody. Crafted of polished mahogany and inlaid with gold leaf, this was by far the most beautiful of the collection and worth more than all the others. It would bring a handsome sum.

Kathryn felt a check in her spirit at the thought, but gently pushed it aside. She believed in her husband's dream as much as he did and would do everything in her power to help him succeed. But if they ran into hard times again, at least they had some security to fall back on.

Lost in the lilting melody, she stood and walked closer to the lamp on the fireplace mantel. She held the box at an angle to the

light so she could read the familiar inscription engraved on the gold underside of the
lid. Tilting it up, she could almost read the
words. . . .

A sudden movement caught her eye and
she turned.

Larson stood close behind her, hurt and
doubt darkening his face. "Planning on selling that one too?"

Heart pounding, she rushed to explain. "I
wasn't planning on selling it. I was only—"

Kathryn felt the music box slip from her
hands. She grabbed for it but couldn't gain
a hold. A cry threaded her lips as the box
splintered into pieces on the wooden floor.
A staccato of clangs and dissonant tings
sounded as the intricate musical workings
scattered beneath the table and hutch as
though seeking safe refuge.

Her throat closed tight and she found it
hard to breathe. How could she have been
so foolish? Hot tears trailed down her
cheeks.

"You bartered the other ones," he said,
accusation edging his tone. "I bet you
could've gotten a good price for this one
too." His voice sloped to a whisper then,

and his eyes glazed with unexpected emotion.

Speaking past the hurt in her throat, she looked up at him. "I was happy to sell those."

"And that's why you kept it from me?"

"I didn't tell you at first because I didn't want you to think that—"

"That I couldn't provide for my own wife? That I'm not capable of giving you the things you need? The things you want?"

The look he gave her cut to the heart, and Kathryn realized, again, what a costly mistake she'd made in not being honest with him from the start. They'd never spoken of it since that day, but that well-intentioned deception had tentacled itself around their marriage.

She blinked against a blur of tears as her memory rippled back in time. "Half our herd died that winter. We needed money for food, for supplies." She reached out to touch his chest.

He caught hold of her wrist and took a step closer, his face inches from hers. "I would've gotten the money somehow, Kathryn. I'm capable of taking care of you."

"I've never questioned that." But her

words sounded hollow and unconvincing, even to her. Were her misgivings written so clearly in her eyes?

A knowing look moved over Larson's face. "Exactly how long *was* Duncan here this afternoon?"

Kathryn frowned and searched the blue eyes glinting now like tempered steel. He couldn't have hurt her more if he'd struck her across the face. Her voice came out a whisper. "What are you asking me?"

"Did you let him touch you?"

She stared, unbelieving. Part of her wanted to laugh at the absurdity of his accusation, while the rest of her knew why he asked, and it tore at her heart. "Have we been together so long . . . and still you don't know?"

The accusation in his eyes lessened, but the set of his jaw stayed rigid.

"I am your wife, Larson Jennings. I pledged myself, *all* of myself to you. I am a woman of my word, and—"

His focus raked to the shattered box strewn across the floor. When he looked at her again, the question in his eyes was clear. His grip tightened around her wrist but not enough to hurt.

Kathryn could clearly see the comparison he was drawing in his mind. She'd faced it before and weariness moved through her at its recurring theme. Would they ever move past this?

"Larson, I am not like your mother. I am not a woman who would give herself to men for their pleasure." She intentionally softened her tone. "I've given myself to only one man . . . to you. And I will never share that part of myself with another man. Not ever."

He didn't answer immediately but let her wrist slip free. "How can I be certain of that?"

Nestled in his question Kathryn heard the echoing cry of a young boy, and she swallowed hard at the answer forming in her throat, realizing it applied as much to her as it did to him. She offered up a prayer that God would somehow teach both of their stubborn hearts. That he would lead Larson past the seeds of faithlessness bred in his youth, and for herself . . .

She looked down at the broken shards of wood and glass and searched her heart. All she'd ever wanted was to be one with her husband in every way. Was she at fault for that? She felt an answer stirring inside her.

It was almost within her grasp. But then it slipped away, like a whisper on the wind.

She steadied her voice. "The answer lies in trust, Larson. You're going to have to learn to trust me."

One side of his mouth tipped in a smile, but it felt more like a challenge. "And does that trust go both ways, Kathryn?"

Again, she felt that same tug in her spirit. "Yes, it does. It goes both ways."

She thought she'd been the one in this marriage to have already opened her heart fully. But she'd been wrong. She hadn't surrendered everything, not yet.

Later that night as they readied for bed, Kathryn felt Larson watching her. Despite the wall of silence between them, she felt a blush sweep through her at his close attention.

The air in the cabin was chilly. She quickly shed her clothes and put on her gown, then slid between the icy sheets. She pulled the layers of covers up to her chin, shivering, and anticipated Larson's warmth beside her. When no movement sounded from his side of the bedroom, she turned back.

He stood watching her. A single lamp on the dresser cast only a flickering orange glow in the darkness, but it was enough for her to recognize the look in her husband's eyes. He opened his mouth as if to say something, then looked away.

Larson moved the lamp to the nightstand and stripped off his shirt. Kathryn knew the lines of her husband's face, was familiar with his physique. She knew all of this and yet so little of the man beneath the exterior.

She had been attracted to him from the start. Everything about him had spoken of determination and dreams, and a passion that ran so deep she feared she might drown in it. When first seeing Larson clad in leather, his brown hair brushing his shoulders, her mother had labeled him a mountain man. A ghost of a smile had passed across her mother's features before she hastily masked her reaction. She cautioned Kathryn about the cost of following her heart. William Cummings branded him a rogue, and though not forbidding Kathryn from seeing him again, her father's cool aloofness toward the subject was answer enough. As it had been in most other areas of her life. And that was the final nudge.

Kathryn had stepped closer and closer to the river's edge until it finally swept her away.

As Larson sat on his side of the bed, Kathryn found her gaze drawn to his back. Spaced at random intervals over his muscular back and shoulders were circular bumps of scarred flesh. She always cringed when thinking about the type of person who would inflict such pain on a little boy. Instinctively, she reached out to touch him, willing his deep inward wounds to heal as the outward had done.

Larson flinched at her touch, but didn't turn.

For a moment he stilled, his head bowed, then he leaned over to turn down the lamp. The yellow burnish of the oiled wick dwindled to smoldering, leaving the room shrouded in shadow.

Kathryn shivered against the sudden draft from the rise and fall of the covers when Larson lay down beside her. She half expected him to touch her, but he didn't. Warmth sprang to her eyes. Would it always be this way between them?

They lay side by side, barely touching, tense and silent. The loneliness inside her deepened until she finally turned onto her side, away from him. She laid a hand over her latent womb, wondering if the sacredness of life would ever dwell within that silent, secret place. A full moon gleaming off the fresh layer of snow cast a pale pewter light through the single window of their bedroom. Kathryn stared at the silvery beams until she felt a stirring beside her.

"I'm sorry, Kat."

His deep voice sliced the stillness of the bedroom, and Kathryn closed her eyes, imagining what his whispered admission had cost him and cherishing the sound of the special name he sometimes used for her. A name she hadn't heard in too long.

She slowly turned back over and was met with his profile. He was looking at the ceiling, and she couldn't help but wonder what unearthed treasures lay in the heart of the man beside her. She reached out and ran her fingers through his hair, then along his stubbled jawline. Not once in all the years of knowing him had he worn a full beard. And she'd never wished for it; she loved the strong lines of his face.

When he didn't respond, Kathryn finally turned back and curled onto her side.

After a long moment, Larson gently pulled her against him. The heat from his chest seeped through her nightgown, warming her back. This was his language. He was telling her he loved her without words. Like when he kept ample firewood stacked by the door or made certain her coat and gloves were still winter worthy.

But she longed for more.

Kathryn felt a tightening in her throat and covered his hand over her chest. She nudged closer to him, answering his unspoken question.

When Larson rose up onto his elbow, he waited for her to look at him, then gently cupped her face with his hand. She looked into his eyes and knew that it didn't matter if he ever opened his heart completely to her or not—her heart was already his forever. She had promised before God to love this man, for better or worse, and it was a promise she wanted, and fully intended, to keep. As their breath mingled and he drew her closer, she begged God to help her see and love her husband for who he was, not for who she wanted him to be.

CHAPTER TWO

Larson awakened before light the next morning, his mind in a thick fog. He lay perfectly still and tried to decipher dream from reality. As the haze of sleep lifted, he felt Kathryn shudder close beside him. Then he heard her soft intakes of breath. Her hidden tears tore right through him, yet he found he couldn't move.

Before his mind had faded into exhaustion hours earlier, Kathryn had whispered, *"Merry Christmas, Larson."* Only then had he realized the injury his self-centeredness the evening before had caused.

He wished he could reach over and pull her to him, but the cause of her tears stopped him cold. He strongly doubted whether his holding her would bring the comfort she sought. He thought he'd loved her thoroughly last night, holding her afterward, stroking her hair until her breathing was feather soft against his chest.

He lay there in the stillness until her breathing evened again. Reliving the disappointment he'd seen in her eyes the night before was almost more than he could bear. His thoughts turned to the request he'd received earlier that week. Still tucked inside his coat pocket, the envelope contained an invitation from a company bearing the name of Berklyn Stockholders, Inc. He'd been invited to attend a meeting to be held in Denver three days from now. He hadn't told Kathryn about the business opportunity. No need to build her hopes up only to dash them again. He'd done that often enough in recent years.

From the darkness enveloping the room, Larson guessed that dawn could not be far off. And in that moment, the decision became clear. This new venture could give him the leverage he needed to make his ranch a success. But even more, he would be a success in Kathryn's eyes.

Within minutes, he dressed and slipped noiselessly from the bedroom. He could make Denver in two days tops, even with the snow. He would conduct his business and return.

Not wanting to alarm Kathryn, yet not wanting to give her false hope, Larson scribbled a brief note and left it on the mantel. He made certain the fire in the hearth was stoked and that ample wood was stacked in the bin.

He opened the door and a bitter cold wind hit him hard in his face, nearly taking his breath away. More snow had fallen than he'd expected, and by the time he made a path to the barn and saddled his mount, faint hues of pink and purple tinged the eastern horizon. Larson took one last look at the cabin and pictured his wife inside, cocooned in the warmth of sleep.

As tempting as it was to go back and share it with her, the hope of her renewed admiration and the chance to give her the life she deserved drove him forward.

By noon, Larson reached the outskirts of Willow Springs. Having once boasted the best route to the South Park mining camps, weeks and savored every minute. He endured it and couldn't wait to return home. He liked the solitary life he and Kathryn lived, busy with ranching and working the homestead. He felt uneasy when he was around too many people.

Larson rode through town, passing Flanagan & King Feed and Flour, Faulkner's Dry Goods and Post Office, Speck's Groceries, and the St. James Hotel. A two-story frame building with a sign that read *Tappan General Store* towered over a smaller bakery to its right. Most of the buildings were constructed of logs or hewed wood, but some were fashioned of quarried stone from the nearby hills. He saw the deserted streets and closed shops and, again, his selfishness hit him square in the gut. The snatches of holly and brightly colored red bows affixed to every storefront and lamppost only accentuated his guilt. He should have written something in his note to Kathryn at least acknowledging what day it was. But in his haste and excitement, he'd forgotten.

Doubting any shop would be open on Christmas Day, Larson still found himself scanning the businesses and reading the shingles hanging above the doors. Despite the darkened windows, he had the uncomfortable feeling of being watched, and he'd learned long ago to trust that inner voice. It had saved his life on more than one occasion. Plodding his mount northward, he scanned the town around him.

By the time he reached the white-steepled church perched at the edge of town, he figured fatigue was swaying his instincts—and that his prospects of finding a gift for Kathryn were doomed. Passing by the cemetery, its headstones shrouded in snow, he suddenly remembered the scores of shops in Denver and his spirits lightened. Surely he would find something suitable for Kathryn there.

Travel proved slower than Larson would have liked. By mid-afternoon a steady wind blew hard from the north and the grayish-blue clouds hooding the mountains to the west held the certain promise of more snow. Accustomed to Colorado's winter, he had worn several layers of clothes and was warm enough but knew a fire and shelter would be needed by nightfall.

Topping a gentle rise of land, his gaze was drawn east. He made out what looked to be a wagon, half blanketed in snow, one side tilted precariously toward the ground. Slowing his pace, Larson hesitated, watching for any sign of life.

Then he spotted it. A man crouched waist deep in the drift, shoveling snow from around the wagon. The man must have sensed his presence because he turned at that moment. He straightened and began waving furiously.

An hour later Larson had the wagon dug completely free of the drift and the wheel mended enough to get the old peddler into town. He loaded the cargo back into the bed of the wagon, marveling at the old man's odd collection of mostly junk amid a few nicer furniture items.

The man's eyes were bright and attentive. "Name's Callum Roberts. I'm just movin' to Willow Springs, and if all the folks is as kind as you, I'll be makin' my home there for sure."

Taking hold of Callum Roberts' surprisingly strong grip, Larson offered his name. "I was glad to be of help, sir." Even if he hadn't planned on the delay. He eyed the sun as it touched the tips of the highest peaks, then shingles hanging above the doors. Despite the darkened windows, he had the uncomfortable feeling of being watched, and he'd learned long ago to trust that inner voice. It had saved his life on more than one occasion. Plodding his mount northward, he scanned the town around him.

By the time he reached the white-steepled church perched at the edge of town, he figured fatigue was swaying his instincts—and that his prospects of finding a gift for Kathryn were doomed. Passing by the cemetery, its headstones shrouded in snow, he suddenly remembered the scores of shops in Denver and his spirits lightened. Surely he would find something suitable for Kathryn there.

Travel proved slower than Larson would have liked. By mid-afternoon a steady wind blew hard from the north and the grayish-blue clouds hooding the mountains to the west held the certain promise of more snow. Accustomed to Colorado's winter, he had ʳn several layers of clothes and was ͻ enough but knew a fire and shelter ᵇe needed by nightfall.

ᵍ a gentle rise of land, his gaze east. He made out what looked to be a wagon, half blanketed in snow, one side tilted precariously toward the ground. Slowing his pace, Larson hesitated, watching for any sign of life.

Then he spotted it. A man crouched waist deep in the drift, shoveling snow from around the wagon. The man must have sensed his presence because he turned at that moment. He straightened and began waving furiously.

An hour later Larson had the wagon dug completely free of the drift and the wheel mended enough to get the old peddler into town. He loaded the cargo back into the bed of the wagon, marveling at the old man's odd collection of mostly junk amid a few nicer furniture items.

The man's eyes were bright and attentive. "Name's Callum Roberts. I'm just movin' to Willow Springs, and if all the folks is as kind as you, I'll be makin' my home there for sure."

Taking hold of Callum Roberts' surpr ingly strong grip, Larson offered his nar was glad to be of help, sir." Even if he planned on the delay. He eyed the touched the tips of the highest gauged the bitter wind and knew he needed to make his destination before nightfall.

"I thank you for stoppin' to help me, son." Roberts worked his right shoulder and gave it a rub. "Don't think these old bones coulda stood a night out here."

Larson pointed back to town. "Follow my tracks straight over that rise and then due south for about three miles. You should make Willow Springs a bit after dark. Jake at the livery should be able to help you."

Larson was astride his horse when he looked down to see the ancient hawker rummaging through his wagon bed. Anticipating Roberts' intentions and eager to be on his way, Larson spoke up. "You don't owe me a thing for this. I said I was glad to do it."

Callum Roberts kept digging through the piles of wooden crates. "Are you married, son?" he asked over his shoulder. "I have some mighty fine personal items for the little woman." He pulled out an ornate brush and mirror set that looked anything but new, much less clean.

"Really. I don't need anything." Larson shook his head. Then he stopped and reconsidered his statement. On the off chance

Roberts did have something of value, Larson much preferred to pay him rather than a mercantile in Denver. The old codger could obviously use it.

Roberts turned, and a smile lit his face as he handed something up to Larson. "Now this, this is something worthy of the kindness you've shown me."

Larson almost hated to look inside the small burlap-wrapped package. Seeing the excitement in the old peddler's eyes, he determined that whatever it was, he would purchase it. Larson pulled back the burlap and felt a jolt run through him at seeing the metal box, hardly big enough to fill his gloved hand. He ran his thumb over the smooth top and around the edges. Larson sensed the man's curious stare and looked down at him.

"It's a music box, son. Made it myself. Well, most of it anyhow. When I got the thing it wouldn't even play. But I fixed it all up. Now it plays a Christmas tune. Here, let me show you." He took the box and wound a simple key on the side. "And see in here." Roberts tilted the box up. "I left a place where you can put your own words inside, where you can make it your own."

Larson couldn't help but smile when the music box started playing a familiar Christmas melody. But it was the man's enjoyment that deepened his grin. "I'll take it, sir. And my wife will be all the more pleased when I tell her how I came by it."

Roberts fairly leapt with pleasure. He refused the money Larson held out to him, but finally took it at Larson's insistence. Larson tucked the box inside his coat pocket and waited for the man to climb up before he started off in the opposite direction.

With each minute, the sun dipped lower behind the mountains, taking its scant warmth with it. After an hour of riding farther north, Larson topped a hill and spotted the vague outline of what he'd been watching for.

Ahead was a thin ridge of land extending eastward from the mighty Rockies. Jutting upward from the prairie, the ridge resembled an arthritic finger, twisted and bent. On the southern side of the crest was a sparse outcropping of scrub oak and boulders. Larson had camped there before. It would serve well to shelter him through the night.

Darkness had descended by the time he reached the ridge. The moon's silvery sheen reflected off the snow and provided enough light for him to make out his surroundings. He soon had a fire crackling and a parcel of earth cleared of snow where he could bed down for the night. Jerky and tack biscuits filled his belly. Coffee warmed his insides, even if it wasn't as good as Kathryn's.

He imagined what she was doing right then and wondered if she was thinking of him.

Reminded of the music box, he took it from his coat pocket and examined it more closely. It didn't begin to compare with any in the collection Kathryn once had. Regret over yesterday passed through him again. The look of loss on her face when the box had shattered into pieces haunted him.

Simple as it was, this box—in his estimation anyway—possessed a quality the others had lacked. It spoke of something more lasting. Something beyond what money could buy.

He laughed out loud at the thought, and the sound of his laughter surprised him. Here he was, setting out for a business opportunity he hoped would bring him wealth, and he'd bought Kathryn something that bespoke the opposite.

As he turned the box over in his hands, the lid fell open. He looked at the scratched and tarnished metal plate that Roberts had affixed inside. What had the old guy said this was for? He nodded, remembering. *"Where you can make it your own."*

An idea struck him. Larson pulled his knife from his boot and moved closer to the fire. He situated the music box on a rock and pressed the tip of his knife into the plate. He smiled when it made a slight indention. Not the highest quality of metal, but that served his purpose at the moment.

Larson lost track of time as he knelt by the fire, making the gift his own. Making it Kathryn's. He hoped she would be pleased and felt somehow that she might be. Even if the value of this gift wasn't as impressive as his gifts one day would be, Kathryn had a soft spot for the elderly and would be pleased that he'd stopped to help the newcomer.

When he finished, he put his knife back into its sheath and slid the music box into the inside pocket of his winter coat. The coat Kathryn had bought for him. He ran a hand along the sleeve and remembered their first Christmas together. Before giving it to him, she'd sewn their cattle brand into the inner lining along with his initials, *making it mine*, he thought with a smile. Not for the first time, he wished he'd done better by her. She deserved so much more than—

A sudden whinny from his horse brought Larson's head up.

He remained crouched by the fire and scanned his surroundings. The spot he'd chosen far into the ravine provided shelter from the wind. Frozen scrub oak and snow-covered boulders bordered him on all sides but one. He squinted and focused on the night sounds around him. A rustle sounded off to his left, but that could be a rabbit or a squirrel.

His heart kicked up a notch when it happened again. He reached for his rifle propped on a rock beside him. He cocked the chamber slowly, deliberately, giving warning.

"Hello, the camp!" a voice sounded to his right.

Larson turned to see a man step from behind a boulder into the shadowed flicker of the campfire.

The stranger extended his hands palm

up, showing he wasn't armed. "Can I share your fire, friend?"

Eyeing him, Larson felt his pulse slow a mite. "Sure, come on in." He kept his rifle within easy reach.

At first glance, the man appeared to be about his age. He wore no gloves, and when he stretched his bare hands over the fire, Larson noticed a tiny tremor in them. He wondered if it was from the chill of the night or if the stranger had another need.

"My horse went lame on me a couple miles back. I been walkin' since dark." The man's pants were caked in snow and ice, and his boots were worn through on one side.

Larson motioned to the coffeepot set on a rock among the glowing white embers. At the man's nod, he tossed the remnants from his cup and poured a fresh one. He rose to hand it to the stranger and heard a horse whinny some distance behind him, on the other side of the ravine.

Too late, Larson realized the man's intent.

The sight of the revolver pointing at his chest sent white-hot emotion pouring through Larson's body. Instinctively, he tossed the hot coffee at the man's face and dove for his rifle. He hit the ground as a thunderclap exploded in his ears. Searing heat tore through his upper right thigh. Sickening warmth and weakness pulsed in his right leg, then spread the length of his body.

Everything swirled in a fog around him. He fought to remain conscious.

When Larson opened his eyes he saw only a dark blanket of sky pierced with specks of light dancing in a nauseating rhythm. He blinked twice to clear his mind.

The night air suddenly felt like an icy blanket hugging him from all sides, and he soon realized why. His coat, boots, and gloves were gone.

He tried to sit up, but a solid kick to his ribcage brought him down. The freezing snow against his face helped keep him conscious. He gulped for air.

Be still.

Larson felt the urging more than heard it. But he didn't want to be still. Everything within him wanted to fight.

He heard movement in the camp and slowly opened one eye. The stranger now wore his coat and boots and was rummaging through his saddlebags. Larson raised himself slowly till he was sitting. He silently reached for the weapon beside him and took aim dead center on the man's back. He cocked the rifle. "Hold it right—"

The man turned, his gun holstered.

The explosion was deafening. But it hadn't come from Larson's rifle.

A look of utter surprise and disbelief contorted the man's features before he fell headlong into the snow. Larson's heart ricocheted off his ribs as he struggled to his knees. He searched the darkness around him. The night grew eerily quiet. Knowing he provided an excellent target in his current position, he gripped his rifle and limped to an outcropping of boulders.

Sinking to the ground, he clamped a hand over the pulsing wound in his right thigh and pressed back against the icy stone. A rifle blast split the silence. A flash of light glinted off the boulder, inches from his head. He fell to his belly and started crawling through the snow and scrub brush, away from the light of the campfire.

Another gunshot sounded, hitting only a few feet to the side of him.

Larson took quick breaths through clenched teeth. His skin suddenly grew clammy even as the wound pulsed hot. Trying to ignore the pain, he prayed like he hadn't done in years. Larson knew the Almighty had no reason to listen to him. Not after he'd ignored Him all these years. Even so, he prayed, with an urgency he didn't know he had in him.

Figuring he'd crawled about twenty yards, he stopped to catch his breath. His throat burned from the cold. He looked down at his right leg and saw the snow staining crimson. His feet and legs were going numb. His fingers ached.

"I know you're in there, mister. Might as well come out and get it over with."

The words were spoken in a singsong tone, lending a macabre feel to the already perilous situation. Larson lay perfectly still, listening to the crunch of the man's boots on frozen snow. He gauged the man to be ten yards south. And moving straight for him.

His options limited, Larson pushed ahead on his stomach through the brush and across a narrow gully. He edged his way up the side of the ravine until he heard the unmistakable *tink* of metal against metal. Loading chambers. At the cock of the rifle, the night went dead quiet.

He waited for the inevitable. But no gunshot came.

Instead, he heard humming. *Humming.* And the sound of it—high-pitched, carefree, something a person might hear at a picnic—made him go stock-still.

"Mighty cold out here tonight, and expectin' a heap more snow. You can die slow or fast, mister. Don't make no matter to me. But I hear freezin' to death ain't no way to go."

The night air pulsed with the absurdity of the voice. Death threats mingled with the weather. Larson pressed back into the brush.

Snatches of prayers Kathryn had whispered at night while he lay silent in bed beside her came back to him. Larson repeated them over and over in his mind as he crawled farther into the dark bramble of rock and brush. When he finally looked up, he thought the night's silver shadows were playing a trick on him.

A wooden shack stood like a sentinel against the rocky wall of the ravine. If he could make it inside, maybe he would stand half a chance. He fired a shot in the direction he'd last heard his assailant. Slowed by his injured right leg, he barely reached the door before another shot rang out behind him.

Larson dove inside and kicked the door shut. Panting, he crawled to the wall farthest from the single window by the door. The cramped space inside the shack was stagnant and musty. A sharp tanginess he couldn't define punctuated the frigid air.

His eyes soon adjusted to the dim light slanting through the window. What looked to be stacks of barrels occupied the wall beside him. A pile of blankets and other items littered the wooden floor.

Another shot fired and blasted out the window. At the same time, Larson heard something shatter beside him. Liquid sprayed his face and neck, and the floor beneath him grew wet. The pungent odor became more pronounced.

A rapid fire of gun blasts punctured the cloak of night, and the shack ignited in blinding white light and flames. Intense heat engulfed the small space as a putrid stench filled his nostrils. Larson knew in that moment that he would die, and that his death would be deservedly painful. He only hoped it would be swift.

CHAPTER THREE

With the ball of her fist, Kathryn rubbed a layer of frost from the icy pane and peered out the cabin window. More than two weeks had passed since she'd awakened to an empty bed to find Larson's note on the mantel. *Kathryn, gone to northern pastures. Back by week's end.*

Though she'd sensed an urgency to pray for him the first few days, that hadn't alarmed her. She was accustomed to the Spirit's gentle nudges, especially when Larson journeyed during winter months.

But it would be nightfall soon, again. And still Larson had not returned.

Seeing movement behind the barn,

Kathryn recognized Matthew Taylor's stocky frame and casual saunter. She raced to open the door and called the ranch hand's name. Matthew turned, his arms loaded down with supplies. He nodded her way before dumping the gear by the tethered packhorse.

Kathryn shuddered at the bitter wind and motioned to him as he approached. "Why don't you step inside for a minute? I have a fresh pot of coffee on."

A hesitant look clouded Matthew Taylor's features, which were boyish despite the maturity of his thirty-odd years. He stopped within a few feet of the door. "Thank you for your kindness, Mrs. Jennings. I appreciate it." He glanced down before looking back, his feet planted to the spot where he stood. "What can I do for you?"

Kathryn wondered at his reluctance but quickly got to the point. "Have you seen my husband recently, Mr. Taylor?"

He shook his head. "Not since before Christmas, ma'am. He gave orders for us to stay with the cattle holed up in the north pasture, and that's where we've been all this time, me and some of the other men." He squinted. "Is there a problem, ma'am?"

Kathryn briefly debated how much to

share with him. Matthew had been in Larson's employ for over six years, longer than any other ranch hand. She quickly decided the situation warranted it. "Larson's been gone since Christmas Day. He left a note stating that he was heading to the north pasture and that he'd be back by week's end." Kathryn felt a sinking feeling inside her chest. Somehow stating the situation out loud made it worse. "He hasn't come home."

Matthew eyed her for a moment before answering. "Five or six feet of snow fell that night, Mrs. Jennings. It was bitter cold." The look of warning in his eyes completed his thought. "I haven't seen him. None of us has. I know because, well . . . we've been wonderin' where he is."

He started to speak, then stopped. Kathryn encouraged him with a nod.

"Me and the other men were due to be paid last Friday. We don't mind havin' to wait again, as long as we know it's coming."

"What do you mean 'again'?" Kathryn asked.

A pained expression creased his forehead. "I don't know if there's anything to but some of the men . . . they've heard the ranch isn't doing so well." He glanced away briefly, shifting his weight. He shook his head before looking back. "They're worried about their jobs, Mrs. Jennings. Winter's a hard time for a ranch hand to be out of work. Your husband . . ."

"My husband what?" she encouraged softly.

"Well, 'bout a month ago your husband fired Smitty right there on the spot. When I took up for Smitty, Mr. Jennings told me I'd get the same thing if he caught me snoopin' around." He shook his head again. "He was real mad."

The part about Larson losing his temper wasn't unimaginable to Kathryn, and that her husband might fire a ranch hand wasn't either. She didn't know any of the men personally, except for Matthew. They never came around the cabin. She suddenly realized how very little she knew about the operation of the ranch.

"Mr. Taylor, is there any chance the man actually did something wrong?"

"A chance, maybe, but not likely. I've worked alongside him now for three year and Smitty's a pretty good man." He glanc down. "You probably don't know any of and maybe I shouldn't be tellin' you."

Kathryn took a step forward. "I'm concerned for my husband's safety, Mr. Taylor. If you know something that would help me, I'd appreciate your telling me."

"There's been more trouble." His voice dropped low, and Kathryn strained to hear. "Just last week we found a portion of fencing torn down again. Cattle are missin'. Some of them are heifers due to drop come spring. The head gates on Fountain Creek are fine though. We shouldn't have much trouble with that during winter months."

"Trouble with the head gates?"

"Last summer our water supply ran low, and after we found that gate rider—"

"*Found* him?"

Matthew hesitated again, his mouth forming a firm line. "Yes, ma'am. By the looks of it, he drowned. We found him floatin' upstream a ways, near the bend in the creek by the hot springs."

Something behind Matthew's eyes, something he wasn't saying, prompted Kathryn to question him. "But the water's not that deep there. Did he slip? Or fall?"

Matthew looked away, unwilling to meet her gaze. "The gate rider had told us he'd found proof that someone was tamperin' with the water gates, takin' more water than they'd a right to and leaving too little for downstream to town. The rider let your husband know he was goin' to file a report. Then the next day . . . that's when we found him."

Kathryn shook her head, shaken by the news but even more puzzled as to why Larson had never shared it with her. "Do you know who was taking the water?"

"Never did find out. Two other ranches have rights to the water in this creek, plus it runs on through to Willow Springs, so the townsfolk have a claim too. But your husband has first rights, so his portions should be guaranteed." He glanced away. "But with the drought the last few years, some don't quite see it that way anymore."

"Do you think we'll have more trouble this spring?"

A spark of disbelief, as though she should have already known the answer, flashed in Matthew Taylor's topaz brown eyes before he blinked it away. He nodded, and a shiver of warning passed through her.

———

Larson fought to open his eyes but felt something pressing them closed. Darkness companioned the pain wracking his body—pain so intense he wanted to cry out. But with every fettered breath he drew, his lungs burned like liquid fire and the muscles in his chest spasmed in protest.

He tried to lie still, thinking that might offer reprieve, but relief escaped him. He writhed as his flesh felt like it was being stripped from his body. Why would God not let him die?

Blurred images swayed and jerked before his shuttered view. His mind grasped at one as though lunging for a lifeline.

Kathryn. Her eyes the color of cream-laced coffee. Her skin like velvet beneath his hands. If only he could—

Jagged pain ripped through his right thigh. The image of Kathryn vanished.

A cry twisting up from his chest strangled in the parched lining of his throat, and he struggled to remember his last lucid thought before this nightmare began.

Instinct kicked in again, and he was prey—a wounded field mouse cowering in muted terror as talons sank deep into his tender flesh. His heart pounded out a chaotic rhythm against his ribs as a fresh wave of pain tore through him. Not for the first time, he wondered if he was in hell.

But as the thought occurred, something cool touched his lips. Wetness slid down his throat, burning a trail to his belly. Then a sensation he craved swept through him.

Liquid sleep.

He waited for it. Yearned for it. It didn't matter where it came from, only that it came. He floated on waves of painlessness, far above the suffering that he knew still existed. And would soon return.

———

With scant minutes of daylight left, Kathryn fought the familiar swell of panic that tightened her chest with every nightfall. She pulled on her coat and gloves and, forcing one foot in front of the other, plodded through the fresh fallen snow for more firewood.

Used to the warmth of the cabin, she winced as the cold air bit her cheeks. Her eyes watered. She took a deep breath and felt the frigid air all the way down to her toes. February's temperatures had plummeted, and their descent brought twice the amount of snowfall as January. With her arms loaded down each time, Kathryn made five trips and turned to make one more.

Her steps slowed as she let her gaze trail upward to the tip of the snow-flocked blue spruce towering beside their cabin. Seeing it almost brought a smile. At her request, Larson had planted the once twig of a tree ten summers ago, shortly after building the cabin.

"I want it to grow closer to my kitchen window, Larson," she'd told him, slowly dragging the evergreen with its balled root toward the desired spot.

"If you plant it there, it'll grow *through* your kitchen window." The smirk on his handsome face told her he knew this was a game. "This spruce is going to grow a mite bigger than the potted bush your mother has in that fancy hallway of hers."

"It's called a *foyer*." Kathryn playfully corrected him using the French pronunciation.

Larson hauled the tree back to the spot he'd measured and used his shirtsleeve to wipe the sweat from his brow. With a shovel, he traced a circle roughly two times the circumference of the balled root and began digging. Kathryn had stood to the side, enjoying the time with her new husband and amazed at the intensity of love filling her heart.

She blinked as the memory faded. A sudden gust of wind blew flecks of snow and ice free from the spruce's branches and onto her face, but she didn't move. The pungent scent of pine settled around her, and she breathed its perfume. Larson had been right that day. He'd planted the tree in just the right spot. Far enough from the cabin to allow room for it to spread its roots and grow—where she could lean forward in her kitchen window and enjoy the magnitude of its towering beauty—yet close enough where she could still enjoy the birds flitting among its branches.

She closed her eyes against renewed tears. *Where are you, Larson?* She'd gone over the events of their last day together countless times, each time hoping to uncover a sliver of a reason as to why he would leave and not return. Had he been displeased with her? She'd grown more discontent in their marriage in recent months. Had he as well, and she'd simply mistaken his reticence as worry over the ranch?

Shaking her head, Kathryn forced herself to focus on what she knew for certain about

Larson's absence—not these imaginings born of fatigue and loneliness. She turned back for one last load of wood and, with each step, sifted possible reasons through the filter of truth.

If he truly had planned to leave her, he wouldn't have penned a note. Nor would he have replenished the wood supply that morning. Tracing her steps back to the cabin, she remembered their last night together.

Intimate relations between them had been . . . well, better than she could remember in a long time. Larson's tenderness had reminded her of their early years together. But even after sharing such physical intimacy with her husband, she had awakened during the night with a loneliness so vast that it pressed around her until she could hardly breathe. She'd turned her head into her pillow so Larson wouldn't hear her cries. How would she have explained her tears to him when she scarcely understood them herself?

As she stacked the logs on the woodpile, one last certainty cut through the blur of her thoughts, and its undeniable truth brought simultaneous hope and pain.

Larson would never willingly give up this ranch, much less desert it.

This ranch was his lifeblood. His dreams were wrapped up in its success or failure.

The truth pricked a tender spot inside her, but Kathryn knew it to be true. Deep down, she'd always known that Larson's making a success of the ranch came before her. However, in recent days, to her surprise, that understanding had nurtured a growing sense of ownership she'd not experienced before. A dogged determination on her part to see the ranch succeed.

When Larson returned—and he *would* return, she told herself as her gloved hand touched the door latch—he would find the ranch holding its own or, by God's grace, maybe even prospering. She would keep her husband's dream alive, no matter the cost.

Muffled pounding on the snow-packed trail leading up to the cabin brought Kathryn's head around. She recognized Matthew Taylor astride his bay mare, but none of the four riders behind him. She swiped any trace of tears from her cheeks and took a step toward them.

"Mrs. Jennings." Matthew reined in and tipped his hat. The other men followed suit.

Kathryn nodded, including the group in her gesture. She easily guessed the reason for their visit. "I gave you my word, Mr. Taylor, and I intend to keep it." Though she didn't know exactly how yet. "You and the other men will be paid, like we agreed."

She couldn't tell if it was the cold or a blush, but Matthew's face noticeably reddened. "I don't doubt your intentions, ma'am. None of us do." He motioned, including the men behind him. His gloved hands gripped his saddle horn. "Have you heard from your husband yet?"

Kathryn shook her head but injected hope into her voice. "But I'm expecting to . . . any day now."

The men with Matthew muttered to each other, but with a backward glance from Matthew, they fell silent.

"Mrs. Jennings, I understand you want to keep hopin', but you have to face the possibility that your husband might not have made it out of the storm that night. He might have—"

"My husband possesses an instinct for direction, Mr. Taylor." Kathryn purposefully phrased it in the present. "He's never owned a compass a day in his life and he's never been lost. He knows this territory better than any man."

Matthew's eyes softened. "And I'm not sayin' otherwise, Mrs. Jennings, but—"

One of the other ranch hands nudged his horse forward. He was a man slight of build but surly-looking—*mean* was the word that came to Kathryn's mind. A ribbon of scarred ruddy flesh ran the length of his right jawline and disappeared beneath his shirt collar. Kathryn would not have wanted to be left alone with him. "Winter storms can make a man lose that sense of direction, Mrs. Jennings. It can blind you. Turn you 'round, where you don't know where you are or where you been." He laughed, and the shrill sound of it surprised her, set her defenses on edge. His eyes swept the full length of her. "You ever been out in a storm like that . . . Mrs. Jennings?"

Matthew turned in his saddle. Kathryn couldn't make out Matthew's response to the man, but his manner was curt and harsh. With one last look at her, the ranch hand turned and rode back down the trail.

Matthew slid from his horse and came to

where Kathryn stood. From the concern etching his eyes, she had the distinct feeling that what he was about to say hurt him somehow.

"I'm here to tell you that we've been offered jobs at another ranch." His announcement felt like a physical blow to Kathryn's midsection. "The rancher's payin' double what we get here, Mrs. Jennings."

"But, Matthew—Mr. Taylor," she corrected. "You each have jobs here. You've agreed to work through the spring." She knew they didn't have formal agreements like her father did with his employees back East. But still, wasn't their word worth something? She took a step toward him. "You gave my husband your word to work through the spring, did you not?"

"Yes, ma'am, we did. We made that agreement with your husband." Kathryn didn't miss the emphasis on his last words. "But he's not here anymore."

"But he will be." Her voice involuntarily rose an octave.

"Yes, ma'am."

"And I'll have the payroll as promised for every man this week."

"Most of the men are taking the other offer, Mrs. Jennings." At her protest, he raised a hand. "You have to understand that a lot of these men have families to feed. They got wives and children dependin' on them. And I gotta tell you . . ." A sheepish look came over his face. "Couple of the men say they spotted an owl yesterday."

Kathryn's confusion must have shown on her face.

"It wasn't just any owl, ma'am. They say it was pure white." He shrugged. "I don't hold much to the Indian lore around here, but the sayin' goes that seein' a white owl's a bad sign. Means more snow's coming, it's gonna get colder. Things are gonna get worse before they get better."

Kathryn tried to mask her mounting frustration. She looked past him to the other men. "Mr. Taylor, if I ask them personally, will they stay?"

"Ma'am?"

"I said if I ask each of the men personally, will they stay and work my ranch?"

A quizzical look swept his face. "*Your* ranch, ma'am?"

Determination stiffened her spine. "Yes, it's my husband's *and* mine."

That simple declaration inspired courage

and strength, and a hope she hadn't known in nearly two months. Was this a small taste of what Larson felt for this land? If so, no wonder he had worked so tirelessly to keep it.

Matthew laughed low and quick. "I don't reckon it'd make much difference if you ask them. Most of them don't take to the idea of workin' for a woman anyhow."

Twilight shadowed the quivering aspen and towering birch canopying them, but Kathryn could see the hint of a smile tipping his mouth. It brought one to hers too.

"I gotta admit, it's not something I ever thought I'd do." His look sobered. "But I gave my word to your husband that I'd work through the spring. And I intend to stand by that."

"I appreciate your integrity, Mr. Taylor. I look forward to doing business with you."

After Matthew and the other men disappeared down the trail, Kathryn turned and walked back to the cabin. She wondered how many ranch hands Larson had to begin with and how many there would still be come Monday.

After latching the door behind her, she stood for a moment in the dark silence of the cabin. The utter stillness held an invitation she wasn't ready to face yet. She lit a single lamp and set about preparing dinner. She hadn't cooked much recently. Her appetite had noticeably, understandably, lessened.

Bending over to get a cup from a lower shelf, Kathryn's world tilted.

She grabbed hold of the back of a kitchen chair, but it toppled under her weight. Her knees hit the floor with a dull thud. The room spun in circles around her. Giving in to the dizzying whirl, she sank to the floor. Her stomach spasmed, and she tasted bile burning the back of her throat.

She called out for help, as if someone would hear. The loneliness she'd been evading suddenly permeated every inch of the cabin. From the methodical ticking of the mantel clock, to the single dish on the table, to the bed in the next room—as barren and empty as her heart.

Curling onto her side, she cradled her head in the crook of her arm and wept. She wept for all that she'd longed for from her husband and had never received. She wept for life's promises that remained unfulfilled, and for the innocence with which she'd once embraced them. Wrapping her arms around her waist, her heart ached for the child she would never have.

The flame from the lamp flickered and sputtered. The dwindling oil gave off a purple plume of smoke before darkness fell over the room.

Staring at the shadowed outline of the cabin door, Kathryn thought back to the first day she'd crossed that threshold—in her husband's arms. She'd known then that God was with her, guiding her steps. The One who stood beside her that day was still beside her now, and somehow already dwelled in the moment when she would breathe her last, whenever that day would come.

Her choked voice trickled across the empty room. " 'Whither shall I go from thy spirit? or whither shall I flee from thy presence?' " She clung to the psalmist's promise. "Lord, I cannot be anywhere where you are not." And the same was true for Larson, wherever he was.

Cradled on the floor, Kathryn surrendered herself—again—to the Lover of her soul, and laid her grief and worry at the foot of His cross.

CHAPTER FOUR

Larson awakened to a cool sensation sweeping across his legs and arms, followed by a heat so intense it seeped all the way into his bones. His skin tingled in response, and though the experience was far from pleasant, neither did it resemble the ravaging of flesh he'd endured and come to dread.

Thick haze surrounded his mind. Moving toward him through the fog, a dull pain throbbed with the rhythm of a steady pulse. He recognized its sickening cadence and fought to open his eyes, but couldn't. Why couldn't he see? He commanded his arms and legs to move, but they too proved traitorous.

As the steady thrum of pain grew louder inside him, Larson begged for waves of slumber to carry him to the place where agony was a distant memory, and where Kathryn waited.

His prayer answered, cool wetness slipped through his lips and down his throat. Murmurs of voices, far away, moved toward him through a distant tunnel. He willed himself to reach out to them, but he couldn't penetrate the veil separating his world from theirs.

Sweet oblivion drifted over him, luring him with her promises of peace and escape. He embraced her whisper and surrendered completely.

When he awakened again, Larson sensed a change. Exactly what, he couldn't figure, only that his surroundings were different. *He* was different. For the first time he could remember, he felt the flutter of his lids and knew he was awake. He slowly opened his eyes.

Darkness still hung close, cocooning him like a thick blanket. But this time it wasn't for lack of sight.

Flat on his back, he sensed his body

stretched out before him, somehow different from how he remembered. He tried his voice, and the muscles in his throat chastised the effort. The back of his throat felt like crushed gravel, and when he tried to move his body, hot prickles needled up his arms and skittered down his legs. He braced himself for the hot licks of pain to return and once again quench their thirst. But none came.

Pain's thirst had apparently been slaked, at least for the moment.

He lay in the darkness, listening for sounds, for anything that might yield a clue to where he was. More than anything, he longed for the voices he thought he'd heard before. Or had they been part of the dream?

One reality was certain—he was alive.

He strained to recall his last memory preceding this nightmare. The recollection teetered on the edge of his thoughts, just out of reach. He shut his eyes in hope of bringing it closer. Scraps of disjointed images fluttered past his mind's eye. Shadowed and jumbled, they wafted toward him then just as quickly drifted away, like ragged tufts of a down blanket ripped and scattered on the wind.

He flexed the fingers on his right hand and lightning bolted up his arm and ricocheted down his leg. He gasped for breath. But with the pain came clarity.

Bitter frost. His legs and feet going numb. Hands aching with cold.

Darkness. Needing to hide. A voice . . . wickedly taunting.

Brilliant light, more intense than he had thought possible.

The metallic taste of fear scalded the back of his throat, and he pressed his head back into the pillow. Memories from that night crashed over him. The stranger at the camp, the gunshot to the man's chest, but not from Larson's own rifle. Then clawing his way through the frozen night in search of a place to hide.

Cool lines of wetness trailed a path down his temples and onto his neck. *O God, were you there that night? Are you here now?*

Then came an image so lovely, so breathtakingly beautiful, that his chest clenched in response.

Kathryn.

He tried to call her name, but the effort languished in his throat. How was she? Was she safe? Did Kat know where he was and that he was hurt? Or did she think him already dead? Wetness sprang to Larson's eyes, but oddly the sensation didn't seem foreign to him. And what of the ranch? He couldn't let all that he'd worked for be wrenched from his grasp—especially when success was so close this time.

His thoughts raced. The sale of cattle this spring was crucial. The increased demand for meat to feed workers in the mining camps would bring more sales, which should result in enough money to nearly pay off the loan they owed on the land. And it would also cover the second loan he'd secured this past fall—a loan Kathryn knew nothing about. He hadn't wanted to worry her. He'd needed some extra to carry them through the winter months and had mortgaged their homestead, the last thing that didn't already have a lien attached to it. But all the years of sacrifice and hard work would soon pay off.

That thought drove him forward. He tried to lift his head but strained at the simple task. It felt like a forty-pound weight was wrapped around his temples. He let his head fall back to the pillow and felt the room sway. His neck muscles bunched into knots.

He wished he could rub the tension away, but his arms would not obey.

A noise sounded.

He went perfectly still, listening for it again. Had he only imagined it?

Despair crept up over him, robbing his hope. Bits and pieces of his life—choices he'd made, goals he'd wanted to achieve but paid far too high a price for—flickered like lit matches against the walls of his heart.

But he hadn't been the only one to pay the price. Kathryn had sacrificed so much for his dreams. She'd given up a life of affluence and certain success. She'd forsaken Boston's wealth, her parents' home, and a privileged upbringing. Not to mention the scores of high-society suitors who, if given the chance, would have lavished upon her every desire of her heart. The way he wanted to.

She'd left it all behind. For him. And what had he offered her in exchange? A rough-hewn cabin and an empty womb.

The creak of a floorboard sent his thoughts careening.

Larson lifted his head, wincing at the spasms already starting in his neck. Darkness enveloped him except for a yellow slash of light that appeared to be coming from beneath a door a few feet from where he lay. A footfall landed beyond the entry-way; he was certain of it.

He laid his head back down and man-aged to coax a moan through his cracked lips, hoping someone would hear.

At the click of the door latch, Larson felt his tears return.

———

Kathryn's gloved hand rested on the door latch. She hesitated, knowing she wasn't ready for what lay beyond. Her gaze trav-eled upward, over the breadth and width of the Willow Springs Bank building. Weak-ness spread through her, and her knees trembled. But she stiffened in resolve. She could do this. She would do this.

For Larson's dream. For their dream.

A chilling March wind ushered in the month and gusted around her as tiny crystals of snow and ice pelted her cheeks. The jour-ney to Willow Springs normally filled her with excitement, but when she'd left the cabin in darkness early this morning, the loneliness inhabiting every corner of her bedroom followed her, strangling her confidence with every passing mile.

Without warning, a sense of Larson's presence stole through her. It robbed her lungs of air, and with fading hope, she turned to search the sea of faces passing on the boardwalk behind her. Nothing. Her grip tightened on the handle. An overwhelming urgency to pray for him hit her. She blew out a ragged breath, white fog clouding the air.

Father, be with my husband in this very moment, wherever he is. The memory of what Matthew Taylor had said about the severity of the storm on Christmas Day hung close. *No matter what Matthew or the other men think, I know Larson is alive. I feel his heart beating inside me. Lead my husband safely home. Bring him back to me.*

She stared at the handle in her grip, summoning courage to complete this task.

Close behind her, a man cleared his throat. "Well, are you going in today or not, ᵗs?"

ᵗathryn turned on the steps with a read- ᵖology. The apology froze in her throat, ʳer, when met with piercing gray eyes ⁿe menacing shade as the storm clouds shrouding the Rockies in the distance. A shudder ran through her and she drew back, careful to keep her balance on the top step.

A broad-chested man stood on the step below, his eyes level with hers. His voice bore a thick Irish brogue but lacked the accent's customary warmth. At his temples, damp copper curls kinked with swirls of gray. His facial features were striking, but while Kathryn supposed some might label them ruddily handsome, nothing within her responded with attraction.

As his gaze penetrated hers, his look of irritation lessened but still bore proof of a foul mood. The hard line of his mouth slowly split into a tight curve. "Perhaps I could offer my assistance. I conduct my business here and know a few of the people inside." He nodded at the door, then back at her. "Maybe I could help you, if you'd let me."

Kathryn caught a whiff of musk and hair tonic. Although he maintained a physica distance that satisfied decorum, and his s and outer cloak designated wealth, sor thing about the man reeked of dishon Yet, remembering why she'd made th all the way to Willow Springs toda wondered if this man might somehow be part of the answer to her prayer.

She decided to risk it. "I'm here to meet with the bank manager, Mr. Kohl—"

"I know Harold Kohlman. What business do you have with him?"

His curt reply took Kathryn by surprise. *"Watch a man's posture,"* she'd once overheard her father counsel younger partners as she sat listening outside the double doors of his office at home—any chance to be closer to her father. *"You can tell a great deal about a man from the way he folds his arms or strokes his chin. You must listen to what a person says, most certainly. But listen even closer to what they don't."*

Kathryn assessed the man before her. His focus briefly moved from her eyes to wander over her face, and what he wasn't saying spoke volumes. Clearly his interests lay elsewhere where she was concerned. Dismissing him with a glance, she reached again for the door handle. His hand beat her to it.

With a smile that provoked warning inside her, he motioned for her to precede him inside. She stepped into the bank lobby, thankful to at least be out of the cold and wind, if not finished with him.

"Do you have an appointment with Mr. Kohlman, Miss . . . ?"

She turned back to find him staring. "No, I don't. I'll address that with Mr. Kohlman's secretary, thank you."

He gave a soft laugh. "Well, my offer to you still stands."

Kathryn raised a brow. Had she not made her lack of interest clear enough the first time?

"My offer to introduce you . . . to Harold Kohlman." He smiled again, and this time it looked almost genuine.

But her instincts told her otherwise. Her youthful days in Boston were not so far removed that she'd forgotten men like this—who routinely sought to play this game in quest of her attention, and something else she'd never given them.

Shaking flakes of snow from her wool coat, she realized again how crucial this meeting was to her keeping the ranch. Swallowing her pride, she nodded. "I would appreciate it if you would arrange a meeting with Mr. Kohlman."

A gleam lit his eyes, telling her his offer

would extend much further. She chose not to acknowledge it.

She followed him, her heeled boots clicking on the polished granite of the lobby floor. She paused to survey the surroundings. Though the intimidating exterior of the Willow Springs Bank building lacked grandeur of any significance, no expense had been spared on the interior furnishings. She grew reflective, thinking of Boston and the office buildings her father owned.

Apparently aware of her reaction, the man stopped beside her. "Beautiful, isn't it? The original building burned to the ground two years ago, almost to the day, as a matter of fact. Two people lost their lives; many others were badly burned. But the community banded together and, with the aid of a wealthy benefactor . . ."

He paused, and Kathryn got the distinct feeling he was referring to himself.

"We rebuilt in grandeur, and"—he flourished a wave of his hand—"you see the results."

She sensed he was waiting for a reaction. Not wanting to encourage him further yet realizing he had offered to help arrange a meeting with Mr. Kohlman, she managed a smile she hoped would suffice. "Yes, it's quite impressive. And so generous of . . . the benefactor."

His own smile broadened, and he held her eyes for a moment too long before continuing through the maze of desks. Kathryn followed his path toward the large—and only—separate office located on the west side of the building. The architect's forethought, no doubt, to offer the best view of the mountain range.

The buzz of nearly a dozen bank employees and twice that many customers filled the spacious lobby and spilled over to the private waiting area outside the manager's office. The low hum of blended conversation suddenly registered as foreign to Kathryn as she realized how long it had been since she'd been around a group of people. For so long it had been only her and Larson. Staring ahead at the massive double oak doors, she wished this meeting were already concluded.

The man indicated a chair where she was apparently supposed to wait. Then he nodded to an attractive blond woman walking past.

Her face lit. "Good afternoon, Mr. Mac-Gregor."

Kathryn doubted that the woman's voice was customarily imbued with such a lilt, nor her smile so bright. It would seem Kathyrn was right about judging this man—this Mr. MacGregor—to be attractive to some.

The nameplate on the closed double doors read *Harold H. Kohlman*, and Mr. MacGregor entered without benefit of announcement. Kathryn watched after him, unimpressed but curious at his apparently close affiliation with the bank manager. Benefactor, indeed.

A wave of nausea spasmed her stomach. She gripped the cushioned arm of the chair and took deep breaths, praying not to be sick again. After a few moments, the queasiness subsided. She put a hand to her forehead and felt the cool perspiration.

Kathryn noticed the lobby area had grown quiet. She turned to discover why and found several employees looking in her direction. Then she heard the voices. They came from behind the manager's door. Growing louder and more intense. She couldn't make out the source of the argument, only that one of the voices, the most pronounced, bore an unmistakable brogue.

Should she leave and come back later this afternoon? That would mean staying the night in Willow Springs. She hadn't the funds for a hotel. Should she wait in hopes of seeing Mr. Kohlman soon? She wished she'd never accepted Mr. MacGregor's help—now it would appear to people that they were friends. Or, at the very least, acquaintances. And she doubted whether that perceived affiliation would play in her favor at the moment.

Kathryn was halfway to the entry leading from the private sitting area when she heard a door open behind her.

"Mr. Kohlman is available to see you now."

She spun around at the voice. MacGregor's brogue was noticeably thicker, and if the annoyance on his face was any indication, his mood was definitely more foul. This didn't bode well for an advance on her loan. "I appreciate your help, Mr. MacGregor, but perhaps it would be best if I came back later."

His scowl darkened. "Nonsense, Kohlman

already knows you're waiting. And he's a very busy man."

A man appeared at MacGregor's side, a portly gentleman a good foot shorter, and thicker around his middle. His thick reddish sideburns matched his full mustache and lent him an air of approachability that abruptly ended at the firm set of his jaw. This was not going as she'd planned.

Breathing a prayer, Kathryn crossed the distance. "I appreciate your seeing me today, Mr. Kohlman."

He turned and walked back into his office.

Not knowing what else to do, she followed. "You know my husband. His name is—"

"What is the nature of your business with me today, ma'am?" Kohlman eased his generous frame into the leather chair, then glanced past her.

Kathryn turned to see Mr. MacGregor pushing the door closed, but from the inside. He was staying? Trying to hide her surprise, she focused again on Mr. Kohlman and approached his desk. She handed him a letter she'd carefully worded the night before. "I'm here to request an advance on our loan with your bank. My husband and I own a ranch outside of—"

He raised a hand, his eyes still scanning the letter. "Let me stop you right there. I'm sorry, ma'am, but do you have any idea the number of ranches that are going under right now?" He let the letter fall to his desk and pinched the bridge of his nose. "I wish I could help you, but I can't loan any more money without solid collateral."

Kathryn stepped closer and pulled the document from her purse. "But I have the deed for our homestead here. I state that in the letter." She intentionally kept her voice level as her determination rose. "I'm offering that as collateral. Certainly it will more than cover the amount I'm requesting."

Kohlman's eyes narrowed. "Perhaps I didn't make myself clear."

Whatever thread of benevolence Kohlman had previously, Kathryn watched it evaporate as his face deepened to crimson. She sensed MacGregor's presence behind her. Was he enjoying seeing her put in her place? Especially since she'd refused his earlier invitation?

"I told you, miss, that I cannot—"

"It's *Mrs.* Jennings, Mr. Kohlman, and I'm

not asking for something for nothing. I understand the nature of business and your need to make a profit, but—"

"What did you say your name was?" Kohlman's face lightened a shade as the room grew quiet.

The tick of a clock somewhere behind her counted off the seconds. "Mrs. Larson Jennings."

He shot a look over her shoulder, and Kathryn had the uncanny feeling that a silent exchange had occurred. Hearing movement behind her, she turned. MacGregor didn't look back as he exited the office.

"Well, Mrs. Jennings." Kohlman's tone turned surprisingly ingratiating. "I'm certain we can come to some sort of agreement."

CHAPTER FIVE

The door creaked open. Lamplight spilled over the darkness.

"I'll sit with him awhile till you get those griddle cakes of yours goin', Abby."

Larson's heart thudded against his ribs as new hope kindled inside him.

Soft humming in a masculine timbre hovered toward him. Burnt-orange flame flickered and played off the walls. Lying prone, he could make out the vague outline of a dresser and cupboard within his limited view. An aroma conjuring comfort and home filtered through his uncertainty. A sharp pang jabbed his abdomen, slowly registering as hunger. The sensation felt both foreign and familiar.

Larson tried to swallow but his throat closed tight. He heard the *plunk* as an oil lamp was set on a table. Then a shadowed figure, barely distinguishable from the darkness, loomed at the foot of the bed.

"Lord, lay your healing hand on this child of yours." The same deep voice, then more humming.

Larson could almost make out the tune. It was one Kathryn sang. Oh, to hear her sweet voice again. A cool draft wafted over his legs and up his chest, and he shivered at the undeniable bond of human touch.

The humming ceased, and the man leaned forward. A chuckle cleaved the silence. "Well, praise Jesus." He turned away. "Abby, come quick."

The laughter gurgling up from inside the man resonated in Larson's chest like a life-giving stream. Larson felt a smile tug the edges of his parched lips. The pale yellow light illuminating the room suddenly curved and swung before arching over the bed. For a moment all Larson could do was stare at the dark face and beaming smile of the man standing over him.

He was older than Larson would have guessed from his voice. Fifty, if he was a day.

The black man reached out a massive hand and gently laid it on Larson's head. The touch felt strange somehow. And while the fatherly gesture offered Larson immense comfort, it opened a floodgate of emotions that were foreign to him.

"My wife said you'd be joining us today." The man laughed as though he'd told a joke. "My Abby has that way about her, you know."

Larson suddenly became aware of his own breathing. Shallow, rasping. He tried to fill his lungs with air, and his chest burned from the effort.

"You just take it easy now." Compassion registered in the dark eyes holding his. "You've been through the worst already."

Soft footsteps drew Larson's attention, and a woman walked into the pale glow. She tucked herself beneath the sheltering arm of her husband, now drawing her close. Her pale blue eyes and silvered blond hair reflected the soft light. She put a hand to her open mouth, looking as though she wanted to speak but couldn't.

Larson stared at the couple, his eyes going wide. The woman's skin, the color of fresh cream from the pitcher, contrasted with the deep mahogany complexion of the man beside her. Suddenly Larson was glad he couldn't speak. He feared he might have said something unfitting. But certainly his expression revealed the whole of his shock.

As though reading his thoughts, they smiled at him, then at each other.

"My name is Isaiah," the man said softly, his voice sounding like the force of mighty waters tumbling over smooth rock. He lowered the lamp and set it on a table beside the bed, then placed a hand on Larson's shoulder. "Abby and I welcome you to our home."

Isaiah rearranged the sheets draped over Larson's body, then slipped an arm beneath his shoulders. Isaiah's touch exuded confidence, and Larson drew strength from it. Abby propped pillows behind his back as he leaned forward. The room swayed as Larson sat up. Shutting his eyes, he fought the disturbing feeling that he hadn't done this in a long while.

As though sensing his unease, Abby laid

a cool hand to his forehead, and he had a peculiar sense of well-being. Once the world stopped spinning, Larson opened his eyes.

He was in a bed under a contraption unlike anything he'd seen before. His arms and legs were draped with sheets and suspended above the mattress by means of ropes. His eyes trailed up the rudimentary pulley-type system to the ceiling and then back down again.

Waves of dread expanded through his chest. Using his right hand, he strained to reach the edge of the sheet. He peered beneath.

A strangled cry rose from his chest. Sickness twisted his gut.

The scarred, furrowed flesh of his legs, arms, and chest blurred before him as reality shredded his hope. The body on the bed resembled nothing of what he remembered. While patches of skin on his legs and arms remained seemingly unscathed, the majority bore the carnage of the flames. His abdomen, once lean and muscled, looked as though fiery talons had clawed him raw, leaving shallow welts of white-ribboned flesh.

An ache started in his throat and he dropped the sheet. The air left his lungs in a rush.

Isaiah laid a hand on his arm. "I know what you're thinking . . . that you'll never walk again. That you won't be able to do the things you did before. But that's a lie."

Larson turned away, but Isaiah gently drew his face back.

"Don't listen to that voice. Part of healing involves believing that you will be healed. Abby and I learned long ago that it means giving the Almighty your mind—" Isaiah touched his broad forehead, then covered the place over his heart—"along with your body and heart, and letting Him take charge."

Despite the assurance in Isaiah's voice and the compassion in Abby's gaze, panic tightened Larson's chest. Isaiah nodded to Abby and she left the room, closing the door behind her. Then Isaiah slowly lifted the sheets.

Cool air prickled the flesh on Larson's legs and arms. It took every ounce of courage within him to look down again.

His stomach churned at the hideous scars.

"Like I told you before," Isaiah said as he

laid a hand atop Larson's, "you're through the worst of it now. But you still have a hard road before you. I've seen men in the mining camps blown up and burned so badly you'd think they'd never live through the night." Isaiah smiled, and the effect resembled the youthfulness of a young boy far more than a huge mountain of a man. "But the Great Physician hears their prayers, and they live.

"I've worked with men before to help them regain their strength. And I can help you too." Fierceness settled behind the man's dark eyes. "You have a fight in you that only a few men possess. I saw it during the first days you were here, then after that in the weeks you fought the infection. You have something worth living for. I don't know what it is. Or who . . ." He paused. A gleam lit his eyes. "But I suspect her name is Kathryn."

Isaiah's words pulsed with Larson. But something in particular made his mind reel. *"In the weeks you fought the infection."*

Straining, he reached over and took hold of Isaiah's shirt. Larson moved his lips but nothing came out. He tried again. The words scraped over the tender cords in his throat. "How . . . long?" he rasped.

Isaiah didn't answer for a moment, then nodded once. "You've been with us for over two months. It's the second day of March."

Larson let his hand fall free. How could so much time have passed? Harold Kohlman at the Willow Springs Bank. The loan payment coming due. What must Kathryn be thinking after all this time?

Isaiah placed his hand upon his head, and Larson suddenly realized why the touch felt so different. He was feeling flesh on flesh.

Understanding weighed Isaiah's expression, and Larson's chest ached.

He thought God had spared his life for a reason, when all along it had been a cruel, horrible joke. How was he supposed to live like this? Provide for Kathryn? Be a husband to her? He imagined what her response would be to him now, and the result sickened him.

He turned away from Isaiah, ashamed of his tears, ashamed of what he'd become. Why hadn't God just let him die that night? Why?

Some time later, Abby appeared by his

bedside cradling a cup in her hands. Steam rose from its contents. "The tea will give you strength and help you find your voice again."

Kindness wrapped itself around her voice, but Larson sensed an iron will at its core. He lacked the strength—or the ability, he thought bitterly—to refuse. He drank as she held the cup to his lips.

The warm liquid burned at first, and he choked on the first two swallows. But after a few sips, the muscles in his throat relaxed and the bitter brew washed down to his stomach. Abby's movements were swift and efficient, and belied the soft lines of age crinkling the corners of her eyes and mouth when she smiled.

Larson found himself self-conscious under her gaze. He looked away. Then it occurred to him that while tending him Abby had no doubt become familiar with his scars, and far more—the same as Isaiah. The realization didn't lessen his discomfort.

His eyes grew heavy, and he suspected the ingredients in Abby's tea had a sedating effect.

When Larson awakened, he saw Isaiah reaching into a cupboard on the far wall.

Isaiah hummed as he took several containers from the shelves. He meticulously measured out ingredients and replaced the containers before grinding what he'd taken with a mortar and pestle. He emptied the contents from the mortar into a wooden bowl, then drew a bottle from the highest shelf. Pouring a dark liquid over all, he began to blend the mixture.

Larson watched him, wanting to tell him not to bother if the concoction was for him. What difference did it make now? On the heels of his hopelessness, he thought of how kind Isaiah and Abby had been to him, of all they'd given. What caused people to be so generous? He was a stranger to them, yet they'd taken him in and cared for him, had tended his wounds and fed him. He looked down at his withered body. Well, they'd kept him alive anyway. Larson doubted that even Kathryn's cooking could layer his bones again.

Kathryn . . .

Isaiah turned and looked at him, and Larson felt as though the man had heard every unspoken thought.

"Good morning." Isaiah brought the bowl with him and sat on a chair beside the bed.

As he mixed the contents, a pungent scent spiced the air. "You've been asleep for two days." He winked. "I forgot to tell you, watch out for Abby's tea."

Despite not wanting to, Larson smiled in response. Something about Isaiah—Abby too—skirted his defenses and infused him with unsolicited hope.

Isaiah lifted a brow. "Well, that's a little something, at least."

Larson swallowed and glanced at the bowl. "I hope that's not breakfast," he whispered, testing his voice. His mood lightened at Isaiah's smile.

Isaiah looked down at the bowl dwarfed in his hands. When he lifted his head, all traces of the smile were gone. "Tell me your name."

Larson stared at him a moment. "Larson Jennings," he rasped.

"As I see it, Larson, God's given you a second chance. You can have your life back. Not as it was, but as it is now." He set the bowl aside and leaned closer. "When I found you in that burned-out shack, the only reason I pulled you out was to bury you. There is no earthly reason why you should be alive right now, so there must be a heavenly one."

Larson watched Isaiah's rugged face fill with emotion. A single tear trailed down the man's rough cheek.

"I normally don't go through that ravine. I travel around it." Isaiah glanced down at his clasped hands. "You might say my former life instilled a sense of caution in me. I like to know what's around me, and I don't like closed in spaces. Especially at night."

Larson read the pain in Isaiah's eyes and suddenly wanted to know more about this man. "Where were you . . . before this?" His voice resembled a rusty hinge.

"I was born in Georgia and worked for a time on a plantation there and in South Carolina. I came out west almost twenty years ago with a man who won a hand of poker. I was the prize. Oh, I didn't mind leavin' the South, not one bit. The man who won me was a physician." He gave a soft laugh. "As it turned out, he was an excellent doctor but a poor gambler. Years later he was shot for cheating. But the day he won me in that card game, bless him, I became a free man."

Isaiah spoke the last words with a sigh,

and Larson suspected that whatever Isaiah's life had become after that day, it wasn't what he had expected. Strangely, that thought brought him hope, and spurred further questions within him. Was there a chance that God hadn't forgotten him after all? And what had Isaiah said about a heavenly reason for him having survived the explosion?

Larson remembered Kathryn sharing a Bible verse with him once that spoke to that thought, or close to it. Something about God's ways being different from ours. Kathryn often read their Bible in the rocking chair by the hearth at night. Recalling how she looked, her features softened by firelight, her honey hair reflecting the glow, sparked a longing inside him.

Unlike Kathryn, he'd never taken much stock in reading the Bible. If obliged to give answer, he would concede that the Bible was God's Word. But the simple truth was, it had never made any real difference in his life. How could dried words on a page, written hundreds of years ago, make a difference in a man's life? Hard work and making a success of yourself were what counted. God invested abilities in a man and then expected a return on that investment. Surely that was what mattered.

Unexpected doubt goaded Larson's certainty. How would he ever make a success of himself now? All of his dreams, money, and energy were tied up in the ranch. If he lost it, he lost everything. He did a quick calculation. On the sixteenth of March the next loan payment would come due. If he was late again, Harold Kohlman would surely follow through with his threat.

"Larson, are you hungry?" Isaiah's voice drew him back. "Abby has breakfast ready."

Larson looked up, distracted. "Sure," he whispered. Then he leaned forward, wincing at the soreness in his back and legs. "But first, I need to ask you to do something for me."

Isaiah's eyes lit, conveying his answer.

"What's the closest town with a tele-
___h?"

___h didn't answer immediately. His
___rehead sunk low. "Why?"

___e I need to send a wire to a man
___ Springs Bank." Larson took a
___?d tried to ignore the pain.
___ get word to him. I could

lose everything I have in this life, everything I own. My ranch, my land."

Isaiah stood abruptly. "I'm afraid that's impossible." He turned away, grabbed the bowl on the table, and stalked back to the cupboard. He kept his back turned. "It's been snowing for days now, heavy and wet. It'll be at least a month before the passes are clear enough to travel. And that's only if we get fair weather." He threw a hasty glance to the window. "That's doubtful at this point."

Sensing his chance slipping away, Larson sought another angle, ashamed that Kathryn hadn't been his first reason for sending a telegram. "But this way I could get word to my wife that I'm alive. I'm sure she's beside herself with worry and—"

Isaiah turned. The keen perception in his eyes withered the excuse on Larson's tongue, while at the same time laying b Larson's true motives.

Larson glanced away briefly, rassed, yet refusing to accept th day of the past ten years spent h ranch was going to end up nothing. "Listen, I'll reimbu' expe es you might—"

Isaiah slammed the bowl down and turned back. "It's not about the money, Jennings!" He didn't speak for a moment, and Larson grew even more uncomfortable beneath his stare. "Have you not learned that yet, after all you've been through? Not everything in life can be measured in dollars and cents."

Larson lay back, stunned. Isaiah's dark eyes were black with fury, along with another emotion he couldn't define.

Isaiah's lip trembled, almost imperceptibly. A small frown crossed his forehead. "I'm sorry, but you don't know what you're asking. I'll tend your wounds. I'll help you gain your strength so you can walk and return to your life again. Everything Abby and I have is at your disposal."

The fear etched in Isaiah's rugged face hit Larson like a physical blow.

Isaiah walked to the door, shoulders weighted, head bowed, then turned back to face him. "Even if I could make it across those passes, which I'm sure I couldn't, this thing you ask comes at too high a price. It would cost more than riches. Last time I went back to that town, it nearly cost me my life."

→ CHAPTER | SIX

Kathryn reined in the chestnut sorrel mare as she crested the top of the ridge. She reached down and rubbed the horse's sleek coat. Chestnut had been a gift from Larson five years earlier and was a faithful mount. Kathryn looked east to the miles of snow-dusted prairie stretching as far as she could see, gentle waves of land swelling and dipping as it raced to greet the sunrise. Divine brushstrokes of pastels swept the horizon and reflected off the snow, proclaiming the Master's touch.

A sense of peace moved over her, displacing her apprehension and fear in a way she'd be hard-pressed to explain to Matthew Taylor, who rode beside her. Her breath puffed white in the numbing March dawn. She pulled her scarf up over her nose and mouth for added warmth.

Matthew turned back. "Mrs. Jennings, we need to keep these cattle movin' if we're to make Jefferson's ranch by noon. We can't afford to leave the rest of the herd with just two men much longer than that."

She nodded, recalling his protests at her coming along at all. "You and Mr. Dunham go on ahead. I'll catch up with you."

Matthew Taylor gave her a look that said he wasn't keen on leaving her. She returned it with one of confidence.

He sighed. "Follow my path when you come down the ridge. And mind you, stay to the middle." With a last look of warning, he shook his head and prodded his mount over the ridge.

Despite the doubt and grief plaguing her in recent days, the unmistakable sense of God's presence stoked to life the dying embers of hope inside her. Kathryn recalled the words she'd read that morning. *The Lord is my light and my salvation; whom shall I fear? the Lord is the strength of my life; of whom shall I be afraid?*

Following her heart's lead, she glanced behind her and scanned the snowcapped peaks shrouded in mist and cloud. In two more weeks, if he did not return by then, Larson would have been gone for three months. Winter's hand was harsh in the Colorado Territory, but she reminded herself of Larson's knowledge of and respect for this land. Surely he'd found his way through the storm that night. Tempted to trust in that thought alone, Kathryn fixed her hope on heaven instead. *Father, I entrust Larson to you. Again.*

Breathing in the earthy scent of cattle and winter and fresh fallen snow, she urged Chestnut forward. As they started over the ridge, Kathryn leaned slightly to the side and searched the plowed mass of snow and earth for Matthew's exact path. Not spotting it, she reined in sharply. Chestnut whinnied, and the horse's footing slipped. The animal strained at the bit, edging closer to the right side.

Kathryn secured the reins, careful not to jerk back. She spoke to Chestnut in low soothing tones, as Larson had taught her, and tried to coerce her back from the edge. A frantic, primitive cry pierced the air just as the sorrel's legs buckled.

Kathryn hit the icy slope face down and

started to slide. A sharp blow to her ribs forced the air from her lungs. She gasped for breath and grabbed for anything to slow her slippery descent. Frozen scrub brush slipped through her gloved hands. Bits of gravel and rock bit into her cheeks. The further she slid, the less pain she felt.

Until she finally felt nothing at all.

A rush of cold air chilled her skin and brought the hovering voices closer. Hands moved over her bodice and down her sides. Kathryn tried to restrain them and cried out at the pain streaking across her chest.

"Keep still, Mrs. Jennings. Just keep still."

Recognizing Matthew Taylor's voice, she did as he said. She opened her eyes, blinking against the bright sunlight. Another man stood above her. Harley Dunham.

He slanted a look at Taylor. "I told ya calicos have no place on a cattle drive. You shoulda said no to her comin', boss."

"Stop talkin', Dunham, and go see to the horse." Mr. Taylor leaned close. Kathryn could feel his breath on her face. "Mrs. Jennings, can you hear me?"

She nodded, her mind still humming from

the pain that exploded in her chest when she moved.

"Don't move, okay?"

"Don't worry," she whispered, trying to manage a smile. It hurt even to breathe.

"I think you may have cracked a rib or two." Taylor bit his lower lip.

A shot sounded, and Kathryn tensed. *Chestnut.* Tears burned her eyes and her throat ached.

Taylor jerked off his hat and forked a hand through his hair. "I'm sorry, Mrs. Jennings. Looks like this wasn't such a good idea after all. I never should have said yes," he whispered, more to himself than to her. He searched her face. "We're still at least three hours away from town. Do you think you can ride?"

She nodded, wondering if she could bear the pain.

"It's just like when I saw that white owl, boss." Dunham came back into view, shouldering his rifle. "I tell ya, a woman runnin' things is just bad luck."

Taylor's jaw clenched tight. He stood and grabbed Dunham by the shirt. "Go mount up. Mrs. Jennings will ride point with me. You take the drag and follow behind."

Dunham strode off, mumbling something beneath his breath.

Kathryn stared into the cloudless, ethereal blue above and wished for only one thing—for Larson to be by her side.

Mr. Taylor knelt down beside her. His eyes darted to hers, then away again. "I'm sorry. This is gonna hurt, but I can't leave you here alone. And Dunham can't drive this herd by himself."

Kathryn nodded again and took a deep breath. "I'm ready."

Taylor slipped his arms beneath her and drew her to his chest. She bit her lip to keep from crying out. She tasted blood and her head swam. As they passed, she caught a glimpse of Chestnut's massive, still body.

As though reading her thoughts, Taylor whispered, "Don't worry, ma'am. I'll come back and take care of her for you. She was a good mount. A lady-broke horse if I ever saw one. Real gentle. I remember the day your husband bought her for you. He had a real eye for—" Taylor heaved a sigh. "I'm sorry, Mrs. Jennings. I didn't mean to sound like . . ."

Kathryn shook her head. "No, that's all right."

He lifted her to the saddle, then mounted behind her. Her head swam again, and she clenched her eyes in an effort to endure the pain. As they reached the front of the herd, her voice sounded like it was traveling through a tunnel back to her. "Let me apologize in advance, Mr. Taylor, if I pass out on you."

"You just go ahead and do what you need to, ma'am." His voice grew dim, but Kathryn felt his grip tighten around her waist. "And I'll do the same. . . ."

With perspiration beading her forehead, Kathryn managed to button her shirtwaist and fasten her skirt behind the screen in the doctor's office. The bandages tightly binding her midsection were uncomfortable but had eased the pain considerably. She smoothed the wrinkles from her skirt, wincing at the already purpling bruise on her midsection that lay hidden beneath the folds. She was fortunate to have suffered only two broken ribs and a few bruises and scrapes in the fall.

Foolishness swept through her again as she thought of what she'd done. Her pride stung.

She had pressed Matthew to let her join them on the cattle drive when clearly he'd been set against it. But she'd wanted so badly to be part of seeing the ranch succeed. Larson's dream, and hers now. She bowed her head as her confidence shed a layer of hope.

Even if Larson failed to return to her, by keeping the ranch she would somehow still have a part of him. Though she'd resisted the idea that he'd intentionally left her, a seed of doubt still clung at the base of her resolve and was slowly taking root. *Lord, if he does not come back, for whatever reason, please help me see his dream, our dream, to fruition.*

The aging doctor rinsed his hands in a basin of water and peered at her over his spectacles. "Mrs. Jennings, what you attempted was foolhardy. You're a fortunate woman, indeed. You could have sustained a serious injury in a fall like that."

The way the doctor dipped his head toward her, piercing her with his gaze, made Kathryn feel like a small child again. She nodded, the weight of her choices of recent days sagging her shoulders. "I'll be more careful in the future, I assure you."

"Have you fared well the past few weeks?"

She frowned at the odd question, then quickly realized that Matthew Taylor must have confided to the physician about her situation. She tried not to feel a bit peeved that he would have shared something so personal. It had been uncomfortable enough when the doctor had done a personal examination for internal injuries, but this too. . . .

"My appetite has suffered, and I've been a little more tired than usual." Recalling the last two and half months and the burden she'd carried—still carried—Kathryn knew she had a right to be weary. She retrieved her coat and gloves from the chair, eager to be done. Though thankful for the doctor's attention to her injuries, she didn't appreciate his gruff manner.

"Well, you should get over that quickly enough. You're a healthy, strong young woman."

His callousness left Kathryn speechless. She took coins from her coat pocket and deposited them on the desk.

The doctor nodded toward the money, indicating his thanks, then followed her to the door. "And don't let old wives' tales stoke fear inside you for something that's been going on since the beginning of time." He lightly patted her back. "Women have been having babies since the Garden of Eden. You'll do just fine."

Kathryn stilled, then felt the blood drain from her face. She turned back. "What do you mean?" she whispered.

The doctor touched her shoulder. "Are you all right, Mrs. Jennings?" Then his eyes went wide. A frown crossed his face. "You mean you didn't know?"

Kathryn felt her knees go weak. She reached out and clutched his arm. He stayed her with a strong grip and led her to a chair. She sank down, the soreness from her broken ribs and bruised body nothing compared to the equal parts of pain and joy now flooding her heart.

She was with child. Larson's child. Finally. After all these years. She swallowed against the bittersweet truth of it.

"When?" Her voice sounded so small.

The doctor lifted his shoulders. "My guess would be September, maybe October. Hard to tell this early."

Tears wet her cheeks. Kathryn didn't bother to wipe them away. She smoothed a hand over her abdomen, over the gift of life blossoming within her once-barren womb. If a son, would he have Larson's blue eyes and thick mane of dark hair? Or would their daughter claim her own coloring? Long-awaited fulfillment pricked her heart, and she gave thanks to God for the child she and Larson had always wanted.

A child that Larson might never hold.

———

Larson lay awake during the night and stared into the darkness, sleep a distant companion. The muted tick of a clock marked off the seconds, reminding him both of time's brevity and its anguishing slowness.

The bold finality of Isaiah's response to his request over a week ago still thundered inside him. Had he really asked so much of the man? With every faint *tick, tick, tick* Larson imagined the swing of the pendulum and could feel the last decade of his life and all he'd worked so hard for being wrenched from his grasp.

At the familiar creak of the door, he turned to see Isaiah's formidable shadow filling the entry. Having spoken little to each other in recent days, Larson found that the seed of their last conversation had taken bitter root inside him. And not until that moment did he realize how lonely he was for companionship, someone to talk to.

Thinking of what Kathryn's reaction would be if she knew tempted him to smile. She was always trying to get him to talk more.

"I couldn't sleep." Isaiah's deep timbered voice came out a whisper. "Sun'll be coming up soon. I was wondering if you'd like to join me."

"It's been forever since I've seen a sunrise," Larson finally answered. He sensed Isaiah's smile, though darkness obscured it.

Isaiah drew back the covers and assisted as Larson painstakingly lowered his legs over the side of the bed. When the soles of Larson's bare feet met the cold wooden floor, shivers shot up his spine. Isaiah draped a heavy blanket around his body, and Larson braced his hands on the side of the bed. He managed to stand but felt his legs giving way beneath the unaccustomed weight.

Isaiah lifted him in his arms, and Larson clenched his jaw tight as shame poured through him. The extent of his injuries hit him all over again, and anger at his dependency momentarily saturated his self-pity. No doubt Isaiah felt his discomfort, yet the man said nothing. Larson purposefully kept his face turned away as his esteem for Isaiah grew.

Isaiah carried him from the bedroom directly into another room—what looked to be the only other room—of the cabin. The promise of coffee layered the room's warmth, and Larson took the chance to inventory his surroundings.

Sparse was the first word that came to mind. A scant arrangement of furniture dotted the small space. An amber-orange fire glowed from the fireplace, radiating warmth. And in the shadows in front of the hearth, he made out a small bundled form lying curled up on one side on a pallet.

An unexpected lump lodged in his throat.

This couple had given so much to him. But why? He'd thought of little else besides his own predicament since awakening. A glimpse of his own selfishness barbed him.

Isaiah flicked the latch from the cabin door, and cold air rushed around them.

Surprisingly, it felt good against Larson's skin. Glancing ahead of him, he quickly realized that this was no chance gathering. A cushioned chair sat catty-corner on the small porch, blankets piled on the floor beside it. Two mugs of what he bet was coffee sat atop a portion of porch rail that had been cleared of snow. Steam spiraled against the pinkish hues of the eastern horizon.

Isaiah lowered him into the chair and covered him.

"Couldn't sleep, huh?" An apologetic smile tipped Larson's mouth, and he wished he had the words to convey his gratitude—and his remorse.

Isaiah handed him one of the cups and their eyes met.

In that brief exchange, Larson knew that Isaiah was a man of unquestionable honor and kindness. Then, as though a mirror had appeared before him, Larson saw himself and lowered his gaze.

Isaiah leaned against the porch rail and looked out across the treetops. Moments passed. Thick stands of aspen and birch cleaved the small clearing around the cabin, and the faint rustle of awakening life stirred in the frosted brush. Larson looked westward over his shoulder and, gauging from the peaks in the near distance, figured he was a good fifteen or twenty miles farther northwest from where he'd camped in the ravine that night.

Isaiah turned to look at him. "How did Abby's chicken and dumplings settle on your stomach?"

"Fine. It's good to have solid food again. Your Abby's a great cook." He took a deep breath. "Look, Isaiah . . . I'm sorry about the other day. I don't know your reasons, but . . . I know they must be important." Larson wrestled the next words off the tip of his tongue. "So I won't ask you again."

Isaiah nodded and turned again to con-centrate on a spot on the horizon.

Larson tracked his focus to a smattering of clouds in the east. They hung low in the sky, like tinted shreds of cotton on a blanket of gray, reflecting the coming dawn in soft wisps of purple and pink.

Larson took a sip of coffee and relished the warmth in his throat. "So what hap-pened after the doctor won you? After you gained your freedom?"

For a moment, Isaiah just looked at the mug in his grip. "Well, at first Doc Lewis gave me work sweeping and cleaning his patient rooms. He was the first white man who ever looked at me like a man . . .

treated me like a man. In time, he showed me where to pick the ingredients for his poultices and remedies, which plants they came from and where they grew. Which wasn't foreign to me because my grandmother was a healer—she'd taught me a lot of that. But I'd never seen some of the plants and trees that grew out here. They're different from down South. Doc showed me how to mix them, like my grandmother had." The edges of his mouth tipped slightly. "So that became my job, which was better than harvesting cotton and pulling a plow for sure.

"People had been coming to the doc's clinic for years. He cared about them. He had me deliver the medicines to families outside of town when he couldn't go himself. Doc treated me well; he was my friend. Taught me how to read and write, how to speak suitably to the townsfolk." The deep timbre of Isaiah's voice accentuated the stillness. "I watched and learned from him, and for some reason, people kept coming to the clinic even after Doc Lewis died. I'd listen to what ailed them and then mix the remedy Doc would've given them."

Larson saw a smile ghost Isaiah's profile, then slowly fade.

"One day a couple of families new to town got sick. Folks around there found out they'd been to see me and figured I was the cause. That I'd poisoned them." Emotion textured his hushed voice. "Some of the men in the town . . . visited me that night. When I woke up again, I was lying in the dirt, naked, with a noose around my neck. At first I thought maybe they just hadn't picked a strong enough branch." He shook his head. "But that limb looked like it had been cut clean through."

Larson noticed the cabin door edge open slightly. Abby's shadowed silhouette stilled.

"The families died, all but one of the women. I know because as soon as I was able I gathered supplies from the clinic and went to their houses by night. When I got there, I found the woman barely alive." Isaiah shook his head, the early dawn giving his dark complexion a bronzed glow. "Nobody was with her. Not a soul. She was sick with the cholera. It swept through the town, took a lot of people with it."

Larson looked from Isaiah back to Abby, who stood in the doorway, silent tears coursing down her cheeks.

Isaiah sighed. "I didn't know if I could help

her, but I knew I couldn't leave her to die. I also knew that if those men found me again, they'd hang me for sure. So I took her and went to an old cabin near a mining town that Doc and I had come across on one of our trips. Thanks to God's mercy, she got better. And I eventually took her back to her home."

"But I wouldn't stay," Abby whispered, opening the door fully. Going to Isaiah, she went and laid a hand on his shoulder. He reached up and covered it with his own. "I'd already found my home."

Larson stared at the two of them. Abby's small white hand covered by Isaiah's large black one. Such an unlikely pair, and with so much against them to start with. His throat tightened as he watched the love pass between them. Had they not known him so intimately already, he might have felt uncomfortable intruding upon the tender moment.

As it was, all he could think about was Kathryn and whether she could ever come to care for him with that same intensity. But even more, could he ever be the kind of man who would inspire such love?

CHAPTER SEVEN

Kathryn gathered her robe about her and peered through the cabin window at the imposing-looking man standing on the other side of the door. The top of his head reached at least a hand's length above the threshold and his powerful build was daunting.

He pounded again and she jumped. What could he want? And so early in the morning. The sun was scarcely up. Almost without thinking, she placed a hand over her still-flat belly in protection of the child inside her. *Lord, keep us both safe.*

She unbolted the door and opened it a crack. "Yes, may I help you?"

"Good morning, Mrs. Jennings." The man removed his hat to reveal a more youthful and decidedly friendlier looking face than Kathryn expected. "I'm here to talk to you about the job." He spoke as though his words were measured, carefully thought out beforehand.

Her fears eased considerably. Despite his size, there was something in the man's deep blue eyes that persuaded her to trust him. Still trying to decide what it was exactly, she nodded. "You'll need to see Mr. Taylor about that. He's responsible for all the hiring, but I'm certain we'll have work for you."

The rest of the ranch hands had quit a week ago. Apparently they shared Harley Dunham's opinion about working for a woman. Matthew had put word out that they were hiring, but so far they'd had only scant inquiries. She felt sure that Matthew would not turn this man away.

He dipped his head in deference. "What would you like me to do first? I can start right now." He accentuated each syllable, and his eyes twinkled.

Seeing his eager expression, Kathryn realized what it was that inspired her trust.

This man possessed an innocence that belied his formidable stature. She couldn't help but smile. It was like watching a little boy at Christmas. "If you're that eager to get started, there are chores to do in the barn. The animals need to be fed and—"

"Oh, I know what to do in a barn, ma'am." He grinned as he slipped his hat back on. "I've been in one of those before."

Kathryn stared across the desk at Harold Kohlman, fighting to hold her temper in check. "But my understanding was that I owed you the amount I borrowed when I was last here. I'm bringing that amount in full today, the second of April, like we agreed. Here, I have the contract we signed together."

Kohlman glanced at the papers in her hand but didn't reach to take them. "I know very well what I signed that day, Mrs. Jennings. The bank has its own copy. But you are obviously unaware that your husband also secured a loan on your homestead prior to that time." His eyes narrowed slightly. "That payment was due two weeks ago—on the sixteenth of March. The loan is now in default."

Silent until now, Matthew Taylor leaned forward in his chair. "Mr. Kohlman, I'm here on Mrs. Jennings' behalf. Larson Jennings has not been seen or heard from in over three months. We don't know his where-abouts . . . or if he'll be returning."

Matthew looked down, and Kathryn saw him wince. She knew he hated to speak so plainly in her presence but was thankful for his offer to accompany her.

"We have reason to think he might have been caught in the storm that hit Christmas Day," he continued. "Fact is, he may not be comin' home. We just don't know."

Kohlman looked at her dispassionately. "Regardless of whether your husband is alive or not, Mrs. Jennings, the loan is now due. The bank has, in good faith, loaned that money to you and your husband. If you cannot repay the loan, we'll be forced to take action."

"What do you mean by 'take action,' Mr. Kohlman?" Mr. Taylor asked.

"Well, foreclose, of course."

Kathryn nearly came to her feet. "You have no right to—"

"I have every right, Mrs. Jennings." Crimson crept up the pudgy folds of Kohlman's neck. "Your husband signed an agreement with me, whether you were aware of it or not."

"But you should have told me about that loan on the day we met. You shouldn't have withheld that information from me."

"Mrs. Jennings, I do not consider it my responsibility to relay business details between a husband and wife. It is a husband's business what he decides to share with his wife." His eyes cooled. "I am not the one who withheld that information from you, ma'am."

At his withering glance, Kathryn felt the fight drain from her. She sank back in her seat. The dream of keeping the ranch was slipping through her fingers. Why had Larson kept this from her? It hurt that he hadn't told her, that he hadn't trusted her enough to help bear this burden. She took a deep breath, struggling to maintain her composure.

"Given Mrs. Jennings' situation, how long does she have to repay the loan before you foreclose?"

Kathryn glanced from Mr. Taylor back to Kohlman.

Kohlman's left eye twitched. "I'll give her

until September, and I'm being generous in that offer. Then all loans will be due in full."

"All loans!" Kathryn prayed she'd misheard him.

The banker laced his fingers over his protruding stomach. The leather chair creaked under his weight. "That's right. The agreement your husband signed last spring clearly stated that if he defaulted on any portion of this loan, then the balance of all loans would be due. That includes the land, the cattle, the homestead. Everything."

Though she was no expert in banking, Kathryn had gleaned some knowledge through overhearing her father's business dealings. "May I see the agreement my husband signed?"

Kohlman opened a file already on his desk and shoved the papers across to her, then eyed his pocket watch.

Ignoring him, she carefully read through the agreement. Though she didn't understand all the legal jargon of the lengthy document, a sickening feeling weighted her chest when she recognized Larson's signature at the bottom. "Is this standard practice, Mr. Kohlman? To call in all loans if one payment is late?"

His look told her he didn't like being questioned. "Only for those patrons who are considered to be high risk."

She blinked. "High risk?"

His brief smile twisted her stomach. "Your husband fell behind in payments last year. We worked with him, of course, as we do with all our patrons." He shook his head and sighed. "If I bear any fault in this it would be that I was too generous in my estimation of your husband's business acumen. And for that, I am indeed sorry. That, however, doesn't change your situation."

The blow of the insult struck Kathryn with more impact than if Kohlman had directed it straight at her. But why had Larson not shared this with her? She thought back, remembering how the previous winter's brutal cold had cost them several hundred head of cattle. Apparently the loss had been more devastating than she'd imagined. What anxiety Larson must have been shouldering alone. . . .

"Mr. Kohlman." Matthew Taylor leaned forward in his chair, his face determined. "I've worked for Mr. Jennings for over six years. He's a good man and has a natural savvy about him when it comes to overseeing his ranch. He wouldn't take any unnecessary risks with it, I can guarantee you that."

When Mr. Taylor rose, Kathryn rose with him. He looked her way and, with a slight nod, she thanked him for his kind words.

"Nevertheless, here we are." Kohlman spread his arms wide as though a banquet had been set before him.

Kathryn got the impression he was almost pleased with himself. Something inside her rebelled. She would fight to keep this ranch if it cost her everything else she possessed. If for no other reason than to give the child secreted inside her womb— Larson's child—a tangible legacy of the father he might never know.

Kathryn waited outside the bank building while Mr. Taylor retrieved the wagon from the livery. The sun played hide-and-seek behind a cloud-dotted sky, and the unseasonably warm temperatures in recent days promised rain instead of the customary snow.

Her chest tightened when she thought of Mr. Kohlman's deception. And that's clearly what it had been. He should have told her about the preexisting lien on the homestead the day she secured her loan. Regardless, as he'd declared so glibly, that didn't change the situation.

Seeing Mr. Taylor bringing the wagon at a distance, Kathryn stepped off the board-walk and into the street. As she walked toward him she froze, unable to move forward. She stared at the back of a man on the boardwalk on the opposite side of the street. The sight of his broad shoulders and thick mane of unruly dark brown hair made her heart leap.

Larson.

Dodging wagons, puddles, and deposits of sludge and muck, Kathryn tracked his path through the crowd. She could barely contain her joy as she climbed the stairs to the crowded boardwalk. Still several paces away, she felt a flutter in her stomach and knew God had heard her prayers. Then the man turned and her breath left her in a rush.

She stopped short when she saw his ruddy, pocked complexion and heavily lid-ded eyes. Though clean-shaven like Larson, the man lacked any hint of her husband's rugged charm and handsome features. She slowly bowed her head and turned away.

Jostled by the crowd, she felt a hand to her arm. Expecting to see Mr. Taylor, Kathryn turned and came uncomfortably close to another man. She took a step back and raised her eyes. As he had been the day she'd met him outside the bank, Mr. Mac-Gregor's suited attire was immaculate and his eyes chilling.

"Mr. MacGregor." She forced a polite nod.

He raised a brow and his eyes shone with obvious pleasure. "You remembered, lass. Now that does give me fresh hope."

The weight of the day's events bore down, and Kathryn's patience evaporated. "If you'll excuse me, please." She brushed past him, ignoring his flirtatious smile. She searched the street for Mr. Taylor.

"Looking for someone, are you?" He followed closely, shadowing her steps.

The remark roused fresh pain from the disillusionment of moments before. She stilled. She'd been so sure the man was Larson. As Matthew had stated inside Mr. Kohlman's office, over three months had passed. He should have returned by now. Kathryn bowed her head to hide her emotion. At the same time, she knew this trick her heart was playing. In past years, she'd caught glimpses of her mother in the way another woman would brush back a strand of hair from her temple or check the brooch at her neckline. It was simply the heart's way of trying to hold onto something that was lost forever.

MacGregor tipped her chin with his forefinger. "Is something wrong, Mrs. Jennings?"

She turned her head slightly to evade his touch. Surprisingly, his compassion appeared to be genuine, but Kathryn's instinct told her otherwise. She wasn't about to share her most private thoughts in the middle of a crowded boardwalk, and certainly not with this man.

"I assure you, I'm fine."

"Well, that's good to hear, because I'd hate to think you were distressed in any way." His gaze dropped from her eyes, lowering briefly before lifting again.

Kathryn felt a blush start in her neck and move upward.

"Would you allow me the honor of your company for lunch today, Mrs. Jennings? And that of your husband, of course. I'd like to discuss a business proposition with you both." He looked up and down the street. "Your husband is with you, is he not? I assume that's who you're waiting for."

For an instant, Kathryn almost believed that he'd spoken the words with intentional cruelty. But when he turned back, she searched his face and knew that her own sense of loss was coloring her judgment.

She spotted Mr. Taylor on the opposite side of the street. "I'm sorry, Mr. MacGregor, but I must decline. Good day."

She crossed the street quickly. Taylor assisted her into the wagon, then climbed up beside her. The horses responded to his command. "Why were you talkin' with him?"

Kathryn wondered at the coolness in his tone. "I wasn't really. He approached me about—"

"Do you know who he is?"

Knowing little more about the man other than his name, she shook her head.

"That's Donlyn MacGregor. He's owns the largest ranch in the Colorado Territory, and he's been buyin' up all the land around here for the past few years." He laughed, but there was no humor in it. "I only know what I've been told, but I'd advise you to steer clear of him. He's a powerful man, and word has it he's not above bending the law in order to get what he wants. Plus they say he has friends in high places, and I don't mean that to his credit." With a flick of his wrist, Matthew Taylor urged the team of horses to a trot.

Kathryn turned around to look behind her and spotted Donlyn MacGregor walking through the doors of the Willow Springs Bank. Facing forward again she stole a sideways glance. The stiff set of Matthew's broad shoulders told her he didn't invite conversation on the matter. Her own instincts partially confirmed Matthew's warning, yet another part of her couldn't help but wonder. . . . A powerful man with friends in high places might be just what she needed to help keep Larson's ranch.

CHAPTER EIGHT

His breath came heavy, but at Isaiah's insistence and against his own will, Larson tried again. The muscles in his legs screamed from the effort just as the makeshift weights slipped again from his ankles. The padded bricks landed on the wooden planks with a thud.

Exhausted, Larson clutched the chair he was sitting in and let his feet fall back to the floor, barely reining his temper. "Like I told you before, it's too soon for this, Isaiah. My legs aren't strong enough."

Isaiah said nothing for a moment, then moved to pick up the bricks. "That's what you said two weeks ago when you tried the walker."

"Yeah, and I couldn't do that either."

"You took a few steps with it. That's a good start."

"I took *two* steps and fell flat on my face!"

Isaiah sighed heavily, but it didn't hint at exasperation. Larson had yet to see the man lose his temper, though they'd been following Isaiah's regimen of exercise for nearly a month now with little to show for it.

Isaiah cradled the two bricks in one massive hand. "Your lack of strength doesn't lie in your body, Larson." With his free hand, he slowly traced the place over his heart. "It lies here."

Larson threw him a scathing look. "What's that supposed to mean?"

"It means you don't want it badly enough yet." The patience in Isaiah's eyes matched the quiet of his voice, and kindled Larson's anger.

He gripped the sides of the chair and bit back a curse. They'd been doing this for the last hour, and he'd barely managed to lift his feet more than four inches off the floor before his muscles would begin to tremble and the bricks would fall. Despite Isaiah's encouragement, he doubted he'd ever regain use of his legs. Between the gunshot wound, the fire, and the weeks he'd spent in bed, his muscles had weakened to the point where Larson hardly recognized his own body.

"Let's try it once more before supper." Isaiah reached out to reposition Larson's legs.

Larson suddenly wished he had the strength to kick him. "No."

Isaiah's hands stilled. He looked up. "What?"

Larson kept his head down and licked his parched lips. "I said no. I've had enough for today."

A moment passed. Isaiah gently laid the bricks aside and stood.

Larson sensed Isaiah's eyes on him but didn't lift his head. His chest tightened as he prepared himself for another of Isaiah's miracle stories meant to bolster his spirits. The tales always stemmed from either the mining camps or the Bible, but whichever the source, Larson knew they contained only false hope. The truth of his situation was undeniable.

Larson cringed as he looked at his legs.

He'd never walk again, much less be able to run his ranch. And Kathryn. Why would she ever want such a broken shell of a man?

"You hungry?" Isaiah asked, pulling Larson's thoughts back. "I bet Abby's got some of her warm corn bread and stew ready by now."

Larson nodded, thankful for the unexpected reprieve. "Sure, that sounds good. I'm starved." Humbled both by Isaiah's understanding and his own need for assistance, Larson held out his arms.

Isaiah placed the walker in front of him. "Come on in when you're ready, then. We'll wait for you."

Larson's head shot up just as Isaiah disappeared through the doorway. He looked from the walker to the door and back, disbelieving. He knew Isaiah well enough to know what he was doing, and it galled him to the core.

He squeezed his eyes shut against a sudden burning sensation and swore aloud. Did Isaiah see this as some sort of game? Or challenge perhaps? Larson gripped the sides of the chair again and shifted his body till his spine was flush with the back of the chair. Part of him wanted to call out an apology and get it over with. Another part of him knew that no matter what he said, Isaiah wasn't coming back. And neither would Abby. Not with Isaiah standing in the gap.

He heard the clink of dishes and Abby's soft voice in the next room, but he couldn't make out what she was saying. Isaiah responded, but their conversation was indistinct.

He reached for the walker with his left hand and dragged it closer. The pine wood was smooth and well sanded, not that Larson could feel any imperfections with his scarred palms. It was obvious Isaiah had painstakingly crafted this for him. That realization did little to quell his anger at the moment.

Larson positioned the walker over his legs. He could move his legs—that wasn't the problem. Sustaining his weight was another story. He gripped the sturdy pine and pushed up, but he barely got out of the chair before his arms burned from the effort and gave way. He fell back with such force that the chair almost toppled over, taking him with it. Catching himself just in time, rage pulsed through his body. He clenched his jaw until it hurt.

Larson positioned himself in the chair again, winded from the exertion. "God, why on earth am I here?" he growled through clenched teeth. Blowing out a breath, he rubbed his hands over his face, noticing the occasional spot of facial hair that was growing back in, patchy and thin. Abby had said she would give him a shave tonight.

He listened for noises coming from the other room. Nothing.

He could well imagine Isaiah sitting at the table, large hands clasped, waiting for him, watching the door and ready to smile in triumph. Larson huffed in disgust and caught a whiff of Abby's stew. His mouth watered at the savory scent of meat.

Adjusting the walker, he managed a firm grip and tried again. His arms trembled from the exertion, but he held on. Once up, he locked his arms and took a second to catch his breath. He gradually transferred a portion of his weight to his legs, certain that at any moment his bones would snap.

A trickle of sweat ran down his left temple.

Thankfully, he was facing the doorway so he didn't have to negotiate a turn. He took one step and paused, then took another.

His heart pounded so heavily he thought he might pass out. But at least he hadn't fallen. Not yet.

He shut his eyes and willed his right leg to move again. His muscles signaled back to his brain and he let out a gasp. Weary from the exertion, Larson leaned forward until his forearms rested on the walker.

"Your lack of strength doesn't lie in your body."

With renewed resolve, Larson refocused all his energy on his right leg—and finally, it moved! He half dragged it forward, but still it moved. By the time he made it to the door, his chest heaved with exertion, his arms felt like wax. He slumped against the doorframe for support, able to make out the edge of the table but nothing else.

He took another step and another, each staggered shuffle a begrudging testament to the determination he thought he'd lost.

He spotted Abby first, seated at the table. Their eyes met and the light of hope filled her gaze. When she smiled, he managed one back. But Isaiah was nowhere in sight. No matter. Determined not to be bested, Larson struggled forward. He lifted his left leg and was midstride when his right knee buckled beneath him. His grip went slack. He braced himself for the impact, but it never came.

Strong black arms like bands of tempered steel came from nowhere, taking hold of him. After a moment, Larson dared to look into Isaiah's face.

"You did it," Isaiah whispered, beaming.

"Oh, Larson," Abby spoke from across the room, tears glistening. She chuckled.

Isaiah squeezed his shoulder tight, and Larson drew from his strength. "I knew you could do it. You and the Almighty."

Surprising himself, Larson laughed in relief and wondered again at how the man holding him could trust so steadfastly in a God who had allowed him to experience such heartache in his life. Abby too. Isaiah had told him the other night that Jesus held him and Abby safe in the palm of His hand, and Larson found himself wanting to believe that.

But how could you trust in someone who promised to shelter you safe in the palm of His hand, when sometimes He still let you fall?

The next morning the three of them shared breakfast at the table. Larson caught the furtive glances Isaiah and Abby shared, along with their secretive smiles. When he finally questioned them about it, Isaiah took something from beneath his seat and laid it by Larson's plate.

Larson glanced at the book, then returned his attention to his food, keenly aware that they were watching him, waiting for his reaction. His first thought was of Kathryn and how she cherished the words that lay beneath a similar well-worn cover. His second thought, mixed with an odd pang of emotion, was that he'd never seen the benefit in reading the Bible. Still didn't.

But neither was he anxious to insult his host and hostess. They read together each morning. He'd heard them. How could he not in a cabin this small? Still, he wasn't one to pretend something he didn't feel.

"Abby and I thought you might like to read with us this morning."

Larson shrugged, trying to think of a way to kindly decline.

"You're not afraid of a book written hundreds of years ago, are you?" Isaiah nudged the book closer to him, hunching his broad shoulders in a blatant attempt at sincerity, but his teasing voice gave him away. "It's only words dried on paper," he whispered, repeating something Larson had said to him. A smile tipped Isaiah's mouth, and Abby laughed softly beside him.

Larson looked from one to the other, knowing he was being baited. But he owed these two people his life. "Where should I start?"

Isaiah's eyes took on new warmth. "At the beginning would be good." He turned past the first few pages, then stopped.

Larson stared at the words on the page, wondering at the increased rate of his pulse. He started reading aloud, but he hadn't read four words when Isaiah stopped him.

"Read that part again, please."

Larson sighed, feeling another one of Isaiah's lessons coming on. He played along anyway. " 'In the beginning God . . .' " He paused, looking up.

"I love that part." Isaiah smiled as though having just tasted Abby's apple pie.

Not understanding the look the couple exchanged, Larson cocked a brow. "And what part is that? I barely got started."

"Don't you see it? In the beginning . . . God," Isaiah answered.

Larson searched Isaiah's face, all too aware of a place deep inside him that was beginning to respond.

Isaiah slowly shook his head. "It's not about you. It's not about me. This life that we live, the reason we're here. It's only when we see our lives through eternal eyes that we find true peace or wealth that will last. Real security can only be found in that which can never be taken from you . . . in a relationship with God."

Intensity deepened Isaiah's gaze, and there was no question that he believed what he said. What must it be like to believe in something so intently? To be so sure. It sparked a yearning within Larson, intriguing him to know more. And for the first time in this second chance at life, he hoped that Isaiah's faith—and Isaiah's God—would stand the test.

CHAPTER NINE

If you keep improving at this rate, you'll be strong enough to travel soon." Larson returned Isaiah's grin across the table and felt a rush of gratitude for this couple sitting opposite him. "Thanks for sticking with me, Isaiah. You too, Abby."

Abby's blue eyes crinkled in answer, and Isaiah merely laid a hand over his heart and nodded.

In the past weeks, Larson's body had responded to Abby's cooking and Isaiah's exercise and medicinal regimen better than he'd imagined possible. This morning, following the normal ritual of exercise, or *torture,* as he'd taken to calling it, Abby had slathered her thick mixture of herbed poultices over his furrowed flesh, commenting on how his chest and arms were filling out. Even Larson was noticing a difference.

He spooned in another mouthful of venison and boiled potatoes, eager to push Isaiah's contraption in the woodshed to its full limit this afternoon.

"How's your leg feeling after this morning?" Abby asked, slicing him a generous portion of apple pie.

He nodded his thanks and washed his food down with water. "Better. That concoction you rubbed into it helped. It drew a few flies, but it helped." He shot her a look he knew would earn a grin.

Abby patted his arm and chuckled.

The wound where the bullet had entered his right leg had healed considerably but still pained him when he overexerted himself—something Isaiah constantly warned him against. Larson hoped to walk without a limp someday, but right now even his limp couldn't dampen his spirits.

After lunch, he followed Isaiah to the shed behind the cabin. Using the staff Isaiah had carved for him, Larson only managed one stride for Isaiah's every three, but at least he was walking on his own now. As with the walker, Isaiah had crafted the walking stick from sturdy pine, and it supported Larson's burden well. Amazing what a difference the independence made in his attitude.

He breathed in the chill of the late April day and smelled the promise of spring. White-laced boughs of towering blue spruce, no longer bent low to earth under the weight of heavy snow, seemed to be declaring their independence from winter's frosty grip. Stands of stalwart birch stretched their icy arms heavenward. All around him were signs of the land's awakening from a frozen slumber, much like the recent stirrings he sensed inside himself.

In the distance, the sun reflected off the snowy mountain peaks with a blinding brilliance that stung his eyes. How could he have lived here all his life and not been more appreciative of this land's beauty? And of God's hand in it all?

The last thought caught him by surprise, slowing his pace. *God's hand* . . . He'd always believed in God. What he hadn't realized, something that Isaiah and Abby were showing him, was . . . that God believed in him.

Larson's grip tightened on the staff in his right hand. He looked from the brilliance of the snowcapped mountains to the modest—and that was being generous—cabin where he'd spent nearly four months. Isaiah's words pierced his heart all over again. Strange how words, even those dried on a page—he smiled ruefully—could rob him of his sense of completeness while fostering a hunger inside him at the same time.

It was a hunger Larson had never known, and he wasn't completely sure what to do with it even now.

"Come on, we don't have all day," Isaiah goaded good-naturedly, holding open the door of the shed.

Isaiah's contraption of rudimentary weights, consisting of rocks of various sizes tied in bundles and hoisted over beams, pushed Larson's strength to exhaustion—far more than the bricks ever had. Without a word they began their rigorous routine, and later that night, after dinner, Larson undressed and fell into bed.

He rose the next morning well before dawn and carefully maneuvered his way through the dark cabin, mindful not to waken Isaiah or

Abby. Once outside, his staff in one hand and their Bible tucked beneath his arm, he wound his way down a wooded path that he and Isaiah had traveled once before. He shuddered in the predawn chill, his muscles stiff, but determination urged him forward.

Within a half hour, he reached his destination, his body tired, but in a good way. Lacking the smooth agility he had once possessed, Larson managed to awkwardly climb up onto a boulder that overlooked a serene mountain lake. His breath came heavy as he stretched out, welcoming the cool of the stone against his back. He cradled his arms behind his head and watched the last vestiges of night reluctantly surrender to dawn.

Despite his peaceful surroundings, a restlessness stirred inside him.

Up until a few months ago, the whole of his life had been centered on seeing his ranch succeed, in making a name for himself—something his illegitimate birth had denied him all his life. And he'd done it all so that Kathryn would be proud of him, so that he could earn her love.

He grimaced, knowing that wasn't the entire truth. No, he'd done it to ensure her faithfulness—though at the time he hadn't been sure if such a thing could even exist between a man and woman.

In watching Isaiah and Abby together over the past weeks, he'd observed their stolen glances and kisses, their quiet exchanges over things he'd once deemed unimportant. And studying how they were with each other had challenged his reasoning. While strengthening his view of marriage in one sense, it also laid bare the shortcomings of his own.

Besides Isaiah's and Abby's obvious differences, which he scarcely noticed anymore, Larson couldn't help but compare their marriage to his. Isaiah had attained nothing in terms of worldly wealth, and yet Abby adored him. Isaiah had no name to bestow on her, yet Abby bore the title of his wife as though it lent her kinship to royalty.

Dawn's first light trilled a finger across the lake, and Larson marveled at the shimmers of sunlight playing off the tranquil surface. He breathed in the air scented of pine.

He used to think that if he provided well enough for her, Kathryn would remain loyal to him. Or if he watched her closely enough, he could keep her from straying, from seeking a better man's arms. But how did a husband entrust his heart to his wife?

Larson scrubbed a hand over his face and sat up. The scant beard still felt foreign to him but helped hide the scarring on his face. His whiskers had grown back in patches, like his hair. He eased off the boulder and went to stand at the lake's edge, remembering his first afternoon here with Isaiah. Not until that afternoon, when he first saw his reflection in the water, had it occurred to him that there were no mirrors in the cabin.

He reached for the Bible resting on a nearby rock and turned to the place Abby had marked for him. He drank in the verses, hearing Abby's voice again as he read.

"Who hath believed our report? and to whom is the arm of the Lord revealed? For he shall grow up before him as a tender plant, and as a root out of a dry ground: he hath no form nor comeliness; and when we shall see him, there is no beauty that we should desire him."

Larson stopped and read that part again.

"This scripture is about Jesus," Abby had explained. *"Isaiah is prophesying about the*

Lord's coming and how Jesus will be treated."

No form nor comeliness. No beauty that we should desire him. The Scripture about Jesus could have easily applied to him. Larson read on.

He is despised and rejected of men; a man of sorrows, and acquainted with grief: and we hid as it were our faces from him; he was despised, and we esteemed him not.

Larson closed his eyes and imagined walking the path home to their cabin, past the grove of quaking aspen and past snowy mountain-fed Fountain Creek. Though the threat of Kohlman having called his loans due haunted him, Larson still clung to the sliver of hope that Kathryn had been able to keep things going. Maybe he'd find her working in the garden or walking back from the creek, her hair still damp from bathing. He pictured her lovely form, the curves of her body he knew so intimately. A fire stirred inside him. He tensed his jaw. Though he still desired to be with Kathryn in that way— how could he not?—he yearned just to be in the same room with her. When he thought of seeing her again, when he pictured her tender brown eyes lifting to meet his . . .

And that's where the image suddenly faded.

How would Kathryn react to seeing him now? Would she despise him? Would she hide her face from him?

Larson laid the Bible aside and bent toward the lake's placid mirror. The man staring back was a stranger to him. He removed the cap Abby had knit for him using yarn from an old sweater, and he ran a hand over his head. His scalp was ridged in places and waxy smooth in others where the fire had melted the layers of skin. Prickly patches of hair grew at random, and at his request, Abby kept them shaved clean. He examined his marred reflection. Could Kathryn ever learn to see past his scars to the man beneath? Would she abide him long enough to see the changes in his heart?

Conviction stung him, and his searching knifed inward. Before all this had happened to him, if their fates had been reversed, would he have extended the same compassion to Kathryn that he would soon ask of her? Without hesitation, he knew his answer—*now*. But before all of this, before the reality of seeing his own reflection repulsed him, would he have possessed the heart to see past it all if it had been her?

A whisper of wind swept across the lake, rippling the water. Larson stood and tugged the cap back on his head, then rubbed his hands together. The scars did little to keep out the cold. It went straight to the bone. He sighed, fighting the familiar sense of failure that dogged his heels. The date the loan payment was due to the bank had long since passed, but he knew Isaiah was right. Not everything in life could be measured in dollars and cents. And the things that were could be stolen in the time it took to draw a single breath. He'd learned that in the crucible.

He picked up the Bible and his staff. He wanted to rebuild his life on something that would last this time. And he wanted to build it with Kathryn, if she would still have him.

Before heading back, he looked up at the sky and cleared his throat. But no words came.

He wished he could talk to God like Isaiah and Abby did. No doubt their prayers reached heaven's throne. His felt anchored to earth, tethered there by the kind of man and husband he had been. *Lord, help me to be the man Kat wants me to be.* As he walked back to the cabin, he thought better and amended his feeble request. *Help me to be the man you want me to be, Jesus.*

Soon his body would command the strength to make the journey home. However, the question remained—would his heart?

———

She couldn't sleep for anticipation of the day before her.

While it was still dark, Kathryn rose and dressed, buttoning up her skirt as far as she could. She would need to make new clothes soon to accommodate the slight swell in her belly. Straightening the bedcovers, she allowed her memory to drift back to the last intimate moments she and Larson had known here as husband and wife. Little did either of them know that night what blessing was being planted deep within.

She pictured Larson's muscled physique, far more at ease in handworked leather and rawhide than silk shirt and tailor-made suit. And his arms, so incredibly strong, yet they possessed a tenderness so intoxicatingly gentle that it wooed her heart even now, leaving her with a physical ache for him.

She ran a hand over his pillow. *O Lord, that you would grant me a second chance.* Instead of wishing her husband to be someone he wasn't, she would love him for who he was. And she would gratefully accept the precious pieces of his heart he was willing to share, without passively demanding more.

In the past weeks of self-reflection, her insatiable need for physical safety and security had also become evident to her. She realized now that she'd sought to obtain them through Larson's aspirations for the ranch. But great wealth hadn't provided it for her in her youth, or for her mother. So what had made her think it would now?

Smoothing the coverlet, Kathryn remembered the emptiness in her mother's eyes and in her parents' less than loving marriage, and the physical longing within her hardened to bitter regret. She stared down at her empty hands as truth wove a grip around her throat. While coveting the dream of something beyond her reach, she had overlooked—and lost—the treasure in her grasp.

Looking down at Larson's side of the

bed, a familiar sense of grief swept through her, but she wouldn't allow herself to dwell on those punishing thoughts, at least not today. Too much was at stake. As she walked to the kitchen, she turned her mind to the hope blossoming inside her.

Tearing a piece of bread from yesterday's loaf, she was thankful that the queasiness had passed. By her estimations, she had just completed her fourth month, and the baby was quickly filling the tiny space inside her. She marveled at the changes her body would go through to accommodate the little one's growth. When could she expect to feel the child move inside her? She assumed that time was near. Oh, for another female, a trusted confidante who had experienced this before. Someone she could share this knowledge with that she kept secreted and who could answer the questions crowding her heart.

But there was One who knew. Who waited for her even now.

Lord, thank you for this child growing within my womb. Make him strong, make him like his father. She smiled as she pulled on her coat. Some nights ago, she'd dreamed she would bear a son, though she would welcome a daughter with equal joy. It didn't matter, so long as the child was healthy. Perhaps it would help to secure the slender thread still tying her to Larson and the fading hope of ever seeing him again.

She walked outside and a mild breeze ruffled her long hair. Leaving her coat unbuttoned, Kathryn watched the first rays of morning reach through the treetops to touch the towering blue spruce. The light mingled with the dew-kissed boughs to create a shimmer of a million tiny crystals on the April breeze. For a moment she stopped, thinking she heard something in the distance.

She searched the cloudless blue overhead and waited. The air around her quivered with an almost tangible anxiety. Finally deciding it was nothing, she walked to the barn to start her morning chores. As she worked, she silently spoke her heart to the One who knew it perfectly already. She scooped feed from the burlap bags, careful not to lift anything too heavy. Footsteps crunched the hay behind her, and she peered over the stall door. She smiled at the unexpected sight.

The hulk of a man who'd pounded her

door weeks ago stood nearby, cradling a kitten against his chest. He stroked its black fur and cooed in hushed tones.

She came around to stand beside him. "Good morning. I see you've found Clara's litter." She'd seen him several times since that morning but only at a waving distance.

His blue eyes danced. "Yes, ma'am. It's so tiny and soft. Wanna hold it?"

Kathryn took the kitten and brushed the shiny black of its coat. The size of the man's hands and strength of his thick fingers belied their gentleness. He was certainly different from any of the other ranch hands she'd met. She was thankful to have him, especially with the task before them today.

"My name is Kathryn."

"I'm Gabe," he said, a grin lighting his face.

Kathryn listened as he told her how he'd found the litter a few days ago and had been checking on them ever since. Two other ranch hands strode in, and Kathryn nodded their way.

"Mrs. Jennings," they murmured back in greeting, touching their hats as they walked to the back to gather their gear.

Gabe gave the kitten's tiny head one last

brush with his thumb. "I better get to work now. Mr. Taylor told me this is an important day."

"Yes, Gabe, it is." She had to remind herself not to speak to him as though he were a child. Gabe was easily her age, if not a few years older, but with his childlike manner it was hard to tell.

She heard riders approaching, so she put the kitten down and went to meet them. Mr. Taylor reined in and dismounted. The four men riding with him stayed astride. Only one of them looked familiar to her, and Kathryn instantly recalled where she'd seen him. The day Matthew had first come to the cabin.

Even smiling, especially then, the man had a reproachable look about him. He rested his forearms on the saddle horn and stared down. "Nice to see you again, ma'am. You're lookin' real nice this mornin'." He grinned and the scar along his jaw bunched and twisted. "I wasn't so keen on workin' for a woman at first, but I might be changin' my mind."

His high-pitched laugh made Kathryn's skin crawl, and she retreated a step.

"Mornin', Mrs. Jennings," Matthew said. "Can I have a word with you, please?" He shot the man a dark look over his shoulder, then took Kathryn's arm and led her inside the barn.

"Is there a problem, Mr. Taylor?"

"No, ma'am, I just need to make sure you still want to do this."

"I'm very certain. You went over the ledgers with me, Mr. Taylor. You know the numbers."

"I just wish there was another way. This is going to leave you with no breedin' stock, no bulls. Nothing."

She laid a hand to his arm. "But at least I'll have the land and my home, and then someday I'll—" She stopped. "Someday my husband and I will start over again."

Something akin to admiration shown in his eyes, and he nodded. "Two days ago I sent men to round up the larger herd from the north pasture." He glanced at the group on horseback waiting outside. "I had to offer higher wages, but I found a few more hands. We'll round up the strays on the south side this mornin', then join up at the pass with the others. I'll get top dollar for the herd, Mrs. Jennings, don't you worry."

"I'm not worried one bit." She wished that were true, but truth be told, she would breathe much easier once everything was settled with Mr. Kohlman and the bank. She could always buy more livestock, but this was their land—hers and Larson's—and she wasn't about to let it go.

"I'll be back in two, maybe three days—but no more than that. I'll oversee the sale of the cattle as well as all the supplies we loaded up yesterday. You'll have the money to pay Kohlman. Don't you worry." He searched her face for a moment and then turned to the men in the barn. "Let's mount up."

He walked a few paces before turning back. He looked at her and then down at the hat he twisted in his hands.

Kathryn laughed softly. "What is it, Mr. Taylor? You'd better be out with it before you ruin a perfectly good hat."

Giving a half-hearted grin, he shook his head. "I'm just wondering . . . are you healing all right from your fall, ma'am?"

She smiled. Matthew Taylor was a good man. He'd become like a brother to her in the last few weeks—showing up to help her with chores, seeing that firewood was chopped and stacked. Larson was right to have entrusted him with so much. "Yes, I'm fine. Still a bit sore, but I'm healing fine."

"If you need me to take you back to that doctor you saw, just let me know. Or to Doc Hadley in town. I'd do it for you."

"I know you would and I appreciate that. But I'm fine, thank you."

Seeing the kindness in Matthew Taylor's eyes, it was on the tip of Kathryn's tongue to share her secret. Then she thought better of it and kept it hidden in her heart.

Loud pounding on the door later that night caused Kathryn to bolt from bed. She got as far as the bedroom door before a dizzying rush pulsed in her ears. She grabbed hold of the doorframe to steady herself.

The pounding continued.

"Just a minute," she called out, groping in the dark for an oil lamp. She struck a match and a burnt-orange glow haloed the immediate darkness. The clock on the mantel read half past four.

She moved to the door. "Who is it?"

"It's Matthew Taylor, Mrs. Jennings. Please . . . open the door."

He sounded out of breath, but she recognized his voice and slid the bolt.

Dread lined his expression, telling her something was terribly wrong. He reached for her hand and squeezed it. Kathryn's chest tightened as the anguish in his face seemed to pass through his grip and up her arm. She shuddered.

It was then she noticed the blood staining his shirt at the waistline. "You're hurt! What happened?"

He waved off her concern, his breath coming heavy. "I'm fine. But . . . I've never seen anything like it."

"The cattle? Did you get the cattle to market?"

"When we got to the pass with the strays, we waited for the others. After a while, I took another man and went to see what the holdup was." He winced and held his side. "Bloated carcasses were everywhere . . . littering the field."

Her body went cold. "The entire herd?"

"All we could see. Been that way for at least two days. And there was no sign of the men I posted with them." He leaned on the doorframe.

Kathryn saw through Matthew Taylor's pained expression to the harsh reality. She waited for a flash of rage to heat her body. Instead, she felt . . . numb.

For ten years Larson had waged war for this ranch. He'd battled disease that siphoned off livestock by the hundreds. He'd taken on this willful, stubborn land with its brutal winters and drought-ridden summers. And though Kathryn didn't know the full depth of it, she knew her husband had fought a war within himself as well. A battle so personal, so consuming, that at times it almost became a living, breathing thing.

A fatal truth arrowed through her heart, taking her breath with it. Larson had come so close to achieving his dream, and she had lost it all in a single blow.

CHAPTER TEN

The stench was overpowering. Kathryn's stomach convulsed. She held a kerchief over her mouth and laid a hand to Gabe's arm. He had brought the wagon to a halt at the edge of the pasture. From a distance, it appeared the herd might have been resting in the warm midday sun among scant patches of snow still dotting the prairie. But as the wagon drew closer, an unnatural stillness hovered in the air, and the bloated carcasses and sickening smell of decay proved the notion false.

Kathryn felt Gabe's gaze and looked over at him. The startling blue of his eyes gave the fleeting impression that their brightness somehow shone from a source within. He laid a rough hand over hers, and comfort moved through her in a way beyond the command of words. But even at his soft smile, she couldn't manage one in return.

"Thank you for coming out here with me today, Gabe. I needed to see it for myself." She sighed and looked out over the fields, recalling the anguish in Mr. Taylor's eyes last night. Their source of livelihood lay rotting before her eyes.

"I'm sorry this happened to you."

Kathryn's tears returned. She was touched by the sincerity in his voice. Nodding, she lifted her eyes to the mountains in the west. *From whence cometh my help.* Before coming out here this afternoon, she'd purposely reread Psalm 121, which spoke of God being her helper and provider. And sitting here now, stunned at the scene before her, she fought to continue believing in its promise. But the breeze encircling her, reeking of devastating loss, tempted her to do otherwise.

Matthew Taylor rode up beside them, a bandanna tied over his mouth and nose. He tugged it down and threw a quick nod at Gabe before speaking. "Mrs. Jennings, we're going to start burning the carcasses soon. . . ." The concern in his voice told her he wanted her to leave. His grimace suggested he bore a weight of responsibility for what had happened here, however misplaced his guilt might be.

"I'll leave," she said, "but before I go I want you to know that I in no way hold you responsible for what happened here. This was not your fault."

He glanced away, his eyes narrowing. "I still haven't found the men I posted here a week ago. They were new hires. I've already sent for the sheriff. Don't know that it'll do any good, but I'd appreciate his seeing this just the same."

She frowned. "Do you have any idea what happened to the cattle? How they died?"

He shook his head. "There was a poisoning down south of here a few years back. They finally traced it back to the feed. There was a cattle drive that passed through these fields not long back, and they coulda brought the Texas fever with them, carried by ticks." He sighed. "Honestly, I just don't know, ma'am. But it sure looks suspicious."

She'd gained respect for Matthew Taylor's opinion in recent weeks. Plus, she'd learned that once he got something fixed in his mind, it would take an act of heaven to move it. When pressed to consider his speculation of an intentional slaughter, she found one person kept returning to mind.

Harold Kohlman.

But surveying the lifeless cattle, she couldn't believe that he would do something like this. That he would sabotage her ability to repay the loan. What motivation would he have? He gained nothing if she couldn't repay her debt. Quite the contrary, the bank stood to lose a substantial amount of money if she defaulted.

She turned back to Mr. Taylor with the intent of putting his concern to rest. But at the look in his eyes, her thoughts suddenly evaporated. His look was less like that of a ranch hand to employer, and more of a man to a woman. Warning sounded within her and she made herself look away. No, it couldn't be . . . surely she'd misread him.

When Taylor prodded his horse closer, Kathryn looked back. The unmistakable sentiment in his face clearly portrayed a desire she did not—and could not—reciprocate.

Deciding to save them both embarrassment and hoping Gabe hadn't noticed, she quickly forced a smile. "As always, Mr. Taylor, I trust your judgment completely. And I appreciate whatever you do on my behalf, as will my husband . . . upon his return."

His features clouded for an instant, then quickly smoothed. "Yes, ma'am, of course. Gabe, you take care of Mrs. Jennings."

"Yes, sir," Gabe answered, giving a mock salute.

Absent of his customary smile, Matthew Taylor tipped his hat.

Watching him ride away, Kathryn wondered if she'd misinterpreted his intentions. It had all happened so fast. Surely she had. And now she felt a bit foolish at the hasty presumption. Still, it would be wise to distance herself from the friendship that had been developing between them recently, if only to avoid further misunderstanding.

"Are you ready to go home, Miss Kathryn?" Gabe's quiet voice pulled her back.

"Yes, Gabe. I am," she whispered, thankful for his company.

But she wondered where home would be in coming days. She'd have to move to Willow Springs—that much was clear. With the ranch being insolvent, she needed to find a job that paid and a place to live. She knew no one in town, and even with selling everything she owned, the amount would fall far short of what she needed.

The wagon jolted as a front wheel slid into a rain-worn rut. She gripped the buckboard and laid a hand over the promise nurtured deep within her belly. Thoughts of the cabin pressed in close, and she realized how lonely she'd been there without Larson. She couldn't imagine staying there without him indefinitely. Strangely, with each passing day, home became less a place and more a person.

Kathryn closed her eyes, uncertain if she would ever truly be home again.

————

She folded the last of Larson's clothes and laid them in the trunk, smoothing a hand over the shirt on top. Kathryn had spent the last two days packing and had saved this task for last. Holding the shirt to her face once more, she breathed in the fading scent of him.

A heaviness filled her chest as her grip tightened on the cotton fabric.

"Can I help with something, Miss Kathryn?"

She jumped at the voice behind her and turned. "Gabe . . ." She blew out a breath. "You startled me." She nodded to the crates by the door. "You could take those to the wagon, if you don't mind." Placing the shirt back in the trunk, she secured the latch.

Gabe carried the crates outside, then returned and hefted the trunk with the customary smile in his eyes. They had worked in companionable silence all afternoon. Having Gabe there brought a comfort to Kathryn that she hadn't anticipated, and with his strength and dutiful attentiveness, the difficult job was finished before the afternoon was spent.

She loaded a light crate into the wagon, then walked back to the cabin. Pausing in the doorway, she drew a slow breath.

Loneliness emanated from every empty corner. Painful reminders of failure. *Her* failure. And of broken dreams. She'd planned on staying here one more night but didn't know now if she could.

Gabe stopped beside her in the doorway. "How long did you and your husband live here?"

"Ten years," she whispered, tracking his gaze around the barren space. It looked smaller than she remembered upon first seeing it all those years ago. Larson had built it for her, and that had made it a palace in her eyes. So when had the silent, subtle comparisons between this cabin and her childhood home started to encroach the happiness of her and Larson's early years together? And had Larson ever sensed her longing for more?

Gabe shifted beside her. "It makes you sad to leave."

She wiped away a tear. "Yes . . . it does. But I hope to return someday." She hesitated, glancing back at the wagon. "Gabe, I was wondering . . . would you have time to help me take all this into town today?"

He looked at her as though considering her request, and Kathryn almost wished she hadn't imposed on him.

Then he nodded, his blond brows arching. "I know a real nice woman you can stay with when we get there too." His fathomless blue eyes lit like a child's. "There're lots of rooms where she lives."

Later that evening, Gabe reined in the horses behind the Willow Springs mercantile and brought the loaded wagon to a sluggish halt. The mere thought of climbing down made Kathryn's aching muscles weak with fatigue. The budding life inside her drained her energy, and she longed for her bed back at the cabin, but she pushed herself to climb down.

She introduced herself to the new owner of the mercantile, a Mr. Hochstetler. After speaking with him briefly, he agreed to sell her items, keeping a percentage for himself, which she deemed as fair. Gabe unloaded the heavier items and carried them into a back room. Overhearing him chat with Mr. Hochstetler, Kathryn learned that Gabe made deliveries for the mercantile on occasion. It would seem he got around and knew more people than she'd figured. Kathryn followed him inside with the lighter crates, but her thoughts kept returning to the bank across the street.

She planned on meeting with Kohlman tomorrow to offer a good faith payment— however modest—hoping to propose a payment schedule for her loan. Imagining his reaction to the idea made her cringe. Part of her knew it was foolish to try and come up with the money, but it wasn't within her to quit. And maybe Larson would return. After all, God was in the miracle business, as her mother had always said.

Exhausted after several trips, Kathryn sank to the back steps of the mercantile and rested her head on her forearms. Feeling a gentle squeeze on her shoulder, she nearly wept.

"You're tired, Miss Kathryn. The woman's house isn't far from here. I'll take you."

Kathryn started to rise, but at the familiar buzzing in her ears, she sat down again. She held up a hand. "Wait, Gabe. Give me a minute to rest, then I'll be fine."

He leaned close and, before she could protest, gathered her in his arms. Kathryn felt her eyes grow hot with tears again. She thought he was carrying her back to the wagon, but he walked on past.

"Where are we going?"

Gabe nodded down the street. "To Annabelle's house. I've delivered stuff there before."

"But what about the things in the wagon?"

"I'll take care of them for you."

After a minute, she tried again. "Gabe, I can walk now, I'm sure."

But he shook his head and held her closer. His embrace was like that of a father cradling a daughter, and it gave Kathryn a sense of security she hadn't felt in a very long time.

"You need to rest," he whispered, looking straight ahead. "You miss your husband, you left your house where you lived for ten years, and you gave all your stuff to the mercantile."

"Actually, I'm selling it," she corrected.

"Still. None of it belongs to you anymore."

Her throat tightened at his blatant observation, and a wave of fatigue moved through her. She couldn't remember a time when she'd been more tired. Knowing Gabe wouldn't mind, nor would he misinterpret her intentions, she closed her eyes and laid her head on his shoulder.

Vaguely aware of being deposited in a soft bed sometime later, Kathryn awakened, groggy. "Gabe?"

"Yes, ma'am," he answered softly, arranging the bedcovers over her body. In the stilted shadows of the dark room, his massive stature appeared larger than life. He stood by the bed looking down upon her like a sentinel, the outline of his shoulders broad and commanding, his stance daring further harm to try and touch her. His body suddenly looked like it was chiseled from marble.

Kathryn reached out, and he took her hand. "Thank you for doing this for me."

He didn't answer, but she sensed his smile in the darkness.

She closed her eyes, unable to hold them open any longer. After a moment she turned back to thank Gabe again. Though she hadn't heard the bedroom door open and close, the place where he had stood was empty. She must have drifted off and he'd left without her hearing. Kathryn curled onto her side and slept.

Whispered voices awakened her sometime during the night. They drifted through the apparently thin walls around her, but she couldn't make out the conversations. A footfall, the creaking of wood, muted laughter. The strong smell of perfume and something else she couldn't quite name scented the air. But she shut her mind to it and slipped back into sleep.

The next time she opened her eyes, a slanted beam of sunlight shone through a window cut high in the wall above her. She yawned and turned onto her back. Picturing Larson's face, as she did every morning upon waking, she spread her hands over the secret blessing that would soon be visible to the world and breathed the familiar prayer. *Lord, please bring him back to me . . . to us.*

Blinking to focus, she listened for any of the sounds she'd heard during the night. A horse whinnied in the distance, then silence. She propped herself up on one elbow and looked around. The room was smaller than she'd sensed the night before, about a third the size of their bedroom at the cabin. In fact, it was mostly bed. A small table sat in the corner.

A knock on the door brought her fully awake. The door opened before she could respond. The first thing Kathryn noticed about the woman was her red hair. But it was unlike any shade of red Kathryn had seen before.

"My name's Annabelle." The woman plopped down on the edge of the bed, remnants of kohl smudging the edges of her eyes. Her lips bore evidence of a claret red long faded, and her dress was cut surprisingly low. The fabric left little to the imagination.

Kathryn caught the faint scent of cloves and noticed the woman chewing something.

Annabelle crossed her legs Indian style, despite the filmy garb. "Gabe said you needed a place to stay and Marcy was away last night, so you got her room. But on the nights all of us are here, you'll have to stay in the room off the kitchen. There's a cot and it's near the stove, so you'll keep warm enough till you find someplace else."

Kathryn pushed herself to a sitting position. "Thank you for letting me stay in your home, Annabelle. My name is Kathryn. Kathryn Jennings."

Annabelle stared at her for a second. "Sure." Her smile had a mischievous quality. "Glad to do it."

"We got in so late last night, and I certainly don't want you to think that . . ." Kathryn paused, then smiled. "What I'm trying to say is that I promise I won't impose on your generosity for too long. I'm planning on looking for a job today."

Annabelle shrugged. Her eyes swept Kathryn's face, then moved down over the rest of her body. She huffed. "Just watch out that Betsy doesn't try and put you to work here." Then she laughed as though she'd told a joke. "The other girls wouldn't like that much, that's for sure."

Kathryn smiled along with her, wondering about this interesting woman. She guessed them to be about the same age, although Annabelle was shorter and claimed a more petite build. The dark brown roots of her hair tattled its true coloring, and Kathryn tried to imagine her without all the extra window dressing, as her mother used to say. Annabelle's blue-eyed gaze was direct, and the slight tilt of her chin portended a stubborn will.

But one thing was certain—Annabelle possessed a kind heart. She'd let Kathryn stay here the night, and for that Kathryn was grateful. Her stomach growled.

"You hungry?" Annabelle asked needlessly, patting the bed. "Come on, let's head to the kitchen before all the good grub is gone. The girls here eat like pigs!"

Kathryn got up and smoothed the covers and then her wrinkled dress as best she could. She followed Annabelle down the narrow hallway, passing door after door.

Two of the doors were ajar. She quickly surmised that all the rooms were about the same size as hers, and with the same sparse furnishings.

Part of her was embarrassed to meet the other women in the boardinghouse in her disheveled state, but Annabelle appeared accepting enough. Hopefully the other women would be too.

A cacophony of women's voices met them in the hallway and soon blended with the delicious aroma of eggs, bacon, and coffee. How long had it been since she'd been in the company of a woman? Much less a group of women? Images of quilting bees and baking for church socials flitted through her mind. She'd asked God for another woman to share the joys of her current condition, and she smiled at how quickly He'd granted her request.

Annabelle pushed open a swinging door, then glanced back and winked. "Betsy may work us hard, but she feeds us good, I'll say that for her."

Kathryn followed Annabelle inside and took a seat beside her at the end of the long wood-plank table crowded with women. The steady hum of conversation suddenly dwindled. Kathryn looked up and scanned the faces now aimed in her direction.

She quickly counted eleven women, besides her, Annabelle, and a bountifully girthed woman laboring over the stove. The eyes boring into hers belonged to women of all ages, shapes, and sizes. Most were younger than she, but two looked older. Much older.

A common thread twined itself through the group. Kathryn couldn't quite put a finger on it, but . . .

The joy inside her flickered. Her smile faded.

"Girls, this is Kathryn," Annabelle announced, waving her hand in a queenly gesture. "She needed a place to stay last night so she took Marcy's room. She'll be with us for a few days till she lands some work."

Gawking expressions darkened to frowns. All but one.

A small dark-haired girl at the end nodded, almost imperceptibly. Her cinnamon almond-shaped eyes flicked to Kathryn's. Away. Then back again. A pretty smile curved her diminutive mouth.

"Well, she's not takin' my room!" a stout blonde declared with authority.

The aging brunette beside her banged the table with her fist. "Mine either. And I don't appreciate Betsy hirin' someone without talkin' to us first!"

Heat poured through Kathryn's body. She fought the impulse to get up and run. Her eyes darted from face to face as tainted images of what these women did—of what they were—turned her stomach. The aroma of eggs and bacon suddenly became fetid.

What on earth had Gabe been thinking? He hadn't found her a room in a boardinghouse. He'd delivered her to a house of ill repute!

CHAPTER ELEVEN

Isaiah accompanied Larson the first day of his journey, explaining that he wanted to make sure Larson found his way back through the obscure mountain pass that led to their secluded valley. Larson didn't bother telling him he already knew the way. Instinctively. He'd grown up reading the position of the sun and had memorized the peaks of the Rockies. Never once had he been lost in this land. Ever.

Isaiah moved over the rocky terrain with surprising agility for a man his size, and though he purposefully lagged his pace, Larson had to work to keep up with him. Close to noon, Larson paused and leaned heavily on his staff, resting for a moment before attempting the steep climb before him. The cool mountain air felt good in his chest, but he still couldn't seem to draw in enough of it to satisfy his lungs.

Watching Isaiah up ahead, he wondered again how the man had gotten him back to the cabin after finding him in the burned-out shack. Later that night he took the opportunity to ask.

Isaiah grew quiet at the question, smiling in that way of his that signaled his hesitance to speak on the matter.

"You're a powerful man, Isaiah, I'll grant you that. But I'm no trifling," Larson needled him, edging back a good ways from the fire Isaiah had built. "Or I didn't used to be."

Isaiah laughed, then grew quiet.

"Seriously, how did you get me back there?" Larson asked again, his curiosity roused.

Isaiah rose, gathered timber in his arms, and laid it on the fire. White sparks shot up into the dark night sky, and the crackle of flame consuming wood sent involuntarily shivers up Larson's spine. He appreciated the fire's light and welcomed its warmth, as long as he didn't have to handle the flames.

Isaiah took his time in answering, a wistful look filling his eyes. "A fine ol' gal named Mabel carried you."

Larson laughed. "Mabel, huh? She must be one brute of a woman." Isaiah laughed along with him. Then, watching him closer, Larson felt his humor drain away. "What happened to her?"

Isaiah stoked the fire with a long branch. "I heard of a man looking for a good mule, so I sold her a while back . . . at a small mining camp not too far over the ridge there." He pursed his lips as though trying to decide what to say next.

Larson stared at the former slave sitting across the fire from him, the words forming in his mind less of a question and more a statement of fact. "You sold her to buy what you needed to care for me."

Isaiah shrugged a broad shoulder and stared into the flames.

Larson tasted the salt of his tears before he realized he'd shed them. Was there no end to this man's generosity? He quickly wiped them away but knew that Isaiah had seen.

"Tears carry no shame, Larson. 'Specially not tears of gratitude. I've shed so many in my life I've lost count. I was afraid to cry in front of Abby at first, but she taught me that every person's been hurt and has wounds. Some scars are just easier to see than others." Isaiah's dark eyes seemed to focus somewhere beyond Larson, on a memory long past. "The outward scars aren't what determine what a man will become. It's the inward scars that can keep a man from living the life God intended."

Long into the night, Larson lay awake thinking about what Isaiah had said. And when Isaiah laid a hand to his shoulder the following morning as they said good-bye, the wisdom had taken firm root.

"You've been led down this path for a purpose, Larson. It's not one you would've chosen—I know that." His laughter mixed with a sigh. "I wouldn't have chosen most of what's happened in my life either, but I've come to trust that my sweet Jesus can see things better from where He is than I can from here . . . as hard as that seems sometimes."

He pulled Larson into a hug and Larson returned it, unable to keep from smiling at how uncomfortable he would've been hugging another man before this. He squeezed his eyes tight against the emotion rising in his throat.

From the slope of the afternoon sun, Larson estimated three more hours of light. He and Isaiah had covered roughly four miles yesterday, and today he would push his body to its limit to cover three. His progress was gratingly slow, and it goaded his pride when he recalled how he used to walk twenty plus miles a day without fatigue. He reached down and massaged his right leg. It was already paining him, but he pushed on.

Near dusk he stopped, his leg throbbing. He eased the pack from his shoulders and sank to the ground. After a quick dinner of Abby's biscuits and jerky, he filled his canteen from the stream running in a fury down the mountainside, evidence of the spring snow melt. Isaiah had told him this particular watercourse fed the lake by their cabin, then flowed all the way to the lower towns at the base of the Rockies. Larson dipped his finger briefly in the icy water, watching it flow downstream and wondering if that same water would soon churn down Fountain Creek past his cabin.

Tipping up his canteen, he drank deeply of Adam's ale, recalling the first time he'd used that phrase with Kathryn.

"What are you calling it?" she'd asked, grinning.

"Adam's ale." He'd pushed back a damp strand of blond hair from her shoulder, enjoying the smirk of disbelief on her face. *"It flows out of the mountains, fresh from the heart of the earth, clear as crystal."* She'd used the term ever since.

Larson walked back to where he'd left his pack and pulled the wrapped bottle of liniment from the pocket. He shed his pants and long johns and rubbed the dark brown mixture into his aching muscles. The welted reddened flesh bunched and rippled beneath his fingers. He winced, wishing again for Abby's firm but gentle touch, and for Isaiah's conversation.

Dressing again, he unrolled his bedding and lay down. He would have liked to continue reading in the Bible Isaiah and Abby had given him but light was fading, and he let the matches at the bottom of his pack lay untouched. The chill from the ground seeped through to his bones, but he shut his mind to the cold.

Instead, he turned his thoughts back to the first time he'd pictured Kathryn as an older woman—one Abby's age, and again the image touched him. As Abby had tended him one afternoon, he'd found himself studying her features and had quickly decided she'd been a beauty in younger years. Abby still possessed a comeliness about her, but it shone now more from within.

He closed his eyes and Kathryn's face came into view, her warm brown eyes and honey hair, the silk of her skin. He'd long appreciated her outward beauty, but he suspected that Kathryn's beauty would one day deepen into a radiance similar to Abby's, and the thought warmed him. His body responded, and he hungered for the intimacies shared between a husband and his wife.

In an unexpected moment of hope, he allowed a fissure in his heart wide enough to entertain the possibility that he might enjoy that with Kathryn again someday. If she were able to look past who he was on the outside now, to what lay beneath.

He slowly turned onto his back to study the night sky and put his hand out as though reaching for the handle of the Big Dipper. How could he have ever doubted the woman Kathryn was? Or her loyalty to him?

But he knew the reason, and his chest ached with the truth of it. Kathryn had borne the brunt of his suspicion and distrust stemming from his mother's faithlessness. Images of mistreatment at his mother's hand, and at the hands of her countless lovers, crowded the night's stillness. One particular memory stood out, and Larson's stomach hardened as he relived the scene. . . .

His mother sat in the corner of the dimly lit bedroom, her expression like a mask, her dark eyes glazed as she watched the man grab her son by the scruff of the neck and shove him down. Larson could still hear the jarring crunch of his bony knees as he hit the bare wooden floor, then the sound of the door latching behind him.

"Take off your shirt." A sickly smile wrapped itself around the man's voice. Then he'd lit a cheroot and slowly inhaled, the smoldering end flaming redder with each exaggerated draw. . . .

Larson shifted to his side on the hard ground, still able to smell the acrid stench of the cigar, and of what followed. His eyes burned. *God, erase it from my memory.* Wasn't it enough to have endured it once? How could a woman—his own mother—be so cruel and void of compassion? What had he done to lose her love?

But Kathryn wasn't like his mother. He knew that now, and he planned on spending the rest of his life proving it to her.

———

Kathryn huddled closer to the boarding-house doorway to avoid the rain pouring off the slanted tin roof. A cold droplet some-how found its way past the protection of her coat and trickled down her back. She shud-dered at the chill. The barren land needed the rich moisture to green the brown prairie grasses and nurture coming crops, but the heavy, overcast skies did nothing to lift the gloom in her heart.

She knocked again and smoothed the wet hair back from her face. Her gaze shot up at the door's creaking, but what she saw wasn't heartening. "May I speak with the proprietor, please?"

A tall bone-thin woman blew a gray wisp of thinning hair from her eyes and shifted the load of soiled linens in her arms. "I'm the proprietor." She eyed Kathryn, her eyes narrowing. "We're all full up on rooms right now, if that's what you're wantin'. Check back with me next month."

She started to shut the door, but Kathryn put out her hand. The thought of spending a second night at the brothel bred uncustomary boldness within her. What she'd heard last night was enough to have kept her slogging through the rain and mud all day. She wouldn't be easily deterred.

"Please, ma'am. I don't need a big room, nothing fancy. Just a place to stay." Kathryn nodded toward the laundry. "And I'll work for you. I can do laundry and clean and cook and—"

"I said I got no rooms right now. I'm full up. And I ain't got no money to pay tenants to cook and clean. This town's hit hard times. Folks have to pull their own—"

"Oh, I don't expect any pay for it. I'll do it plus pay you for the room." As long as it wasn't more than the scant amount she had left after seeing Mr. Kohlman that morning.

The woman's gaze traveled the length of her. "You in some kinda trouble, girl?"

Yes. But not the kind you think. Kathryn

shook her head. "I just need a place to stay."

"Well, can't help you none with that." She moved to close the door, then must have read the desperation in Kathryn's face because she paused. Her lips pursed. "You might check across town with the preacher. Sometimes he and his woman take in folks who's hit hard times."

Kathryn nodded, feeling a tear slip down her cheek but doubting the woman noticed. She was wet to the bone as it was, and besides, the woman had already closed the door.

She started back down the boardwalk, her pace as sluggish as her hope. This was the last boardinghouse in town, and she'd already been to the preacher's house first thing that morning. A passerby had said they were away visiting family and had directed her to the boardinghouses in town. Late afternoon relinquished its fading vestiges of light to the laden pewter skies, and though everything within her rebelled at the thought, Kathryn turned back in the direction from which she'd come that morning.

She waited for a wagon to pass, then crossed the muddy street, avoiding the deeper puddles and deposits as best she could. Back on the planked walkway, she stomped the mud from her boots and quickened her pace as she passed the saloon. Kathryn avoided eye contact with two men lurking just inside the doorway. One of them let out a low whistle, which she didn't acknowledge, but her cheeks burned at the lewd remark that followed.

Minutes later she passed the bank and recalled her meeting with Mr. Kohlman earlier that day. He had laughed—literally laughed—at her suggestion of paying him back the loans. Remembering his flat denial to offer her a payment schedule brought a scowl. But he *had* acquiesced upon discovering that she'd brought enough for one monthly payment—Mr. Hochstetler at the mercantile had paid her a goodly sum, and Jake Sampson at the livery had been generous in buying back their tackle and gear—but even then Kohlman had accepted the money with a begrudging air.

It seemed Kohlman actually preferred to see her default and lose the land. But why?

A sign in a store window caught her attention. She slowed as she read it.

Shielding her eyes from the heavy drop-

lets, she looked up. *Hudson's Haberdashery.* Feeling as though this might be her last
chance, she glanced down at her rain-
soaked skirt and muddied hem and hoped
that, whatever kind of man this Mr. Hudson
was, he would be forgiving when it came to
first impressions.

That evening, Kathryn crept through the
back door of the brothel and into the small
room—more like a closet—off the kitchen
that Annabelle had shown her earlier that
morning. She lit the nub of a candle left on the
cot and closed the door behind her, nearly
stumbling over her trunk. Gabe must've
brought it sometime during the day. She
looked forward to seeing him if only to ask
him what on earth he'd been thinking in
bringing her to a place like this!

After fumbling for a lock for a moment,
she realized there wasn't one—as though
she would get a good night's rest here anyway. She shed her damp dress and hung it
from a sagging nail. Though the lack of privacy bothered her, she couldn't very well
sleep in wet clothes.

She puffed out the anemic flame and
crawled beneath the blanket that smelled

faintly of dust and storage, all the while promising herself that she wouldn't cry. But her flesh proved stronger than her will. One more night and she could leave this horrible place.

Mr. Hudson had indeed been a gentleman who looked past initial impressions and, being satisfied with her mending skills on a pair of trousers, he'd agreed to give her a chance as well as accommodations in the back of the store, where the pressing was done—starting the following day. Not her own room exactly, but it was enough. Far better than where she was now. She'd come close to telling him where she was having to stay tonight but thought better of it. No need to tempt the limits of his benevolence.

Curling herself into a ball, Kathryn tried to ward off the chill and sense of loneliness pressing close in the darkness. The gnawing in the pit of her stomach reminded her that she'd forgotten dinner, but her hunger bothered her far less than the sounds of what was going on around her and above on the second floor.

An image flashed through her mind, and her heart ached again for Larson. Was he still alive? It'd been so long since Christmas Day. Though she had wondered about it many times, she'd never fully understood what it had been like for him as a child. Even her worst imaginings couldn't match the brutal truth of this life. How could anyone treat a small boy with such—

Kathryn's breath caught as footsteps sounded in the kitchen just beyond the door. A burnished glow shone through the crack beneath the door.

"Kathryn?"

Her heart regained its normal rhythm. "Annabelle?"

The door creaked open. Annabelle's shoulders were bare, and Kathryn wondered if she wore anything beneath the thin shawl she held gathered about her chest. The material of her skirt invited the eye as well. Surely this woman couldn't have— wouldn't have—intentionally chosen a path of easy virtue for her life. What had brought her to this end? Kathryn drew the blanket closer around her and questioned, again, why Gabe had ever delivered her here.

"I'm in between clients so don't have much time, but I wanted to make sure you got back all right. That nobody bothered you when you came in."

Unexpected concern softened Annabelle's voice, and the sound of it made Kathryn feel less alone. "No, no one bothered me. I made it fine."

"Just checkin', cuz I saw Conahan head back here a bit ago. He's a creepy sort, that one. Just plain mean if you ask me." Annabelle cringed. "He normally asks for Ginny, and that suits the rest of us just fine. So, did you find a job today?"

Astonished at how casually Annabelle changed topics, Kathryn nodded. "I saw a sign in the haberdashery window and stopped in. Mr. Hudson hired me after I demonstrated my work. I start tomorrow, and he's letting me stay in the back room of his store."

The glow of lamplight illumined Annabelle's face enough for Kathryn to detect a slight narrowing in her eyes. "He said you could stay in the back, did he? And did he happen to tell you how you'd be payin' for those lodgings?"

"No, Annabelle, it's nothing like that. I assure you, Mr. Hudson is an honest—"

"All men are like that, Kathryn, if given

half the chance." She shook her head. "Mark my words, you better sleep with one eye open."

Kathryn started to respond but then paused. Apparently Annabelle had never known any other kind of man, and Kathryn doubted that she would be easily convinced otherwise. Not by words anyway. Then the irony of Annabelle's word of caution struck her and she smiled. "I'll be careful—I promise. And you be careful too. All right?"

Grinning, Annabelle tossed her red hair over her right shoulder in a saucy move. "I'm always careful, honey. You don't have to worry about me."

On impulse, Kathryn reached out and took hold of her hand. "I'm serious, Annabelle. Please look out for yourself."

Annabelle's grin faded. Her eyes flicked to Kathryn's, then away again. She gently pulled her hand back, and Kathryn got the distinct feeling that she'd overstepped her bounds.

"Well, I need to get back to work." Annabelle's voice came out soft at first, and higher than usual. Then she took a deep breath and Kathryn could see the façade slipping back into place. "Heavy crowd tonight. The miners just got paid, and that always means good business. Things'll quiet down around three o'clock or so; then the gals always sleep till around noon. Hopefully you'll get some sleep too." She turned to go.

"Annabelle?"

She paused, her silhouette softened in the warm yellow light.

"I don't know where I would be tonight if you hadn't helped me. Thank you."

Annabelle nodded once, then noiselessly latched the door.

Kathryn lay awake long into the night, trying to block out the raucous laughter and occasional high-pitched squeal by reliving every memory she had of Larson. There were so many good things she'd forgotten that had been glossed over by her selfish desire for more. More from Larson, more from life. Some recollections brought tears, others a smile. But one thing stood out above all the rest—her fault in not appreciating what she'd had at the time.

What she wouldn't give to turn back the clock and relive every moment of those years—both the good and bad—with him again.

CHAPTER TWELVE

Kathryn quickened her pace, glancing back at the clock on the front of the Willow Springs Bank building. Ten minutes to get to her next job. Her hands ached from sewing all morning at the haberdashery, and the space between her shoulder blades burned with muscle fatigue. She reached up and massaged the tightness, reminding herself to be thankful despite the fatigue and long hours. The past week had seen her gain not only one job, but two, and a safe place to live. For the time being anyway.

The bell hanging over the entryway to Myrtle's Cookery jangled when she entered, and as they had more than once in recent days, her thoughts turned to Matthew Taylor. Wondering how he'd been faring, she slipped out of her coat and shook off the droplets of water clinging to the wool before hanging the garment on the hook. Tying an apron loosely about her expanding midsection, she paused, realizing her condition would soon be evident to all. Still, somehow it felt right to keep it to herself for now. She wanted Larson to be the first to . . .

The bell above the door sounded, and she spoke without turning. "We'll be serving lunch in about an hour. Today's special is fried chicken and mashed potatoes. Can you come back then?"

"Well, that depends on who's cookin' today . . . you or Miss Myrtle."

Kathryn turned at his voice. He stood in the doorway, his customary smile softening his eyes. Matthew Taylor removed his hat and slapped it against his thigh.

"Mr. Taylor." The delight in her own voice surprised her, as did the warmth she felt at seeing him again.

He crossed the room. "I've been wondering how you are . . . Mrs. Jennings."

"I'm fine." She quickly decided by the eagerness in his eyes not to divulge she'd been wondering the same about him. "Did Jake Sampson at the livery give you—"

"He gave me your note. Yes, ma'am. And the money. But I came to tell you that I don't feel right takin' the money from you like this. I don't feel like I did right by you." He glanced down at the hat in his hands, his voice growing soft. "Or by your husband."

The sincerity in his tone, coupled with the earnest look in his eyes, caused Kathryn's heart to skip a beat. Such a fine man. "Mr. Taylor, you did everything you could to help me keep the ranch." She swallowed against the tightening in her throat. "And you did right by my husband. Never doubt that. You're an honorable man and I appreciate your friendship."

He stared at her for a long moment, a muscle working in his jaw, looking as though he were weighing his words. "Yes, ma'am," he finally answered quietly, and his soft brown eyes conveyed emotions that Kathryn prayed he wouldn't give voice to. "If you need anything. Anything at all . . ." His gaze locked with hers. "You let me know."

Unable to speak, Kathryn nodded and

managed a smile. When the door closed behind him, she let out her breath.

Kathryn skirted down the darkened board-walk toward the brothel, unable to keep from glancing behind her every few seconds. Though she'd stayed at the brothel for only two nights and had moved out several days ago, she was acutely aware of how her being seen there again would easily be miscon-strued. And as much as she'd come to care for Annabelle and some of the other women in that short time, truth be told she didn't want to be associated with what they did.

The boisterous shouts coming from the front parlor told her that business was going well that night. Clutching the cloth bag in her hand, she stopped just inside the back alley and tried to imagine what Jesus would do in this situation. He had befriended pros-titutes and social outcasts, had loved them despite the vicious rumors that accompa-nied his befriending them, and then paid the price for it. Not a comforting thought at the moment.

With one last glance, she edged her way toward the back porch stairs.

Surprisingly, she'd moved past the point

of merely being sickened by what went on here to feeling an ache so deep inside her she knew it was one only God could heal. She'd quickly come to recognize a depth of loneliness in Annabelle's painted eyes, and in the diminutive dark-haired Sadie, that could only be filled by the Lover of their souls. God desired to fill them to overflowing with His love, while the evil lurking here sought to ravage their bodies of innocence and rape their souls of hope.

Kathryn opened the back door to find Annabelle seated at the kitchen table. Perfect timing. "Annabelle, just the woman I wanted to see."

Annabelle turned, and Kathryn's smile faded.

"What happened?"

"Nothing. I'm all right." Holding a bloodied cloth to her head, Annabelle waved Kathryn away when she came closer. "One of the men got a little rough is all. I was handling him fine until he threw that right hook." She cursed softly, working her delicate jaw. Her tongue flickered to the left side of her mouth, where purpling flesh bordered her swollen lips. A dark circle was already forming around her left eye. "I didn't see it comin' this time."

"This time?" Kathryn gasped.

Annabelle sighed and shook her head, her eyes mirroring disbelief. "You really are an innocent, aren't you? Didn't your husband ever hit you?"

The question took Kathryn by surprise. Though she and Annabelle had talked on several occasions, she'd not spoken of Larson yet. "No," she whispered, laying the cloth bag on the table. "My husband never laid a harsh hand to me."

"What about when the stew was burned or his clothes weren't washed?" Annabelle's eyes flashed with anger and a pain so raw that Kathryn felt sure few had been allowed to see it. "Or when you didn't please him to his liking?"

Kathryn's eyes watered and she shook her head. "No, not even then. We had our disagreements, don't get me wrong, but . . . he never hit me." She remembered Larson's sullen moods. "He would withdraw and wouldn't talk to me, sometimes for days. I wondered what was going on inside him and would've given anything for him to let me in."

As soon as Kathryn said it, she regretted it. Seeing the bruises and cuts on Annabelle's face, she knew there was no comparison between the existence Annabelle endured and the life she shared with Larson. *Had* shared. Her heart beat faster. No, not past tense. She would share it again. He would come home; she felt it inside her.

"What happened to him?"

Kathryn blinked.

"To your man." Annabelle's focus dropped to Kathryn's abdomen. "Does he know about the child?"

Kathryn's jaw went slack. "How did you know?"

Annabelle gave her a look. "I've seen lots of it through the years—the start of it anyway. So it's not really so hard to tell." Her smile grew wistful. "The full cut of your dresses and skirts, your visits to the water closet. And the way you're shieldin' the little one right now."

Kathryn looked down to see her hand resting over the gentle swell she'd thought well hidden by the gathers in her skirt. She smiled and shook her head. "And here I thought I was keeping a secret."

A shadow flitted across Annabelle's marred features, and Kathryn had the feeling she was about to gain a glimpse into the woman's battered heart. Then just as quickly, she looked away.

Annabelle cleared her throat and nodded to the sack on the table. "So what'd you bring me?"

Kathryn smiled. "Blackberry cobb—"

"Annabelle!" The door to the kitchen swung open. One of the other women ran in, out of breath. Her lacy bodice gaped open at the top. "Come quick, it's Sadie!"

Kathryn climbed the stairs, right on Annabelle's heels. She pushed through the crowd of half-dressed men and women standing in the hall and arrived at Sadie's room. Sadie lay motionless on the bed, her naked body half draped in a sheet. Annabelle knelt beside her, her face ashen.

Kathryn moved to the other side and lifted Sadie's limp wrist, checking her pulse. Relief trickled through her fear. "She's alive. Did anybody hear what happened?"

The brunette who had so vehemently voiced her displeasure at Kathryn's first night at the brothel leaned against the doorway. "Her next appointment just came in and found her like this. I saw Conahan with her downstairs a while ago, but I don't know if he followed her up here or not."

Annabelle's hand shook as she pulled the sheet up to cover Sadie.

Kathryn brushed the hair back from Sadie's delicate features. Sadie's smooth brown skin glistened with perspiration and her breath was thready. She looked so much younger close up, where Kathryn could see past her heavily lined almond eyes and rouged cheeks. "How old is she?"

"Thirteen," Annabelle told her.

Kathryn thought she was going to be sick. Someone handed her a cool cloth. She smoothed it over Sadie's forehead and cheeks and beneath her chin. She pulled back the long dark strands of hair clinging to Sadie's throat, and that's when she saw them.

Faint red stripes flared out on either side of Sadie's neck, extending around to the back. Kathryn placed her fingers in the subtle outline on the right side of Sadie's slender throat and shuddered.

Silent tears coursed down Annabelle's cheeks. Kathryn reached out to touch her hand, but she pulled away. Layers of hurt, betrayal, and anger twisted Annabelle's pale expression. Her clenched jaw evidenced her resolve not to cry, and yet the tears forced their way out, as if there were no more room inside to contain the pain.

Kathryn had seen this look before, and her heart flooded with sudden understanding.

The debauchery she'd witnessed here, however brief, had branded her heart forever. How would being raised in this violence warp an impressionable child's heart? She remembered the scars from a smoldering cheroot on Larson's back. After he'd fallen asleep on their last night together, she'd kissed each scar and then had ached for the wounds inside him that he wouldn't—or couldn't—let her touch. Once again she had wondered how he had survived the brutal world of his childhood.

But now she understood. He had pulled everything in. Every need, every emotion, anything that could be used as a weapon against him. In a survival instinct, he'd stuffed it all down deep inside him. As Kathryn stroked Sadie's cheek, it was Larson's face she saw. *Oh my beloved, if only I had understood. I would have loved your scars even more.*

———

With the protective nature of a mama bear guarding her cub, Kathryn linked her arm through Annabelle's as they walked to the mercantile. Secretly, and shamefully, she was glad that the boardwalk was mostly emptied of traffic at this early morning hour. She'd never been in public with Annabelle before, but she couldn't help but know that others would easily detect Annabelle's profession, and Kathryn wondered how they would treat her.

She chanced a look beside her, amazed at how her initial judgments about Annabelle had changed. The morning sun played off the aberrant scarlet hue of her hair, contrasting with her pale skin.

In the last week the swelling had gone down on Annabelle's face and the bruised flesh was nearly masked by powder. Sadie had recovered physically as well, but had yet to speak about the incident to anyone. Betsy allowed Annabelle two days to recuperate, then promptly put her back to work. But Kathryn had quickly seized those days as an open door from God and had taken the opportunity to plant the seeds of friendship—and faith.

Annabelle had visited her after hours at the haberdashery, entering through the back door after the store was closed, and Kathryn had read to her—first from a book of Annabelle's preference, then from her Bible. Kathryn purposefully chose the story of Rahab and had secretly delighted in Annabelle's rapt attention.

As they now turned down an alleyway, Annabelle looked over at her and smiled. "You didn't have to come with me this morning, you know. I'm used to doing this myself."

"I know, but I wanted to come." Kathryn didn't share her former concerns or that she was thankful to have her mind occupied. Anything to keep from dwelling on the possibilities that haunted her, each day with stronger force. She'd awakened that morning long before dawn, unable to sleep. Surely Matthew Taylor was mistaken—Larson couldn't have gotten lost in that storm. But something else must have happened. . . . Almost five months had passed since he'd left.

Annabelle's huff pulled Kathryn back.

"You might just change your mind once we get there." She waved her arm at the empty boardwalk. "And not many people are out yet, but later it'll be a different—"

"Annabelle, I'm glad to be with you. All right?"

She nodded, but doubt lurked in her eyes.

Noticing the stubborn tilt of Annabelle's chin, Kathryn smiled to herself, feeling somehow privileged to have glimpsed the wounded, fragile, yet remarkably resilient woman beneath the façade.

The back door of the mercantile was locked. Annabelle knocked twice.

Kathryn glanced at the stairs and thoughtfully remembered the night she'd been here with Gabe. She hadn't seen Gabe since and wondered where he was. She wanted to thank him for introducing her to Annabelle, although, recalling her initial discovery at his choice of accommodations, she smiled, knowing gratitude had hardly been her first reaction.

The back door opened to a gray-haired woman waving them brusquely inside. "You're late! Hurry. Hurry, already." She scanned the back alley before she slammed the door shut. "We need to open for regular customers in a few minutes, and I want you both gone."

The warmth in Annabelle's eyes turned to frost. "And good morning to you too, Mrs. Hochstetler."

Mrs. Hochstetler? Kathryn looked at the red-faced, tight-lipped woman standing before her. How could this woman be the wife of the kind gentleman who'd helped sell her goods?

"How are you this fine day, ma'am?" Annabelle continued. "You're looking lovely for this early in the morning." Her tone had acquired a chill to match her expression, and Kathryn looked at her, stunned. Annabelle's words were as smooth as cream but as sharp as daggers, and Mrs. Hochstetler's loathing only seemed to deepen Annabelle's arsenic sweetness. This was a side of Annabelle Kathryn had not seen.

Mrs. Hochstetler glowered. "Give me your order and be quick about it." She snapped her fingers twice.

"I left my order with your husband two days ago, just like you asked. Once we get those things, we'll leave."

With a huff, Mrs. Hochstetler disappeared through a side door and returned minutes later toting two burlap bags, stuffed full. She stooped under the weight of them and dropped them unceremoniously at Annabelle's feet. Her husband followed behind her, shouldering a crate.

Mr. Hochstetler set his load on the counter and heaved a sigh. "We expect payment up front. Just like the arrangement you had with the previous owner."

As Annabelle paid the man, his eyes flickered to Kathryn, then narrowed.

"Hello, Mr. Hochstetler," Kathryn offered politely, hoping to ease the tension. "We've met before, if you remember, when I first arrived in town."

He stared at her, his face reddening. He shot a look at his wife beside him, whose glare seethed venom.

Kathryn swung a glance beside her. Annabelle's eyes clearly said "I told you so."

Once outside, Annabelle burst out laughing as the door slammed behind them. "Did you see the look on that old bat's face when you said you'd met him before?" She laughed so hard she had trouble keeping a grip on the crate in her arms. "Oh, that was priceless."

Kathryn walked on ahead. "I don't see what's so funny." The heat of embarrassment still tingled her upper body. She opted for the street instead of having to climb the stairs to the boardwalk. Her shoulders already cramped under the weight of the two bags. Not wanting to be late for work at the haberdashery, she quickened her pace. "It was horrible the way they treated you."

"Oh, that doesn't bother me. I'm used to it," Annabelle said with a bit too much bravado.

But it bothered Kathryn. How could people be so hypocritical? So intentionally cruel? Thinking themselves better than . . . She noticed Annabelle's steps had slowed. She turned back just as Annabelle set down the crate. "What is it?"

The woman's expression grew watchful. "It wasn't so much the way they treated me as it was the way they treated you . . . was it."

Her words were like a blow. Kathryn started to respond but then stopped, surprised and ashamed to discover bits of truth in Annabelle's observation. She glanced

away, only now aware of how the few people already out that morning were staring at
them as they passed. And going out of their
way not to walk by them. "I'm sorry,
Annabelle. Yes, that's part of it, but it also
hurts me to think of you being treated that
way." No doubt the same way the child of a
prostitute would be treated. "That's not the
way God sees you. He sees us as we are,
certainly, but He also sees us as what we
can be with His grace."

"But that's the way you first saw me,
when you realized what I was." She uttered
the same word Larson used when referring
to his mother. "Wasn't it?"

Kathryn looked into Annabelle's eyes,
and the truth deepening their blue depths
daggered her heart. *Oh, God, I'm so
ashamed. How do I answer her?*

But she already knew how to answer.
With the truth.

After a moment, she slowly nodded.
"Yes," she whispered. "Please forgive me,
Annabelle, but that's exactly how I saw you,
until God showed me differently."

A smile tipped Annabelle's mouth. "Well,
you're honest. That's sayin' a lot." Her smile

spread into a grin. "I think we might just turn out to be good friends, Kathryn Jennings."

Kathryn laughed in surprise, then set down her sacks and hugged Annabelle tight. The tiny seed of friendship had sprouted.

The next morning, Kathryn hurried to finish her duties at the haberdashery. She checked the clock, knowing that Myrtle would be expecting her soon. She had one last fitting, and the customer was waiting in the back room. She paused at the door to catch her breath.

A sharp pang stabbed her abdomen and she gripped the threshold for support. Annabelle had said she should feel the baby moving any day . . . a soft fluttering movement. But the pain she experienced now didn't fit that description in the least. It soon passed and she calmed.

Drawing a breath, she opened the door and stepped inside. Her throat went dry.

"Mrs. Jennings, what a pleasant surprise." Donlyn MacGregor crossed the room to stand before her. He reached for her hand and brushed his lips against her skin. "I'd heard you'd moved into town. Though I must say I was disturbed to learn of the circumstances. I'm sorry about your stock, and that you're losing your ranch." His dark brow furrowed. "If I may, I'd like to—"

"Thank you, Mr. MacGregor." Kathryn had heard enough. "But I haven't lost it yet. I'm still working with the—" Remembering what Matthew Taylor had said about MacGregor buying up all the land surrounding his ranch made her stop short. "I'm still working things out."

Something vaguely resembling compassion ghosted his gray eyes, perfectly complementing the material of the fashionable waistcoat and trousers he wore. "Well, my apologies, again, Mrs. Jennings. I misspoke. I was under the impression you'd sold everything relating to your business."

She indicated where she wanted him to stand and pulled her pincushion from her apron. Donlyn MacGregor seemingly feigned a look of concern as he eyed the pins in her hand. Normally Kathryn might have smiled, but not under the circumstances.

"I've sold everything pertaining to the ranch, Mr. MacGregor, but I plan on keeping the land, and the homestead. Now, please turn to the side." Looking at the waistcoat, she clearly saw where the tailor had made his mistake, and it was one easily made. He simply hadn't allowed enough taper for MacGregor's lean waist. The side seams of the coat and the waist of the trousers were both too generous.

Being this close to him, Kathryn could smell the spicy scent of his cologne. "Please button the coat for me."

"As you wish, my lady." His brogue thickened in faint mockery.

"Extend your arms, please," she continued, ignoring him. She pulled pins from the cushion and held them between her teeth. Standing in front of him, Kathryn gathered the extra material from both side seams of the coat. "There, how does that feel?"

"That feels . . . perfect."

Hearing the tease in his tone, Kathryn also felt his eyes on her. Matthew Taylor hadn't mentioned anything, but she suddenly wondered if MacGregor had a wife waiting at home, though she highly doubted that even marriage would be deterrent enough for a man like him.

On a whim, she decided to test the waters.

"Now lower your arms slightly," she said

around pins clenched between her teeth. She knew from seeing him before that he wore his suits fitted. "Perhaps you'd like your wife to see this before we make the final adjustments?" Thankfully, the question came off sounding more normal than it felt.

When he didn't answer immediately, Kathryn secured the alteration with one last pin and stood. His expression stopped her cold. She took a half step back.

His eyes held hers for a moment and then cut away, focusing anywhere but on her, and she got the distinct impression that she'd wandered into forbidden territory. If Kathryn didn't know better, she might have thought he was uncomfortable by the way he fidgeted with the coat sleeve and wouldn't look at her. But surely not—this man was a silver-tongued devil if she'd ever seen one.

He turned back to the mirror and appraised the suit, giving each sleeve a gentle tug. "This will do nicely, I'm sure. Thank you, Mrs. Jennings." An undercurrent played beneath the surface of his voice when he spoke her name, and Kathryn couldn't shake the feeling of being somehow put in her place.

She hurriedly marked the lines for the tapered seams with a row of pins, doing the same for the trousers. "The suit will be ready next week." She closed the door for him to change.

She put her supplies away and was halfway to Myrtle's when she felt a touch on her arm.

"Mrs. Jennings."

She turned and, seeing him, quickened her pace.

MacGregor fell into step beside her. "Mrs. Jennings, please . . . a moment of your time."

"I'm late for work, Mr. MacGregor."

"But you just left work."

"Is there something else you need?"

This time he smiled, a sparkle lighting his eyes. Obviously he'd recovered from whatever he'd felt moments before. She walked faster, hearing his soft chuckle behind her.

"No, Mrs. Jennings, please. I just have a question for you. A proposition of sorts. Not the kind you're thinking," he added quickly. "It's about helping you keep your ranch."

Her steps slowed even as her defenses rose. "You want to help me keep my ranch."

"Yes, and no. I'm a businessman, Mrs.

Jennings. Not a philanthropist. I'd want something in exchange for my investment."

She stopped and gave him a withering look. She should have seen this coming.

He smiled and shook his head. "That's not what I had in mind, lass. Although I'm always willin' to negotiate."

She had to concede—this man had charm. But not nearly enough to entice her. Nor earn her trust. "Good day, Mr. Mac-Gregor."

"Will you not at least listen to my proposal?" he called after her.

Kathryn kept walking, feeling his stare. The jangle of the bell as she entered Myrtle's sounded like the sweet ring of victory. She hung up her coat and walked back to the edge of the front window. MacGregor still stood where she'd left him. Absently, her hand covered the child nestled not far from her heart.

Everything she knew about this man screamed at her not to trust him. But God help her, she was so desperate to keep the ranch—the last remnant of Larson and the life they'd shared together, the legacy for their precious child—that for a moment, she'd actually contemplated asking him about his offer.

Later that night, Kathryn slid her key into the back door lock of the haberdashery when someone touched her from behind. She nearly jumped out of her skin.

In the instant it took her to turn, she imagined that it was Larson and a flurry of thoughts filled that hopeful moment. Why hadn't she thought to leave him a note at the cabin? He'd probably been searching for her for days, and why had he thought to look for her here of all places? Then she imagined telling him that they were finally going to have a . . .

In the faint glow of the half moon Kathryn recognized the silhouette, and the fragile hope died in her chest.

"Betsy sent me out for more whiskey, so I thought I'd run over and see if you were home yet. Got somethin' for me?" Annabelle cocked a brow, eying the cloth bag in Kathryn's grip. Kathryn handed it to her, and she lifted the opening of the bag to her face and inhaled. "Mmm, bread pudding?" She followed Kathryn inside and leaned against a crate as she pinched off a bite with her fingers.

"A man was here when I came a while before, knocked on the door a few times. He didn't see me though. Didn't want him gettin' the wrong idea about us being *acquaintances* and all."

Annabelle smiled and Kathryn caught the sincerity in it.

"But I don't mind tellin' ya, that fella was *mighty* easy on the eyes." Annabelle drew out the last part and licked her lips.

Kathryn glanced back at the door, her beleaguered hope wary of another false start. Could it have been Larson? "You didn't recognize him?"

Annabelle shook her head. "No, and I'd remember him for sure. Tall, dark hair about to his shoulders, and had a certain—" she took another bite of the bread pudding and paused, as though trying to choose just the right word—"I don't know . . . confidence about him. Not meanlike, mind you, just sure of himself. You know, like he knows somethin' the rest of the world doesn't."

A knock on the door caused them both to jump. Kathryn forced a laugh at the comical wide-eyed look Annabelle was giving her, clearly saying she hoped it was that man. Kathryn's hands were shaking so badly she could hardly manage the latch.

Matthew Taylor filled the doorway, hat in hand. He had a wounded look about him, his expression somber. "Mrs. Jennings." The smile he managed looked forced. "I came by a bit ago but guess you weren't home yet."

The flatness of his voice drew Kathryn's curiosity. "I just arrived a few minutes ago. Mr. Taylor, are you all right?"

"Yes, ma'am, I'm fine. But . . ." He looked past her. "Would you mind if I came in for a minute?"

She nodded and pulled the door open. "Yes, certainly." From the corner of her eye, she saw Annabelle move to leave. "Annabelle, please stay. Mr. Taylor," she offered, extending a hand in Annabelle's direction, thankful Annabelle was there but already wondering how Matthew would react. Matthew was a decent, God-fearing man and Annabelle was . . . well, Annabelle was Annabelle. And she was dressed for work, as she often called it, and her clothing, her rouge-tinted cheeks, and her painted lips bespoke a woman of easy virtue. "This is

Miss Annabelle Grayson, a *friend* of mine,"
Kathryn added with purposeful inflection,
hoping Matthew might take her lead and extend Annabelle undue social courtesy.
"Annabelle, this is Mr. Matthew Taylor. Mr.
Taylor was the foreman on my husband's
ranch. On *our* ranch."

"Nice to meet you, Mr. Taylor."

When no reply came, Kathryn looked
back at Matthew. She watched his gaze
quickly travel the length of Annabelle's
body—not in a licentious way but as though
struggling to make sense of her presence
here. The somber edge of his expression
gave way to surprise, then unmistakable
shock. Little by little, another emotion
emerged through the fog of Matthew's responses. He glanced back at Kathryn and
she recognized the look in his eyes. She'd
experienced the same affront to her sense
of dignity the first time she'd realized what
Annabelle was, what she did for a living.
Kathryn turned her attention to Annabelle
and watched, silently hurting for her friend,
as the smile on Annabelle's face gradually
slid away.

Kathryn tried to think of something to say,

still absorbing Matthew's reaction and the thick layer of silence that weighed the room.

Matthew finally managed the briefest of nods. "Miss Grayson . . . it's nice to—" He hesitated, lips in a thin line, as though unable to force the words out. "It's nice that you have such a good friend in Mrs. Jennings."

Matthew's response had been honest, yet painfully devoid of warmth. But could Kathryn really blame him? After all, Annabelle wasn't someone Matthew would normally associate with. And if she had been, Kathryn thought again, looking between the two of them, she wouldn't have thought as much of Matthew as she did. Unable to fault him for his reaction, Kathryn waited for the frost to move into Annabelle's eyes, as she'd witnessed yesterday with Mrs. Hochstetler at the mercantile. Or for Annabelle to have a quick comeback, something she'd say to put Matthew squarely in his place. Kathryn's ears burned just thinking about it.

But Annabelle didn't say a word. The silence in the room became oppressive as she openly searched Matthew's face for a moment before slowly lowering her eyes to the floor.

Sharing her friend's hurt, Kathryn tried again to think of a way to ease the moment.

Matthew glanced down briefly, then turned back to face her. "Mrs. Jennings, I'm sorry to be the one to have to tell you this . . ."

The seriousness in his tone caused the thoughts forming in Kathryn's head to evaporate.

"I've just come from the sheriff's office." He blew out a breath. "A body was discovered late this afternoon."

Kathryn felt something anchored deep inside her give way. She clutched her waist and felt Annabelle's hand on her shoulder.

Taylor's eyes filled with emotion. "They think it's your husband."

CHAPTER THIRTEEN

The following morning, a crowd gathered outside the paint-peeled clapboard building of the Willow Springs undertaker's office. The buzz of speculation hummed beneath the overcast skies, and a late May drizzle dampened the air. Kathryn shivered and searched the unfamiliar faces around her. Most of them stared back, watchful, waiting. She supposed it was nothing more than morbid curiosity that drew them.

"A man's body was found in a ravine a few miles from town," Matthew Taylor had told her the previous night.

That's all he'd said, but Kathryn had the feeling he knew more. She stared at the door that Taylor had disappeared through a half hour ago, fear of the unknown knotting her stomach. If the body beyond that threshold was Larson's, then she had indeed lost everything.

She wished Annabelle had come with her, but Matthew Taylor had insisted against it. Kathryn had glimpsed the sting of rebuff in Annabelle's eyes when Matthew had voiced his strong opposition to her accompanying them. Annabelle had hugged Kathryn tight and hadn't looked in his direction again.

Kathryn pulled her coat tighter and wrapped her arms around herself. *Lord, please let them be wrong. Don't let it be him.*

From the corner of her eye, she spotted Gabe standing at the edge of the crowd. Their eyes met, and he smiled gently. He worked his way through the clusters of people, careful not to jostle anyone in his path. Then he came and stood close beside her.

Kathryn looked up into his face. After not having seen him for days, she wanted to speak with him but was completely bereft of words. In his eyes she sensed a depth of compassion she would have guessed him incapable of with his childlike purity. Without a word, he slipped an arm around her shoulders in a brotherly fashion, and she found herself leaning into his strength. What pain had this gentle man endured that he could so thoroughly, with a simple touch, render such peace?

"Mrs. Jennings?"

Kathryn lifted her head to see Matthew Taylor walking toward her. People drew back as he approached. Her gaze fell to the object in his hands, and she heard a guttural cry leave her throat.

Larson's coat. The one she'd bought for him in Boston for their first Christmas. Dark stains marred the tanned leather.

She saw her own hand reaching to touch it while another part of her tried to hold it back. Maybe if she didn't touch it, it wouldn't be real. And he wouldn't be dead. The leather felt cold and stiff and damp. Kathryn sank to her knees.

Taylor knelt in the mud beside her. "I'm sorry. I'm so sorry."

She took the coat from him and in one last frantic hope, opened to the inner lining. The images blurred as she ran her fingers over the initials LRJ, then over their unique cattle brand she'd embroidered inside.

"I want to see him."

He shook his head. "No you don't. You don't understand. The body is . . . Your husband's been dead for several months now."

With his help, she rose. She started in the direction of the undertaker's office.

Matthew touched her arm. "Kathryn, please. Don't do this. He's not like you remember."

She stilled at his use of her name and looked up, her resolve holding fast.

As though sensing it would take more than pleading to change her mind, he grimaced. "His body's been ravaged. First by the cold, then by the spring thaw." His voice lowered. "And by . . . animals."

She closed her eyes as she imagined Larson's body—the body she'd drawn next to hers and had clung to so tightly—being so horribly defiled. "Even so, Mr. Taylor," she said quietly, so only he could hear, "it is my husband's body and I will see him one last time before I bury him."

After a long moment, his determined look faded. Before he led her inside, he handed her a handkerchief. Kathryn realized why as soon as she entered.

She held the cloth to her nose and stared in disbelief at the body on the table. Surely this couldn't be Larson. Her eyes scanned the torn clothing and deteriorated flesh. Her stomach convulsed.

With his coat still in her arms, she saw Larson's boots on the table.

"Mrs. Jennings." A man's voice sounded softly beside her.

Kathryn turned. She hadn't noticed the gray-haired gentleman standing there. She guessed him to be the undertaker.

"My condolences to you, ma'am." He slowly extended a bundle to her. "These papers were found near your husband's body. They're hardly legible now, but I thought you might want them. And there's something else. I found it in the pocket of his coat." He held a crudely fashioned metal box in his hand.

Swallowing, she took the box and opened the lid. Her eyes filled when she read the inscription inside. She saw the key on the side and gave it a slight twist, doubting anything would happen. Her lips trembled as a tinny Christmas melody plinked out from the mechanism within. *Larson, you remembered after all. . . .*

Matthew Taylor stepped closer, paused for a moment, then laid a hand to her arm.

"I'm sorry, Kathryn. Your husband was a good man. A lot of snow fell Christmas Day. Even the best tracker would've gotten lost in that storm."

She nodded. But how could he be gone? She still felt him with her. Inside her.

The gray-haired gentleman turned, drawing her attention. He nodded to the table. "Oh, this man here didn't die from the elements, leastwise not that alone." His expression flashed to Matthew and then back to her. Regret lined his face. "I . . . I'm sorry, ma'am. I thought you'd already been told. Your husband was shot before he died, square in the chest. No doubt he died quickly, if that's any consolation."

Kathryn felt her mouth slip open. "But, I don't understand. . . ."

The look the man gave her clearly told her that he didn't have the answers either. And even if he did, it wouldn't bring Larson back.

Her eyes flashed briefly again to Larson's body, then to his left hand. She wished, not for the first time, that he would've allowed her to purchase a wedding ring for him. She looked down at the simple band of gold adorning her left hand and wondered why such a silly thing would matter at a moment like this.

True to Matthew Taylor's word, Larson's body was not as she remembered. Nor as she wanted to. Kathryn almost wished the painful image could be erased from her mind even as the talons of truth sank deeper into her heart. Her loss was complete. She turned to leave.

Then a slight flutter quivered in her belly, and her breath caught tight. In that instant, she knew she was wrong. She hadn't lost everything.

———

Larson skirted the boundary of Willow Springs and made his way up the mountain pass. He still held hope that Kathryn had kept the ranch, but even if Kohlman had called the loan in, Larson knew that, by contract, Kathryn could continue to live in the cabin until the bank foreclosed. To that end, he gently nudged his aging mount around an outcropping of boulders and down the familiar path toward home.

In the past, he'd never have given his swayback horse a second glance. But using the money he'd found stashed in his pack a few days into his journey, he'd managed a fair barter for the pastured mare with a few bills to spare. He reached down and ran a gloved hand over her less than lustrous coat, thankful for every grueling mile she'd spared him from walking. Then he aimed his thanks heavenward again for the gift of Isaiah and Abby.

He carefully tugged off the leather gloves and looked at his misshapen hands. Gently flexing his fingers, Larson winced at the unpleasant sensation shooting up his right arm. The skin was nearly healed but was stretched taut over the back of his hand, much as it was over half of his body. He may have denied death its victory, but the grave had certainly claimed a bit of him in the struggle.

A sense of dread washed through him. What would Kathryn's reaction be at seeing him like this for the first time? He pulled the gloves back on.

His yearning to see her, to hold her, had deepened with each mile. But along with his anticipation mingled a foreboding that tasted far more of fear than festivity. He shifted in the saddle and stared ahead at the winding trail of dirt and rock that had been the haunt and haven of his dreams, both waking and sleeping, for the past five months.

He'd lived this moment a thousand times over, and it still sent a chill through him.

Maybe if he'd been a better husband to her, a better provider, or perhaps if he had treated her more gently, he'd feel differently about coming back. The truth of their marriage was as real to him now as the scars marring his body. And the fault of the relationship rested mostly with him. Hadn't God chiseled that truth into his heart in the past months?

After several hours of riding, Larson's pulse kicked up a notch when he rounded the bend and the familiar scene came into view. It still took his breath away. The cabin, nestled in stands of newly leafed aspen and willow trees, crouched in the shadow of the rugged mountains that would always be his home.

His stomach clenched tight as he watched for movement from the homestead. He hadn't seen signs of cattle yet, but they could've already been herded through the pass to the lower pasture. He frowned as he rode past the unkempt garden. Normally Kathryn would have the plot cleared by now, the soil tilled and ready for planting. More than likely she was overworked from the ranch. His lack of provision for her thrust the stab of guilt deeper within him.

An explanation for the shape of things corralled his thoughts. His emotions argued against it, but a heaviness weighted his chest. What if Matthew Taylor and the ranch hands hadn't been able to keep the ranch going? What if they'd lost the land he'd worked so hard to claim? But remembering Taylor's skill lessened Larson's unease. Taylor was a hard worker and an honest man. He would've helped Kathryn in any way he could, Larson was certain of that. Taylor was a man he could trust.

As he rode closer, a breeze swept down from the mountain, whistling through the branches overhead. The door to the cabin creaked open and Larson's eyes shot up. A rush of adrenaline caused every nerve to tingle.

"Kathryn?" he rasped. Though Abby's tea had worked wonders, his voice still reminded him of a music box whose innards had been scraped and charred. The comparison tugged hard at a well-worn memory, but he resisted the pull and stuffed it back down.

He eased off his horse and glanced at the barn. Eerily quiet.

It took him a minute to gain his balance and get the feeling back in his limbs. His right leg ached, and he was tempted to reach for the staff tied to his saddle but he resisted, not wanting Kathryn's first image of him to be that of a cripple. With each stuttered stride toward the cabin, he fought the urge to feel like less of a man. Would he ever be able to look at himself again and not flinch? But more than that—would Kathryn?

He stopped and briefly closed his eyes, wishing he could mimic the simple eloquence of Isaiah's prayers. Vulnerability flooded his heart, sweeping away all pleas but one.

God, let her still want me.

He continued toward the cabin, his eyes trailing upward to the smokeless chimney. A light mist filtered down through the hearty blue spruce he'd planted their first spring here. Remembering that day gave him hope. Larson pulled his knit cap farther down over his scalp and turned up his coat collar to meet his sparse beard—partly to protect the still-sensitive skin on his neck from the chill and damp, but mostly to lessen the initial shock for her.

He gently pushed open the door. "Kathryn?"

He stepped inside and scanned the room. Deserted. Empty. Dust covered the wood plank floor. He heard something scurry in the far corner. The door to the bedroom was closed, and he crossed the room and jerked the latch free. The room was empty but for the bed they'd shared. Scenes flashed in his mind of being here with Kathryn that last night. Disbelief and concern churned his gut.

He strode from the cabin and searched the barn. It too was empty. He called her name, but his voice was lost in the wind stirring among the trees. Chest heaving, he ignored the pain and swung back up on his mount.

Later that afternoon, exhausted from the hard ride back to Willow Springs, Larson's body ached from the unaccustomed abuse. If anyone would be able to tell him what had happened to Kathryn, it would be Jake Sampson at the livery. He'd dealt with him for years, and Jake kept up with all the town's business, whether he had a right to or not.

The livery doors stood open. Larson walked in and spotted Sampson bent over an anvil by the fiery forge, pounding red-hot steel. Larson stopped in his tracks.

He watched the rhythm of Jake's body as he worked, the muscles flexing and bunching in his forearm as he brought the hammer down with practiced expertise. Larson couldn't help but stare. A whole body, healthy and unmarred, was a masterful thing—something he'd never fully appreciated until now, until it was too late.

He took a step forward. "Jake?"

His head didn't turn. Larson took another step and called out again, motioning this time.

Jake's head lifted slightly. He acknowledged him with a nod. "Let me finish this and I'll be right with you, sir."

"Jake?" Larson repeated.

Jake looked up again and paused. Hammer in hand, he took a step through the smoke-layered air and into the sunlight. "You got a horse you need boardin' while you're in town, mister? I charge fifty cents per—" His eyes took in Larson's face, and his smile faded. He turned away but not quickly enough to hide his grimace.

The revulsion Larson saw in Jake's eyes caused an unbearable ache. Disbelief jolted him. He lowered his face and took a step back into the shadows, struggling to maintain his composure. Jake hadn't even recognized him. How was that possible? Was he so different a man now? A thought pierced him. If Jake looked at him this way, how would Kathryn see him? Surely there was enough left of the man he'd been that would stir Jake's memory. Part of him wanted to turn and leave, but he thought of Kathryn and knew he had to find her.

Summoning the last of his pride, Larson stepped forward and looked directly into Jake Sampson's eyes.

Jake wiped his hands on a soiled cloth but kept his face down, as though determined not to look at him again. "What exactly is it that you need, sir? I'll be happy to help, if I can."

Larson didn't answer. Instead, he willed his old friend to look at him, to know him.

When Jake did look up again, his expression was a mixture of shock and pity.

But it wasn't pity Larson sought. He wanted some semblance of recognition. Anything but the thinly veiled aversion he saw in Jake's response. For the first time, Larson saw himself through eyes other than Isaiah's and Abby's, and the reality sent a shudder through him.

If given a choice, of course he'd choose his former appearance and powerful build over this ugly mask and crippled stride. How had he ever thought Kathryn would see past his wretched appearance? She'd always wanted more from him, more of what was inside. But he hadn't fully understood what she'd meant until that very moment. Until the only good left in him was masked by a hideous shroud. Just imagining Jake's reaction mirrored in Kathryn's eyes was more than he could take.

He thought of what Abby had said about her loving Isaiah despite his scars. But Isaiah's deep scars had been on his back and arms. They hadn't disfigured his face, hadn't irrevocably altered the man she sat across the table from each morning and slept with each night.

Larson's courage withered inside him. Shame filled him. His eyes burned, and he knew he needed to leave quickly. "If you could direct me to a hotel, I'd be obliged," he said quietly, eyes down.

Jake said accommodations were hard to come by but gave him directions to a place Larson knew well two streets down. Larson thanked him and left. Back on his horse, he urged the animal down a less crowded side street. Still reeling from Sampson's reaction, he tried to convince himself that Kathryn's response could be different. In a way, the woman Kathryn was had become clearer to him during their separation. Her honesty, purity, and loyalty were more real to him now than they ever had been.

Clinging to that fragile hope, he gave his horse the lead as his mind searched the possibilities of where she might be.

If the ranch had become too much for her, which by all signs it had, she would have surely moved here to Willow Springs. He thought about checking the hotels and boardinghouses, but then his mind lurched to a halt.

What if she'd gone back home to her father, back to Boston? His body tensed. He had been gone for five months. What if she had assumed him to be dead and returned to the East?

Kathryn's mother had passed away years ago, and though she and Kathryn had written letters through the years, Kathryn's father had maintained a wall of silence. It was still hard to fathom that William Cummings had taken so little interest in his only child.

Not having thought about it in years, Larson recalled a conversation with Kathryn's father that occurred before he'd taken Kathryn as his bride. The sting of Cummings' words wounded afresh.

"My daughter can do better than you, Jennings. Kathryn has beaus lined up, just waiting for even a cursory glance. But she won't look at them because of you. Those men are able to give her the opportunities she deserves, provide the kind of life she's accustomed to." William Cummings had higher aspirations for his daughter and was accustomed to getting his way. *"Name your price, Jennings."*

Remembering that day in Cummings' plush study, how he'd felt so out of place while trying hard not to show it, brought back a flood of uncertainty. Kathryn had sworn to him that she didn't care about any of it—the money, the inheritance, the social status. All she wanted was him. But Larson had watched the fire inside her die through the years, and he suspected her inability to conceive contributed to that in large part. Though they'd never spoken of it, he wondered now if she'd grown to resent him for it through the years.

Pulled back to the present, his attention was drawn to a small gathering of people huddled in a fenced off portion of land behind the white steepled church. He remembered visiting the church once with Kathryn, years back, when she'd begged him to stay over for Sunday services on one of their supply trips. He'd begrudged every minute of it. The tightness of the pews, the hushed whispers and grave expressions that hinted to him of disapproval.

Kathryn had thanked him no less than five times on the way home for taking her, but the hour wasted that Sunday morning only confirmed within Larson that he best communed with God among His creation and away from His people.

As Larson moved closer to the gathering, he realized their purpose. Two men worked together to lower a coffin suspended by ropes into a hole in the ground. Three other people looked on in silence. A woman dressed all in black and two men beside her. Larson guessed that from the Bible in his hands one of the men was a preacher, but it wasn't the same sour-faced fellow he remembered behind the pulpit all those years ago.

Watching the sparse gathering, Larson suddenly felt for the departed soul and wondered what kind of life the person had led that would draw so few well-wishers. Then the woman turned her head to speak to one of the men beside her.

A stab of pain in his chest sucked Larson's breath away.

Kathryn.

He dismounted and started to go to her, but something held him back.

She walked to the pile of loose dirt and scooped up a handful. She stepped forward and, hesitating for a moment, finally let it sift through her fingers back to the earth. Larson was close enough to hear the hollow sound of dirt and pebbles striking the coffin below. He was certain he saw her shudder. Her movements were slow and deliberate, as though carefully thought out. She looked different to him somehow. He drank her in and could feel the scattered pieces of his life coming back together.

His thoughts raced to imagine who could be inside that coffin. She knew so few people. His mind quickly settled on one. Bradley Duncan. While rubbing the numbness from his right leg, he remembered the afternoon he'd found the young man at the cabin visiting Kathryn. Despite the past months of pleading with God to quell his jealous nature and for the chance to make things right, a bitter spark rekindled deep inside him.

He bowed his head. Would he ever possess the strength to put aside his old nature? At that moment, Kathryn turned toward him, and he knew the answer was no.

Larson didn't want to believe it. He knew his wife's body as well as his own, from vivid memory as well as from his dreams, and the gentle bulge beneath her skirts left little question in his mind. Larson's legs felt as though they might buckle beneath him.

He hadn't recognized his ranch foreman at first, but Larson watched as Matthew Taylor put a protective arm around Kathryn as though to steady her. An uncomfortable heat tightened Larson's chest at the intimate gesture. Kathryn nodded to Taylor and casually laid a hand to her abdomen. He'd trusted Taylor with the two most important things in the world to him—his ranch and his wife. It would seem that Taylor had failed him on both counts. And in the process, had given Kathryn what he never could.

With Taylor's hand beneath her arm, Kathryn turned away from the grave. Taylor whispered something to her. She smiled back, and Larson's heart turned to stone. They walked past him as though he weren't there. He suddenly felt invisible, and for the first time in his life, he wasn't bothered by the complete lack of recognition. Defeat and fury warred inside him as he watched the couple walk back toward town.

When the preacher had returned to the church and the cemetery workers finished their task and left, Larson walked to the edge of the grave. He took in the makeshift headstone, then felt the air squeeze from his lungs. Reading the name carved into the splintered piece of old wood sent him to his knees. His world shifted full tilt.

Just below the dates 1828–1868 was the name—

LARSON ROBERT JENNINGS

CHAPTER | FOURTEEN ←

The days ran together, yet they were always the same.

Kathryn worked from dawn until well past dusk, ate when she wasn't hungry, and slept to escape. She hadn't realized what strength the hope of Larson's return had instilled within her. Now, with that hope abandoned, the only thing that kept her moving forward was the remnant of their love growing inside her. Even the fervor to keep the land had lost some of its urgency. What good was the land if she and her child couldn't share it with Larson? But she knew she had to keep struggling—she had to make a home for his child.

She rose early one morning, forcing one foot in front of the other, and parted from her normal routine. Myrtle had asked her to help serve on the breakfast shift, so Kathryn had rearranged her schedule with Mr. Hudson. She wove a path through the crowded boardwalk on her way to Myrtle's. She brushed a hand over the spacious front panel of the black dress she'd worn to the funeral, and every day since. She'd sewn it to allow for coming months' growth, and the recent changes in her body were proof that the space would soon be filled.

Looking down the plank walkway, Kathryn spotted Matthew Taylor speaking to an older gentleman unfamiliar to her. She quickly crossed the street, keeping her face averted. Mr. Taylor's back was to her, and she hoped he hadn't seen her. Though thankful for Matthew's friendship and support in recent days, she'd grown increasingly awkward around him. The emotions his brown eyes had only hinted at before were now painfully obvious.

Glancing behind her and realizing she'd escaped Matthew's notice, Kathryn slowed her pace. A definite twinge fluttered within her belly. They were growing more frequent. She warmed again, remembering the way Sadie's cinnamon eyes had lit up when hearing about the baby. Asking beforehand if it'd be all right, Annabelle had brought Sadie over one morning that week. Kathryn had been thrilled to see her again. The quiet, reserved girl, only a child herself really, rarely smiled these days, according to Annabelle, so her reaction had been especially meaningful.

The day crawled by, but not for lack of work. Back at the haberdashery for the afternoon, Kathryn mended until the muscles in her fingers burned. Then she set to ironing the freshly washed shirts hanging on the rack in the back room.

"Excuse me, Mrs. Jennings?"

Mr. Hudson, her employer, was standing in the doorway. He held a mass of red roses in his hands.

"These just arrived." His eyes twinkled. "There's an envelope attached."

Her curiosity piqued, Kathryn set the iron back on the grate positioned above the hearth's glowing embers and wiped her hands on her skirt. "Who brought them?"

"I haven't a clue," he answered with a shrug, handing her the bouquet. "I went to the front counter a moment ago and found them there. It would seem you have an admirer, Mrs. Jennings. And an extravagant one, at that."

He purposefully twitched his mustache, and Kathryn had to smile. A man well into his years, Mr. Hudson treated her more like a daughter than an employee. She thought of her own father and her smile faded.

The mischievous twinkle in his eyes softened. "There're twenty men to every woman out here, Mrs. Jennings, and I told you it wouldn't be long until one of them started taking notice of you. You're a beautiful young woman. You need time to grieve your late husband, and that's only right, but I've a feeling—and please take this the way it's meant—that you grieved for your husband long before they found his body." He looked away briefly. "I mourned my Rachel for nearly eight years before I was ready to love another woman in that way. But I was much older than you are now, and . . ." His eyes regained the twinkle as he rubbed his bald head. "I didn't have hair the color of sunshine on wheat and eyes that could melt a man's heart at a glance."

Kathryn blew a limp curl from her forehead and wiped the beads of perspiration.

She tried for a smile. "Yes, I'm quite a catch, Mr. Hudson. If my charm and good looks didn't win them, I'm certain my generous dowry would."

With an endearing look, he shook his head and walked back to the front.

Kathryn lifted the flowers to her face, and Matthew Taylor immediately came to mind. He shouldn't have gone to this trouble. Even if he, or another man, were to some day want her in that way, she couldn't imagine opening her heart to someone else. She'd been avoiding Matthew Taylor, and he deserved better. She would find him and thank him for the flowers, then be honest with him about her feelings.

She opened the envelope and pulled out the stationery. Her mouth fell open at the name engraved across the top.

Dear Mrs. Jennings,

I've learned of your husband's death and extend my deepest sympathies. My offer to help you still stands, as does the invitation for dinner.

Most sincerely,
Donlyn MacGregor

Katherine read the note again. A mixture of emotions stirred inside her—disbelief at Mr. MacGregor's gall at inviting her to dinner while she was still in mourning, followed by a shameful spark of interest in his continued offer to help her keep the ranch.

The rest of the week passed in a fog, and as Kathryn walked home late that Friday night, she continued to weigh the options for trying to maintain ownership of the ranch. She couldn't bring Larson back, but perhaps she could still keep his dream alive.

After all, he'd wanted to see the ranch succeed above anything else.

Sensing more than hearing a presence behind her, she slowed her steps and turned. The boardwalk was empty and dark. Still, she felt . . . something.

That presence stayed with her as she walked to the back of the men's shop and bolted the door behind her. When she lay down to sleep on her cot sometime later, it was still with her. She cradled the music box against her chest. Gently lifting the lid, she fingered the inscription she didn't need to see to read.

To Kathryn,
For all your heart's desires.
My love, Larson.

In that moment, the decision about whether or not to accept Donlyn Mac-Gregor's offer to help her became clear.

———

Kathryn waited outside Mr. Kohlman's office. She pulled the watch from her pocket and checked it for the seventh time in almost thirty minutes. His secretary had said Mr. Kohlman was in and could see her. So why had he kept her waiting? She stood and crossed to the woman's desk. "Excuse me, miss, but I'm already late for work. I'll need to come back to see Mr. Kohlman some other—"

The door to his office opened.

Harold Kohlman's thick sideburns bulged around his cheekbones as he grinned. "Mrs. Jennings, what a delight to see you again. Won't you come in?"

Shoving aside her frustration, Kathryn nodded. Entering his office, she heard the metallic catch of a latch and noticed another door on the opposite side that she hadn't seen before.

"Sit down, Mrs. Jennings, please. As a matter of fact, I was going to be contacting you soon, so you saved me the trouble."

Kathryn turned her attention to the chair she'd occupied during their last meeting and quickly decided to remain standing. Somehow she felt more in control that way, less like a beggar. "No thank you, Mr. Kohlman, I don't have much time this morning. I've brought another payment for my loan." She laid an envelope on his desk, wondering how to work up the nerve to voice the real reason for her coming.

"You don't have to see me for that, Mrs. Jennings. You can leave it with someone at the front counter. They can credit your account." He flipped through the bills in the envelope. "However, you are still in arrears, and I'm afraid that—" He looked up sharply. "This is hardly a week's worth, and you're already several months behind."

"Yes, I realize that. I'm bringing you all the money I have, and I promise to bring you more as soon as I can."

His smile hinted at artful hypocrisy. "If you're here to plead for another extension on your loan, Mrs. Jennings, I'm afraid my answer will be the same as last time."

"No, Mr. Kohlman." She worked hard to keep the anger from her voice. "You made yourself quite clear on both those points. I'm here about something else entirely."

"Well, before you begin, please allow me to give you my good news, because it may shed new light on your situation."

Her suspicions rose. "Good news?"

"Yes, yes indeed." His smile spread to a grin and puffed his ruddy cheeks. "Just this morning I received an offer on your behalf. Quite a substantial offer, I might add. Enough to pay off the loan with the bank and leave a bit to spare to provide for you and your child. I told the buyer that I would present—"

"You can refuse the offer, Mr. Kohlman. My land is not for sale."

His eyes lit. "Oh, but it's not for the land, Mrs. Jennings. It's for the water."

Kathryn thought she'd misunderstood. "The water?"

"Yes, or more exactly, the water rights in your husband's name. He had certain rights to the water that flows down the pass through Fountain Creek." He sat up straighter. "What

I'm telling you is that I'm offering you a chance to keep your land and your ranch. All you need do is sign over your husband's shares. A very simple procedure, actually, and then you can have your money, move back to your little cabin, and resume your life."

Little cabin? Resume my life? Kathryn's thoughts collided as a flurry of emotions clamored for priority—indignation at how he dared suggest that she simply take the money and resume her life, and shock as she realized that, while focusing so intently on the cattle as the key to keeping the land, she'd overlooked another answer, a possible solution.

"They're willing to pay you handsomely." Kohlman quoted the sum of money, and Kathryn felt her eyes grow wide. "And they would pay you in cash, Mrs. Jennings. You'd receive the funds by week's end." He opened the top drawer of his desk and pulled out a document. "You'd be wise to seriously consider their offer."

Kathryn reached for the document even as a sense of warning stole through her. She scanned the pages of tiny print, little of it registering. Then her eyes locked on a phrase. "What does this mean? 'Right to dam and store,' " she read aloud. "'The pro-prietary owner shall retain rights to all sur-face water and groundwater, and shall re-serve the right to dam and store said watercourse. . . .' " She let her voice trail off as the silent question hung between them.

Kohlman focused on something past her shoulder. "All of that simply means that the new owner will have the same rights your husband possessed."

"But my husband never dammed the creek or tried to stop the flow of the stream into town. He took what he had a right to, only what he needed for the ranch and our livelihood. The water in Fountain Creek also belongs to the people of Willow Springs, doesn't it?" He didn't answer. "Doesn't it, Mr. Kohlman?"

Kathryn's thoughts immediately went to the gate rider who had drowned and what Matthew had told her—that someone had been tampering with the head gates on the creek. She stared at the paper in her hand. Water was a precious resource in this arid climate, and it was scarce at times. Three years ago they'd suffered a drought so dev-astating that the territory's supply of bread-stuffs, vegetables, and feed for stock had been wiped out. She could sell the water rights and keep her land, but what would she have? What legacy could she give Larson's only child? Land without water. That was worth nothing. Fountain Creek was her property's life source, and the life source for Willow Springs. This town wouldn't survive without it.

Suddenly the document felt like a coiled snake in her hand. She dropped it on Kohlman's desk and backed away.

He eyed her, his smile intact but all other signs of graciousness gone. "Mrs. Jennings, don't let the specifics of the contract sway you. Your responsibility is to yourself and to your child. You owe your child the safety and security this agreement will provide. And you won't find another buyer who will match this price, I assure you."

"I'm not looking for a buyer, sir. As I told you before, this land, this water, is not for sale. I mean to keep them both."

Kohlman leaned back in his chair and laced his thick fingers across the broad expanse of his middle. "And just how do you aim to do that, Mrs. Jennings?"

Her defenses rose at his caustic tone. "I don't know exactly. But I do know I will not sell." She'd spoken the last words softly, but with quiet resolve.

His face hardened. "Very well. Was there something else you needed to see me about today?"

As if he would be willing to help her now. Kathryn sighed. Best to come right out and say it. "I'm wondering if you could let me know how to get in touch with Mr. Mac-Gregor."

He leaned forward. "Donlyn MacGregor?"

"Yes, I need to see him for . . . business reasons."

Kohlman's mouth took a suggestive turn. "Well, I see . . ."

The high collar of Kathryn's black dress suddenly felt overly snug. How dare he think . . . "No, sir, I'm certain you do not!"

"Really, Mrs. Jennings, it's of no concern to me whom you choose to spend your evenings with. After all, you are a young widow . . . though still in mourning," he added, his leather chair creaking as he rose. "But I can easily see how Mr. MacGregor would be a desirable man to someone of your . . . current position." He opened his office door and, with a wave of his hand, indicated she was to precede him. "I'll make known your . . . desire to meet with him."

"Mr. Kohlman, it's nothing like that," she said in a low whisper, hopeful that his assistant sitting within earshot hadn't overheard. "And I would appreciate your not implying those intentions to Mr. MacGregor."

Kohlman smiled. "Oh, I won't imply a thing. I'll let him do that, Mrs. Jennings. Good day to you." The door closed with a thud.

By the time Kathryn reached Myrtle's, anxiety knotted her stomach and her jaw ached from biting back the responses she wanted to hurl in Harold Kohlman's face. Unfortunately, or perhaps fortunately for her, she'd thought of them all after the fact.

At closing time she was in no better mood. Since she'd been late to work, Kathryn offered to clean the kitchen and lock up. Not long after bolting the door behind Myrtle, Kathryn heard a tap on the front window and threw down her dishrag. Could people not read the *CLOSED* sign? She strode to the front.

Silhouetted by the coal-lit street lamps, Matthew Taylor's broad-shouldered stance was instantly recognizable. The bell jangled when she opened the door.

"Am I late for dinner?" A tentative smile tugged the corners of his mouth.

The humor in his voice worked to thaw Kathryn's anger, and something inside her eased. "Only by about two hours."

"Well, that being the case . . . would you allow me to walk you home when you're done?"

She hesitated. "It'll still be a while. I have work left to do."

"Not a problem. I'll wait out here."

Kathryn finished, and true to his word, Matthew Taylor sat on the front steps waiting for her. An easy smile stretched his face as he stood and offered his arm. Kathryn slipped her hand through. Walking beside him, she couldn't deny how good it felt to have someone watching over her.

"Hard day?"

She glanced up at him. "How could you tell?"

"When you answered the door, I nearly ran."

Kathryn winced playfully, then smiled. "Was it that noticeable?"

He shrugged and covered her hand on

his arm. They walked in silence down the empty boardwalk for a moment. "I talked to the sheriff earlier. They sent the samples of the carcasses to Denver for testing and got the results back today. Somebody poisoned your cattle, that's for sure. But they still don't know with what."

"So we really don't know any more than we did before." She briefly considered telling him about Donlyn MacGregor's offer to help but decided against it. Matthew would encourage her not to do it, but Matthew didn't share her passion for keeping the land. And it was unlikely he would understand it.

His grip on her hand tightened. "No, I'm sorry we don't know anything more."

Hearing the underlying guilt in his voice, Kathryn stopped. "Mr. Taylor, as I told you before, none of this was your fault. And I don't blame you for any of it. I wish I could make you see that."

"And I wish I could make you see how much I care for you, Kathryn. How much I want to help you through this, if you'd only let me."

He leaned closer, and Kathryn instinctively stepped back. Suddenly all she could picture was being with Larson that last night, of him holding her in their bed, touching her, kissing her. And she didn't want to mar that memory with another man's kiss, however good or sincere that man might be.

"I'm sorry, Matthew. I can't."

"Larson is gone, Kathryn." His voice was soft, and he didn't move to close distance between them.

His statement sounded more like a plea than a fact, and tears sprang to her eyes. "I know that," she whispered, looking away.

"Do you?" He stepped closer and brushed his thumb across her cheek, wiping away her tears. "Your husband was a good man, but he's not here to take care of you anymore. To take care of his child."

At his mention of the child, she looked up.

"I know the baby is his, Kathryn. But I also know what some people are saying."

She frowned.

"Willow Springs is a good-sized town, but it's small when it comes to this kind of thing. People talk; they speculate. Some folks are saying the baby's mine. Some are saying it's a result of you staying at the brothel."

"But how did you know about that, Matthew? I was only there for—"

"Word gets around, Kathryn. Some of the ranch hands saw you coming and going from there."

She tried to look away, but he gently turned her face back. His thumb traced her chin, and Kathryn felt an involuntary shiver pass through her.

"Like I said, some of the ranch hands are saying the child is mine, and I haven't corrected them because what others are saying is far worse. People here don't know you, and since you stayed at that brothel and—" his lips firmed—"you've been seen in town with that whore, they're saying the child is a—"

She held up a hand. "I understand what you're saying. You don't have to repeat the rumors."

"You're living in the back of a men's store, sleeping on a cot. I can give you better than that, Kathryn. Let me try."

Looking into Matthew's warm brown eyes and feeling her fatherless child move within her, it would have been easy to convince herself to give him a chance. Matthew was indeed a good man. Larson's having employed him for six plus years affirmed that, and Larson's trust hadn't been easily earned. "I appreciate what you're offering me, Matthew, but . . . I still feel Larson with me. In here," she whispered, laying a hand over her heart, willing him to understand. "It's like he's not really dead."

"But he *is* dead, Kathryn. You held his coat. You saw his body. So did I. He's not coming back."

Her throat tightened. "I know that. But just because I've buried my husband doesn't mean I'm ready to bury what we were together, the life we shared. To completely forget him."

"I'm not asking you to forget him. I'm only asking you to consider what's best for you, for your child. Some folks are saying—"

"Why should I care about what people are saying behind my back! Perhaps if you'd correct their assumptions instead of remaining silent on the matter, they'd—" She stopped short, hearing the accusation that had crept into her tone. "Oh, Matthew, I'm sorry." She let out a breath. "I didn't mean for it to come out that way. I'm simply not ready for this yet. I may never be."

Kathryn saw the emotion—the love—in

his eyes, but it was a love she could not return. Not now anyway. She also saw something that ran deeper—a patience that said he understood. He pulled her against him, and Kathryn didn't fight against his embrace.

How could the strength of Matthew Taylor's arms around her feel so good when she still loved her husband? It felt like a betrayal somehow.

"Whenever you're ready," he whispered against her ear, "I'll be here."

She felt his kiss on her forehead and nodded, doubting she ever would be.

———

Having witnessed his own funeral and seen his wife betray him in a way he'd never imagined, Larson spent the next two weeks looking for her. With no money for food, he took a job mucking out stables at a small ranch on the edge of town. It was mindless work, which suited him fine because his every thought was centered on one thing: finding Kathryn again.

Willow Springs wasn't that big, but he hesitated to draw more attention to himself by asking a lot of questions. After glimpsing his face, people responded with looks of either disgust or shock, then acted like he wasn't there. Jake's reaction at seeing him still stung, and remembering the way Kathryn had allowed Taylor to touch her that afternoon by the graveside only deepened his disappointment and uncertainty.

Every time Larson's thoughts returned to the child in her womb, not of his doing, his throat would close tight. How could she have put him aside so quickly?

But still he searched. Patience had never been a virtue he possessed, but it would seem he was destined to learn it now. Each day, after finishing his chores at Johnson's ranch, he walked the alleys of town, keeping an eye on the respectable hotels and boardinghouses from one end of Willow Springs to the other, hoping to see her.

Then late one evening, weary from work and losing heart, he headed back to the ranch. A bell jangled on the opposite side of the street and, following the noise, Larson looked over. And froze.

It was dark, but he recognized her instantly. A mixture of longing and bitterness streaked through him. He pressed back into the shadows of the empty boardwalk.

Kathryn closed the door to the eatery, checked the lock, then crossed the street. His pulse raced as she walked toward him. And in that instant, he realized he wasn't ready for this yet. He wasn't ready for her to see him like this. *Oh, God, no . . .* He held his breath as she climbed the stairs and turned, never looking in his direction. He waited, then followed at a distance.

She quickened her steps along the darkened boardwalk, a bag of some sort clutched in her hand. Larson worked to maintain her pace, not using the staff in his hand for fear she might hear him and turn. She passed the well-lit boardinghouse where he'd first thought she might be staying, then continued past the mercantile and livery. Where was she going? They were nearing the edge of town. Finally, she disappeared into an alleyway between two run-down buildings on a side street, and for an instant, Larson felt concern for her safety.

Then he rounded the corner and saw her enter a simple two-story clapboard building through the back door. Staring at the building, he took a step back.

Instinctively, he knew what the place was.

The furrowed skin on his back tingled in sickening recognition even as his concern for Kathryn cooled.

He counted ten narrow windows on the second floor and couldn't help but think of each room in terms of time and money. Absently, he wondered which one was Kathryn's. But his heart rejected the thought even as the harsh truth glared back at him. No, it wasn't possible. It couldn't be. . . . Not *his* Kathryn.

Glad for the building at his back, Larson leaned against it and slid to the ground, reliving the last five months of his life. He thought he'd come to understand what God had been doing all that time—making him into the man He wanted him to be. The man he needed, and wanted, to be for Kathryn.

The smell of liquor assaulted him and his stomach churned. Raucous noises and sounds from another life, long dead to him, resurrected themselves and cloaked him like a heavy shroud. He knelt in the dirt.

All the nights he'd dreamed of her, living only to be with her again. He hadn't thought he could tolerate more pain than his physical wounds had inflicted, but this pain cut deeper to a tender place he hadn't even been aware existed. And still one breath followed another and his heart continued to beat. The weeks and months he'd endured excruciating pain, then the slow healing of his body and spirit, for what? Why had God allowed him to survive all that only to return and face a different kind of death? One proving even more painful.

He cursed Kathryn for her unfaithfulness. And while the words still tainted his lips, a swift stab of conviction penetrated his chest.

Bone of my bone, and flesh of my flesh.

Larson went completely still. Prickles rose on his neck and back at the gentle thunder inside him. Was this the still, small voice Isaiah and Abby had taught him to listen for? His breath came heavy. His heart raced. He closed his eyes, frightened of the response invading the anger in his heart. His lips moved but nothing came out at first. "But, Lord, Adam said that about a wife who was faithful." Eve hadn't given herself to another man. Or men.

The vivid images filling his mind twisted his gut—the things he'd seen as a boy, that he'd tried to block out and forget. *Lord, she scorned me. Kathryn sold herself and traded my love for a pittance.*

For an instant, Larson considered blaming God for his circumstance. After all, God was the one who had allowed him to live. But having blamed Him before, Larson knew it wouldn't change anything. He covered his face with his hands.

After all these years, the Lord had finally begun to soften his stubborn heart. What did it matter now if Kathryn didn't want it?

Larson awakened from a restless sleep. He barely remembered walking back to the farm last night and hadn't slept in the bunkhouse with the other hands. Not in the mood for company and needing time to take in what he'd witnessed, he'd chosen the barn loft instead. He sat slowly and stretched, and the weight of last night's discovery hit him all over again.

Elbows resting on his knees, he rubbed his hands over his face and slowly let out his breath, feeling his last bit of hope being siphoned away by Kathryn's deceitfulness. If he hadn't seen it with his own eyes, he never would've believed it. And it struck him then that, even with the layer of distrust that had shadowed their years together, nothing had prepared him for this.

Muscles in his right thigh resisted the chill morning air and movement, and he massaged them until the tightness eased. Wincing, he flexed the waxy ribboned flesh of his hands until they too bent to his command.

As the pewter sky gradually lightened to a pale blue, he rushed through his chores, not knowing what he was going to do when he saw Kathryn again but knowing that he had to see her, even at a distance. Even after all he knew.

It was almost noon by the time he made it into town. He waited down the street and watched the brothel, unable to make himself walk up to the door. The setting looked oddly tranquil, so different from last night, which was no surprise for this time of day. After a while, on a hunch, he shadowed his path from the previous evening back to Myrtle's Cookery, the homey-looking eating establishment where he'd first seen Kathryn.

From a bench across the street, he kept vigil on the people walking up and down the boardwalk, and it wasn't long before the object of his search appeared.

Kathryn was still a good distance off, on

the other side of the street, but seeing the black dress she wore, the respectable shroud of a mourning widow, Larson felt a flush of anger. She carried herself with such quiet dignity. His unexpected anger frightened him. Never would he have thought himself capable of wishing his wife harm. Seeing her again, though, discovering where she was living and what she was doing, wreaked havoc with his emotions.

Even draped in black, she stole his breath. Men turned as she passed, some tipping their hats, but she seemed oblivious to them. Memories of his mother drifted toward him, her head held high as she'd walked through town holding his hand. Men he'd seen visiting her room, some who returned with frequency, looked at her in open disgust and called her names as she passed. Yet her ivory complexion, as though chiseled from marble, had revealed nothing. Only the slight tightening of her hand around his gave any indication that the taunts had struck their mark.

Larson's vision blurred. He hadn't thought of that in years. He looked down at his clasped hands. Two things struck him in that moment, reliving that thinnest of reactions from his mother—the tightening of her hand around his, and the fact that she'd been holding his hand in the first place.

Kathryn crossed the busy street and disappeared into the mercantile. Larson rested his arms on his thighs, bent his head, and waited. Now that he'd found her again, he didn't know what to do. The thought of following her, watching firsthand as she built a new life without him certainly wasn't a desirable option. Especially with the life she'd chosen.

Everything within him wanted to confront her. But how could he approach her? What would he say? Imagining the look in her eyes at seeing him now, how he looked, was enough to stay that course of action for the time being.

From cautious inquiry at the feedlot earlier that week, Larson had learned about the loss of his entire herd and that his land was scheduled to go to auction in the fall. "Shame about all that cattle though." The worker had punctuated his statement with a stream of well-aimed tobacco juice. "I hear disease got 'em, but I'm thinkin' it was tick fever come up from Texas. Don't know much about that Jennings woman, other than that she done moved to town and took up with her husband's foreman. Least that's what folks is sayin'. Good piece'a land up there though—right on Fountain Creek. I'd make a claim for it if I had the means."

But even if Larson came forward to claim the land, *his* land, he had no money to pay the debt. He'd lose it anyway. Plus, he'd face the devastating humiliation of Kathryn's rejection all over again.

He looked down the block occasionally, keeping an eye on the mercantile. His thoughts were jumbled and he didn't know where to turn. Isaiah would tell him to talk to God. Larson tried remembering one of Isaiah's prayers, but couldn't.

"Talk to Him like you're talking to me," Isaiah had said countless times with that smile of his. *"Be honest. Tell Him exactly what's inside you. Only remember that He's the Alpha and Omega, the First and the Last. And you're not."*

At that moment, an attractive young woman passed by, her gaze connecting with Larson's. She stared at him for an instant, then grimaced and turned, hurrying her steps. Dropping his attention to the boardwalk, Larson pulled his knit cap farther down and turned up his collar. He rubbed a hand over his unkempt beard. Before all this, women had looked at him differently. *Much* differently. Realizing just how much he'd enjoyed their attention, their second glances, bothered him now. Especially when he recalled how he'd hated catching men looking at Kathryn.

He closed his eyes and hunched over further. Isaiah sometimes started his prayers with *Father God* but, never having known his father and imagining what kind of man he must've been, that particular phrase turned to sand in Larson's throat. *God, I don't know why I'm here. I don't know what to do, where to go.* He paused. Isaiah had said to be honest. *You're the one who brought me back here, so I guess I'd appreciate you tellin' me what you're thinking and what you'd suggest I do next.*

Larson waited for an answer. For the silent whisper he'd heard all too clearly the night before. Nothing came. Emptiness, thick and suffocating, rushed in to fill the void.

He spotted Kathryn leaving the mercantile. She had something tucked beneath her arm—a newspaper, maybe. His eyes narrowed. She was no longer alone. Matthew Taylor casually slipped her hand into the crook of his arm as they walked down the boardwalk, conversing. He'd never seen Kathryn interact with another man that way, and something twisted inside him. He could hear their laughter even over the pounding in his ears.

Taylor walked her across the street and as far as the door of the restaurant, and then Kathryn smiled and nodded at whatever he had said to her. Larson couldn't miss how his once-trusted foreman hesitated, then watched his wife walk inside and close the door.

Instinctively, Larson reached for his cane but then realized he hadn't brought it. He mentally counted the steps it would take for him to reach that door, and Matthew Taylor. Thirty at best, even with his irregular stride. Then a wave of hopelessness suddenly crested inside him. For every reason he could think of to confront Taylor and Kathryn at that moment, there were a hundred more that kept him anchored to the bench where he sat. The most compelling being the illegitimate child now growing in his wife's once-barren womb.

A swift knife of truth bladed through him at that thought and brought his inadequacies into the harsh light of reality. His throat suddenly felt parched. Indeed, through all these years, the burden of sterility had rested upon him after all.

The afternoon faded into evening and the distance to that door—to the life he remembered and had cheated death to reclaim—might as well have been a chasm forty miles wide, with no bridge in sight.

As it neared closing time, Larson watched her through the large glass window of the restaurant, skepticism warring with the courage he'd tried gathering all afternoon. He knew he needed to talk to her, but all the words just tripped over themselves in his head. He'd already lost everything, hadn't he? So why this tightness in his chest and the impending need to escape? The single prayer he'd held onto as he'd walked up to their cabin upon his return whispered back to him.

God, let her still want me.

Heaviness settled over him. What a fool he'd been, helplessly hoping. But even as he punished himself for having trusted her, a sense of uncertainty still haunted him. Something kept eating at him, something that didn't make sense. How could Kathryn work all day *and* all night? And be with child?

A disturbing image came to mind and he winced. He'd been about seven or eight years old when his mother had sent him up-stairs to get one of the women. He remem-bered knocking on Elisa's partially opened door, and when she didn't answer, he gave it a gentle push. One look at the bed, and the room started spinning. He'd never seen so much blood. Turned out Elisa had come to be with child and had tried to perform her own abortion, with tragic results. The other women had railed at her for not using the normal aloes or cathartic powders to end the unwanted pregnancy. Larson still re-membered the regret on his mother's face, the detached look in her eyes that night when she'd explained to him that some-times the powders failed to work.

It hadn't made sense to him then, but a few years later he'd come to understand what his mother had been saying. The truth of her actions had clearly told him what she'd never possessed the courage to say aloud. That she wished he'd never been born.

The squeak of hinges brought his eyes up. He blinked to clear his vision.

Kathryn exited the restaurant, locking the door behind her. She paused and peered up and down the boardwalk as though looking for something or someone. Then she turned in the direction of the brothel.

He followed her, looking down occasionally for uneven planks in the boardwalk that might hinder his altered stride. He turned over in his mind what he was going to say, wondering if she would even recognize him before he revealed himself. The pounding of a slightly off-key piano carried on the night air and helped to mask the occasional stutter of his step. He worked to catch up with her as she rounded the corner.

"There you are. I wondered if you were going to show up."

Her voice halted Larson midstride. His courage fled along with the air in his lungs. Kathryn was stopped about ten paces in front of him.

"I'm sorry, Kathryn. I tried to get here sooner, but . . ."

Larson recognized the voice first, then

the man. But the rest of Matthew Taylor's response was lost in the lilt of Kathryn's laughter.

Sick-hearted regret twisted his insides until an ache formed in the pit of stomach. He told himself to move, to close the distance between them and get it over with, to expose their betrayal, but his body refused. He stood watching, immobile, as the two of them walked away, arm in arm.

Ashamed of his own cowardice, he turned and walked in the opposite direction, needing to put some distance between himself and Kathryn—and Kathryn with Matthew Taylor.

But her voice, her laughter, played over and over in his mind as the darkened storefronts passed. Hearing it again affected him in a way he'd not expected and that he was loath to acknowledge. Remembering it, a softening somewhere deep inside him unearthed feelings he wished would have remained hidden and revealed a remnant of love for his wife.

But after all she'd done to him, how could he still care for her?

When he glanced up a while later, the faint outline of a white steeple stood out against the dark prairie sky. He walked past the church to the cemetery. Staring down at a grave, *his* grave, he'd never felt so vacant inside. He'd sold his horse two weeks ago, needing the meager funds for livelihood. He had no mount. No place to call home. No family. Nothing. He might as well be inside the pine box buried at his feet.

He stooped and sifted the mounded dirt through his fingers. Since he wasn't in that coffin, who was?

Moments passed. He finally stood and brushed the dirt from his hands, then stared up into the star-speckled sky. "So what now, Lord?" he whispered, waiting.

Heaven remained silent, but Larson couldn't. Not anymore.

Tomorrow he would confront Kathryn and find out why she had betrayed him.

CHAPTER FIFTEEN

Before the faintest hint of light challenged the night shadows, his timidity in prayer ceased and Larson poured out every anguished thought to God.

As the sun rose, splintering multicolored rays through the top of the barn loft, it brought peace with it, though still no answers. Larson likened his experience to the night Jacob had wrestled with the Lord. For the rest of his life, Jacob had borne the physical reminder of that struggle. Larson stood and stretched. Like Jacob, he too asked that the Lord would bless him. Then he smiled wryly, massaging the sore muscles of his right leg. God had already seen to giving him the limp.

He thought of Kathryn and prayed again for His timing in all of this, still not having felt a strong confirmation about facing her. But he was tired of waiting. Isaiah always said God's timing was perfect. Larson only hoped he was following it now.

Kathryn tossed Annabelle a tight smile as she closed the back door to the haberdashery shortly before noon, her nerves in a jumble. "Thank you for coming over and doing this with me. I feel a bit more prepared for it now."

Annabelle waved a hand as though to say it wasn't any big deal. "You'll do fine. You answered every question perfectly." Seriousness sharpened her expression and she glanced away before speaking again. "I really am proud of you, Kathryn. Of how you've gotten along since they found your husband's body and all. I know it hasn't been easy. . . ."

For a woman who had life so easy beforehand was the unspoken phrase Kathryn heard in her mind. Though Annabelle didn't say it, probably didn't even think it, she had a right to. Kathryn had thought about that a lot—about how easy her life had been, and was, in comparison with Annabelle's. She wished she could change the situation for Annabelle, help her out of the life she seemed trapped in. Kathryn had yet to broach the subject but hoped this morning's meeting would provide her a way to do just that.

They parted ways, and Kathryn smoothed her hair and black dress, thankful for Annabelle's mock interview. Kathryn had checked the newspaper on a regular basis and found a position that sounded promising. She had been hopeful when she'd received a response to her inquiry about the possible new employ, and she didn't want to be late for her interview with Miss . . .

Kathryn pulled the letter she'd received yesterday from her pocket. With Miss Maudelaine. If she made a favorable impression this morning, the position could be the answer to her prayers.

Much better pay. Room and board. No more working two jobs from dawn to well past dusk. And most importantly, a better environment in which to raise her son or daughter. A twinge of guilt chided her conscience. She hadn't mentioned being with child in her inquiry letter and hoped that wouldn't influence Miss Maudelaine's decision. *Lord, open a door for me, please.* Considering the opportunities this job would make in her life and in that of her child, Kathryn's nervousness lessened. Anticipation quickened her pace.

She cut a path across the busy main street and reached into her pocket to finger the delicate metal box, an ever-present reminder she kept close. After her meeting this morning, she would go by the cemetery. It'd been at least a week since her last visit, and that had been late one evening, with Matthew. He'd insisted on going with her, even though she actually preferred to visit alone.

Donlyn MacGregor hadn't contacted her since the day he'd sent the flowers. Harold Kohlman apparently hadn't given him her message. She had roughly three more months before the land would be auctioned in Denver in September; then she would lose it for certain. She decided it was time to seek Mr. MacGregor out on her own.

Crowds of midweek shoppers thronged the plank walkway and trailed out the front door of the post office and mercantile. Fearing she would be late for her interview, Kathryn finally gave up trying to push her way through and made a beeline to cut down an alleyway instead.

And ran headlong into someone standing just around the corner.

Air left her lungs at the impact. Her footing slipped.

But the man caught her and steadied her.

Kathryn finally managed to regain her balance. "I'm so sorry, I wasn't watching where I—"

She glanced up, but he turned before she could glimpse his face.

"Sir, my deepest apologies," she offered again to his back, her heart still racing. "I was in such a hurry."

The man wore a knit cap and long sleeves buttoned at the wrists, despite the June warmth. He was tall and of thin build, and the shirt he wore looked two sizes too big, the seams passing well below his shoulders. His breath came raspy and quick, and she suddenly wondered if she'd hurt him.

"Are you all right, sir?" she tried again, gently touching his shoulder.

He flinched and sucked in a sharp breath.

Kathryn drew back. "I'm sorry," she whispered.

Only then did she notice the scarred flesh stretched taut over his fists clenched at his sides. He turned slightly, his head bowed, eyes closed. Seeing the furrowed white flesh of his neck and upper right cheek, a barely audible gasp escaped her. He winced at the sound, and Kathryn instantly regretted the thoughtless reaction. What had this poor man been through?

She thought of the fire that had destroyed the bank building and the survivors Donlyn MacGregor had told her about. Then her mind flashed to a badly maimed and scarred man she'd seen visiting the brothel one night. "Men like him got damaged in the war back East. Either that or the mines," Annabelle had stated matter-of-factly. "Nobody else wants them, I guess. They're still men, though, so they come here to get that need met."

Determined not to gawk, Kathryn stole a quick glance at the man beside her. Had he experienced that kind of rejection? He turned farther away, as though her presence somehow caused him more pain, but something about him spoke to her heart. Perhaps it was the way his shoulders were stooped, giving the appearance of nearly breaking beneath an unbearable load.

Unable to think of anything else to say, she turned. When she got to the corner, she hesitated, then looked back. The man was leaning against the building, his face in his hands.

———

Larson's heart pounded out an erratic rhythm. He blew out a steadying breath.

Kathryn's gasp at seeing him had wounded him more deeply than he could have imagined. Certain she was gone, he raked his hands over his face. He didn't know which hurt him more—her reaction to him or the raw truth that she hadn't recognized her own husband.

But the question lingering in his heart had been answered.

Even if he were to come back from the grave, she wouldn't want him. Not like this.

He'd been waiting in the alleyway on the chance of seeing her, planned on approaching her sometime before she reached the restaurant. But then he'd lost her in the crowd. And then . . . *Oh, God!* He wiped his forehead with the back of his hand. With her face so close to his, seeing her eyes in that instant—his mind had gone completely blank. His courage had evaporated.

The scent of lavender, and of her, still lingered in the air around him. Her hair like silk against his face, her body pressed briefly against his in the fall. She was so beautiful.

He looked in the direction she'd gone. Her stride had held purpose. Not knowing what else to do, he headed in that direction.

Larson spotted her minutes later at the far end of the street. She'd stopped at an outdoor café and now stood searching the tables of people. An elderly woman seated alone looked in Kathryn's direction and arched a brow. The woman's white hair glistened like morning frost in the sun. She had a regal air about her, and she smiled as Kathryn approached.

Feeling slightly emboldened by his confidence that she wouldn't recognize him, Larson chose an empty table within earshot of theirs. It was partially obscured by a large cottonwood, but that suited his purposes well. He sat with his back to them and willed his pulse to slow.

"So tell me, dear, what job would you currently be holdin' here in town?"

Larson leaned slightly backward upon hearing the older woman's voice. Smooth and inviting, it bore a lyrical inflection that hinted of Irish heritage. He strained to hear Kathryn's answer above the other conversations drifting around him.

"Well, I've been working at Hudson's Haberdashery for a while now as well as at Myrtle's Cookery," Kathryn answered. "Both of my employers said they'd be willing to pen letters of reference for me, if you'd like."

"So you're an accomplished seamstress and cook?" The woman's question carried approval.

"Well, probably a better cook than seamstress, but yes, I have skills at both."

Larson could well imagine the telling crinkle in Kathryn's forehead as she answered, and he surprised himself by hoping she actually got the job. Wherever it was had to be better than her current situation at the brothel.

"May I ask why you're seeking to leave your current employ?"

From the corner of his eye Larson saw a young girl, no more than seven or eight, approaching his table with a pot of coffee. The aroma had already enticed him, but he shook his head. Keeping his face turned, he held up a hand, still trying to follow the conversation behind him. "No thank you, miss," he whispered. "I . . . I have no way to pay."

But the child pulled a mug from her apron front and set it before him anyway. "Sorry, sir, but I've got my orders," she said, her tiny mouth pulling into a bow. Tucking her lower lip beneath her front teeth, she gripped the cloth-wrapped handle of the pot with petite hands and poured with practiced care.

Larson stole a glance at the girl as steam rose from the cup. She was a beautiful child, with flawless skin and hair as black as a raven's. Her violet eyes seemed especially brilliant set against such coloring. Her eyes suddenly flashed to his, and Larson held his breath, steeling himself for her shock.

But her expression softened. She looked directly into his face and smiled, then pointed back over her shoulder. "That man over there says this one is on the house." Then she giggled.

Larson looked in the direction she motioned. A tall, slender man standing by the cook's table nodded to him. Larson sent his silent thanks with a tilt of his head, wondering why the man seemed familiar to him. He looked a bit like the late president Lincoln, tall and willowy, a little younger than Larson, with features that bespoke quiet strength and rightness. Then Larson realized where he'd seen him before. At his own funeral!

"Is that man a preacher?" he asked the girl.

"Yes, sir, and he's my papa too. My name is Lilly," she proclaimed, her eyes bright. "Go ahead and taste it. People say my mama makes the best coffee in all of Willow Springs."

Larson started to take a sip, then noticed the child's irregular gait as she walked away. He looked down to where her calico dress fell just above her ankles. The sole of her right boot was markedly thicker than the left. How had he missed that before? He took a sip of the coffee. It was smooth and strong and soothed his throat, washing down to warm his belly.

Suddenly realizing that he hadn't been paying attention, he half turned in his chair to make sure Kathryn was still behind him. The women's voices had grown hushed.

"Yes, very well stated, my dear," the older woman was saying. "We all have circumstances we'd rather change in our lives, to be sure. And I dare say that, if given the opportunity, we'd all prefer to choose our adversities. However, I doubt it would matter much, because in the end, seems as though we're all learnin' the same lessons."

The older woman's tone had grown soft with measured consideration, and Larson silently scolded himself for having missed the other half of the exchange.

"I don't have any further questions for you, my dear. My employer has reviewed your letter and qualifications, and I'm certain he'll approve of my decision."

A long silence followed. "So . . . Miss Maudelaine." Kathryn's voice was tinged with surprise. "You're saying that I have the position as housekeeper?"

The older woman laughed. "Yes, you do. Unless you're to be wishin' for the job of stableman instead, which I hardly think suits you . . . especially in your present condition," she added softly.

Larson detected the gentle reprimand in the woman's tone and the fact that Kathryn apparently hadn't revealed her "present condition" in the letter. He leaned closer, wondering how Kathryn would respond to being caught in the deceit.

"Thank you, Miss Maudelaine. I'm sorry I didn't mention being with child in my initial letter to you." Contrition weighted her voice. "I didn't want that to influence your decision, but I should have been honest with you from the beginning. It was wrong of me to exclude that information. If you'd like to change your—"

"I accept your apology, my dear, and admit I was a bit surprised upon first seeing you a moment ago. But I believe you'll work hard to do a job well done. I've already spoken with your current employers, and they have only the highest of praise for your work. As to the care of the child, I'll be leavin' that to you when the time comes. I think you'll agree that your wages are most generous and will afford you the opportunity to hire someone to help as you might be needin'. So write down your address for me, and I'll send a man to gather your things. I'd like you to start within the week, if possible."

Larson sensed Kathryn's hesitation and could imagine what she was thinking. She could hardly tell this cultured woman to pick up her new employee at the local brothel.

"I can start on Monday," Kathryn said

finally. "But I'm sure I can find my way out there if you give me directions."

Another pause. "You mean you don't know where Casaroja is?"

Larson's stomach hardened at the name. Every muscle within him tensed. *Not Casaroja. Lord, she can't go there. Anywhere but there.*

"No, I don't, but I have a friend who can take me there."

Larson's grip tightened around his cup. A friend. Matthew Taylor, no doubt.

"Well, if you're sure," came the response after a moment. "Take the road leadin' east from town. It's about ten miles out."

"Is there a turnoff? How will I—"

"Don't worry, my dear." The woman's lilt thickened with what sounded like amusement. "You'll be knowin' it when you get to Casaroja."

Once Kathryn left, Larson followed the elderly woman to a black carriage parked on the street. He prayed that the opinion he had formed of her was accurate and that he was hearing God's direction clearly. Once Miss Maudelaine was situated in the carriage, he approached.

"Excuse me, ma'am. May I have a word

with you?" His voice sounded surprisingly strong to his own ears. When she looked at him, she didn't flinch. Her features remained smooth. She studied his face closely, as though measuring the man behind the mask. He liked her immediately.

"Yes, what may I be doin' for you, sir?"

"I understand you're looking for a stable-man. I'd like to apply for the job."

Her right brow rose slightly. "Do you have experience with runnin' a stable and han-dlin' horses?"

"Yes, ma'am, I do." Best to keep his an-swers simple.

"And can you supply me with references?"

Lord, you know what I have a mind to do here. If it's your will, please open the door.

"No, ma'am, I don't have any references."

"So you're new to the area, then?"

"You could say that." He'd been away for a while, and he'd certainly returned a differ-ent man.

She nodded as her gaze swept him. Her eyes narrowed, but not in a way that made him uncomfortable. "Are your injuries pro-hibitive to your doin' this job, sir?"

"I'm getting stronger and I'll work hard. I know I can handle the job." He looked away briefly. "But I can't do everything that I used to."

Miss Maudelaine chuckled and shook her head. "And who among us can? Time sees to that with amazin' efficiency, I'm afraid." Her smile faded. "You'll have to be approved by the ranch foreman, but . . . I'll tell him to expect you. Be at Casaroja no later than week's end."

"Yes, ma'am. I'll be there."

"I'm Miss Maudelaine. I oversee the main house. And what would your name be, sir?"

His name. Larson hadn't considered that. "Jacob," he finally answered, feeling a confirmation within him. "My name is Jacob."

———

"I'm sorry about your husband, Miss Kathryn."

"So am I, Gabe." Kathryn looked up at her former ranch hand as he loaded her single trunk into the back of the wagon behind the haberdashery. She was thankful he'd shown up on her doorstep when he did. The breeze ruffled his blond hair, and his muscular arms were already bronzed.

His blue eyes held hers. "Do you miss him?"

"Every day," she whispered. Hearing footsteps behind her, she turned.

Kathryn winced at the fresh bruises on Annabelle's face and wished again that she could take both Annabelle and Sadie with her. But maybe she could do something even better.

She reached into her pocket for the envelope and pulled Annabelle aside. "I want you to reconsider and take this for—"

"I'm not takin' your money, Kathryn." Annabelle shook her head, but Kathryn detected a lessening in her determined response from the night before.

"You and Sadie could share a room somewhere in town, away from that place."

"I'm afraid it's not that simple to leave this place. And besides, it's not right, me takin' the money from you." Annabelle pushed the money away. "You'll need that for the child."

"My child will be fine. You and Sadie could both get jobs and—"

Annabelle huffed a laugh. "Yeah, doing what? Quilting with the ladies at church? Or maybe Mrs. Hochstetler would give us jobs at the mercantile. I hear they have some openings."

Kathryn smiled at Annabelle's droll tone.

Then she sighed and brushed a wayward red strand from her friend's forehead. They'd had this conversation before. "God sees you so differently, Annabelle. He didn't make you to live like this, to do the work you do."

"Do you think I enjoy doing this?" Annabelle's eyes hardened for an instant before she looked away. She shook her head. "I'm sorry, Kathryn. I know you mean well."

"And I'm sorry too. I didn't mean to imply that you . . ." She sighed. "What I'm trying to say is I've got room and board where I'll be working. I'll be making a good wage. I want to give you this. Please take it."

Annabelle's eyes filled. "Put it to that land you're tryin' to keep."

In truth, Kathryn had considered doing just that. But she felt God prodding her to do this for Annabelle, and she couldn't ignore His lead, no matter the cost to her and her dream. "If I lose the ranch, it won't be because of this small amount. I am going to try and keep the land, or at least the homestead and the rights to the stream." Kathryn laid a hand to her unborn child. "But even if that fails, I've got something far better, and I wouldn't trade this gift for the finest ranch in the Colorado Territory."

A single tear slipped down Annabelle's cheek, but she made no move to wipe it away.

Kathryn warmed at the subtle softening. "You have no idea what you've given me, do you?" Swallowing, she noticed the quickening of her pulse. "I haven't talked much about my late husband—not because I don't love him and miss him terribly. I do, but . . . but sometimes when people you love are taken away, their absence creates a hole so gaping that you fear even the slightest shift will send you plunging. My husband was a very loving man."

"I bet he was handsome too."

Kathryn pictured Larson and nodded. Her smile took effort. "Yes, he was very handsome. He had the clearest blue eyes, eyes that could see right through you." Her throat tightened with regret. "But he suffered a great deal of pain earlier in life. Pain I couldn't even begin to understand . . . until Gabe brought me to you that night." She glanced back at Gabe, who stood silent by the wagon. "I thought he'd made a mistake in bringing me there. But God was guiding his steps." She squeezed Annabelle's hand. "You helped me to see who Larson really was. All my married life I was so busy wanting my husband to be what I thought I needed that I missed the man that he was. The man God had chosen for me."

"Larson," Annabelle whispered. "I wondered what his name was." She glanced at the wagon, then bit her lower lip until it paled. Her jaw tensed, and she let out a shuddering sigh. "I'm gonna miss you, Kathryn." Sniffing, Annabelle wiped her tears with the back of her hand, then looked at Gabe. "But ol' Gabe'll stay and watch over me. Won't you, friend?"

Kathryn's gaze swung to Gabe's and her heart nearly stopped. The love in his eyes—the absolute purity and power of it—stole her breath.

"Gabe showed up last night at just the right time, again. I don't know how you got into that room, but thank you. That man would've killed me for sure this time." Annabelle walked over and touched Gabe's arm.

His large hand covered hers completely.

Kathryn took a step forward, taking in the bruising on Annabelle's face and marks on her throat, already suspecting the answer to her question. "Who did this to you?"

Annabelle shrugged. "It doesn't matter

now." Then seeing Kathryn's expression, she added, "Betsy finally told him not to come back, so we won't be havin' trouble from him anymore."

When the wagon pulled away minutes later, Kathryn looked back over her shoulder. Clutching the rough plank seat with one hand, she turned and waved. Annabelle stood in the alley, her hand raised. Kathryn's throat ached. Hadn't God meant for her to do more in Annabelle's life in this short time? She felt like a failure for leaving Annabelle in that evil, hope-starved place. A life so full of cruelty and selfish desires.

"Sometimes people can be real mean." Sitting beside her, his voice quiet, Gabe's face was pensive. He tugged the reins as he negotiated the wagon around a curve.

Kathryn turned to face forward on the bench. "I was just thinking that." Larson used to say the same thing, in so many words. She wished her husband could have experienced the generosity people were capable of, instead of all the deception and meanness. Perhaps then things would have been different between them.

Nearing the outskirts of town, Kathryn spotted an old man. From the looks of the rickety handcart he dragged behind him, he was a peddler. The sort she'd seen before while visiting here with Larson. Under different circumstances, she would've made a point to approach the wizened gentleman about his wares. Thinking of what Larson's response would have been tugged at her heart, and she pulled the music box from her skirt pocket. Two cranks of the key and the familiar tune tinked out in staccato rhythm.

"That's my favorite Christmas song, Miss Kathryn," Gabe said after the music stopped.

She nodded. "Mine too, Gabe."

Larson had always told her those peddlers sold mostly junk, but his smile always lingered as he watched her converse with them. And on the rare occasion when she actually bought something, she anticipated and almost looked forward to the long-suffering shake of his head as he helped her back into the wagon. But the gentle squeeze of his fingers around hers had conveyed his true opinion.

Larson had shown his love for her in so many ways. Quiet, unadorned ways. Kathryn only wished she'd been more aware of them at the time.

CHAPTER SIXTEEN

The fenced boundary of Casaroja began about twenty minutes out of town, and it companioned Kathryn and Gabe for the rest of the hour-long ride. Kathryn couldn't help but anticipate what the house might look like. In her mind's eye she imagined the home she and Larson would've someday built together. But her mouth dropped open when Casaroja's main house came into view.

Situated on a bluff of land rising gently from the eastern plains, the home was far grander than her imagination had indulged. No wonder Miss Maudelaine had smiled at her question about finding the place.

Two stories high with red brick, white-painted wood, and gray-stained eaves, Casaroja rose from the dusty brown plains like a pearl in a pool of dross. The massive white columns bracing the expansive upper porch glistened in the golden summer sun. Miss Maudelaine had been right—Casaroja was impossible to miss.

Gabe drove the wagon around to the back of the house. He helped her down, then carried her trunk to the back porch.

"I've got to get back to town, Miss Kathryn," he said, climbing back into the wagon.

Kathryn nodded, wishing he could stay awhile longer. She felt . . . safe with him.

"You take care of yourself, Miss Kathryn. And your baby," he added quietly, his mouth turning in that knowing way of his. He looked toward the house, then to the stables and fields. A gleam lit his eyes as though he knew a secret she had yet to discover.

"What is it?" Kathryn finally gave in, wondering at the grin on his face. She narrowed her eyes inquisitively.

He shook his head. "I'll be back to visit you soon." He gave the reins a flick.

Kathryn brushed the road dust from her black dress, still taking in the wealth of this place. Not only the main house, but the rows of bunkhouses, the stables and corrals. Even a separate livery, where the blacksmith was hard at work, if the dull pounding coming from within was any indication. An enormous field lay east of the house with workers bent over perfectly furrowed rows of soil. Kathryn couldn't help but think of what her and Larson's ranch might have been like one day, if only . . .

The back door swung open, drawing Kathryn's attention.

Miss Maudelaine appeared, looking pleased. "Welcome to Casaroja, Mrs. Jennings. You're just in time to be helpin' with dinner for the ranch hands." The older woman glanced around. "But how on earth did you get here, darlin'? I hope you didn't walk all this way."

The lovely Irish rhythm in her voice coaxed a smile from Kathryn. "No, ma'am, I got a ride. The wagon just left."

Miss Maudelaine's hands went to her hips. "I usually hear a wagon comin' up the road. I must have been lost in my work. There's never a lack of it around here. I have a surprise for you," she added with a lilt, pointing to a small white house some short distance away. "That's the guest cottage our employer built for me a few years back. But as I've gotten older, I find bein' in the main house is easier on me, plus it helps me keep up with the servants." She winked. "I had it cleaned for you, thinkin' you might enjoy the privacy and extra space."

Kathryn stared, speechless, at Maudelaine and then at the white cottage trimmed in gray to match the main house. It was perfect, and far more than she'd anticipated.

"But, dear, if you'd rather stay in the main house, I can have a room fixed up for you."

"No, it's beautiful!" Kathryn said after a pause. "I just didn't expect it, that's all."

Miss Maudelaine's smile conveyed her pleasure. She extended her hand and raised a brow in question. Kathryn nodded in approval, and the woman laid a hand to her swollen belly.

"You're small for bein' as far along as you told me. You must be carryin' that little one close to your heart, lass."

Kathryn smiled, warming at the truth of that statement.

Maudelaine hesitated. "Might I ask you a

personal question, dear? And please don't be takin' any offense in my askin' it. I have a reason for my pryin', I assure you."

Unable to imagine what the question might be, Kathryn told her to go ahead.

The woman smiled softly. "Would this be the only dress you have to wear during your mournin' time?"

Looking down, Kathryn smoothed a hand over the dusty skirt of the black dress she'd worn every day since Larson's funeral, noting the obvious wear along the hemline and sleeves. "Yes, ma'am. I made it myself and would've sewn another, but I've had other obligations to meet, and . . . Well, I'm sorry if it's not—"

The woman gently touched her arm. "Don't you dare be sayin' you're sorry to me, dear. I told you there was a reason for my pryin'. My younger sister, God rest her soul, was about your size, and after her husband passed on . . . Well, let's just say she wore the widow's color for a long time, and she was with child too. If you're willin', I'll go through some of her dresses and pick a few for you to make good use of. They've been packed away for years but have plenty of wear left in them, to be sure."

For a moment, in the company of such generosity, Kathryn found herself too moved to speak. "That's most kind of you to offer. Yes, I'd appreciate that very much. Thank you, Miss Maudelaine."

The older woman made a tsking noise. "Oh, there'll be no 'Miss Maudelaine' for me, dear. I'm Miss Maudie here at Casaroja. That's what all the servants and ranch hands call me." She turned and led Kathryn toward the cottage. Pulling a key from her pocket, Miss Maudie continued, "Even Mr. MacGregor calls me that."

Kathryn slowed at hearing the name. "Mr. . . . Donlyn MacGregor?"

"Yes, dear. He owns Casaroja, and you'll meet him soon. He meets everyone who works on his ranch. It's a strict rule of his to know his employees."

While picturing her meeting with her new employer, Kathryn took in the magnificent surroundings again. Larson had never mentioned Casaroja or even the name MacGregor for that matter, but something didn't make sense to her. Why would a man like MacGregor, who had all of this, want more land?

"Are you all right, child?" The older

woman looked back from the cottage's small porch.

Kathryn nodded and joined her. "Have you known Mr. MacGregor long, Miss Maudie?"

"Oh my, yes." Her voice grew quiet and her expression indicated she might say more, so Kathryn waited. But then Miss Maudie turned and made a sweeping gesture with her hand. "Mr. MacGregor has done very well for himself. He built all this from nothing, I'm proud to tell you. I dare say that not one thing he's set his cap to has remained out of his reach."

Kathryn followed Miss Maudie inside the cottage, wondering at the hint of motherly pride in the woman's voice. The cottage was pristine in every way. From the shiny oak paneled floor to the yellow and white flower print curtains adorning the windows. The kitchen sat off to the right with a separate sitting area opposite it, and a bedroom ran along the back. It far exceeded Kathryn's expectations and needs.

"Miss Maudie, this is lovely! Are you sure this is included in our agreement? I fully expected to be sharing a room with at least one other woman."

The older woman put up a hand. "Nonsense, this has been sitting empty for some time now and needs to be used. In fact, Mr. MacGregor insisted that you have it. There's even a water closet off the bedroom there." She chuckled. "And if memory serves right, that should come in handy in the wee night hours."

"So you have children, then?"

A shadow crossed Miss Maudie's face, and she cleared her throat. "No, actually . . . I don't. None of my own, but I was very close to my sister when she was with child."

The light in her eyes dimmed despite the smile on her face, and Kathryn wished she could take the question back.

"Well, it's time to be gettin' dinner on." Maudie turned. "We feed fifty-seven ranch hands morning, noon, and night around here, and I can sure use another pair of hands." She glided a fingertip along a side table, then held it up for inspection before rubbing her fingers together. "You take an hour to get settled, Mrs. Jennings, and then come help me in the main kitchen. We'll go over your specific duties after dinner in the study."

Kathryn stepped forward. "Please, Miss Maudie, call me Kathryn."

"Kathryn it is, then," she said, her eyes softening. "And may I add . . . I'm thankful you're here, lass. You've a brightness about you, despite what you've endured of late. I'll enjoy watchin' the wee babe grow within you, and I'll be here to help you when your time comes." She gave Kathryn's hand a squeeze. "Now get some rest, then meet me in the kitchen at four o'clock. I'll have a man tote your trunk here later."

The coordination of dinner in the main house that night was a sight to behold. Miss Maudie ran a tightly scheduled crew. Everyone had a job, and though Kathryn understood her basic responsibilities as housekeeper, she quickly learned another important duty—to do everything Miss Maudie said, exactly when she said it. A poor girl by the name of Molly dawdled once too often during the evening and paid the price dearly. Miss Maudie never raised her voice, but her disapproving expression earned immediate respect and a swift change in behavior. Kathryn vowed to never be on the receiving end of that unpleasant look.

Expecting to see Donlyn MacGregor during the course of the evening, she discovered with relief that he was away on business. No doubt their meeting would come soon enough, and she didn't look forward to it, nor did she particularly like the idea of being in his employ. But this job seemed like a godsend, and to think of it in any other light left her feeling selfish and ungrateful. She thought again about MacGregor's offer to help her and wondered what it would mean being indebted to the man.

Returning to the cottage later that evening, well after dark, she made it through the darkness and to the bed before collapsing on top of it. Her hands were chapped from washing stacks of dirty dishes, and her legs ached from standing so long in one place. Plus the amount of cooking she'd done before that! And to imagine, this happened three times a day! Despite her exhaustion, Kathryn thanked God for His provision of this job and a much more suitable place to live.

She didn't have to wonder what Annabelle and Sadie were doing at that moment, and she hurt because of it. *Lord, please be with them, and the other women. I wish I could have made more of a difference in their lives while I was there. Keep chipping away on Annabelle's heart, Lord. She's got such a soft heart beneath it all. . . .*

As Kathryn lay there, loneliness crept over her. She pulled the music box from her pocket and lifted the lid. Unable to see the inscription in the darkness, she ran her fingers over the words she knew so well. *For all your heart's desires.* In slow arching circles, her hand moved over her abdomen, caressing their unborn child. *But you were my heart's desire, Larson.*

She turned the key three times and the simple tune filled the silence, sprinkling it with soft tinny notes. Over and over the song played, repeating itself, until finally it slowed to intermittent chimes, then nothing. A familiar pang tightened Kathryn's throat, and she turned onto her side. *Father, it feels as though half my heart has been ripped away. I have so many questions about what happened to him. And no answers.*

A rapping on the front door brought her head up. She sat slowly to avoid the dizziness that was becoming less frequent, then picked her way through the darkness. She looked out the side window first.

A man stood on the porch, with what looked like her trunk at his feet. Smoothing her hair and dress, she went to open the door.

Larson had recognized the trunk immediately, and he'd wanted to tell Miss Maudie to ask someone else to take it to the cottage. But from the ranch foreman's frank appraisal days ago, Larson knew he was at Casaroja by God's will working through that woman's kind nature. And he aimed to please them both.

As he stood on Kathryn's front porch, waiting for her to answer the door, a bead of sweat trickled between his shoulder blades and inched down his back. She hadn't recognized him before, and it had been daylight then. He had little to fear now. So why did his heart race?

He adjusted the smoky-colored spectacles he'd purchased before leaving town from the same old peddler who had sold him the music box. He didn't know if they would keep Kathryn from seeing who he was, but they did help mask the pain he felt every time someone stared at him. He still saw their shock, but at least they couldn't see how deeply it wounded him.

He heard footsteps and fought down the panic rising in his chest. Again, he questioned God's wisdom in his coming to Casaroja. He was so close to Kathryn here. But wasn't that why he'd taken the job? To be close to her?

Yes, but not this close. He backed up a step.

That put him in the moonlight, so he shifted again. Kathryn opened the door, and for an instant, Larson thought he'd gotten her out of bed.

"Miss Maudie asked me to bring this to you." His voice came out raspy, and he swallowed.

Slivers of pale light shone through the cottonwoods and fell across the threshold, enabling him to see her face. She looked at him briefly, then glanced away. The cottage behind her was dark, especially through his glasses. Her hair was mussed, beautifully so. Something stirred inside him.

She smiled and pulled open the door. "Thank you for carrying that up here for me. If you'll just put it over there, please." She pointed to a space by the cold hearth. "I can carry the clothes to the bedroom later."

Larson walked inside, keenly aware of his

limp. He tried to compensate, but he'd worked especially hard that day and his body ached. Kathryn had swung the door open wide and left it that way, purposefully so, as though suddenly fearing for her virtue. As if she had any left. A metallic taste filled his mouth at the thought.

The curtains were open, and shafts of light gleamed off the polished wood floor in the moonlight. Larson easily made out the path to the bedroom and carried the trunk on back.

"Sir, I said you could—"

The bedroom was nice. Much nicer than the one they'd shared for ten years. Larson set the trunk below a window and slowly turned to look at her from across the bed—a feather mattress at that. Not stuffed with straw like the one they'd shared. He saw the rumpled blanket and the imprint on the bed where she'd been. She had been asleep, or at least lying down.

She stood in the darkened doorway, watching him, her hands gently clasped over her illegitimate child. Larson winced at the harshness of his thoughts. Then he saw the glint of something on her left hand. Her wedding ring. No doubt she thought it lent credibility to her situation.

His boldness to look at her surprised him. But then again, it was dark and the moon was at his back. Did she even recognize him from their brief encounter last week? Part of him hoped she would, while the greater part of him preferred to remain in the background, unnoticed.

She motioned toward the trunk. "Thank you for bringing it in here. That was very kind of you, sir."

Larson heard the smile in her voice. The same smile he'd seen her give to countless other ranch hands during the course of dinner earlier that night. Though meals were served beneath the stand of cottonwoods behind the main house, he chose to eat closer to the stable, alone. His second day here, he'd worked that out with Miss Maudie, with surprisingly little exchange between them.

Miss Maudie possessed an intuitive nature that encouraged his trust on one hand, while making him wary on the other. Not that he thought she was dishonest. Far from it. But the woman saw into people in ways most others didn't. And Larson couldn't afford her doing that with him.

"I'm sorry about . . ." Kathryn's voice was soft. She glanced away. "About running into you the other day."

So she did remember. Why should that silly fact matter to him? And why were his hands shaking? In the veil of darkness, Larson looked his wife up and down, rapidly ticking off the reasons why he should walk out that door and never come back. But no matter how many of Kathryn's sins he piled on the scale, he couldn't make it tip in his favor. Some unseen hand seemed to stay the balance. The same hand tightening a fist around his heart right now.

He walked out of the bedroom, intentionally breathing in her scent when he passed. "Good night, ma'am."

He didn't hear the front door close behind him. Larson felt her watching, but didn't turn. After a few strides, his right leg gave out. He stumbled and nearly fell. His body went hot thinking that she might have seen. Not looking back, he gathered his right pant leg in his hand and dragged his leg forward with each stride, gritting his teeth.

Back in the stable, he took off his dark glasses, threw a blanket on the straw, and sank down. Wishing for one of Abby's warm mineral baths, he peeled off his pants and shirt and poured the last of the precious brown liniment into his hands. He rubbed it into the taut muscles of his legs and shoulders, then lay back. His body welcomed the reprieve, but his mind was too full to sleep.

After a while, he picked up his Bible and limped back outside, past the rows of bunkhouses to a spot where lamplight still burned in a window. Voices drifted out to him from the open windows. He sat down beneath the window and leaned against the side of the building, holding the Bible up at an angle. He began reading where he'd left off the previous night, in Peter's first letter.

Another week and he'd have read through the entire Bible for the first time. He sighed, thinking of how proud Isaiah and Abby would be of him. For a minute, he wished he were back with them, safe in the cabin, cared for, even loved. Kathryn would have been proud too, but she would never know.

Larson's eyes tripped over a phrase, and he suddenly realized he hadn't been paying attention. He backed up and read the verses again. His throat tightened as he mouthed the words silently.

Though now for a season . . . ye are in heaviness through manifold temptations: That the trial of your faith, being much more precious than of gold that perisheth, though it be tried with fire. . . .

Tried with fire.

He ran a finger over the words, unable to feel the smoothness of the page beneath his seared flesh. He'd heard this Scripture somewhere before. Most likely Kathryn had read it to him one night as he'd halfheart-edly listened. His heart devoured the words as his eyes moved down the page.

For all flesh is as grass, and all the glory of man as the flower of grass. The grass withereth . . . but the word of the Lord en-dureth for ever.

He didn't understand everything he read, but some of the verses sounded like God had meant them just for him.

Laying aside all malice, and all guile, and hypocrisies, and envies . . . desire the sin-cere milk of the word. . . . He continued to the bottom of the page. *Christ also suffered for us, leaving us an example, that ye should follow his steps . . . Who his own self bare our sins in his own body . . . by whose stripes ye were healed.*

The beginning of chapter three left a bitter taste in his mouth, and Larson knew that during their marriage, he hadn't treated Kathryn as a fellow heir to the grace of life. And it had hindered his prayers. Hers too, no doubt. He kept reading to chapter five.

Humble yourselves therefore under the mighty hand of God, that he may exalt you . . . Casting all your care on him; for he careth for you.

When the lamplight in the window above him extinguished some time later, Larson quietly got up and made his way back to the stable. He lay down and, for the first time in months, slept the night without waking.

CHAPTER SEVENTEEN

Hanging laundry the next morning, Kathryn saw him again from a distance. The man who had delivered her trunk. She recognized him instantly—the knit cap pulled tight over his head, the scruffy beard. And though his scars had been obscured in the shadowed half light, she could never forget them.

As he led a horse from the stable to the fenced corral, Kathryn watched him, staring at the reason why sleep had eluded her the night before. How did a man communicate so much while speaking so little?

Last night she'd gotten the distinct impression that he didn't want to be in the same room with her. It still puzzled her.

Something about him drew her, as it had that first day. Compassion most likely, or at least that's what she'd originally thought. But as she'd lain awake considering it, remembering his darkened silhouette against the moonlight, she'd figured out what it was.

He reminded her of Larson.

Not so much physically, she decided. It was more his . . . presence. And the way he looked at her.

The man tethered the buckskin mare to a post, then turned her direction and adjusted his spectacles. He stilled.

Kathryn's eyes went wide. She felt like he'd caught her spying. She managed a half smile, but he chose that moment to turn. If he'd seen her, he didn't acknowledge it. She hung another sheet over the line and watched him furtively from behind its folds.

He was shorter and definitely older than Larson had been. At least fifty pounds leaner, his build would never rival Larson's well-muscled stature. And the poor man's scars . . .

She cringed, remembering how she'd gasped at first seeing them in the daylight back in town. Kathryn pulled another sheet from the basket. A dull ache throbbed inside her, and she briefly closed her eyes. Would missing Larson always hurt this much? And was she destined to continually see him—or the qualities she'd loved about him—mirrored in other men?

When she looked again, the ranch hand was rubbing the mare's forehead. The horse nudged closer to him and, though Kathryn couldn't hear what the man said, his lips moved as though he were cooing to the animal. He bent and ran a hand over each of her legs. When he touched her left hind leg, the horse whinnied and shied away. He stood and came close to her again, looking directly into the mare's eyes. She calmed and moved back toward him.

Such gentleness. Again, a quality Larson had possessed. But not to this extent. . . . Whatever this man lacked in human civility, he certainly possessed with animals. He walked to the fence and picked up a currycomb, the limp in his right leg less pronounced than it had been the night before.

After he'd delivered her trunk, she'd seen him nearly fall on his way back to the stable. But she hadn't dared approach to help him, certain he would refuse. Was it pride or bitterness, or perhaps both, that kept a person from accepting help from others? Annabelle came to mind, and Kathryn turned back to her work. She could hardly stand in judgment of either Annabelle or this gentle, scarred man. Though she'd faced trials in her own life, she certainly hadn't endured the same kind of pain. And if she had, who was to say her heart would have been any less embittered than theirs.

That afternoon, Kathryn climbed the stairs leading to the second floor of the main house and looked down the hallway to the closed ornate double doors. The master bedroom was next on her list, but she wasn't going near that room until she was absolutely certain Donlyn MacGregor was not in it.

She'd overheard a kitchen maid say that Mr. MacGregor had returned home late during the night from his trip. Perhaps today she would have the opportunity to speak with him about his offer to help her keep the ranch.

Placing her bucket of cleaning supplies aside, she polished the marble-topped rosewood table on the landing, then walked down the hallway. She checked inside each of the three unoccupied guest-rooms to ensure everything was in proper order.

Miss Maudie had given her a thorough tour of the home the night before. The house was much larger and far more exquisitely furnished than what Kathryn had first imagined. Boasting vintage Chippendale furniture crafted from the finest mahogany with curved cabriole legs and claw-and-ball feet, the pieces rivaled the splendor of those in her parents' home in Boston. Kathryn wondered if her father even lived in the same house since her mother's passing.

She ran the dusting cloth along the scrolled edges of a mirror hanging over the table, wishing her mother could have lived to see the child Kathryn carried. The two people most precious to her were gone. She thought of her father and wondered if writing to him now might make a difference. Maybe if William Cummings knew he would soon have a grandchild, he might feel differently toward her. But she'd written him twice shortly after her mother had died and had never received any response. Apparently his interest in her life, or lack of it, remained unchanged.

Kathryn came to the last door on the right and stopped, not remembering this room on Miss Maudie's tour. She'd already cleaned the servants' quarters downstairs and the guest bedrooms on this level. Could she have missed one? She tapped on the door.

No answer. She quietly turned the knob, and it gave easily in her hand.

Half-opened shutters diffused the sunshine, sending slanted beams of light across a massive desk and leather chair. Rows of books and ledgers lined the shelves on either side of the desk. Kathryn quickly ran a finger along one of the shelves and blew away the dust. She would earn Miss Maudie's disapproval for certain if she missed this room. Whoever held this duty before had shirked their employer's office. From her impression of Donlyn MacGregor, his expectations would stand for nothing less than perfection, and she wanted to stay in his good graces. She closed the door behind her, opened the shutters, and pulled the bottle of lemon wax from her apron pocket.

Nearly an hour later, footsteps sounded from the other side of the office door. Atop a stool cleaning the upper shelves, Kathryn paused and looked behind her, waiting for Miss Maudie to breeze in for an inspection and hoping the woman would be pleased.

But whoever it was didn't come in. Kathryn went back to cleaning.

Piles of neatly stacked papers layered each other on the left side of the desktop. Kathryn carefully lifted each one to clean beneath it. The embossed name titling one of the pages caught her attention. Something about it tugged at her memory and made her look at the stationery more closely.

Berklyn Stockholders.

Why did that name sound familiar? Perhaps a company her father used to do business with? But somehow the memory felt closer than that. She ran a finger over the pressed parchment and scanned the body of the missive. Her eyes honed in on the words *Colorado Territory River Commission.*

"'Regarding your inquisition about First Rights of Appropriation on Fountain Creek,'" she read, her voice barely audible. Her focus dropped down the page. "'Your conditional filing will be reviewed—'" The closing of a door in the hallway drew her head up.

Kathryn quickly returned the business letters and legal documents to their place, her hands suddenly shaking both at the possibility of being caught reading these documents and for having read them in the first place. She grabbed the dirty cloth and hurried from behind the desk. Reaching the door, she glanced back. Were all the stacks in the right order? And what had possessed her to look at them to begin with? It was none of her business, but . . . why was MacGregor inquiring about Fountain Creek?

A footfall sounded again, this time on the stairs. She turned to the door, her heart in her throat.

Moments passed, nothing happened.

Calming, Kathryn nearly laughed out loud at her own guilty conscience. She shook her head, breathed in the lemon-scented air, and admired her handiwork. The shelves and desk fairly gleamed. Surely Miss Maudie would be pleased.

Quickly exiting the office, Kathryn latched the door quietly behind her and noticed the doors to the master bedroom now stood open.

She knocked on the doorjamb. "Mr. Mac-Gregor?" She waited, then called his name again.

Stepping inside, the opulence of the room made her pause, as it had the night before. Everything in this room bespoke money and success. But given the choice, she would still choose the cabin Larson had built for her—if only he were still alive to share it with her.

Pushing aside the awkward feeling that accompanied being in Donlyn MacGregor's private quarters, Kathryn picked up a pair of trousers and a coat slung over a wingback chair. She walked around the corner to the mahogany wardrobe, lining up the ironed folds of the pants. She heard the bedroom door slam shut.

"Of all the . . ."

Kathryn's eyes widened at the string of curses that followed, and then she jumped at the sound of breaking glass. Recognizing the thick brogue, she stepped from behind the wardrobe door to make her presence known.

Donlyn MacGregor's dark eyes shot up, and for a moment, he simply stared. Then a slow smile, one she'd seen before, curved his mouth. "Well, maybe heaven will yet smile on me this day." His gaze swept her front, then stopped abruptly around her midsection. His eyes narrowed.

For some unexplained reason Mr. Mac-Gregor's obvious displeasure at seeing her with child pleased her immensely. Apparently Miss Maudie had not shared that piece of news with him. Kathryn's affection for the woman grew even as she remembered that MacGregor was now her employer—and her sole prospect for keeping her land.

"Mr. MacGregor." She offered a deferent nod. "I'm sorry. I thought you'd left the room in order for it to be cleaned."

His mouth drew into a thin line. "Mrs. Jennings. You're looking . . . in full health today." His voice grew flat.

She gave a half smile, said, "Thank you, sir," then quickly hung the pants and coat in the wardrobe, eager to leave.

"I'm sorry I wasn't here yesterday to give you a proper welcome to Casaroja. I would've preferred to give the tour myself. But no doubt Miss Maudie did that in my stead."

"She showed me the house. Yes, sir."

"But not the lands?"

"No, sir. But Miss Maudie's a kind woman and I felt welcomed by everyone." Well, almost everyone. Kathryn glanced out the large window overlooking Casaroja's stables, but she didn't see the ranch hand or the buckskin mare. She closed the chifforobe door and turned. "I hope you had a pleasant trip, sir. I'll come back to finish at a more convenient time."

MacGregor walked to the edge of the bed and stopped before her. "Now is quite a convenient time for me, Mrs. Jennings. I was hopin' for the chance to see you again. Though I must admit, I never did dream you'd be so agreeable as to meet in my private quarters." He glanced down at the bed, then back to her. "You can't have been in here very long, lass. You haven't even made the bed yet." A gleam lit his dark eyes. "Maybe we could be doin' that together."

Kathryn's mouth fell open, her face heated at the insinuation. Was this man always so single-minded? "If you'll excuse me, Mr. MacGregor. I'll come back later." She picked up her bucket of supplies and skirted past him. Something crunched beneath her boot and she stopped. Shards of crystal littered the floor. From the broken remnants and pungent aroma, it appeared to have been a brandy decanter at one time.

"I knocked that over on my way in, Mrs. Jennings." His tone didn't even approach believability, and they both knew it. "Would you be so kind as to clean it up for me?" When she didn't respond, he reached out and brushed the tips of his fingers over the back of her hand. "Please," he added softly.

Kathryn stared back at him. The ardor in his eyes had been replaced by a challenge.

MacGregor had known he was hiring her—that was clear from what Miss Maudie had told her about her employer having reviewed her letter. Kathryn suddenly wondered if his expectations of her being here at Casaroja extended beyond what she and Miss Maudie had discussed. Better to set that straight right now.

"Yes, I'll clean it up, Mr. MacGregor. But not with you in the room." She paused for a beat before moving past him.

He let out a laugh. "It seems you're always doin' this to me, Kathryn."

Reaching the door, she turned, not caring for the sound of her name coming from him. "Doing what, Mr. MacGregor?"

"Walkin' away from me . . . Mrs. Jennings." He dipped his head in mock deference. "And especially when we have so much yet to be discussin'."

Kathryn fought the anger and disappointment tightening her throat. How quickly she'd pinned her hopes for herself and her child on this new position, and how foolish she felt for doing so. "I thought I understood my duties here at Casaroja, but apparently I did not. I'll let Miss Maudie know I'm leaving."

MacGregor quickly closed the distance between them and put out a hand to stay the door. Kathryn could smell the spice of his cologne and feel his breath on her cheek.

A moment passed. "Look at me, Mrs. Jennings."

She wouldn't.

He sighed. "I was only toyin' with you just now, lass." The lilt in his voice thickened. "I don't know why I do it—you just seem to bring it out in me. I came in here angry, and then you stepped from behind there with no warnin'." From her periphery, Kathryn saw him shrug. "Frankly, you were a bit of a welcome sight to me, darlin'. Too much of one, I fear," he added, his voice almost ringing sincere. Almost.

But Kathryn didn't believe a word of it. Other than the part about him toying with her. She tried to open the door. "I wish to leave now, please."

He held the door fast. "I apologize for my behavior, Mrs. Jennings. It won't be happenin' again, I assure you."

"Now, Mr. MacGregor," she said more forcefully.

He removed his hand. But the door opened before Kathryn could turn the knob.

The young maid's eyes went round. "Oh, excuse me, sir," Molly gasped. "I didn't mean to interrupt anything."

The girl's assumption was written in her shocked expression. Kathryn reached for her hand. "No, Molly, it's fine. Mr. Mac-Gregor returned and didn't realize I was in the room. I'm leaving. I'll come back later to clean, once he's through."

Molly looked from one to the other. "Yes, ma'am. Of course." The girl nodded, but suspicion crept into her eyes before she turned and hurried down the hall toward the stairs.

Kathryn followed her into the hallway.

"I'll take care of clearing up the misunderstanding," MacGregor said close beside her.

"No. You've done quite enough already. I'll speak with Molly myself."

"As you wish. But we still need to discuss my business proposal. Beginning immediately, I'd like to lease your land for grazing my cattle. That would provide you with a steady income from the ranch land while giving us time to discuss other options. Or are you no longer interested in my offer?"

Kathryn studied him. Donlyn MacGregor was a powerful man—in every sense. And certainly not the most trustworthy. Did she dare pursue a partnership with him? But if she wanted to keep the ranch, did she have a choice? And his offer to lease the land was generous. She thought about the course of events that had placed her here at Casaroja. Certainly that was God's hand, right? So was it her own selfishness that was driving her now, or God's will?

Swallowing her pride, she finally nodded. "Yes, I'm still interested and want to speak with you about it. But not in your bedroom," she added quickly, putting more distance between them.

"Give me your requirements for our next meeting, madam, and I'll meet every one."

His smile looked sincere enough, but not wanting to encourage further teasing, Kathryn kept her tone serious. "A more public place would be nice. And next time, leave the door open."

He didn't answer for a moment; he appeared to be considering what she'd said.

"Your every request is my pleasure, lass," MacGregor finally said softly, then let his focus slowly move beyond her.

Kathryn turned. The bucket nearly slipped from her hands.

At the top of the stairs, Miss Maudie and two ranch hands stood staring. Kathryn heard the bedroom door close behind her, and with it, the sealing of her apparent guilt.

Miss Maudie's eyes were wide and displeasure lined her expression. The taller ranch hand with curly dark hair grinned in a way that left no doubt as to his assumption. But the other man's attention seemed to be burning a hole straight through her.

Kathryn couldn't see his eyes through the smoke-colored glasses, but he wasn't smiling. Neither did surprise register on his face. Yet his condemnation was tangible. Her cheeks burned with it.

"Where have you been, Kathryn?" Miss Maudie's voice sounded unnaturally bright. "I came lookin' for you earlier."

Kathryn blinked and drew a quick breath. "I was working, Miss Maudie." Heat prickled from her scalp to her toes. "I was cleaning in the—"

"Very well, Kathryn. Finish your chores

downstairs, then wait for me in the study, please." Miss Maudie turned to the ranch hands. "It's the second bedroom there on the right. There's a wardrobe that needs to be carried downstairs."

Kathryn kept her eyes downcast as she passed, afraid they would mistake her tears for an admission of guilt.

Later that afternoon after finishing her duties, Kathryn sat in the study, waiting as Miss Maudie had instructed. Regardless of her innocence, she still felt the sting of guilt. And hearing the other servants whisper behind her back hadn't helped. Molly had obviously wasted no time in retelling the tale. Kathryn cringed again when remembering the look on Miss Maudie's face. She so wanted to please the woman, and to keep this job.

The door opened. She jumped to her feet.

"Be seated, Kathryn." Miss Maudie's tone held a hint of benevolence, as did her eyes. She sat in the chair opposite Kathryn. "Tell me exactly what happened this morning."

Kathryn quickly summarized the events, from knocking on Mr. MacGregor's bedroom door to the moment when Miss Maudie saw her leaving the room. Remembering the pride in Maudie's voice when she spoke of Mr. MacGregor, she chose to leave out the part about his crass suggestions. Sharing that would only raise more suspicion, and besides, he'd promised not to do it again. "I assure you nothing happened. Mr. Mac-Gregor came back into the room unexpectedly, that's all."

Miss Maudie studied her for a moment, then sighed. "I believe you, Kathryn."

"You do?" she asked, feeling immediate relief. "Thank you."

"But you must be more careful in the future. Gossip spreads quickly at Casaroja, and an incident such as this does a lady's reputation little good."

Kathryn nodded in understanding and started to rise.

Miss Maudie put out a hand. "There is one more thing, Kathryn dear. Mr. Mac-Gregor's office was cleaned earlier today. Was that your doin'?"

"Yes, ma'am," Kathryn answered, looking at her hands in her lap. She smiled, secretly glad for the chance to redeem herself.

"Was cleanin' Mr. MacGregor's personal office on your list of duties today?"

Kathryn blinked at the crisp turn Miss Maudie's voice had taken. "No, ma'am, it wasn't," she answered softly. "But when I saw that it hadn't been cleaned in a while, I thought that—" She fell silent at the look in the older woman's eyes. "No, it wasn't on my list."

"I appreciate your willingness to work hard, Kathryn. It's quite commendable. But Mr. MacGregor has strict rules about who's allowed on the second floor, and into his personal office, for certain. So, keep to the list that I give you, my dear, and you'll do well here at Casaroja."

———

Larson watched her from the shadows of the barn stall, his heart pounding. Kathryn stood just beyond the double-planked doors—near enough for him to see the soft shimmer of highlights in her hair and the crinkle of her brow. What was she doing down here at the stables? And in the middle of the afternoon? He looked at his glasses that lay on a workbench a few feet away.

He'd seen her every day since having caught her leaving MacGregor's bedroom. He'd said nothing to anyone, but word had traveled fast among the other ranch hands. Within two days, the whole episode was common knowledge. Within a week, they knew she'd lived in a brothel back in town and were labeling her child as the product of the place. They used a word Larson knew well and a label he'd spent most of his adult life trying to escape.

Earlier that morning he'd been working with the buckskin mare when a group of wranglers rode by. They yelled things at Kathryn as she was hanging laundry. She acted like she didn't hear, but Larson knew from the stiff set of her shoulders that she'd heard every word.

Kathryn took a step closer into the stable, and he pressed back against the timbered wall. The hay crunched softly beneath his boots. She was so beautiful it almost hurt. Her delicately arched brow, her dainty mouth, the clouds of silken blond curls falling over her shoulders. . . . He took in the full swell of her black skirt and the tenderness inside him waned.

She squinted her eyes as though trying to decipher the shadows beyond the open stable door, but she seemed hesitant to come any farther.

Larson relaxed a bit at the discovery. Hidden, he studied her again—the tender curves of her face, her eyes the shade of cream-laced coffee. The tightness in his throat made it difficult to swallow. Why was he here at Casaroja? He'd thought it was God's voice he was following, and yet, at this moment, that didn't seem like enough. A hot burst of anger poured through him again. And how could God bless her womb with another man's seed?

His gut twisted thinking of Matthew Taylor, and he winced at the image of him touching her. He hadn't seen Taylor at all in the two weeks Kathryn had lived here. Did that mean Taylor wasn't going to claim the child? Or maybe he wasn't the child's father after all.

Larson swallowed the bitter taste rising in his throat. He couldn't seem to shrug off the weight bearing down hard inside him, like a hundred pound load of bricks resting squarely on his chest.

Kathryn turned back in the direction of the main ranch house, and Larson slowly let out his breath. She made her way up the gently sloping rise. He watched her slip a hand behind her and massage her lower back. As she walked away from him, a familiar sense of loss welled inside him.

He rubbed the back of his neck and wondered again how differently things might've worked out had he not left so abruptly Christmas morning, and what it might have been like to father a child with his wife. Kathryn's child. Lost in his thoughts, he turned.

He sucked in a breath at the huge hulk of a man standing next to him.

His heart racing, Larson took a step back and knocked a metal bucket off its peg. It crashed into an empty tin trough. The clangor resonated like a church bell, and Larson put out a hand to steady himself.

"Don't be scared," the man said.

Larson tipped his chin up and stared, unable to speak.

"My name is Gabe." The young man's deep voice was hushed, and he pronounced his words slowly, giving each syllable emphasis. "Why are you hiding in here?" he asked in a childish half whisper, his thick shoulders hunched forward.

Larson eyed him, taking in the slabs of muscles layering his arms and chest, and then willed his pulse to slow. The pure guilelessness of the man's voice and manner contrasted with his powerful stature and muscular build. Was he completely daft or simply a bit slow?

"I wasn't hiding, *Gabe*," Larson finally managed. "I was . . . working." It didn't come out as convincing as Larson would've liked but would probably work on this innocent.

A surprisingly knowing look deepened the lines of Gabe's face. The child giant looked from him over to where Kathryn had been standing, then back again.

Larson experienced an unexpected stab of guilt. "I *was* working," he said again in defense, wondering why he felt the need to explain himself to this oaf. He picked up the bucket and hung it back on the peg. "I manage the stables here at Casaroja." Stating his job that way made it sound better than it was. He enjoyed working with horseflesh and training cold backs to be saddle worthy and bridle wise, but his pride was still adjusting to mucking out stalls and filling feed troughs.

The only time he felt even a bit like his old self was when he helped herd cattle or allowed his borrowed mount the lead on miles of open range east of Casaroja's boundaries. In those brief moments, he could almost glimpse the fading shadow of the man he used to be. Almost. But those pleasures took a heavy physical toll on him now.

"Does it still hurt?" Gabe asked, eying Larson's face. Gabe took a step forward, and a splinter of sunlight knifed through the rafters and spilled across his face.

Larson had never seen eyes so blue, the purest cobalt, like windows to the soul. He looked away. "You don't belong in here, Gabe. Only hired help is allowed."

"But the boss sent me down to help. I can lift heavy things." He paused and looked straight into Larson's eyes. "When people hide, it's mostly 'cause they've done something wrong. Have you done somethin' wrong?"

Suddenly tired of this massive simpleton, Larson attempted a dark look. "I don't have time for this. And I don't have anything for you to do right now, Gabe," he lied. "So you need to leave."

Larson limped to the far wall and grabbed his glasses. Ignoring the sharp pain in his lower back, he lifted a bale of hay. He took three steps before the muscles in his arms spasmed. The bale dropped to the barn floor, and he gritted his teeth to quell a curse. Dust and hay particles filled the air around him. He was already breathing heavily, and now his throat felt as if it were coated with sawdust. He coughed and tried to swallow, then reached for the canteen he always kept close at hand. After several swallows, he was able to catch his breath. He took his knife, sliced the thick twine binding the hay, and reached for a rake.

From the corner of his eye, he saw Gabe still standing by the wall, watching silently. Larson wondered why Stewartson, the ranch foreman, hadn't spoken with him about having hired someone. Larson liked working alone, and this Gabe seemed a bit odd. But at least he wasn't causing problems. Not yet anyway.

Deciding to let the situation play itself out, Larson swallowed against the burning in his throat and pulled the bandanna around his neck back up over his mouth and nose. He began spreading the fresh hay into the shoveled stalls. The jerky movements made the muscles in his arms and back burn. This job pushed him to his physical limit, but he had to work to live. Being at Casaroja—at Donlyn MacGregor's ranch—rankled his pride, but the work was steady and the horses and cattle were the finest in the territory. And though most the other hands avoided him, which suited him fine, Miss Maudie treated him well. Last night she'd added an extra portion of pot roast to his plate.

But the real reason Larson was still at Casaroja was because God hadn't given him permission to leave yet. He'd felt the confirmation to come there and had obeyed. Now he wanted to leave and couldn't. Hearing movement behind him, Larson's frustration at Gabe's loitering breeched the last of his patience.

He jerked his bandanna down and turned. "Look, I told you once that only hired hands are—"

The words caught in his throat.

Kathryn stood inside the doorway. Sunlight spilled in behind her, framing her in a soft glow. She took two steps and stopped. A tentative smile played at the corners of her mouth.

"I'm sorry to bother you, sir."

Weakness washed through him at the sound of her voice, and Larson was thankful for the rake in his hand. Leaning heavily against it, he welcomed the shadows of the stall.

He looked past Kathryn to the far wall. Gabe was gone. Great, just when the big guy might've proved useful.

"Sir, I feel rather foolish coming here, but I just wanted to . . ." She glanced down and walked toward him.

He raised a gloved hand to his jaw and suddenly remembered he'd removed his bandanna. He touched his temple and, with relief, felt his glasses. Thinking she might recognize him this close up sent a cold wave through him. It had been dark that night in her cottage. Then in the main house, she'd looked at him only briefly before passing. Seeing her affected him in ways he tried not to acknowledge. Her eyes flashed to his, then took in his face.

Her smile faded slightly. Then a shadow, hardly perceptible, crossed her expression before the lines on her brow smoothed again.

He'd seen the reaction countless times before. People never knew how to act or what to say, even when seeing him for the second or third time. Most resorted to practiced indifference, while others stared outright. But what he hated most was their pity. And pity was something he definitely did not desire from Kathryn. Not after what she'd done to him.

Larson held his breath, waiting for the light of recognition in her eyes. He wondered if she was aware of how her hands traveled over her round abdomen in smooth circles, as though comforting the child growing inside her.

The maternal act did nothing to warm his heart.

"I'm sorry to have bothered you, sir. I can see you're busy. I should let you get back to your work."

A shudder of reprieve passed through him, followed by astonishment. Here he was, her husband of ten years, standing before her, and she didn't see him. How could people be so blind to what was right in front of them? With rash courage, he decided to test the boundaries of his cloak of scars.

"You been here long at Casaroja, ma'am?" he asked, watching for the slightest sign, the subtlest change in her expression at the sound of his voice.

Nothing. Instead, a trace of sadness crept into her eyes.

She shook her head. "No. I haven't been here long. And you?"

He limped to the far wall and hung up the rake, acutely aware of his stuttered stride and the way her eyes followed him.

"Been here about two weeks myself." He nodded toward the open doors. "This is a beautiful place. Finest ranch around these parts." *And the kind of place I wanted to build together with you, Kathryn. That I wanted to give you.*

"Yes, Casaroja is beautiful," she agreed, slipping her hand into her skirt pocket. He half expected her to withdraw something, but she didn't. Instead, she surprised him by closing the distance between them. "My name is Kathryn Jennings."

So she still carried his name. That discovery didn't soften him toward her. Larson looked down at her hands now clasped at her waist and remembered the silk of her skin . . . and the grotesqueness of his own.

"Oh, I almost forgot." She reached into her other pocket and pulled out a wrapped bundle. The checkered material reminded him of Miss Maudie's kitchen cloths, like the ones she draped over his dinner plate before she set it off to the side, keeping him from having to wait in line with the other ranch hands. "Miss Maudie made this last night." Kathryn pulled back on a corner of the cloth. "She said she didn't remember you getting a piece last night, so I saved some back for you. It's her special spice bread."

Larson reached out a gloved hand, but Kathryn simply stared down at it, then back up at him.

She smiled a little, as though questioning whether he was going to remove his glove. Typical Kathryn. Always direct, but with a femininity belonging only to her.

He tugged on his right glove, gritting his teeth at the soreness in his fingers, then at the pain reflected in her face when she saw his hand.

She gently took his hand in hers, as a mother might a child's. A sigh escaped her. "How did this happen?"

The empathy in her tone caught him off guard, and Larson was stunned by his physical reaction.

Her face reflected nothing but innocence, but he didn't welcome the feelings being this close to her stirred inside him. He pulled his hand away.

Surprise lit her eyes.

"I was in the wrong place at the wrong

time, that's all." He took the small bundle from her and set it aside. "Thank you for thinking of me," he mumbled, pulling his glove back on.

"You should come up to the ranch house some night. Miss Maudie often doctors the men's bruises and cuts. I bet she'd have something to help you. I'd be happy to help too, if I could," she added after a moment.

Larson looked away. He wanted her to leave. He hadn't expected, nor did he welcome, her compassion. But Kathryn had always possessed a tender heart. She'd been quick to help wanderers when they happened by their cabin, offering them food in exchange for work that she could've easily done herself. Anything to help a man keep his dignity.

A thought pierced him. Even if Kathryn hadn't betrayed him by being with other men and carrying another man's child, what did he have to offer her anymore? He was a broken shell of a man with a carved out, discarded dream—with no chance of ever waking. Oh, but he had loved her. And she had loved him too . . . at one time—he was certain of it.

"Well, I'm sorry to have bothered you."

The sound of her voice pulled him back. Disturbed by her being here, yet suddenly not wanting her to leave, he cleared his throat. "You never said what it was you came down here for, ma'am."

She turned back and shrugged, but she didn't look him in the eye this time. "I was out for a walk and just wound up down here somehow." Kathryn paused, then shook her head. "No, that's not truthful. I came down here specifically to talk to you about something."

His pulse skidded to a halt.

"You saw me that afternoon . . . leaving Mr. MacGregor's bedroom. I've spoken with Miss Maudie, and she believes me. I really was cleaning his room that day, no matter how it may have looked. I would never do something like that. Mr. MacGregor came back in and shut the door. He didn't even know I was there, I assure you."

Larson didn't answer. Kathryn watched him, unblinking, waiting for his response.

He could easily lose himself in those eyes again. Eyes so warm, seemingly full of compassion. The honesty in them captivated him. He wanted to look away, but some invisible hand kept him from it. Then the certainty inside him wavered, like a candle fighting for flame at the sudden opening of a door.

Was she telling the truth?

But as hard as he tried, Larson couldn't make it fit the reality he knew to be true. *Lord, she was living in a brothel. I saw her there.* Though his eyes never left hers, his mental focus dropped lower. *And she's obviously been with another man.*

Kathryn's eyes filled and she looked down. "You don't believe me."

"What does it matter if I believe you or not?"

She lifted her chin and squinted ever so slightly, as though she were trying to penetrate the brown tint of his glasses. "It matters a great deal to me."

He shifted beneath her scrutiny. Part of him wanted to reach out and brush the tear from his wife's cheek, but he made his gloved hand into a fist instead. *God help me, I don't know what to believe right now.* But he was sure of MacGregor's guilt in the situation. No doubt that man had a hand in Kathryn being at Casaroja, and Larson intended to discover the reason behind Mac-

Gregor's sudden interest. He didn't have to look very far in front of him to start.

Larson tried to sound convincing despite his doubt. "I do believe you, ma'am."

She wiped her tears and the tension eased from her expression.

"Thank you," she whispered, then tilted her head to one side. "I just realized . . . you never gave me your name."

"Jacob."

The edges of her mouth twitched. "A biblical name. It suits you."

"I'm not sure that's a compliment. Jacob deceived and cheated his brother out of his birthright, then lied to his father."

Her brow rose. "You're familiar with the Bible?"

Larson shrugged and reached for a shovel, needing something to occupy his hands. "I've read certain parts." It unsettled him how much he enjoyed talking with her again, especially when nothing could ever come of it.

She took a small step closer to him. "While Jacob had his faults, he was also a very determined man. A man willing to work long and hard for what he wanted."

"But his methods weren't always respectable."

"No, they weren't. But, then, whose are?" She smiled as though enjoying the exchange as well. "Well, I need to get back to work. It was good to meet you, Jacob."

"Same to you."

Larson stood at the door for several minutes, watching her walk back to the main house. She'd looked so sincere. Had she been telling him the truth? And if so, then what about the brothel? And Matthew Taylor? None of it made any sense. He sighed and went back into the stable.

But over the next few days, he decided that a trip back to the brothel was in order. If only to find out once and for all what Kathryn had been doing there.

CHAPTER EIGHTEEN

"Jacob's a nice man," Gabe said, holding the other end of the brocaded wool panel. "Yes, he is a nice man. Now, sling it up and over. On the count of three. Ready?"

At Gabe's nod, Kathryn counted to three and they both swung the heavy drapery over the line. The thick rope strung between her cottage and a cottonwood held, but it dipped under the weight. "Thank you, Gabe." She grabbed the broom and began sweeping the cobwebs and dust from the pleated folds. No easy task with her growing belly.

"I saw you talking to him in the barn the other day."

"Yes," she said, feeling the child move inside her. "I needed to talk to him about something." Kathryn wondered if Gabe had heard the rumors about her yet. She didn't like bringing it up, but if he had heard them, she didn't want him to think they held any truth. "Gabe, now that you're working here at Casaroja, if you ever hear anything about me and wonder if it's true or not, would you please ask me directly?"

"Yes, Miss Kathryn. I will. And you'll always tell me the truth."

He said it with such conviction, Kathryn looked back at him. His blue eyes sparkled in the morning sun. "Yes, Gabe, I would. No matter what."

"Do you like being here at Casaroja, Miss Kathryn?"

She smiled. *Testing my honesty already, Lord?* She set the broom aside and started beating the drapery lightly with a cushioned paddle. "No, Gabe, not really." Dust plumed from the rich burgundy fabric, and she turned her face away. "I wish I were back at the cabin with my husband, but that's not possible anymore. My life has changed in ways I wouldn't have chosen, but I'm trusting that God sees all these changes and that somehow He'll help me accept them, in time. He's given me a safe place to live and good friends." She placed a hand on her midsection. "And He's given me this precious child."

Gabe's look turned quizzical. "How do you trust so much in someone you've never seen, Miss Kathryn?"

She stilled at the question. "The same way you do. The same way anyone does— by faith. And besides," she added with a wink, "I *have* seen Him." The boyish crinkle of Gabe's forehead made her chuckle. "I've seen Him in you, Gabe. Now you'd better hurry up and eat your lunch and get back to work, or Jacob will come looking for you again."

Gabe grinned. "Do you know what Jacob did last night?" He stuffed his mouth with a piece of bread and cheese.

"No, what did he do this time?" Kathryn played along, turning her face away from the dust. She could easily tell who Gabe's new hero was.

"Last night there was a mama cow trying to have a baby, except that baby was comin' out all wrong. Jacob talked to her, right up in that mama's ear where she could hear him. Then he reached up inside her and helped that calf come out the right way. You should come down and see it tonight."

"I'll try and do that," she said, wondering if Jacob would mind her being there. He seemed friendly enough last time, after he'd gotten past her seeing his scars. She wondered again how he'd gotten them. Despite the summer heat, he always wore a long-sleeved shirt and that same knit cap, and she couldn't help but wonder what lay beneath.

Jacob took his meals alone, so she didn't see him unless Miss Maudie asked him to do something at the main house. Kathryn hadn't been able to come up with a reason to visit the stables again, plus she was being extra careful not to be alone with any of the men. But thanks to Gabe, she had a proper chaperone now and a reason to visit. She looked at the big man sitting beneath the cottonwood tree eating his lunch. Thanks to Gabe, she had a lot of things.

Physically, he was all man, but he possessed the heart of a child. She remembered when he'd appeared at her cabin door all those months ago. He'd scared her to death at first. But he'd been a good friend to her, and she owed him so much.

"Gabe," she said, laying her paddle aside, "I don't think I've ever thanked you for all the things you did for me back at my ranch. I'm glad Matthew Taylor hired you and that you came to work for me when you did. I thought then that you were a gift straight from God, and I still do."

He smiled, shrugging as though he'd done nothing.

"No, really, Gabe. If there's ever anything I can do for you, please tell me."

He stopped chewing. "Does tomorrow count?"

"Does tomorrow count for what?"

"Would you do a favor for me tomorrow?"

Kathryn picked up the broom and brushed away the lingering dust from the curtain panel. "Why don't you tell me the favor first?" she said, smiling. She arched her back and rolled her shoulders to loosen the tight muscles.

Gabe laughed. "I promise it's something you'll like, Miss Kathryn."

"Mm-hmm . . . I've heard that before." She threw him a wink.

"Beggin' your pardon, Mrs. Jennings."

Kathryn turned at the high-pitched voice. "Oh . . . hello, Molly."

The kitchen maid curtsied and held out an envelope. "Mr. MacGregor asked me to deliver this to you, ma'am. Said for you to read it right away. I'm supposed to wait for your response."

As Kathryn took the note, she noticed Molly steal a quick look in Gabe's direction. Oblivious, Gabe took another bite of cheese and then happened to look up. He smiled at Molly, who immediately dipped her head in response. But Kathryn could see the sudden color rising to her cheeks.

Smiling to herself, Kathryn lifted the unsealed flap of the envelope and read the letter. Her face heated.

Though she was glad to finally get a chance to meet with him about his offer, Donlyn MacGregor certainly wasn't helping her situation any by asking her this way. She had little doubt the maid had already read the contents of the letter. Kathryn had quickly learned that Molly held a confidence like a sieve. Apparently Mr. MacGregor lacked that knowledge of this particular employee.

"Molly, please tell Mr. MacGregor that I

must decline having dinner with him as he requested, but that I'll look forward to meeting with him later that evening."

The girl nodded, cast one last glance in Gabe's direction, then turned and hurried back inside the house.

Kathryn tossed a look back at Gabe and winked. "I see you've caught someone's eye, Gabe."

He stood up and brushed the crumbs from his shirt. "The same could be said of you, Miss Kathryn."

But for once, he wasn't smiling.

———

Kathryn woke early the next morning to get ready for Gabe's surprise. He wouldn't tell her what it was, but thanks to Miss Maudie's help the night before, she had everything ready. Plus, thanks to the woman's generosity, she had four more black dresses from which to choose, each sensible enough for every day and with room enough to last her until the baby was born.

Like she did every morning upon rising, Kathryn gave the music box key three full twists and set it on the side table. She sang along softly, pulling back the curtain from the open bedroom window to gain a view of the stables and eastern prairie. The sun crested the horizon and the last of the stars were quickly fading. Despite being July, a cool morning breeze blew in, carrying with it the scent of prairie grass and cattle.

Kathryn closed her eyes and, for a moment, was back on their ranch. She could picture the cabin, the barn, the towering blue spruce and quivering aspen; she could hear the creek that ran behind the cabin and could even smell the pungent pine. A gentle wind lifted the hair from her shoulders, and she let herself imagine it was the soft brush of angels' wings. Angels from on high, like the words of the song.

She opened her eyes and spotted a rider coming in off the range. In dawn's pinkish light, the horse's hooves barely seemed to touch the ground as it flew across the open plains. The rider and mount moved as one. Kathryn remembered that feeling—freedom. Larson had taught her to ride like that, many years ago.

The rider slowed the buckskin to a canter, then reined in while still a ways out. Dismounting, he stretched and rubbed his right thigh, then stroked the horse's forehead. He loosely took the reins, and the horse followed. He wasn't close enough yet for Kathryn to make out his face, but even at this distance she saw Jacob wasn't wearing his glasses or his cap. His head was completely bald except for darker patches where it looked as if the hair had been shaved.

Kathryn stepped back from the window as Jacob got closer. The tune from the music box slowed, as though struggling to reach the last few notes. As Jacob passed by, she heard the horse whinny, then Jacob's soft whisper of a voice as he answered back. Curiosity begged her to take a closer look, but somehow she knew Jacob didn't want her to see him like this, and respect for him outweighed the temptation.

Half an hour later, a wagon pulled up outside the cottage. Kathryn laid aside the blanket she was knitting for the baby and looked out to see Gabe climbing down dressed in a crisp white shirt and brown trousers. She'd never seen him look so handsome.

"Where on earth are we going this early in the morning?" she asked minutes later as they pulled onto the main road leading to town. "Miss Maudie and I fixed enough food for a small army, so I hope you're hungry."

Gabe's grin said he still wasn't going to tell her their destination. He started to sing a hymn Kathryn knew, so she joined in. She hadn't sung with anyone in years and found comfort in singing the hymns with Gabe now.

"Okay, you pick one next," he said a while later.

"There's one I know from my childhood. It's not as fast paced, but let's see if I can remember it." She began singing, but Gabe didn't join in. Kathryn stopped and elbowed him good-naturedly.

He shook his head. "I don't know the words. But I like hearing you sing, Miss Kathryn."

She smiled, then started again. "'Father and friend, thy light, thy love, beaming through all thy works we see. Thy glory gilds the heavens above, and all the earth is full of thee.'"

When Gabe turned to look at her, his eyes held a sheen. "Are there more words to that one?"

Touched by his response, Kathryn closed her eyes. "'Thy voice we hear, thy presence feel, while thou, too pure for mortal sight, enwrapt in clouds, invisible, reignest the Lord of life and light.' "

She sang another verse and then let the silence settle around them. Gabe looked deep in thought, so Kathryn sat back, enjoying the sunshine on her face and the hint of secret on the breeze. Whatever Gabe had planned for her today couldn't be more special than what he'd already given her. This was the lightest her heart had felt in—

A spasm of pain gripped her midsection. She doubled over, clutching the buckboard for support. A cold sweat broke out over her body, and she squeezed her eyes tight, gasping.

Gabe slowed the wagon and put a hand on her back. "Miss Kathryn, what's wrong?"

"I don't know," she finally managed, cautiously drawing in a deep breath. As swiftly as it came, the pain left. She leaned back and spread her hands on her belly, caressing her unborn child. "I think maybe it's too much singing." She forced a laugh and saw the seriousness in Gabe's face.

"Do you want to go back?"

She laid a hand to his arm. "No, please, Gabe. Let's go on, I'll be fine."

"Are you sure?"

She blew her breath out slowly. "As long as you don't have me running any three-legged races, I think I'll make it." But she decided to take it easy that day and not to overdo. It wasn't worth risking the health of her child.

When they reached the edge of town, Gabe guided the wagon to the road leading to the white church. "This is your surprise."

She looked at the seemingly empty building. "But it's not even Sunday."

He smiled. "We're early, but they're having a schoolhouse raising right over there later this morning." He pointed to a plot of land west of the church building, where stakes already marked the four corners and boards lay neatly stacked. "The women will be making lunch and quilting." He shrugged. "I thought you might like that. But I figured you might go see Annabelle first." His voice softened. "Then maybe spend some time with your husband."

Kathryn threw her arms around him and hugged him tight.

————

Larson stood in the alley looking up at the two-story clapboard building. The flesh on his back prickled. His mind filled with the dazed look on his mother's face as the man closed the door, then the acrid scent of the cheroot. He shook his head to break the memory's hold.

This was not the same place, and he was not that little boy any longer.

He closed his eyes, trying to gather his nerve.

Larson climbed the back stairs and knocked on the door. He waited a full minute and then knocked again. It was noon. Someone should be awake by now. Stepping back, he looked up at the row of windows on the second floor. He waited a few minutes, then as he turned to leave, he saw the curtain on the door move.

The door opened a crack. "You need to come back tonight." The young girl's dark eyes quickly took in his face and his cap. She didn't flinch. "We are not entertaining now."

She moved to shut the door, but Larson put a hand out. He guessed her to be about thirteen or fourteen. He'd like to think she was kitchen help, but he knew better. The combination of her youthful beauty and her smooth brown skin and almond eyes would be considered exotic, and some men paid extra if they were young. The thought still sickened him.

"I'm not here to be entertained, miss. I'm here to find out about one of the girls who used to work here."

Suspicion flashed in her wide-set eyes.

Larson pulled a few dollars from his pocket. "I just want to know if someone worked here before, that's all," he tried again, holding out the money. She reached for it, but he pulled it back slightly. "Answer first—then I pay."

The girl shook her head and started to close the door.

He wedged his boot in the threshold. "Half now, the rest after."

She nodded and took the offered bills. "What do you call this girl?"

"Her name is Kathryn, but she might have gone by another name." Faint recognition registered in the girl's eyes, and Larson waited for her to answer, but she only stared. Practiced nonchalance—he knew the look well. "Listen, I know she lived here because I saw her coming back here one night. I want to know if she worked here."

"I do not know this lady," she said

abruptly, pushing the money back through the crack. She slammed the door, and the lock clicked into place.

Larson knocked again, already knowing the opportunity was lost. After picking up the loose bills, he made a trip to the mercantile for supplies before heading out of town. Still turning over in his mind what the girl had told him, he passed by the church and reined in.

Wagons clustered in front of and behind the building. Beyond the cemetery, farther below in the clearing, a group of men worked together to set the skeleton of a wall into place. One group shouldered the wall higher while another group hoisted it by ropes. Blankets were spread on patches of prairie grass while children ran over and around them. A hive of women hovered around a makeshift table covered with so much food he couldn't see the table top.

As their high-pitched chatter rose to him, one woman in particular caught his eye.

Sunlight shone off of Kathryn's long blond hair as she walked toward the gathering. He retraced her steps and guessed she'd come from the cemetery. Did he dare think she'd been visiting his grave? The possibility touched him. Her form was getting fuller by the day it seemed, and she was more beautiful to him now than in all the years he'd known her. His mind suddenly flashed back to the last time he'd made love to her, and the experience was so clear in his memory that he ached with the wanting of it. With wanting *her*.

Then he remembered their wedding night, the first time he'd ever known Kathryn in an intimate sense. She'd come to him pure and untainted, shy and unsure. And as he'd held her tenderly, loving her with experience, he had looked into her eyes and wished he'd shared her innocence. He would have liked to have given her that same gift, but his upbringing had left little chance of that.

Kathryn hung back from the crowd of women gathered around the table, and Larson could almost feel her tension, her desire to be part of them. A dark-haired woman finally noticed her and walked up to take her hand. Larson felt a smile tug his mouth.

"I do not know this lady," the girl at the brothel had told him moments ago. *"This lady."*

The women in his mother's brothel had always referred to each other as girls. The term *lady* was reserved for . . . well, just that. A lady. Could it be that—

"We sure could use another pair of hands down there," a man said beside him.

Jerked back from his thoughts, Larson turned in the saddle.

A youthful-looking man resembling Abraham Lincoln sat astride a piebald mare. Larson quickly placed him and tried to remember his daughter's name. The little girl with violet eyes—Lilly.

"I'm Patrick Carlson."

Larson shook the preacher's outstretched hand. "My name's Jacob," he said, hoping Carlson wouldn't ask for a last name.

"Well, Jacob, as I see it, you and I could head on down there, pound a few nails, maybe help raise a wall or two and then get fed like kings, all in a few hours time. Whadd'ya say?"

Carlson smiled, and the first word that came to Larson's mind was *genuine*. But still he hesitated. He glanced back to the gathering, running a hand along his freshly trimmed, if patchy, beard. He'd love to see Kathryn today, if only from afar. But was he up to being around all those other people?

"One thing I like about this church is the people." Carlson continued as though he'd never paused. "They're fine folks. Friendly, generous, a bit sinful at times, but God hasn't run out of forgiveness yet, so I guess we're okay."

Larson detected the gleam in the man's eyes and smiled. "Maybe there's a job that needs doing on the side somewhere, a ways from the crowd?"

"Sawing boards sounds good to me, and that's a two-man job. You up for it?" At Larson's nod, he pointed to a pile of boards off to the right of where the men were working.

"Thank you," Larson said quietly.

"Don't thank me yet. Save that for when you taste Lilly's blackberry pie. She's been asking about you. Our Lilly never forgets a fa—" Carlson stopped suddenly and his chest fell. "Jacob, I'm sorry. I didn't mean to imply that . . ."

Eyeing the younger man beside him, Larson slowly removed his glasses, hoping Carlson would see his sincerity. "Any chance your wife has some of her coffee made? That tasted mighty good that morning."

Carlson held his gaze for a moment, then nodded. He leaned over and gripped Larson by the shoulder. "Hannah's coffee is like God's grace. It's always good and it never runs out. I'll grab us some and meet you over there in a minute."

———

Kathryn spooned a piece of blackberry pie onto the boy's plate and laughed at the grin splitting his face.

"My big sister made that," he said with a lisp before running back to the blanket.

Kathryn couldn't help but watch him. His thick brown hair and hazel eyes set her to wondering again—was she carrying Larson's son or daughter in her womb? Whichever, she prayed the child would bear his handsome features.

Annabelle hadn't been at the brothel that morning. In fact the back door was locked and no one answered. Next, Kathryn had stopped by the undertaker's to check on the headstone she'd ordered to permanently mark Larson's grave, but he informed her it wasn't ready yet. Just as well. She didn't have the funds to pay for it in full anyway. After that she had bought fresh flowers and visited Larson's grave.

At the touch on her shoulder, Kathryn

turned. She'd only met Hannah Carlson that morning, but already she felt a kinship with the woman.

"Patrick says he's going to take his meal with a newcomer and asked me to join him. I know I asked you to share our blanket, but I'm wondering if you'd be willing to do that instead."

Kathryn eyed her new friend suspiciously. "You've already managed to introduce me to every single man here today, Hannah Carlson. Are you sure this isn't a trick?" About the same age, Hannah was the exact opposite of Kathryn in coloring. But from all indications, their teasing temperaments were identical.

"No, that's not what this is, I promise." Hannah playfully pinched her elbow. "But one Sunday after lunch you're coming to my house for that exact purpose." Her grin lessened to a regretful smile. "I wish I'd been at your husband's funeral, Kathryn. I normally accompany Patrick as he ministers, but Lilly was sick that day." Her dark eyes glistened. "I wish we'd met each other sooner."

"Well, we know each other now," Kathryn said, remembering the day she'd visited all the boardinghouses in town, "and I'm thanking God for that already. I'll get my food and join you in a minute." She gave Hannah a reassuring look and then began filling her plate. Wondering where Gabe was, she searched for him as she cut through the maze of blankets. She'd last seen him helping with the schoolhouse by securing the heavy crossbeams as men drove the spikes in. Though already familiar with his strength, his sense of balance was no less impressive.

Kathryn spotted Jacob from a ways off, and she knew the instant he saw her. His mouth curved in a quick smile before he pulled his collar up about his neck. She doubted if he was even aware that he did it. She smiled back at him.

He stood as she approached, acknowledging her in his soft, rasping voice. "Kathryn."

His voice wasn't hoarse-sounding exactly, but close. Sometimes when he spoke, Kathryn wondered if the simple action hurt him. "It's nice to see you again, Jacob."

She chose a seat beside Hannah on a log, directly opposite Jacob and Pastor Carlson. Seeing the looks of mild surprise on the pastor and Hannah's faces, Kathryn chuckled. "Jacob and I both work at Casaroja."

"So you two know one another, then?" Pastor Carlson glanced between them, as Hannah was doing.

Kathryn waited for Jacob to answer, and when he didn't, she chimed in. "Not really, Pastor. Not very well anyway. I'm working as a housekeeper at Casaroja now and Jacob manages the stables."

Jacob's face came up at that, and Kathryn wished she could see beyond his smoke-colored spectacles to his eyes. Despite his quiet nature, she got the impression that Jacob missed nothing, and she would like to have known his thoughts at that moment.

Patrick insisted that Kathryn dispense with calling him Pastor, and the conversation moved comfortably between the four of them as they ate their lunch.

"Patrick, it is, then," she agreed, taking a bite of potatoes.

"So, Jacob . . . we already know a bit about Kathryn and her life"—Patrick speared a pickle—"but we don't know much about you. Why don't you tell us about yourself. Have you been in town long?"

Jacob looked in her direction, but Kathryn couldn't tell whether he was focusing on her or not. "Not too long, really. But I've lived in the Colorado Territory for the past few years."

"Well, I figured that from our earlier conversation. You seem to know these mountains well enough. Where did the couple live that you were telling me about before? The ones who helped you after your accident."

Kathryn pretended to concentrate on her pie, but her attention was riveted on what Jacob would say next.

He didn't answer immediately. "They live up north from here a ways. West of Denver in the mountains." He cleared his throat and took a drink from his cup. "I wouldn't be alive today if it weren't for them. They doctored me after the fire and . . . gave me a reason to live when I'd lost my own."

The sadness tingeing Jacob's voice, the subtle depth of emotion, drew Kathryn's gaze. Though his eyes were hidden, somehow she knew he was looking at her.

"And they led you to Jesus as well?"

He nodded and turned his attention back to Patrick, a slight smile touching his lips. In the ambiguity of that moment, with Jacob looking away, Kathryn found herself staring at him. One side of his mouth remained relatively unscathed by the flames, while the other was drawn tight and sloped gently to one side.

"I'd heard of Him before then, but because of them, and what happened to me . . ." He shook his head. "Well, now I guess you could say that I've seen Him with my own eyes."

Patrick squinted as though trying to recall something. "Oh . . . wait . . . Job chapter forty-two . . . verse five?"

Jacob laughed. "I don't know what verse it is, but you've got the chapter right."

Patrick turned to Hannah, his eyes gleaming. "Jacob and I were quizzing each other on Scripture while we sawed. I think I've met my match."

"Nah, I just got lucky before. But you and Isaiah, the man who found me, would get along real well, I think. He's hidden a bunch of the Word in here." He covered the place over his heart. "And Abby is as fine a woman as I've ever met. I wish I'd met them earlier in my life."

As Jacob talked, he looked to the side and Kathryn caught a glimpse of the scarring surrounding his left eye. Coupled with listening to him talk about the man and woman who apparently meant so much to him, her own eyes burned in response.

"Uh-oh . . ." Hannah suddenly whispered, glancing over Jacob's shoulder. Smiling, she winked at her husband. "Here comes Lilly."

"Jacob, you'd better prepare yourself." Patrick's voice dropped to a conspiratorial whisper. "Looks like you're about to be ambushed."

Kathryn watched as a breathtakingly beautiful child sneaked up behind Jacob. She couldn't help but smile at the pure mischief lighting the girl's face. Jacob casually laid his plate aside right before Lilly let out a scream and pounced on his shoulders. Jacob caught the girl's arms about his neck and stood with some effort.

"Wait! I thought I heard something," he said, turning from side to side and flinging Lilly with each turn. "Preacher, did you hear something? Mrs. Carlson, did you?"

Lilly's high-pitched giggles only spurred Jacob on, and Kathryn watched, amazed at the transformation in this soft-spoken man.

She soon found herself laughing along with everyone else.

"It's . . . me . . . Lilly," the child finally said between breaths.

"Oh, Lilly, I didn't see you back there," Jacob answered, securing her tiny hands in his. Lilly laid her head on the back of Jacob's shoulder and let her legs dangle. He reached up and tugged a long black curl hanging over his shoulder before lowering her to the ground.

Jacob laughed softly, more like a chuckle really, and the sound of it caused Kathryn's own laughter to thin. It sounded so like Larson's. Jacob and Lilly blurred in her vision, and she blinked her eyes quickly to stave off the unexpected emotion. Oh, how she missed hearing Larson's laughter. But even before he'd left that Christmas morning, it had been a long time since she had heard it.

The afternoon slipped into evening, and Kathryn was glad when everyone started packing to leave. Placing Miss Maudie's last empty dish in the wagon, she saw Gabe walking toward her.

"Where have you been, Gabe?" she chided playfully, hands on her hips. "I've been searching for you all afternoon."

He looked at her as though she'd sprouted horns. "I've been workin'. I helped with the schoolhouse, then I had to run into town. Besides, the last time I looked, you weren't searching for me too hard." He shot her a look that drew a smile. "Is Jacob still around?"

Kathryn accepted his help up to the bench seat. "Yes, he's over there talking with the pastor."

"Maybe he wants to ride back with us. I'll ask him," he said before Kathryn could suggest otherwise.

Jacob had worked hard that day. He'd grown quiet through the afternoon, and Kathryn sensed he was tired and might prefer his solitude. But to her surprise, Jacob nodded and walked toward them. The longer the day had gone, the worse his limp had gotten. She determined to ask Miss Maudie for one of her liniments that might help him.

Jacob tied his horse to the back and climbed into the wagon bed. Gabe sang on the way home. Jacob didn't join in, and Kathryn felt hesitant to for some reason.

Finally Gabe nudged her arm playfully. "Come on, sing that one you sang this mornin', Miss Kathryn. That one's real pretty."

Reluctantly, Kathryn sang the first verse, then looked west to appreciate the burnt-orange afterglow of daylight slipping behind the highest snowcapped peaks.

They rode in silence for a moment, accompanied only by the sound of horses' hooves on hard-packed earth and the constant whine of wagon wheels.

"Will you sing some more?"

Barely able to hear Jacob's request, Kathryn looked back at him but found him facing west, watching the sunset. She sang the rest of the song and then three others, one of them Larson's favorite. Strangely, singing that song brought her peace instead of sadness. Maybe that was a good sign. Perhaps she was coming to accept the loss of Larson and their life together.

But if that were true, why did she still feel as though he were with her even now?

CHAPTER NINETEEN

"Good evening Mrs. Jennings." Larson spoke quietly as he approached, not wanting to frighten her as she walked from the main house to her darkened cottage. Following dinner, he'd been sitting outside the stable enjoying the uncustomarily cool July breeze and hoping to see her before she retired for the evening.

He'd spoken with her twice since last Saturday's schoolhouse raising, and Kathryn had seemed preoccupied to him, quieter than usual. He wondered if she was all right. Having heard the purity and clarity of her voice again that night, the songs she sang, somehow they had woven a furtive path through his defenses and were undermining his doubts even as he watched her now.

"Jacob." A smile lit her face that made him think she was glad to see him. "How are you tonight?"

"Fine, ma'am." She wore another black dress, one he hadn't seen before. No matter the sameness of the color she wore from day to day, Larson was glad his glasses masked his eyes so he could appreciate her beauty without fear of offending her. "I thought I'd let you know that another calf dropped early this morning, just in case you wanted to come see it sometime. The mother won't have anything to do with it, so the calf's here in the upper stable. Gabe said you might be interested in seeing it. You can come whenever you like. I'll make sure Gabe'll be there."

Kathryn eyed him thoughtfully. "Yes, I'd like that. Thank you, Jacob."

Nodding, he turned to leave.

"H-how about right now? Tonight . . . if you have time?"

He looked back, surprised at the hesitance in her voice. "Now would be good." He smiled. "Let me make sure Gabe's still there."

"What if I bring some dessert with me? I made a pecan pie earlier. If you like that kind," she added, her voice going soft.

It was his favorite. "Yes, ma'am, I do."

Larson stood outside the stall, enjoying watching Kathryn and Gabe with the baby calf. He doubted he'd ever get used to Gabe's childlike innocence. His personality was such a contrast to what Larson had expected when first seeing the man. Gabe was a hard worker, and his strength helped on many occasions when the job demanded more than Larson could give. Larson's body was growing stronger, and Miss Maudie's steady diet of hearty beef was building his muscle. His arms and chest were filling out again.

"She likes it right back here, behind her ears." Gabe took hold of Kathryn's hand and guided her as she stroked the orphaned calf. Larson waited for her to tell Gabe she already knew that, but she didn't. She just smiled and followed his instructions. "She reminds me of ones you used to have, Miss Kathryn. Back at your ranch."

"Yes, she does." Her voice sounded oddly reminiscent, and Larson watched as she drew her hand back and stood. She walked out of the stall and over to where he stood. She glanced around. "It's getting dark in here."

Larson hadn't noticed. He'd grown accustomed to the dark tint of his glasses and to living by the sun's schedule, except for when he snuck off to borrow the glow of a lamp from the bunkhouse. He hadn't handled a flame since before the fire, and the thought of doing so now sent a shiver through him. He looked up to find Kathryn watching him.

"Do you have a lantern in here, Jacob?" she asked quietly, a smile in her voice.

"There's one in the back, I think," Gabe offered, closing the stall door behind him. "I'll go find it."

Larson panicked when he saw Gabe return with it unlit. Gabe placed it on a workbench beside him and Larson stared down, unable to move. He closed his eyes, heart pounding, hands trembling. He clenched his fists at his sides, having dreaded this inevitable moment for the past few months.

A grown man, afraid of the flame.

"Would you like for me to light it?"

Larson felt a touch on his arm and

opened his eyes. Kathryn stood close to him. He hadn't heard her move. He nodded, the silent admission slicing his pride as she lit the wick.

In the soft glow from the lantern, Larson saw her tender smile, her unspoken understanding, and shame filled him at her having seen this side of him. He moved to a hay bale and sat down.

"Well, I hope you men are hungry. I cut big pieces." She handed them each a slice of pie and set the basket back on the workbench. Gabe finished his piece quickly, then walked back to the stall to check on the calf.

"May I?"

Larson looked up to see Kathryn eyeing his Bible on a shelf above the workbench where he'd left it that morning. He gave a nod. "This is delicious pie, ma'am."

Considering everything that had happened in the past seven months, it amazed him to be sitting here with his wife, enjoying her company and eating her pecan pie. He was hard-pressed to take it all in. Probably because Kathryn wasn't really his wife anymore. Maybe on paper, officially, but not in her mind. She didn't even recognize him.

But did he really want her to know him? Hadn't he taken extra precautions so she wouldn't?

Larson watched her turning the pages of his Bible. He wished he could walk over and put his arms around her like he'd once done—to have the freedom, the right, to touch her again. Briefly, he let himself imagine that she might respond in a way that would tell him she still wanted him. Then he caught a glimpse of his misshapen fingers awkwardly gripping the fork. He let his attention wander the stable.

This was where he lived. His blanket lay on a bed of hay. He couldn't even offer Kathryn a decent bed, much less a home. Larson set aside his half-eaten piece of pie.

William Cummings had been right. Kathryn deserved better. She always had.

"This Bible belonged to the couple you were telling us about." Her voice drew him back. She had opened the Bible to the front, and her fingers were moving over a page. "Isaiah and Abby. But it doesn't give their last name."

Larson smiled, not having thought of it before now. "You know, I can't even tell you their last name. I never asked."

She stared at him for a second. "But they mean a great deal to you, don't they? They sound like very special people. I wish I could meet them."

Her voice sounded so sincere. He nodded, wishing she could meet them too, wishing she could see him like she used to. "You'd really like them, Ka—"

Larson stilled instantly. He'd almost called her Kat. A lifetime had passed since he'd used that name with her. He forced a cough to cover his near misstep. " 'Cause you and Abby have a lot in common. You'd get along well with each other."

Kathryn smiled, appearing unaware of his near slip. She opened to his marked page and lifted the stem of dried prairie grass. "Is this where you're reading right now?" At his nod, she began. "'Who shall separate us from the love of Christ? . . .'"

Larson's heart tightened as he watched her lips move. He listened to the rise and fall of her voice. She read the Scripture with conviction, then glanced at him with a look of pure pleasure. "This is one of my favorite passages. 'For I am persuaded, that neither death, nor life, nor angels, nor principalities, nor powers, nor things present, nor things to come, Nor height, nor depth, nor any other creature, shall be able to separate us from the love of God, which is in Christ Jesus our Lord.'"

The gradual tightening in Larson's chest twisted to an ache. "Do you believe that?"

"Yes." Her answer came quick, followed by a shake of her head. "But I don't always live like I do. Sometimes I look at my life, at decisions I've made." She gave her shoulders a slight shrug. "I think about the things that have happened to me and feel like maybe God has lost track of me, or maybe that He just doesn't love me very much anymore." She smoothed her right hand over the child in her belly and sighed. "Then at other times, I feel His presence so close beside me that I can almost feel His breath on my face." She laughed softly, her expression growing suddenly shy. "I know that must sound silly."

"No . . . it doesn't sound silly at all." Larson saw her eyes glistening, and something inside him responded. She'd worn her hair down, and it fell in a thick swoop over one shoulder. How many years had he wasted living with this woman, day after day, sleeping beside her at night, and yet completely missing who she really was? Not sharing this part of her? This part that would never fade or die. What a fool he'd been.

"Well, it's getting late." She laid the Bible aside. "I'd better be getting home."

Larson walked her back to the cottage, drinking in the sound of her voice as she talked about the day they'd spent at the schoolhouse-raising. She went on about the preacher, his wife, and their children. The night air smelled especially sweet to him, and he was certain it had more to do with the woman walking beside him than the summer breeze.

They stopped at her porch, and he watched her hands move in cadence as she spoke. And in that moment, he knew that no matter what Kathryn had done, no matter what choices she'd made or promises she'd broken, he would love her for the rest of his life. Time suddenly stopped, and an awareness moved over him. *Is this the way you love me, Lord? No matter what I do . . . you'll keep on loving me?*

The inaudible answer reverberated inside him, and a shiver of understanding raced up his spine. How he regretted the years of selfishly seeking his own path, of not knowing God's Word and not caring that he didn't. He'd failed to treat Kathryn with the gentleness and respect she deserved.

He remembered the way Abby looked at Isaiah when Isaiah wasn't watching, and Larson yearned for the chance to win Kathryn's heart all over again. So that she might look at him that same way.

His gaze dropped briefly to the child growing inside her. Was he partly to blame for what she'd done? For her wandering? Had his sin somehow contributed to hers?

As he had in younger years, Larson wondered how God felt about a child born without a proper name. Were the sins of the father and mother passed down to the child? He knew the public disgrace of their sin certainly was, but did God mark the child with the sin? The scornful looks the townspeople had given him and his mother, the names they'd called, were forever in his memory. And these were the same people he'd seen walking to church on Sundays. Some of the men's faces he knew especially well.

"So . . . do you think you'd like to go, Jacob?"

Hearing Kathryn's question pulled him

back. Her head was tilted to one side as she obviously waited for an answer.

"Ah . . . sure," he heard himself say. She smiled and he panicked. What had he just agreed to?

"Then I'll meet you here this Sunday morning. And you'll see if Gabe wants to go to church with us too?"

Church? Larson had to stifle a laugh. The last time he'd been to church had been with Kathryn, years ago, and he'd hated every minute of it. So Isaiah had been right after all, the Lord *did* have a sense of humor.

He looked into Kathryn's eyes and saw the hope there. He also saw his past—a past he couldn't change. But he sure had a choice now, and this Sunday he would take his wife to church.

―――

Kathryn stepped down from Donlyn Mac-Gregor's carriage and looked up at the restaurant, then back at the driver. "Are you certain this is the right place?"

"Yes, ma'am. It's eight o'clock sharp, and Mr. MacGregor is already waiting for you inside."

The bellman opened the restaurant door,

and Kathryn nodded her thanks. Once inside the lobby, she quickly realized this was not the business meeting she'd anticipated. Women patrons wore gowns of fine silk, and the men dressed in suits much like the one she'd fitted for Mr. MacGregor. Kathryn fingered the cotton of her own homespun black dress as her boots sank into the plush pile of the Persian rug.

"Mrs. Jennings, how fine of you to join me, and you're right on time." Donlyn MacGregor appeared at her side and gently looped her arm through his. He wore the very suit she'd tailored for him weeks ago. "You're lookin' radiant this evening."

"Mr. MacGregor, I hardly think this is a proper place for—"

A waiter appeared and bowed slightly at the waist. "This way, sir, madam." He led them away from the room of candlelit tables and down a hallway to a private alcove with windows overlooking the mountain range. The evening sky was awash with color. "I'll return in a moment, sir."

Thankful for being spared the embarrassment of walking through the restaurant, Kathryn carefully withdrew her arm from MacGregor's hold. "Mr. MacGregor, I thought

I was clear about not having dinner with you tonight."

"Ah." He raised a finger. "You declined having dinner with me at Casaroja. You never said anything about dining out, lass." He held a chair for her, his eyes glinting.

Kathryn gave him a pointed look. "I was under the impression that we were going to discuss your offer . . . in a more businesslike setting."

He flashed a smile that she imagined many a woman had succumbed to previously. "Let me see, I believe your exact words were 'a more public place' and 'to leave the door open next time.' This is definitely a public place, Mrs. Jennings, and . . ." He pointed to the door. "I left it open for you. Besides, more deals are decided over a meal of prime rib and fine wine than over any desk, I assure you. Now if you'll kindly wipe that frown from your lovely face and be seated, we can get started with our meeting."

Smoothing the frustration from her expression, Kathryn took a seat. A waiter appeared at her side with a napkin. She nodded, and he laid the lace-edged cloth across her lap. In a flash, memories of the formal dinners and parties she'd attended in her youth came back with startling clarity. Candlelight flickering off fine crystal, its glow reflected in gold-rimmed china, white-gloved servers . . . All reminders of a life she'd willingly traded long ago. But how differently her life had turned out from what she'd planned.

Kathryn waited patiently through the appetizer for her employer to steer the conversation toward business. She was thankful now that she'd eaten such a small meal earlier that evening. The baby had been more active than usual, and she'd simply not been in the mood to eat much.

When he hadn't addressed the matter at hand by the time their meals were served, she decided to do it for him. "Mr. Mac-Gregor, while I appreciate this lovely dinner and your company, I would like to discuss your offer to help me keep my land."

MacGregor took a sip of wine and studied the stemmed glass in his hand. His blue gray eyes looked almost black in the dim light. "Why don't we start by you tellin' me exactly what it is you're wantin', Mrs. Jennings?" His soft brogue came out light and teasing.

Matthew Taylor suddenly came to Kathryn's mind, followed by a twinge of doubt about dealing with Donlyn MacGregor. Matthew's warning rang clear in her memory, along with distrust of her employer's overtures of friendship. MacGregor had introduced her to Mr. Kohlman, sent flowers when Larson's death was made public, and offered her a job at Casaroja. And he was making an offer to lease her land to graze his cattle. Weighing what she knew about him, Kathryn still found him lacking. Yet MacGregor was the only person she knew who had the financial backing at his disposal to help her.

Upon reflection, she couldn't help but wonder if Matthew's warning had been motivated by his affection for her in some way. She pushed the nagging doubt aside, determined to convince Mr. MacGregor to help her.

"I've received a notice from Harold Kohlman about the formal auction of my land. If I don't pay the amount due, it will be sold at an auction in Denver. I only have about two months to obtain the funds I need to pay off the loan."

He rocked his head up and down slowly. "Have you spoken directly with Harold

Kohlman about this? Perhaps something can be worked out between the two of you."

Kathryn took a sip of water to wet her throat. "Yes, I've spoken with him, but he's unwilling to make a concession of any kind."

"You sound bitter toward the man."

"Not bitter," she said, regretting the harshness she'd let harden her tone. "But at my last meeting with him, he—"

MacGregor leaned forward. "Did he say something to upset you, lass?"

Kathryn wished she'd never brought it up. "I'm sorry for implying anything like that, Mr. MacGregor. Honestly, I'd rather keep the topic of our conversation tonight limited to the two of us."

"Nothin' would please me more, Mrs. Jennings." A smooth grin tipped his mouth. He glanced at her plate. "Is there something wrong with your meal? You're for sure not eatin' much."

"No, it's delicious." She picked up her knife and began cutting her steak. "But what I'd like for you to consider, Mr. Mac-Gregor, and I have carefully thought this through"—she looked directly at him—"is for you to advance me the money to pay off my loan with the bank. I promise I'll pay you back every penny within five years."

He nodded in the way an adult might to a small child spinning a fantastic yarn. "And how much money are we talkin' about?"

Ignoring his paternal look, Kathryn finished chewing the bite of steak in her mouth and swallowed. "Fifteen thousand dollars."

His eyebrows rose as he repeated the sum. "That's an enormous sum of money, Mrs. Jennings—especially for someone with no collateral. I'm not aware of any bank that would be makin' that kind of unsecured loan to a man, much less a woman."

"Yes, I realize that. But within five years, if the price of beef holds steady, which I believe it will," she quickly added, "I'll pay you back the entire amount."

"With interest, of course," he said, cocking a brow.

"Yes, of course." But Kathryn hadn't remembered to calculate that and mentally scolded herself at the oversight. She wondered if he would be fair in his percentage.

"So let me get this straight. You're wantin' a fifteen-thousand-dollar loan, which you'll be payin' me back over the next five years, in order to revive a ranch you lost because you lacked the ability to make it successful in the first place? And you havin' no cattle, no ranch hands, nothin' to begin it all with."

His congenial expression contrasted his condescending tone, and Kathryn didn't know quite how to respond to such frankness.

"Actually, losing the cattle wasn't all my fault," she finally managed after a moment, her voice smaller than she would have liked. Bruised pride left her with a bitter aftertaste. "I lost the cattle, true. But there's evidence that they were poisoned."

His eyes flashed to hers. "Evidence they were poisoned? Who would do such a thing to you, lass? And why did you not have men posted to keep watch?"

"Men were posted, but they disappeared. We don't know how it happened, but the examiner said he thought it was intentional."

"That hardly sounds much like evidence to me." MacGregor laid his fork aside and leaned forward, sighing. "Mrs. Jennings, all of that put aside, do you have any idea what an insecure risk you represent? You're an unmarried woman, with a *child*." He accented the word as though it were distasteful. "A woman whose late husband left a pile of debt and a less than stellar business reputation for her to follow."

Kathryn sat numbly as he ticked off the reasons on his fingers. How could he sound so kind when he was tearing her to shreds? Or did he not realize how much he was hurting her?

"Although you're an intelligent woman, you clearly lack the expertise to run a ranch. And may I dare add, this is a man's business, Mrs. Jennings. Hardly fittin' for the weaker gender." He took a bite of steak and chewed slowly. "Plus, the value of land in your region has dropped drastically in recent months." A questioning look moved over his face as one side of his mouth tipped. "You differ with me on this point?" he asked, apparently sensing her disagreement.

"I believe good land will always hold its value, Mr. MacGregor." How many times had she heard Larson say that?

"I'm curious, Mrs. Jennings, has anyone been showin' interest in your property?"

She looked down at the napkin she

fingered in her lap, remembering the day Kohlman had presented that offer to her in his office. Was she foolish not to have taken it? It would have meant security for her and her child. Yet how could she have? It would have—in essence—cost her the land, Larson's land. And possibly the town's rights to the water as well. Random thoughts collided, and she fought to make order of them.

After a moment she lifted her gaze, hoping the businessman would see her determination. "There was one offer, a while back, but I told Mr. Kohlman to refuse it. Next to my child, Mr. MacGregor, this land means more to me than anything else. I haven't advertised it because my earnest desire is to keep it, not sell it."

He waved her last comment off as though it were of little consequence. "There are plots of land for sale all over this area, and the simple fact is, hard as the truth may be to accept, your land is not the most desirable."

Kathryn disagreed but kept her opinion to herself. A grandfather clock on the far wall chimed the ninth hour, and with every slice of its pendulum, her hope of keeping the land seemed to be cut into ever-thinning threads. Larson had specifically chosen that acreage of land. Remembering the first day he'd shown it to her, she could still see the pride shining in his eyes.

MacGregor reached across the table and took her hand. "I'm not sayin' these things to be cruel to you, Mrs. Jennings. I only want you to see what potential risk I, or any-one else for that matter, would be undertak-ing in grantin' you this loan."

"I understand," she whispered, pulling her hand back and wishing the evening were over.

"It's late, and you appear to be tiring." He stood and moved to help Kathryn with her chair. "I'm willin' to lease your land for my cattle, lass. That will provide you with some additional income at least." He mentioned an amount that seemed fair to Kathryn, but she was so discouraged, all she could do was nod her agreement.

By the time they reached the carriage waiting outside, the expensive meal had turned to ash in Kathryn's stomach. She ac-cepted MacGregor's assistance up the steps and was relieved when he chose to occupy the bench seat across from her. The carriage jolted forward. She gripped the molding on the side panel with her left hand—partly to steady herself but mostly to keep from crying.

Larson, I tried to keep your dream alive. I tried. . . . Her wedding ring cut into her palm, but she squeezed harder, suddenly furious with him for not having trusted her enough to tell her about the financial standing of the ranch. Why hadn't he shared that with her? She'd made it unmistakably clear to him she wanted him to succeed.

With that thought, the force of Kathryn's anger deflated. Had her expectation for Larson to make a success of the ranch—of himself—been the very thing that had caused him to keep the truth from her in the first place? She closed her eyes as truth laid bare her motives—motives she now wished she'd been made to question long ago.

They'd passed through town and were on the road leading to Casaroja when Mac-Gregor leaned forward. "Mrs. Jennings, again, I did not say those things to be intentionally cruel to you." He moved to claim the seat beside her on the bench.

Not looking at him, Kathryn scooted closer toward the window.

"I feel like I've hurt you in some way, and that was never my intention, lass." His brogue thickened. "Perhaps you'll allow me to join you for a cup of tea back at your cottage when we return home." He trailed a finger down the side of her arm. "Give me a chance to smooth things over between us."

Kathryn narrowed her eyes at his invitation and continued to stare out the window. The idea of smoothing anything over with Donlyn MacGregor held not the least bit of interest to her. And if he hadn't intended to wound her with what he'd said earlier, she couldn't begin to imagine what he might say with malice aforethought.

As the vague outline of Casaroja's main house came into view, a possibility began to weave itself through Kathryn's mind. The driver pulled around to the back of the main house and stopped in front of her cottage. When MacGregor offered his hand in assistance, she took it and climbed down.

Her plan still forming, Kathryn turned when she reached the porch. "While I cannot say that I appreciate the things you've said to me tonight, Mr. MacGregor, I do appreciate your honesty. It's helped me to see my situation—and my opportunities—more clearly."

"Actually, that was my exact intention." Gently taking hold of her arm, he inclined his head toward her as though they shared a more intimate relationship. "I hope some of what I've said will help you decide on what steps to take next."

"Oh, it has." Kathryn reached down deep for confidence and forced herself to look him in the eye. "I've decided to sell the land myself, in parcels, before it goes into fore-closure."

For an instant, his hand tightened un-comfortably on her arm. "But you said that land meant more to you than anything else, that you could never—" A tight smile turned his mouth. "You said earlier tonight that you wouldn't sell."

"I was mistaken, Mr. MacGregor. There *is* something that means far more to me, and you've helped me see that. I won't sell the entire property. I'll keep the homestead and the acreage around it, including first rights to the stream. But by selling off the rest, with proportional access to Fountain Creek, perhaps I can manage to secure the funds I need. My husband chose that land with great care, and I believe others will see its worth, even if you do not." She put a hand on the door. "Thank you again for a lovely dinner. Good evening."

Kathryn closed the door to the cottage behind her and quickly flicked the lock into place.

———

Two days later, as she went about her duties, Kathryn heard footsteps in the main hallway and saw MacGregor striding toward her. Something about the determined look in his eyes sent her pulse racing. Had she pushed him too far the other night with her clear lack of interest?

"Will you accompany me to my office, please, Mrs. Jennings?" Once she was inside, MacGregor closed the door behind her and motioned for her to sit.

Kathryn prepared herself for the worst. Would MacGregor go so far as to dismiss her simply for refusing his advances? Surely not. Nevertheless, her mind tumbled forward, wondering where she would live, what her next employ would be, and who might hire a woman seven months heavy with child.

"Mrs. Jennings, I've been thinking about our conversation two nights ago and deeply regret some of what I said to you."

A look bordering on contrition edged his thin smile, and Kathryn felt a wind of caution sweep through her. Donlyn MacGregor was only a man, she reminded herself as she watched him. A powerful one, yes. Wealthy, most certainly. But still, just a man. One who could help her realize a dream if he so determined. She reminded herself to breathe.

He glanced away, his gaze settling somewhere on the bookshelves lining the walls. "Frankly, Mrs. Jennings, I was angry at the way you refused my attention. At the way you have repeatedly refused me since the day we met." He looked up then and placed his hand, palm down, on a thick legal document atop his desk. Kathryn's eyes immediately went to it. "But after much consideration, I have decided to give you what you've asked of me. I'll loan you the money so you can keep your land. All of it. But first, we need to discuss the terms of our agreement."

CHAPTER TWENTY

Larson pulled the curry brush over the mare's coat, working in smooth, rhythmic strokes, thankful for the breeze that helped cool the heat of the midday sun. At the horse's whinny, he looked up and across the corrals to see Donlyn MacGregor peering inside the stable. Apparently MacGregor hadn't noticed him yet.

Though he'd glimpsed Casaroja's owner several times since being here, Larson hadn't seen him up close. Not since he'd met with him the previous fall when Mac-Gregor had come to him wanting to buy the south pastureland as well as the homestead acreage. MacGregor had said he needed additional grazing land and had pushed him hard to sell, but Larson had refused. Twice. He knew it was a lie. MacGregor already had enough land to keep twice his herd.

MacGregor turned in Larson's direction and stilled.

Larson straightened as the man approached. He offered his hand first. "Sir." He worked hard to keep the spite from his voice.

MacGregor openly studied his face, distaste clearly written in his steely eyes. "I'm Donlyn MacGregor, the owner of Casaroja."

"Yes, sir. I know who you are. My name's Jacob. Jacob Brantley," he added, thinking quickly.

"Brantley," MacGregor repeated. "Stewartson was tellin' me we had a new hire a while back. I thought I knew everyone here, but I don't recall seein' you before." His tone clearly stated that he would have remembered such an encounter.

"I've been here about a month. I mostly keep to myself and just do my job."

MacGregor eyed him, then gave him a look that said he understood why. Larson turned back to currying the mare.

His employer walked around the horse to

face him. "Where were you before you came to Casaroja?"

"I ran cattle down south at Johnson's place for a while. He has a nice spread there. Then before that I was up north of Denver for a few months." That was stretching it a bit, but technically it was the truth.

MacGregor laughed in his throat. "Johnson's stock doesn't come close to comparing with Casaroja's. I'm sure you can see the difference."

"You do have fine animals." The compliment nearly choked him.

"I only purchase the best." MacGregor ran a hand over the sleek black coat of the mare. "It's costly, but worth the investment. You'll discover that after workin' here for a while." He paused for a moment. "If you want the best, you must be willin' to pay to get it."

Noting the shift in MacGregor's tone, Larson looked back to follow the man's line of vision. Kathryn was walking toward them from the house.

"Now there's a real beauty, man." MacGregor's voice dropped low. "Somethin' worth an investment, for sure."

A stab of possessiveness twisted Larson's insides.

MacGregor went to meet her. "Mrs. Jennings, what a nice surprise."

Larson watched her but didn't say anything. Kathryn nodded politely to MacGregor, then looked over the man's shoulder. She offered Larson a smile, and he felt the tightening lessen in his gut.

Her hair shone like gold in the afternoon sun. She'd never been more beautiful to him.

"You're needed at the main house, sir," she told MacGregor. "Mr. Kohlman is here to see you. He's waiting in your office."

"Indeed," MacGregor answered, taking hold of her arm. "And would you do me the great honor of accompanyin' me back, Kathryn? I enjoyed our evenin' together and look forward to many more like it."

Larson's eyes met Kathryn's just before she turned away. He didn't know what to make of the look of surprise on her face.

Not watching them leave, he worked the brush over the mare's coat until the black coat gleamed almost blue in the hot sun. When he was done, his long-sleeved shirt was soaked clean through and his shoulder throbbed with pain.

———

Jacob sat quietly beside her as the wagon jostled along the parched, rutted road. From the moment he'd helped her onto the bench seat, Kathryn had tried drawing him into conversation. They still had a good half hour before arriving at church, and she'd so looked forward to talking with him again. Jacob's responses, though kind, were reserved. She'd caught him staring at her twice since they'd left Casaroja, and for some reason, that gave her hope.

Kathryn turned her head slightly to try to read his mood. Unfortunately, the right side of Jacob's face bore more damage than did the left, and any tension in his jaw or slight turn of his mouth that might have hinted at his feelings lay masked beneath the scarring.

Despite the heat, Jacob wore his customary long-sleeved shirt and loose-fitting dungarees, with a knit cap almost totally covering his ears. His beard grew in much thinner and in patches on the right side of his face. He'd let the whiskers grow, to help cover the scarring no doubt, and kept them neatly trimmed, much different from the first time she'd seen him in town. It looked like he'd gained weight in recent weeks, and his shirts didn't look nearly so large on him. Even sitting silently beside her, Jacob radiated a gentleness that drew her, and Kathryn wished she could hear him laugh again.

Jacob suddenly cleared his throat and repositioned his glasses. Kathryn glanced away, not having meant to look overlong. He was sensitive about people staring, and that's exactly what she'd been doing, but not for the reasons he might imagine.

"Thank you for taking me to church this morning." She tried again after a moment. "I'm sorry Gabe couldn't join us."

Jacob urged the pair of bay mares to a faster trot. "I did ask him, like I told you I would. He said he'd come, but this morning he said the boss needed him to work."

Kathryn caught a trace of defensiveness in his tone. "I didn't mean to imply that you hadn't asked him, Jacob. I'm fine with it being just the two of us. Really. I've been looking forward to your company."

He said nothing.

Waiting for him to respond, Kathryn sighted a post about a hundred feet down the road and promised herself that if Jacob hadn't said something by the time they reached it, she would inquire about his sullen mood.

They passed the post, and Kathryn wondered if promises made to oneself really counted. She sat up a little straighter, summoning her nerve.

"Jacob—"

"Mrs. Jennings—"

They both turned to each other and gave a nervous laugh.

"Please, Jacob, you go first."

He kept his gaze trained forward, his thumbs rubbing the worn leather of the reins in his hands. "You can tell me this is none of my business, ma'am. And you'd be within your right, but I've been wondering about something the Carlsons mentioned when we were at the picnic."

"And what is that?"

"The pastor said something about your having gone through a recent loss."

He turned and looked at her then, and from the tilt of his chin, Kathryn got the feeling he wasn't looking only at her eyes. Strangely, it didn't bother her, because she sensed nothing inappropriate in his stare, and besides, hadn't she been studying his face just moments ago? The morning sunshine hit his glasses just right and, for an instant, she saw the faintest outline of his eyes.

He faced forward. "I'm just wondering what your loss has been. 'Course I can guess some of it from the dresses you wear."

Kathryn looked down at her dress and then rested a hand on her abdomen. She hadn't expected this sharp of a turn in the conversation. "Have you always been this straightforward, Jacob?"

He shook his head. "No, ma'am. Guess I picked it up somewhere along the way."

Kathryn thought she detected a smile fighting the edges of his mouth. The church building came into view, and she wondered how much to share in the brief time they had left. She quickly decided that Jacob had been honest with her and the Carlsons about parts of his life, and she owed him no less.

"I buried my husband earlier this year.

That's when I first met Patrick Carlson, in fact. He spoke at my husband's funeral. And he did a fine job remembering him too, especially never having—" Her voice caught, and Kathryn realized how long it had been since she'd spoken her husband's name aloud. "Especially since he'd never known Larson." She looked across the valley toward the cemetery. The warm breeze suddenly felt cool on her cheeks, and Kathryn dabbed the tears on her face. She felt Jacob watching but didn't turn.

"So your husband wasn't a church-going man?"

"No, he wasn't. But he was still a good man. He just had a . . . a difficult upbringing that made it hard for him to be around people. I remember the day he agreed to come to church with me, just that once. It was years ago, before the Carlsons moved to town." She sighed, remembering the hymns they'd sung. "The songs we sang filled my heart to overflowing, but with every note we sang, I sensed his discomfort. He didn't want to be there—I felt it. So I finally told him I'd had enough and that we could leave."

Jacob kept his focus on the road and

Kathryn did the same. The prairie grass growing tall by the road's edge quivered as they passed.

"But you hadn't had enough, had you?"

A rush of tears rose without warning. Kathryn swallowed hard and shook her head. "No. That hunger has always been inside me." She turned to him. "Same as dwells inside you, I think."

Jacob started to speak, then stopped. His hands tightened on the reins. "Did he know? Your husband, I mean. About how you felt?"

Kathryn wondered how they'd drifted down this delicate path, a path she hadn't had the courage to walk yet, but part of her welcomed the reflection. Perhaps it would help provide some clues to the answers she still sought about her marriage to Larson and how they'd grown apart, especially toward the end. "I did tell him once that I wanted . . . more. More of him, more of us. But then time goes by and things between a husband and wife settle. Even if life isn't what you thought it would be, nevertheless, you're there. And you get used to things the way they are. Time passes, and you almost forget what it was that you wanted at the outset. Then all of a sudden, out of the blue, things happen that make you remember. Then it almost feels selfish to ask for something more when you're not even certain there's something more to be had. And yet, sometimes I . . ." She looked down at her hands clasped in her lap. "I still felt so empty inside."

Kathryn bowed her head, suddenly self-conscious at having rambled on and afraid she might appear selfish in Jacob's eyes. She looked across the fields to the nearly finished schoolhouse. Uncomfortable as it might be, it did feel good to talk about Larson to someone else, to finally give voice to misgivings that still haunted her solitude.

"In answer to your question, Jacob, I think he knew. It was always a kind of . . . unspoken boundary that separated us."

Jacob guided the team of horses down the lane leading to church. "Why didn't you ever just tell him outright?"

Though she doubted he intended it, Kathryn sensed accusation in Jacob's question. And she acknowledged the guilt laid at her feet. "I should have been more honest with him, I know that now. I shouldn't have expected him just to know what I needed or wanted." She closed her eyes as the truth surfaced. "I guess I was always afraid it would hurt Larson in some way if he knew I wasn't completely happy, and I didn't want to do that. I loved my husband very much, even though there were times when—"

Kathryn suddenly caught herself. She blinked to clear the memories and forced a smile. "I'm certain that's more than you wanted to hear, Jacob. Maybe that'll keep you from asking me such a straightforward question next time." She tried for a light-hearted laugh as she smoothed her skirt.

A few wagons dotted the yard, and she spotted Patrick Carlson standing in the doorway greeting people. Jacob brought the team to a halt in the churchyard and set the brake. They sat in silence for a moment, neither moving. The breeze whistled through the cottonwoods overhead.

"How did your husband die?"

Surprised again by Jacob's directness, Kathryn slowly let out a breath. "We really don't know for certain. Most people seem to think he got lost in the storm on Christmas Day, but I find that hard to believe. In all the years I knew him, Larson never lost his way in this land. Not once. He loved it." She decided not to mention that he had been shot—it somehow seemed unimportant now—plus she didn't want to risk planting doubt in Jacob's mind about the kind of man Larson had been. Tears stung her eyes. "He loved this land more than anything else." *Even more than me.* She suddenly wished they would change the subject.

Jacob climbed down and came around to help her. Kathryn offered him her hand and was surprised when he slipped his arms around her to help her down. The strength in his arms was unexpected. He steadied her, his hands lingering on her shoulders. She felt his stare but didn't look up. Why did her pulse skip to such an unnatural rhythm?

But she knew the reason. It was the reminiscing about Larson, followed by the unquestionable certainty that though their marriage had been far from perfect, he had taken a part of her with him when he died. A part she needed in order to feel complete.

"I'm sorry you lost your husband."

Moved by the emotion in his roughened whisper, Kathryn lifted her eyes. "Thank you, Jacob. But I think I lost my husband years ago."

———

"We want you both to join us for lunch today, and I'm not taking no for an answer," Hannah Carlson said following the service. "Lilly's even made another pie."

Larson noted the look that passed between the two women and wondered at Kathryn's frown.

"Hannah, I hope you didn't . . ." Kathryn whispered. Larson recognized the undercurrent of displeasure in her tone.

Hannah squeezed Kathryn's arm tight and leaned close. "I didn't, Kathryn, honestly. But there is another guest coming, someone Patrick invited just a moment ago. He's new in town and is a widower himself, for five years now." Her look grew soft. "Despite my kidding, I know it's too soon for you to be thinking of courting. Everyone realizes you're still in mourning, and I've made certain he knows this is only lunch, nothing more. Please come, Kathryn. I'd love to spend some time with you, and Lilly and Bobby will be so disappointed if you don't." She glanced back behind her. "Listen, I've got to go stand with Patrick for a minute. You two can go on to the house. I've already given Jacob directions on how to get there." She touched Larson's arm before turning. "I'm so glad you're joining us today too. Lilly can't wait to show you her new pony."

Larson helped Kathryn back into the wagon, watching as she searched the crowd. No doubt she was looking for the gentleman Patrick had invited. He climbed up beside her and waited for the wagons to clear out before flicking the reins. Kathryn was quiet next to him, which suited him just fine. Taking the long way through town to the Carlsons' house, he welcomed the time to think.

He'd tried listening to Patrick's sermon, but the things Kathryn had said to him kept churning in his mind. And no matter how he looked at it, he kept coming back to the same conclusion he'd reached the other night. Kathryn deserved better than what he could give her. He'd had his chance and failed. The question he struggled with now was . . . did he love her enough to stay in the grave?

He maneuvered the wagon down a side street and saw the brothel looming ahead.

Sensing Kathryn's awareness of it, he stole a look at her. Her eyes were narrowed, and a slight frown creased her brow.

Through all this, Larson couldn't help but think of Matthew Taylor and wonder how he fit into Kathryn's life. He hadn't seen Taylor since Kathryn had moved to Casaroja. Did that mean Taylor wasn't the father of Kathryn's child after all? Or that they'd reached some sort of understanding?

As they passed the brothel, Larson studied the row of curtained windows on the second floor of the clapboard building. Maybe the child wasn't Taylor's. . . . Maybe Kathryn didn't know who the child's father was.

Though it still wounded him to think that the baby Kathryn nurtured wasn't his own, somehow it hurt him even more to know that her child would share his name after all—a name he'd heard repeatedly as a young boy when he walked through town, the name he'd been running from his entire life.

Hannah Carlson was as gifted at cooking as she was at making coffee. The meal was delicious, and Larson felt especially grateful for Lilly's insistence that he sit by her. It had helped him feel less out of place. Despite Hannah's assertion that their male guest wasn't interested in Kathryn, from his vantage point, interest was written all over the man's face.

Larson looked across the table to Kathryn and the man seated beside her. He guessed Michael Barton to be about Kathryn's age, maybe a little older. Tall with dark blond hair and a mustache, Barton seemed to be a nice enough fellow. Regrettably so. He'd been attentive to Kathryn throughout the meal, asking questions about her upbringing and how long she'd been in town. Kathryn's answers had been truthful but hadn't invited further discussion.

When the conversation turned to her deceased husband, Kathryn deftly turned the topic of conversation back to Barton. To the man's credit, he seemed sensitive to her move and didn't push. Regardless, Larson kept looking for something to dislike in him.

Hannah stood and started clearing the dishes. Kathryn did likewise.

Lilly tugged on Larson's sleeve. "Mr. Jacob, do you want to come see my pony out back? I named her Honey because she's so sweet." Lilly giggled.

"Sure, I'd love to see her."

Michael Barton rose. "Mrs. Jennings," he said a bit too quickly. He looked down at the table, then back to Kathryn. "Would you like to take a walk with me? I could show you my law offices just around the corner. It's not too far."

An awkward silence followed. Larson read the expressions around the table. Sincere surprise lit the Carlsons' faces, and Kathryn's as well. Except he saw a hint of empathy in hers.

Barton's face reddened as the pause lengthened. "Perhaps another time would be better."

Kathryn gave him a genuine smile. "Actually, Mr. Barton, let me help Hannah with these dishes and then a walk would be nice. Perhaps Bobby could join us too?"

Barton noticeably relaxed. "Yes, ma'am. That'd be fine."

Half an hour later, Larson leaned on the top rail of the fence outside the corral and watched the two of them walk side-by-side down the street, Bobby running on ahead. Admittedly, Kathryn and Michael Barton made a striking couple. He turned his attention to Lilly, who sat astride her new pony.

Lilly had a natural rhythm as she rode, especially for one so young, except she tended to lean forward too much. "Keep your feet down," he tried to call to her, but his voice wouldn't sustain the effort. He'd made do without Abby's tea over the last few weeks, but wished he'd asked her for the ingredients so he could make more.

"I take it you haven't told Kathryn your secret?"

Larson's heart misfired at the question. Patrick took a place at the fence beside him, but Larson didn't dare look at the man.

"As intuitive as they think they are"—Patrick waved at Lilly as she rode past—"sometimes women just don't see what's right in front of them."

Larson finally turned and stared at his friend, wondering how Patrick could approach this so casually. How had Patrick learned about him? Could Larson convince him to keep his secret? "Listen, Patrick, I don't know how you found out, but I guarantee you I have my reasons for handling things like this. I beg you not to say anything to Kathryn. She's better off this way. We both are."

Patrick shook his head, smiling. "You

don't give yourself enough credit, my friend. Have you ever noticed the way Kathryn looks at you? I don't know if she's even aware of it herself. I thought I saw something at the picnic but wasn't sure, but I definitely saw her stealing glances at you during dinner today. I dare say Kathryn Jennings is far more interested in you than that successful young lawyer."

Realizing he'd misunderstood Patrick's question, Larson's pulse slowed. "So what you're saying is that you think I'm interested in Kathryn and that *she's* interested in . . . me." Relief trickled through him. He coerced a laugh and leaned against the fence, thankful for the support. "Kathryn is just staring at the scars, that's all."

Patrick huffed and shook his head. "And I thought you were a man of wisdom." A smile softened the mild rebuke. "Only a fool denies the truth when it's clearly set before him, Jacob." He nodded toward the street. "I'm afraid Michael Barton is a man destined for disappointment." He clapped Larson on the back. "And you, my friend, need to decide whether Mrs. Kathryn Jennings is worth the risk."

CHAPTER TWENTY-ONE

A warm August breeze rippled the curtains of the half-opened bedroom window, and Kathryn managed to reposition herself in bed, wishing she could go back to sleep. Her gaze fell on the shadowed contours of the cradle in the corner, an unexpected gift from Miss Maudie earlier that week. The baby blanket Kathryn had knitted was draped over the side, as were two sets of booties she'd finished recently. A sudden movement in her belly got Kathryn's full attention. Apparently her little one didn't know it wasn't dawn yet. Kathryn pushed herself up, then slowly swung her legs over the side of the bed, glad for the convenience of the indoor water closet.

Today was Friday, and the hours stretched before her unspoiled. Miss Maudie had decided she'd been working too hard and had insisted she take the entire day to rest and relax. Kathryn hadn't argued. The weight she'd gained in the past month, along with the heat of late summer, made her uncomfortable, but she tried not to complain.

She lit an oil lamp and sliced pieces of bread and cheese, then sat down at the small breakfast table. Kathryn picked up the letter she'd penned the evening before, fully expecting nothing to come of it. While her father had never openly rejected her, even after her marriage to Larson, his continued lack of initiative to be involved in her life had been deterrent enough. But Kathryn felt certain her mother would have wanted her to give the relationship with her father another try, especially now.

She sealed and addressed the envelope and tucked it into her Bible. After dressing quickly, she snuffed out the oil lamp, grabbed the Bible and a blanket and left the cottage.

While she still missed the seclusion of her

cabin in the foothills and the beauty belonging to the mountains and the stream, she'd discovered a bluff a short distance beyond the corrals that afforded a semblance of privacy and a spectacular view of the sunrise. It was no more than half a mile away, and Kathryn easily found her way in the pink light of dawn.

She spread the blanket, sank down, and placed her hands over her unborn child, cradling it as best she could. In little more than a month, she could actually be holding the precious gift. The doctor she'd seen all those months ago had said late September, but Kathryn hoped it would be a little early.

Lying back on the blanket, she watched the fading smattering of stars gradually surrender their brilliance. *Thank you for my relationship with you, Lord. For my child, for a safe home, even for MacGregor's willingness to loan me the money so I can keep my land.*

She hadn't spoken with MacGregor since signing the loan papers, and he'd been clear on the point that the agreement was to remain between the two of them—along with Kohlman, who would personally handle the transfer of funds. Kathryn had read through the thick document, but admittedly, some of the legal jargon had gone over her head. MacGregor encouraged her to have an attorney in town review it, and when the lawyer she met with gave his approval, she'd signed. Her child would have a legacy from his father after all.

As the sun rose, Kathryn continued to count her blessings. But no matter how many times she counted, Jacob kept returning to the list.

The man remained a mystery to her. Last Sunday on the way home from church, he'd been more talkative than she could remember, which surprised her because he'd been so quiet at the Carlsons'. Except with Lilly. That sweet girl could draw a laugh from him with hardly any effort, and Kathryn loved hearing Jacob laugh.

A bird trilled a morning song nearby, and Kathryn turned onto her side to lessen the ache that had started in her lower back. Jacob was so different from Larson, yet there were similarities. She loved Jacob's laugh, his gentleness with the stock, his quiet manner . . . and the way he looked at her. Two days ago she'd felt someone's stare and had turned to see Jacob standing by the corral, watching her. Having been discovered, he'd smiled and waved before disappearing back inside.

Somehow it felt wrong for her to think of Jacob and Larson in the same breath. She would give anything to have Larson back, but that would never happen. She would see him again some day, she held hope. But not in this life.

Dawn gradually spilled over the prairie and turned the pewter sky a cloudless blue. Kathryn read for the next hour in the book of John. The words of Jesus drew her in. *I am the good shepherd, and know my sheep, and am known of mine. As the Father knoweth me, even so know I the Father: and I lay down my life for the sheep.* "You know me perfectly, Lord. Help me to know you that well."

As she read on, she sensed a stirring inside her. *My sheep hear my voice, and I know them, and they follow me: And I give unto them eternal life; and they shall never perish, neither shall any man pluck them out of my hand.* She liked that thought especially—that no one could snatch her out of His hand. "No matter what happens to me, Lord, you are with me. I may lose everything else—like Larson and our life together—but I will always have you." After reading a while longer, she decided to head back.

She stood and bent to gather the blanket.

A sudden tightening in her abdomen doubled her over. She sank to the ground, panting. The pain gradually receded but the next one hit seconds later. Gasping, she fisted the blanket in her hands until her knuckles turned white. The tightening eased, but she braced herself for another.

Nothing came.

Letting out the breath she'd been holding, she glanced over her shoulder. The roofline of the main house crested above the stables and bunkhouses in the distance. She called out but doubted anyone would hear. Putting a hand to her forehead, she felt the cool layer of perspiration.

It took her twice as long to walk the short distance back, but at least the cramping didn't return. She went directly to the stables and heard the sound of feed hitting a tin trough. She spotted him in the last stall, hefting a burlap bag to his shoulder.

"Jacob?"

He turned. "Kathryn!"

The alarm in his voice made her stop. In the dim light, she could almost make out the outline of his eyes. He wasn't wearing his glasses. She took a step, curiosity driving her forward, but he quickly turned away.

Jacob dropped the bag and mumbled something Kathryn couldn't hear. Seconds later he walked from the stall, feed bag in hand, glasses in place. "How are you this morning?" His brow creased as he came closer. "Are you all right? You look pale."

"I'm worried about . . . my baby." Another pain, a small one this time, twinged her abdomen and fear overcame her awkwardness at speaking about such private things. "I went for a walk this morning and started having pains. They're not as bad now, but I think something may be wrong. I was wondering if you could take me into town to see the doctor."

Jacob dropped the feedbag and looked up to the loft. "Gabe!"

Seconds later, Gabe peered over the railing, smiling. "Morning, Miss Kathryn."

"I'm taking Mrs. Jennings into town. Can you take care of things here for a while?"

"Sure, Jacob. No problem. You take care of Miss Kathryn."

Kathryn carefully eased back on the doctor's table and slipped her hand down and around the full swell of her belly. She whispered a prayer in her heart, assuring her baby that all would be well, then tried to believe it herself.

"You'll feel a bit of pressure during the examination, Mrs. Jennings." Dr. Frank Hadley's voice heightened the quiet of the small room off of his office. "Try and relax. It'll be over soon."

Kathryn blew out a shaky breath and in the same instant, wondered if he'd say the same thing if he were the one on the table. But at the sudden spasm in her loins, her humor fell away.

Oh, God, I'm scared. Please don't let anything happen to my baby.

She clenched her eyes shut and forced herself to breathe slowly. In and out. In and out. Every muscle in her body seemed to constrict. *Concentrate on something else.* She thought of Jacob waiting on the other side of the door and felt unexpected comfort. They'd passed the cemetery moments ago on their way into town. If Jacob didn't mind, she hoped to have some time to visit there before they headed back today. *Larson, I wish you were here with me now. To watch our child grow inside me. Then to hold our son or daughter—*

"You may feel a slight twinge now, Mrs.

Jennings," Dr. Hadley said quietly from the end of the table.

Kathryn winced at the momentary discomfort and felt a tear trail down the side of her temple and into her hairline. After all the years of praying and waiting for a child, this was not as she had dreamed it would be. Instead of her first child's birth being filled with wonder and hopeful anticipation, fear had swiftly marched in and set up camp in every corner of her heart.

Nothing can snatch you out of my hand.

So real was the whisper, Kathryn almost felt the soft breath of it on her face. Her whole body trembled.

Dr. Hadley's hands stilled. "Are you all right, Mrs. Jennings?"

"Yes," she answered softly, still cherishing the hushed echo of the voice. *Yes, I will trust you, Lord. I'm safe in your hands.*

Then a feeling swept through her, one not new to her. Kathryn knew the thought was ludicrous—she'd buried him months ago—but it still felt as though Larson were alive. With everything in her, she could still feel him, see his handsome face, his dark hair curling at the back of his neck, the strong line of his jaw, and those blue eyes that captured her so completely.

"Please, Mrs. Jennings, you must relax." The doctor's voice intoned a firmness it hadn't before.

"Yes, sir." And she tried to comply.

Though Dr. Hadley's manner was gentle enough, the necessary intimacies of soon-to-be-motherhood were unnerving and foreign. She'd come to marriage a virgin, and Larson's touch had been her only experience. He'd been a patient lover, exquisitely gentle, even in the midst of passion.

The doctor stood. "Have you noticed any bleeding, Mrs. Jennings?"

Panic tightened Kathryn's chest. *Bleeding?* "Is something wrong with my baby, Dr. Hadley?"

"No, no, your baby is fine, I assure you." He lightly touched her knee. "But you were right to come in and see me." With kindness, he leveled his gaze. "Now, has there been any bleeding?"

Seeing assurance in his eyes, Kathryn calmed. "No, there hasn't."

"Good. I'll check one more thing, and then we'll be done." He reached beneath the sheet and gently probed her upper abdomen.

The child inside her protested, and Kathryn drew in a breath, marveling again at the miracle of life so quickly overtaking the space inside her. She wondered too, with a brush of fear, what it would be like when the child decided to push its way into the world.

Finished with his examination, Dr. Hadley crossed the room and washed his hands in the basin. "Would you like me to call your husband in before we talk?"

Kathryn sat and repositioned the sheet over herself for privacy. "Oh, Jacob's not my husband," she corrected. Then seeing the rise of the doctor's brow, she quickly added, "My husband died earlier this year. Jacob is my friend." She covered the unborn baby with a hand. "But that's why this child . . . my husband's child . . . is especially important to me."

Dr. Hadley nodded with understanding, a sad smile turning his mouth. "I'm sorry for your loss, Mrs. Jennings, but you needn't worry about yourself or your child. The pains you experienced this morning are normal. They're your body's way of preparing for the baby's birth. You're a strong woman in excellent health, and the baby appears to be fine. A strong, healthy heartbeat, and right where he, or she, needs to be for almost eight months along." He encouraged her to eat plenty to nourish the life inside her and to get ample rest. She could maintain her normal routine but was to rest immediately if fatigued.

"Well, Mrs. Jennings, if you don't have any other questions for me, I'll leave you to dress. I'll be happy to help deliver your child when the time comes. And if you need anything, please call on me." He closed the door behind him when he left.

Kathryn carefully stood and moved behind the screen to dress. Stepping back into her dress, she felt the bulge in her pocket and pulled out the music box. She gently rotated the key on the side and set it on the chair as she finished dressing.

The fragile notes seemed especially slow, as though the very act of striking the chords inside presented a strain. The music box wasn't of the finest quality, but Kathryn hoped the parts weren't already failing because she played it so often. As she buttoned her bodice, she listened to the tune. Somehow the slower, stuttered syncopation better matched the cadence of her mood today.

When she emerged from the exam room, she found Jacob standing by the window, waiting for her.

He stepped forward. "Are you all right? Is the baby . . . ?"

She smiled. "I'm fine and the baby is too. The doctor said what I experienced was normal." She looked down. "I'm a bit embarrassed to have made you bring me all the way into town for nothing."

"It wasn't for nothing. We know you're all right and that your baby is too."

Kathryn laid a hand to Jacob's arm. *What a gentle, thoughtful man.* "Thank you, Jacob." When he covered her hand with his, the tingle from his touch moved through her body. Surprised by her response to him, she gently withdrew her hand. "Well, we can head back now, if you're ready."

He paused. "You're sure you're okay?"

Concern layered his soft, raspy voice, and Kathryn would have given much to see his eyes at that moment. "Yes, I'm fine, Jacob. Really."

He headed to the door, but the sound of one opening behind her drew Kathryn's attention.

Dr. Hadley appeared. "Ah, good, Mrs. Jennings, you're still here. There was one more thing I wanted to tell you. Moderate walks are fine, even encouraged. But please ask someone to accompany you from now on. It wouldn't do for you to be alone and have a recurrence of what happened this morning. Especially as your time approaches."

"Certainly, Doctor. Thank you."

Kathryn accepted Jacob's help into the wagon and noticed a smile tilting the left side of his mouth as he climbed up beside her.

"Personally, I've always enjoyed a good walk," he said, then gave the reins a flick.

Kathryn couldn't help but chuckle at his implication. How was it possible? The closer she looked at the man beside her, the more she got to know him, the less she saw his scars.

———

The relief Larson felt at discovering that Kathryn's baby was all right, that Kathryn was all right, still coursed through him. But when she'd laid a hand to his arm a moment before, a reckless seed of hope had taken root inside him—entirely without consent. A hope that perhaps Kathryn might someday learn to see past his ugliness to the man he'd become, to the husband who still loved her and who would love her child, if given the chance.

In a way, he felt a kinship with the tiny life growing inside her womb. From reading the Bible, he'd come to know that God didn't love her baby any less because of the way it was conceived. He sighed to himself, wishing he'd learned that sooner in relation to his own life.

"Jacob, would you mind if we made a brief stop before leaving town?" Kathryn's voice sounded hesitant. "If you can spare the time."

"Sure, where to?" Anything to prolong being with her.

She slipped something from the pages of the Bible she'd left on the buckboard. "I'd like to stop by the post office and mercantile, and then . . . visit my husband's grave."

It took him a minute to process her question, and Larson noted again the hesitance in her tone. "Sure. . . . I'd like to visit his grave with you, if that's okay." Her smile was answer enough.

He waited in the wagon while she went inside the post office and then the mercantile. Visiting his own grave with his widow wasn't something he'd thought he'd ever do, and frankly he was surprised that he'd even suggested it.

Kathryn walked from the mercantile minutes later with a bouquet of fresh flowers wrapped in paper. Larson climbed down to help her.

"Kathryn!"

They both turned. Seeing the man walking toward them, a mixture of jealousy and dread curdled Larson's stomach.

Kathryn's face lit when Matthew Taylor hugged her. "Matthew, it's so good to see you. How've you been?"

Taylor's hands rested a mite too long on her shoulders before releasing her.

"How have *you* been is more like it." Taylor's gaze swept over her. He shook his head. "You look beautiful, Kathryn."

A blush colored her cheeks. "Thank you." Then she glanced back at Larson. "Matthew, I'd like you to meet a good friend of mine."

As she made the introductions, Larson measured the man beside him. Things he'd not noticed about Taylor before, and would rather not have noticed now, caught his attention. The man's broad-shouldered stance conveyed undeniable strength and command. His hair was thick, cropped close at the base of his neck, and his jaw was freshly shaven and smooth. Larson imagined women might consider Taylor handsome and wondered if Kathryn did.

"Jacob and I work together at Casaroja. We both started working there about the same time and . . ." Larson thought he detected a slight frown in Taylor's eyes. Did Taylor disapprove of Kathryn's working there? "Jacob manages the stables at Casaroja," she continued, drawing Larson into the conversation with a look. "Matthew Taylor used to work on my husband's ranch." She looked down briefly. "Things were hard after Larson died, and Matthew helped me get through a very difficult time."

Yeah, he helped you, all right, and himself. Larson forced himself to meet Taylor's eyes, waiting to see disgust there—waiting for the reaction that would give him reason to hate Matthew Taylor all the more.

Taylor extended his hand. "It's good to meet you, Jacob." His grip was firm, his eyes taking in the obvious scarring but returning only warmth. No condemnation. "So, Kathryn, you work at MacGregor's ranch now?" he asked, turning his attention back. "Exactly how did that come about?"

"Actually, I believe it's by God's design that I'm there." Her smile looked coerced. "It's been a very good situation for me, and the pay is excellent."

Taylor's look held doubt but he finally nodded. "Well, that explains why I haven't seen you around town. And I've been looking," he added softly.

The man's obvious affection wore on Larson. First because it was his wife Taylor was looking at, and second because the look in the man's eyes appeared to be genuine. And the glow in Kathryn's face didn't help. If not mistaking the signs, Larson guessed that Matthew Taylor truly loved Kathryn. But even if he did love her, it didn't make right the wrong that he and Kathryn had done together. *If* he was the father.

"I'm sorry, Matthew. It all happened so fast. I got the job and then moved out there soon after. I've been busy with work since then, and being so far out of town, I . . ." She stopped abruptly. "Honestly, Matthew, I think I just needed some time away from . . . everything."

". . . from you," is what Larson heard her

saying. Seeing Taylor's expression, Larson knew he'd caught her meaning as well. Larson recognized the look in Taylor's eyes— that of a man clearly trying to gauge a woman's feelings and wondering how much to reveal, how much to risk.

Apparently not sure of his wager, Taylor only nodded. "So the two of you are in town for the day?"

This was the chance Larson had been waiting for. "Actually, Kathryn and I were about to leave."

Kathryn glanced at him as though surprised to hear him speak. "Yes, we were just heading back. Jacob was kind enough to bring me into town to see the doctor this morning."

Taylor frowned. "There's nothing wrong, is there? With you or the—"

"No, everything's fine," she assured him, and laid a hand to his arm.

Larson saw the gesture, and suddenly it didn't mean quite what he thought it had before. Kathryn looked at him and as though reading his thoughts, gently withdrew her hand from Taylor's arm.

"The doctor said I'm fine, and that the baby is too. I was being overprotective."

Taylor glanced at Larson, a shy look in his eyes. "Would you mind if I spoke to Kathryn for a minute? Alone?"

You bet I mind. "No, not at all." Larson walked to the other side of the wagon and climbed to the bench.

As Taylor spoke, his voice grew more urgent, and Larson heard bits and pieces of the conversation between them.

". . . maybe things moved too quickly between us, but it was unfair for you to . . . I don't care what people are . . . You know I still feel the same way. . . ." Finally, Taylor sighed. "At least tell me you understand what I'm saying to you."

"Yes, I do, Matthew. Thank you," Kathryn answered. "But this way is best, at least for now."

Larson stole a glance behind him. From the look on Taylor's face, he clearly didn't agree.

Taylor briefly leaned close and whispered something to Kathryn and then stepped back. "If it's all right, I'd like to pay my respects to your husband too."

Larson couldn't believe it. Here Taylor wanted to pay his respects, and the man hadn't even waited until Larson was dead and buried before staking claim to his wife. Larson silently willed Kathryn to say no.

"Of course, Matthew. You're welcome to join us."

His grip tightened on the reins. Taylor helped Kathryn into the wagon and then climbed into the back himself. Whatever else Taylor said had apparently moved Kathryn, because Larson saw the sheen in her eyes.

He waited in the wagon while the two of them visited his grave. He'd visited it already, and he certainly didn't care to do it again with Taylor standing over him. Larson's eyes narrowed as he watched them. How many men got the chance to die and then come back to life and see the choices their wife had made? It sure had a way of putting things into perspective. Larson huffed a laugh, not feeling the least bit of humor.

Kathryn knelt by the makeshift headstone and laid the flowers down. Taylor stood wordless by her side. Why was Kathryn visiting his grave anyway? And with the very man she'd so quickly abandoned him for? Taylor was obviously willing to take Kathryn as his own and to take responsibility for his mistake, yet Kathryn refused. Somehow that didn't make Larson feel any better.

He shook his head. None of it made any sense. No matter how he worked it in his mind, this didn't fit the picture of the woman Larson thought he'd known all these years. A stirring started deep inside him. More importantly, it didn't fit the portrait of the woman he'd been given the chance to know and love again, for the second time in his life.

Kathryn snuck a glance at Jacob seated on the pew beside her. He wasn't singing with the rest of the congregation, but somehow she felt him following along. He'd dressed up more today than she'd ever seen him before, and she couldn't help but wonder if he'd done it for her. The possibility coaxed a smile.

"Please be seated," Patrick Carlson said when the song ended. "Turn in your Bibles with me to Matthew chapter five. We'll be reading from the Sermon on the Mount. . . ."

Kathryn opened her Bible. Balancing it with one hand, she shifted on the hard pew to ease the dull ache in her back. The Bible slipped and landed with a soft thud on the wooden floor. Jacob retrieved it along with the papers that had fallen out. It was a bit foolish, but she still couldn't part with the documents found in Larson's coat pocket, despite the papers being crinkled and the writing indistinguishable.

Jacob gathered them but then paused as though staring at one in particular. After a moment, he handed them back.

Kathryn leaned close. "Thank you," she whispered, catching a faint scent of musk. Jacob's thin beard was neatly trimmed. Looking at the knit cap covering his head, an idea came to mind and she wondered why she hadn't thought of it before. Making a mental note, she started to slip the papers back into her Bible, but she stopped when she read the faded letterhead.

Her stomach dropped.

Printed across the top—in barely legible faded type—was the name *Berklyn Stock-holders.*

"How about another piece of cake, Jacob? I'll throw in a fresh cup of coffee." Hannah Carlson rose from the porch swing.

"No, ma'am, I can't eat another bite." He stood and walked to the edge of the front porch. "But it was delicious. Thank you for such a fine meal."

Hannah's look turned conspiratorial. "Then I'll just wrap it up and you can take it with you for later. I'll put one in for Kathryn too." She glanced at Kathryn's tummy. "You'll be hungry later tonight."

"Oh please, Hannah, don't. I don't need it." Kathryn laughed along with everyone else, but only on the surface. She loved the child inside her more than anything else on earth, and nothing would ever change that. So how could she explain feeling bigger than a barn and not the least bit attractive? As though her attractiveness should matter. But it did matter for some reason. Especially today.

Kathryn looked across the porch at Jacob. He didn't smile or nod, so she had no idea whether he was watching her or not. Her thoughts turned back to church this morning, and she wondered again why Larson had been carrying a letter from Berklyn Stockholders with him that day. What kind of company was it? She guessed it involved cattle markets somehow, since Donlyn MacGregor had also corresponded with them. But MacGregor's letter from them had mentioned something about water rights. If only she'd had more time while in Mac-Gregor's office that day. She would check with the bank about Berklyn Stockholders. Certainly someone there would know. But she wouldn't ask Kohlman. The less she had to do with that man, the better.

"Kathryn?"

She looked up to see Jacob standing beside her chair.

"It's time for us to head back. Are you ready?"

For a moment she wished Jacob would offer his hand and help her up. But his hands were stuffed into his pockets, away from sight—like his eyes and his emotions. Hidden. Like so much of him was to her.

"Yes, I'm ready," she answered, seeing her faint reflection in Jacob's glasses when she would have much preferred to see him.

Halfway to Casaroja, a warm breeze swept down from the north across the plains, bringing with it the sweet smell of rain. Gray clouds gathered in the northwest, piled high one atop the other over the steep rocky range. The farmers and ranchers would welcome the rain, but Kathryn hoped she and Jacob would make it back to Casaroja before the thunderhead unleashed its fury. While the rain didn't bother her, being caught in a thunder-

storm on the prairie was another thing altogether.

Closing her eyes, the distant memory of
another summer thunderstorm made her
skin tingle. She could still hear the claps of
thunder crashing overhead. Without warning, gusting winds had swept down late that
afternoon as she and Larson traveled back
from Denver, and Larson had sought refuge
in a ravine he'd stayed in before. He'd made
sure she was safe in the cleft of an over-
hang before going back for the horses.
When he disappeared into the driving wind
and rain, she feared he wouldn't find his
way back to her. How could he? She could
barely see two feet in front of herself. Once
he returned, she'd asked him about it. Larson had shrugged as though it was something he'd never considered before. "I just
know the way . . . in here," he'd added,
lightly touching his chest. Half wanting to
smack him for treating her fear so casually,
she had sought the reassurance of his arms
instead. And through the night, even as the
storm subsided, Larson had chased away
her fear and any chill that might have come.

Kathryn's eyes filled with tears, and her
chest tightened painfully. Her skin tingled

again, but this time with the longing for Larson's touch. For the chance to again look into his eyes and see the fire that burned there for her.

"Are you all right?" Jacob asked, quiet beside her.

She turned to find him watching her. Whether he noticed her tears or not, when she nodded he just looked back to watch the road, and Kathryn felt strangely bereft. She remembered the many times in the past when she'd wished Larson would have held or touched her at a moment like this. She could've asked him to and he would have, no doubt. It was silly, she knew, but somehow it wasn't the same if she had to ask. And she wasn't about to ask Jacob to do such a thing. It wouldn't have been proper, nor would—

Jacob's hand covered hers on the bench between them.

Kathryn closed her eyes, and tears slipped down her cheek. A part of her heart long cordoned off slowly opened, and she gasped softly at the loneliness hoarded inside. The warmth from Jacob's hand seeped into hers. She shivered and gripped the buckboard tighter, hoping he wouldn't move it away. He didn't.

Neither of them looked at the other, yet it felt as though they were joined somehow. Connected in a way Kathryn had never been with another person before.

CHAPTER TWENTY-TWO

Walking back to the stable, Larson saw the wagonload of women pull up behind the row of bunkhouses. It was hardly dusk, and the party was already starting. Several of the men had made a point of telling him about tonight's remuneration.

"It's MacGregor's way of thankin' us for a job well done," one of the hands had said, jabbing his buddy in the side. "They stay till everybody's had a turn. That means even you, Jacob."

Larson turned away from the women strutting into the bunkhouse amid hoops and hollers and instead looked to Kathryn's cottage. A faint yellow glow came from the bedroom window, and he wondered if she would be up for a walk tonight. They'd been on several in the past few days, and he'd begun to look forward to them, probably more than he should. But the more time he spent with her, the more he wanted to spend. He was getting to know his wife in a way he'd not known her before. Larson recalled finding his papers in her Bible that Sunday—that had made him feel special in a way he couldn't put into words.

Kathryn answered on the second knock. "I was hoping you would come by tonight." The look in her eyes reflected her words. "Wait here for just a second. I'll be right back." She left the door open and walked back to the bedroom.

When she returned, Larson saw her stuffing something into her pocket. It looked like a pair of knit gloves. "I doubt you'll need gloves tonight," he said teasingly.

Her smile only deepened. "Better safe than sorry."

He purposefully took a path in the direction of the stables, well away from the bunkhouses. The silhouette of a thumbnail moon lit the twilight sky as the sun took refuge behind the mountain peaks, and conversation came easily as Kathryn talked about her day.

As they rounded the corner to the back of the stable, Larson gently interrupted her. "I was hoping you'd feel up to taking a short walk tonight, and maybe . . . a hayride." He motioned with his hand.

Kathryn's eyes went wide and she chuckled.

Gabe stood beside the hay-filled wagon bed dressed in his work shirt and dungarees but with a ridiculous-looking hat on his head—something a fancy carriage driver might have worn. He bowed low and swung an arm wide, apparently intent on playing the part.

Larson laughed. "I asked you to drive the wagon, Gabe, not steal the show."

He motioned for Kathryn to precede him and helped her onto a blanket in the back of the wagon. He climbed up beside her, her expression warming him. Larson settled down a fair distance away, not wanting to give the wrong impression. He recalled covering her hand the other day on their way home from the Carlsons'—the fragile strength of hers lying beneath his—and the feeling was still with him.

Seated on the buckboard, Gabe gave the signal and the horses responded.

Kathryn tipped her head back and closed her eyes. Neither of them spoke, and that suited Larson fine. He enjoyed the chance just to be near her. Staring at her now, drinking in her unflawed beauty, he had a hard time imagining her living back in that brothel or having another man's child. And though he was certain he could love Kathryn again, that indeed he did love her still, he couldn't deny the wish inside him that she'd remained faithful, that she'd kept herself pure.

Like you were when you came to her, beloved?

Truth arrowed through Larson's chest. He lowered his face. His heart pounding, no words rose within him in defense of his past sins—sins that were covered now in Jesus' blood, completely forgiven by God. And that Kathryn had willingly forgiven years ago.

Thankful for the darkness and the noise of the wagon wheels over the prairie, Larson searched the night sky. Forgiveness was a strange gift. One that had to be shared in order to be kept. He might not understand everything the Bible said, but God's Word was clear on that point.

Gabe returned to the stable about an hour later, and Larson helped Kathryn down from the back of the wagon. He plucked pieces of straw from her hair.

Her eyes shimmered. "Thank you, Jacob. This was a wonderful evening."

Larson's gaze went to her mouth, and the urge to draw her close to him was nearly over-powering. But the memory of his scars and the fear of how she would surely react swiftly doused the reckless desire. He cleared his throat. "Well, it's not quite over yet," he said, enjoying the crinkle of her brow.

"Refreshments are served," Gabe an-nounced with a flourish and then threw open the stable doors.

Kathryn covered her mouth in surprise, a giggle sneaking past her fingers.

Larson offered his arm, and she slipped her hand through. As Gabe cut slices of a cake that Miss Maudie had made at Lar-son's request, the three of them talked, sit-ting on bales of hay huddled around an old crate.

"Did I do it right, Jacob?" Gabe whis-pered after a minute.

Larson laid a hand to his massive shoulder. "You did very well, my friend. Thank you."

Kathryn leaned over and placed a kiss on Gabe's cheek. Larson smiled at the sweet gesture and the blush it drew from Gabe. "Thank you both, but how did you know?"

Larson attempted a look of nonchalance. "Know about what?" he asked, the surprise in his voice almost convincing himself.

"That August ninth is my birthday."

Gabe's sincere look of shock clinched it, and Larson was glad he'd kept it a secret from him. This way, Gabe was party to the fun and not the well-intentioned deception.

A while later, Larson escorted Kathryn back to her cottage. "I'm sorry for getting you home so late. Time got away from me."

"Oh, don't you dare apologize for anything, Jacob. This evening was perfect. It was the best birthday I've ever had."

The sincerity in her voice told him it was true. The evening had turned out far better than he'd planned. He wished he could have done more, something fancier, perhaps, but he hoped it had made her feel special.

They fell in step beside each other again, and without provocation, Kathryn placed her hand in the crook of his arm. Larson covered her hand with his, silently loving her with a passion that ran deeper and wider than he'd ever imagined possible.

How much longer could he work and live this close to her without revealing who he was? Without her discovering it for herself?

When they reached her porch, Kathryn turned and looked at him. "Oh, I almost forgot. I made something for you." She pulled the gloves from her pocket and held them out.

Larson looked at them, then back at her, not sure why she was giving him a gift— much less gloves in the middle of August!

"It's not fancy, I know. But . . . I thought you could use another one."

He took what was in her hand, then realized what it was.

His eyes burned with emotion. "Thank you," he rasped, fingering the knit cap in his hands. How had Kathryn described him to Matthew Taylor the other day? *"A good friend"*—that's what she'd called him. How could Larson remain merely good friends with Kathryn—and still be an honest man? The cost of the truth was great. Was he ready to risk it?

"Kathryn, I—"

A scream split the night.

She stepped closer. "What was that?"

They heard it again, more muted this time. Larson shoved the cap into his shirt pocket, then put a hand to Kathryn's arm. "Stay here. I'll go see what's going on."

Thinking the screams might have come from a supply building next door to the bunkhouses, he tried the side door. Unlocked. When he pushed it open slightly, a pale slice of moonlight illumined the inside of the building.

He heard a hard slap, then a thud.

The opening of a door on the opposite wall let in a second brief wedge of moonlight. Whimpering, like that of a child, sounded from a far corner. It was a pitiful cry, and it stirred a mixture of anger and protectiveness inside him. Larson felt his way along the shelves, then heard a shuffling noise.

"I'm not going to hurt you," he said softly, realizing the child was trying to hide. "I'm here to help you." A crate toppled from a shelf directly in front of him. He easily avoided it. Cautiously, he rounded the corner and spotted a young girl cowering in the corner.

"Get away from me," she hissed.

Even in the pale light, Larson recognized

the long dark hair, and he had heard the voice before. "Are you hurt?" He took a step forward.

"I said stay away from me!" she screamed. Her face contorted as she pushed her body against the wall. Only then did Larson notice her dress. It was ripped across the shoulder and down the front. Her hands clutched the pieces, holding it together.

"I'm not going to hurt you, I promise. I want to help."

The girl screamed at him in a language Larson had never heard before. He heard a door opening.

"Jacob?"

"We're over here." Intentionally keeping his voice calm, he met Kathryn in the aisle. "There's a girl in the corner. She's from the brothel in town. I think she's been—"

Kathryn pushed past him. "Sadie!" she gasped, going to her.

The young girl fired a rapid response in the foreign tongue, switching to English intermittently, but this time her voice came out broken and raw. The girl clung to Kathryn until Kathryn finally ended up on the floor beside her. Larson watched as the two held each other, the girl holding her arm in an awkward-looking position. The older cradled the younger against her chest, nodding at whatever it was the girl whispered between sobs. Kathryn rocked Sadie back and forth, stroking her hair like a mother would her child.

Watching the scene, Larson was struck with a difficult truth. All the things he'd desired to give Kathryn through the years, all the earthly goods he would've lavished on her if he'd been able—they all fell away in a moment's passing. The one thing Kathryn had wanted most was the one thing he had not given her. And never could give her. Another man had done that, and that other man deserved to watch his child grow. Matthew Taylor could give Kathryn the life that she deserved. Larson's chest heaved. Taylor could give his wife the desires of her heart. In truth, he already had.

"Can you help me with her?" Kathryn's voice was hoarse with emotion.

Wishing he could help, Larson raised his hands in a helpless gesture. "She won't let me get near her."

Kathryn gently drew up Sadie's chin and stroked her cheek. "This is Jacob. He is a good man. He won't hurt you. He won't try to touch you like that; I give you my word."

Sadie looked from Larson back to Kathryn. "He is like the man you told me about?"

"Yes," she said, a sob escaping her, "he is like that man." With effort, she stood. "I think her arm is broken, Jacob."

Larson approached slowly. It was clear from Sadie's posture that she didn't trust him. What held her there was her trust in Kathryn. The girl winced and went stiff when he tenderly gathered her into his arms.

"It's okay, child," he whispered as he carried her out of the building. She looked at him but said nothing.

Kathryn caught up with them. "Sadie needs a doctor. She told me she was running to catch the wagon heading back to the brothel when someone grabbed her from behind and dragged her in there. She told me she's not hurt badly on the outside, but I'm not sure about . . ."

Larson nodded, understanding. "I'll take her into town to see Doc Hadley."

"I'm coming with you."

"No, Kathryn, you're not. I'll be gone most of the night, and you need to rest."

And he didn't need to be with her right now. The knowledge that he would never have her again was killing him. "I'll take care of Sadie—I give you my word."

He carried Sadie behind the stable to the wagon filled with hay and laid her in the back. Fierce distrust sharpened her dark eyes as she backed away from him. He quickly hitched the team and made to leave. Kathryn covered the girl with a blanket, whispering to her in low tones, which the girl answered in her own whisper.

Before Larson could climb to the bench, Kathryn put a hand to his arm. "Sadie says she's seen you before in town . . . at the brothel." A clear question rang in her voice.

The irony of the sudden role reversal might have seemed comical to Larson earlier, but not now. "I wasn't at the brothel for that reason, Kathryn. Ask Sadie yourself."

"I did. She said you were there asking about me."

His mouth went dry. *God, is this your way of forcing the truth from me? I'm not ready yet. I'm not ready.* He searched for a way to answer—and avoid—her question. "It's true. I was there asking about you." His mind raced. He wished he could see Kathryn's face better in order to gauge her reaction. "It was after I'd met you here at Casaroja. I'd heard that you worked at the brothel in town, and . . ."

"And you wanted to see whether it was true or not."

He cringed at the cool edge to her tone. "Yes," he finally answered.

"And what have you discovered?"

He shook his head. "Sadie wouldn't tell me anything that day."

Kathryn stared at him for a long moment, and Larson would have given much to see her eyes. "I know that, Jacob. Sadie told me she turned you away." Her tone softened and her question was clear. "But what I'm asking you right now is . . . what have you discovered since then?"

Larson knew what she wanted him to say—the same thing he'd said to her back in the stable that day about leaving Mac-Gregor's bedroom. That he believed in her innocence, completely and without reservation. But he couldn't lie to her, not again.

He swallowed against the tightness in his throat and measured each word, wanting to get them right. "I've discovered that it doesn't matter to me if you worked there before or not. God has . . ." His voice broke as truth filled him. "God has forgiven me a debt I can never repay," he whispered. "Who am I to demand payment from someone else after having been forgiven so much?" Larson wanted to touch her face, just one last time, but he didn't dare. "So you don't owe me any explanation, Kathryn. Instead, I owe you an apology. I'm sorry."

When she didn't answer, he bowed his head. It wasn't the answer she'd wanted, but it was the truth. Well, part of it anyway. He started to climb up to the buckboard but stilled at the touch on his arm.

He stood speechless as Kathryn reached up, drew his face down next to hers, and gently kissed his scarred cheek.

———

"Bring Sadie in here," the red-haired woman said, keeping her tone soft. "The other girls have just now gone to sleep."

Cradling the sleeping girl against his chest, Larson followed down a second-floor hallway. Pale pink dawn peeked from beneath a curtain drawn closed at the end of the narrow corridor. The house was quiet. He passed door after door, then waited in the hall as the woman turned back the ornately trimmed bedcovers.

He'd left Casaroja shortly after midnight and, an hour later, had awakened Doc Hadley. The doctor didn't hesitate for a moment to offer his help—not even when Larson told him who he would be treating. "We're all God's creatures, no matter what we've done" was all the doctor said before grabbing his bag and meeting them in the clinic.

"Okay, put her down here." The woman motioned to the bed.

Larson felt the woman staring at him but didn't look at her. He gently laid Sadie down, careful of her bandaged arm. She stirred but didn't waken. Doc Hadley had given her something for the pain in her body, but Larson wished there was something he could give her for the pain he'd seen in her eyes. Especially the distrust— she reeked with it. And why wouldn't she?

He'd been raised in this environment as a boy, but she had grown up living it as a girl. His scars were nothing compared to hers.

Sadie's eyes fluttered, and he backed up a step, not wanting his closeness to frighten her when she wakened.

"Sadie, honey, it's Annabelle. I'm here with you." She leaned over the bed. "This man told me what happened to you last night." Annabelle cursed none too softly. "I'm sorry I wasn't there to take care of you. I should've gone out there with you."

Sadie shook her head. "I'm okay." But her voice sounded flat and lifeless. She blinked and then focused on Larson. "Jacob," she said softly, "look at me."

He slowly did as she asked, not sure if this was her or the drugs talking. She beckoned him forward with a tiny brown hand. Larson couldn't explain it, but he felt a command in the simple gesture and obeyed.

"Let me see your eyes."

He shook his head. He knew neither Sadie nor this Annabelle woman would recognize him—they hadn't known him before the accident—but the skin around his right eye made him especially self-conscious. In healing, the scarring had pulled at an awkward angle and gave his eye a sloped look.

Larson clenched his jaw at the shame pouring through him. "I'm not really worth looking at, miss."

Sadie laughed in her throat. "I'd like to decide that for myself, mister. If you don't mind." Her tone sounded too old for her age. "Take off your glasses." Her smile faded. "Please . . ." she added, the simple word holding a pleading quality.

Slowly, Larson reached up with his right hand and removed the spectacles, wishing the early morning light from the window wasn't so bright on his face.

"Come closer," she whispered.

He did, his heart hammering. She took his hand and pulled him down. Larson went to his knees beside the bed. Her dark eyes shone as her fingers traced the disfigured mask he knew only too well. The skin around his eyes was still sensitive, but her touch was featherlight.

Sadie smiled. "You were a handsome man . . . before this."

Larson gave an uneasy laugh, not knowing how to respond to such honesty.

"But I wonder," she continued, "were you as kind?"

His throat tightened. He let out a quick breath as her tiny hand tightened around his—as though she were comforting him.

"Thank you, Jacob." She blinked heavily, the laudanum apparently taking effect. "Kathryn is right to look at you . . . the way she does. You are . . . good man. You are like . . . the man she . . . told me about."

"Kathryn?" Annabelle asked, her voice both excited and wary. "You know Kathryn? How is she?"

Larson stood. "I work with Mrs. Jennings at Casaroja. She's doing fine."

Annabelle briefly touched Sadie's hand, then motioned Larson into the hallway. She closed the door behind her. "Her baby. Has Kathryn had her baby yet?"

"Not yet, but the time isn't far off."

The intensity of the woman's gaze deepened, making Larson uncomfortable. "I bet she looks wonderful, all big and glowin'." Annabelle laughed and the hard lines of her face softened. "Oh, I'd love to see her again. What a fine woman she is."

"Yes, ma'am, there's none finer," Larson said quietly, putting his glasses back on.

Annabelle stared at him briefly before leading him back down the hallway. "Thank you for seeing to Sadie's hurts. I try to take care of her, but I can't always be there." Her tone hinted at frustration, and deep regret.

"She's young to be in this business," Larson said more to himself than to her, looking around the small front parlor and then following Annabelle back through the kitchen. No matter which part of the building they were in, it all smelled of cheap perfume, stale smoke, and depravity.

So much of this building, this life, felt painfully familiar to him. Even so, strangely he wasn't repulsed at being inside like he'd imagined. The sickening feeling he'd expected had been filled instead by a dull ache in his chest. One he could only describe as . . . compassion. He looked at Annabelle's hair, at the revealing cut of her dress. Then he tried to see her through God's eyes. It was a stretch for him, but deep down he knew that the love that had saved him was the same love God offered to this woman.

Annabelle stopped at the back door, her hand poised on the latch. "So, Jacob, how long have you worked at Casaroja?"

He shrugged. "A few months."

"You new to this territory?"

"No, not really. I've been around."

Larson suddenly wondered how close this woman had been to Kathryn. From Annabelle's earlier response at discovering he knew Kathryn, Larson guessed they'd known each other fairly well. Most likely, Annabelle would be able to answer every question he had about Kathryn, if he still had any worth asking. But he'd laid those questions to rest at the foot of the cross and he determined, again, to leave them there.

"You've never been here before, have you? To the brothel, I mean. I would have remembered you, even before all this." Annabelle studied his face. "Sadie's right, you know. I bet you were a real fine-lookin' man once."

Something in her expression stirred Larson's discomfort. He cleared his throat, suddenly eager to leave. "Well, I'd better be getting back. I've got work to do."

She didn't move. "How long have you kown Kathryn . . . Jacob?"

Larson stared at Annabelle's hand on the door latch, and a slight tremor passed through him. There was something in the way she was looking at him. . . . He tugged on the right side of his cap, pulling it down a bit farther. "Like I said, I've gotten to know Kathryn at Casaroja."

Annabelle's bottom lip slipped briefly behind her front teeth. "Do you and Kathryn have some sort of understanding? I mean, Sadie mentioned something about the way Kathryn looks at you."

"No, ma'am, there's no understanding between us. We're . . . good friends, is all."

Annabelle nodded, then lifted the latch and smiled. "Well, you tell Kathryn I said hello and ask her to bring herself around sometime. Maybe after the baby's born. I'd like to see her again, and her little one."

"Yes, ma'am, I'll do that." He stepped through the open door. He forced himself to take the back stairs one at a time and was nearly to the corner when he heard Annabelle call his name.

He turned back to see her standing in the alley, hands on her hips, a look of unspoken challenge on her face.

And then it hit him.

Chills shot up and down his spine.

Larson. She'd just called him by the name Larson.

CHAPTER TWENTY-THREE

Larson fought the instinct to run. Instead, he cocked his head to one side and hoped the wave of dread inside him would somehow translate into surprise. "I'm afraid there's been some misunderstanding, ma'am."

Annabelle huffed a laugh. "You bet there has been," she said, slowly walking toward him. With each step she took, Larson felt his carefully constructed world crumbling. "It was your eyes that gave you away, you know. Eyes that could see right through you, that's what Kathryn told me. That and the fact that Kathryn Jennings wouldn't look twice at another man this soon, less'n it was her husband." She bit her lower lip and laughed to herself. "And I'd bet my life that I'm lookin' at him right now."

Larson shook his head and worked to keep his voice even. "I'm not who you think I am, ma'am."

Annabelle's eyes filled with tears, and from the angst in her expression, she wasn't comfortable with the emotion. "I just wanna know one thing. Why haven't you told Kathryn you're still alive?"

Larson was stunned with what he saw on this woman's face. She was completely devoted to Kathryn. No, more than that. A protectiveness radiated from Annabelle that almost frightened him. This woman would fight to protect Kathryn at all costs.

He felt a spark inside him at the thought and took a deep breath. "Kathryn Jennings' husband died last December. I know that for a fact because . . . I was there with him."

"I may just be a whore to you, mister, but I know more about the inside of a person than you ever will. So you take off those glasses and try tellin' me that again."

Larson fisted his hands to ease their trembling. Then he did as she asked.

Head bent, he rubbed his eyes, unaccustomed to the light. Then slowly, he looked up. Annabelle's eyes were disturbingly blue, and dangerously discerning. Larson forced himself to maintain her gaze. Clearly, she didn't believe his story, so he would have to find another way to convince her.

"What I'm telling you now is the truth. Larson Jennings died in a fire last December. He was so badly burned there was hardly any of the old man left in him. Kathryn has buried her husband and moved on with her life, and that's how things need to stay."

Annabelle shook her head. "Kathryn always told me you weren't dead. She said she felt it"—she put a hand over her heart— "in here."

Larson clenched his jaw against the churn of emotions inside him. He reminded himself that he was doing what was best for Kathryn, for the baby. For everyone. But why did it have to hurt so much? "Even if her husband could come back from the grave, he wouldn't have anything worth giving her. He lost everything when he died. He wasn't the man she married anymore, or a man she would've wanted." Larson prayed for Annabelle to see the truth. "Kathryn deserves far better than that. She deserves better than him."

She didn't answer immediately. Her voice was a whisper when she finally spoke, but her expression was fierce. "Do you have any idea what she's been through?"

Larson looked past Annabelle to the place where he'd stood and watched Kathryn enter the brothel that first night, after following her back through town. That night seemed like a lifetime ago. He didn't even feel like the same man anymore. He sighed, wondering how to convince Annabelle. Then it came to him. The words were like rust on his tongue.

"There's one thing Kathryn has now that her husband was never able to give her. That he never will be able to give her. And it's something Kathryn has wanted all her life."

Annabelle's brow wrinkled, then her mouth fell open slightly. "You're talking about the baby?"

He nodded. "Matthew Taylor is ready to take full responsibility for what he did. Kathryn cares for him, and in time, she'll let him take care of her." Saying the words aloud scathed what little of his pride remained. "He can give her the life her husband never could."

"You think Matthew Taylor . . ." Annabelle looked at him as though trying to piece together what he'd said.

Larson nodded, and then, as he'd hoped, comprehension registered in her expression. Her features grew hard, and her loathing was almost tangible.

"You know, Jacob, I think you're right. Kathryn Jennings does deserve better."

———

It was nearly noon and still Jacob hadn't returned from town. Kathryn dusted the shelves in the main study and peered out the window, eager to find out how Sadie was faring this morning—and to see Jacob again. Maybe he'd come in the back way and she'd missed seeing him. She walked to another window and looked out. Gabe was working with a horse in the corral, but there was no sign of Jacob. She carefully bent down to clean the lower shelves.

Thinking about the previous night and reliving Jacob's gift of the evening to her, Kathryn acknowledged how drawn she was to him. To his kindness, his gentleness. He

made her feel so special when they were together. Jacob was *aware* of her—not just
about what she liked or didn't like, but of
her. And he went to the trouble to find out
her birthday, a date Larson had always
seemed to let slip his mind. Jacob was
slowly becoming the center of her thoughts,
and that discovery left Kathryn feeling
slightly off-balance.

She remembered the feel of her lips on
his cheek and the faint scent of musk and
hay. He was a man of gentle strength. His
love for God and his respect for God's Word
drew her with an attraction Kathryn had not
experienced before. Not even with Larson.
What would it be like to be loved, to be
cherished, by a man like Jacob?

Larson's looks were the first thing that had
attracted her to him—his eyes specifically.
Eyes that could see right through her. She
sighed. And that's just what they'd done—
seen through her, but never really into her.
She'd always placed too high a value on the
outside of a person and not enough on the
heart. How many times had her mother
warned of the danger of that miscalculation?
Kathryn wished she'd learned that lesson
earlier in life.

Standing with effort, she caught a glimpse of her profile in a glass-fronted bookcase. Her protruding belly halted her frivolous thoughts.

What was she thinking? She was a recently widowed woman about to have her husband's child. How could she be entertaining thoughts about Jacob when the precious remnant of her husband bloomed inside her? She would never do something to intentionally dishonor Larson's memory. *The only interest I have in Jacob is as a friend.* Hadn't she called him that just the other day when introducing him to Matthew? A *good friend.* That's all Jacob was to her, and that's how it would stay.

Kathryn pushed through her chores that afternoon so she could leave early to go see Sadie and Annabelle. Standing by the kitchen door, she untied the apron from her middle and reached to hang it back on the hook. The baby within her kicked in response, and Kathryn gasped. She smiled and ran a hand over her abdomen, gently rubbing the definite protrusion of a tiny arm or leg. "Patience, dear one. It's not quite time yet."

Soon she would hold her precious child, and a part of Larson again.

"Are you done for the day?"

Kathryn inhaled sharply. "Oh! Miss Maudie, you startled me." Then she laughed. "Yes, I'm all done. Gabe offered to drive me into town to see a friend. We're leaving in a few minutes."

"Time away from here will do you good, dear. You just take your time and get back when you can. I have plenty of help with dinner, so there's no need to be hurryin'." She tilted her head, a twinkle in her eyes. "How was your surprise last night?"

"Oh, it was wonderful. The best birthday I ever had." Kathryn's face grew warm. "Jacob is a very nice man, and your cake was delicious. Thank you."

"It was my pleasure. You deserve some wonderful things after all that's happened. And that Jacob is a fine man indeed. Sometimes the greatest treasures are found where no one else is lookin' deep enough to see." She winked before she turned away.

Kathryn stepped outside and stood on the back porch step, breathing in the languid summer breeze and pondering what Miss Maudie had said. By the time Gabe pulled the wagon up behind the brothel an hour later and set the brake, she'd decided to take a deeper look into Jacob, to make the effort to get to know him better as a friend, if he was willing, which she believed he would be. No doubt, treasures lay within his heart that few had taken the time to see.

"I'd like to go in with you to see Sadie, if that's okay," Gabe said, helping her down.

Kathryn squeezed his hand. "Certainly, and Annabelle will want to see you too."

The back door to the brothel opened, and Annabelle stood framed in the doorway. Her eyes dropped to Kathryn's front, and slowly, she shook her head and smiled. Her expression was a mixture of pleasure and pain, and Kathryn wondered if Annabelle's seeing her so far along with child made her friend long for another chance at a different life.

"It's good to see you again, Annabelle." Kathryn climbed the stairs and warmed when her friend's arms came around her, and then she had to laugh. "That's about as close as we can get with this baby between us." She drew back slightly. "How is Sadie this afternoon?"

"Doc says she's gonna be okay." Annabelle seemed unusually quiet, subdued. "She's up in bed asleep right now, but I know she'll want to see you." She offered Gabe a weak smile. "How are you, old friend?"

"Better now." Gabe pulled her close in a big hug before letting her go.

Annabelle stepped back, her eyes swimming. "Sadie'll welcome a visit from you too, Gabe. She's always liked you, which is sayin' a lot, 'cause she doesn't take to most people. Especially men." She turned to Kathryn. "So, have you seen Jacob today? Since he left here this morning?"

Kathryn shook her head, wondering if she'd imagined the subtle shift in Annabelle's tone. She sounded . . . disturbed. "No, I haven't seen him since he left to bring Sadie into town last night. Why?"

Annabelle opened her mouth to say something. Then, apparently thinking better of it, she motioned for them to follow her upstairs. "Doc Hadley already came by this afternoon to check on her. He said she's gonna be fine. Her arm is broken, but it'll heal, in time."

Annabelle's voice was thick with regret, and Kathryn wished again that she'd been able to talk her and Sadie into leaving this terrible place. Maybe now that she had her land, thanks to Donlyn MacGregor's generosity, another opportunity would present itself.

Annabelle poked her head into Sadie's room. "You awake? You've got some visitors, girl." She motioned for them to follow her.

Kathryn had to force a bright countenance when she saw Sadie. The girl looked so small and helpless lying in the bed, her arm bandaged and her left cheek swollen and purpled. "I hear Doc Hadley is taking good care of you." She leaned down and laid a hand to Sadie's forehead. It felt warm to the touch.

"Mmm, your hand feels good. It's so cool." Sadie sighed and blinked heavily, her eyes slipping closed again.

Kathryn glanced back at Annabelle.

"It's okay," Annabelle said. "Just the medicine the doc gave her. Said it'd make her real sleepy."

Gabe entered the room, went around to the other side of the bed, and stood quietly. Kathryn was about to make sure Sadie knew Gabe was there too when Annabelle's name echoed down the hallway.

Annabelle huffed. "I swear these girls

can't do anything by themselves. I . . ." Mumbling, she finished the sentence to herself. "You go ahead and visit. I'll be right back."

Kathryn eased herself down on the side of the bed. "I see things haven't changed much around here." Smiling, she gently cupped both sides of the girl's face, sharing the coolness of her hands. Sadie's eyes fluttered open, and Kathryn relished the rare softness in them. *She's so young, Lord. Give her hope. Help her to see your love.* "I'm so sorry this happened to you, and I'm glad you're going to be all right. You're very special to me, you know. Do you remember my first day here?"

Sadie nodded.

"You never said anything, but the way you smiled at me . . . Somehow it made me feel not quite so alone." Kathryn paused, and her heart began to beat faster as she realized what she truly wanted—and needed—to say to Sadie. "You're not alone either, Sadie. You're very special to God. He knows your name, and He loves you more than you know."

Sadie's expression clouded. She closed her eyes and turned her face away.

Kathryn ached at the wordless denial. How often had she herself felt unloved by God, especially during these past months? How often had she questioned that love? She wanted to help this child understand that you couldn't judge God's love by your circumstances, but where to begin? How did you describe the ocean to someone who had only lived in desert?

"You probably don't think God loves you very much right now, Sadie, and I don't blame you. But please don't be fooled into measuring His love by the bad things that happen to you or by how other people treat you or see you. Or especially by whoever did this to you last night. God has a better life planned for you than this. You're worth so much more than what you've been told."

Slowly, Sadie looked back, her eyes glazed, her expression guarded. "You are a good woman, Kathryn. . . . I'm glad you came here . . . and that you were there with me last night. I'm also glad for Jacob." Her brow creased. "What do you know of this Jacob?"

Curious at the question, Kathryn sat up a little straighter. "Why do you ask?"

"He is a different kind of man than I have known before."

That brought a smile. "Yes, I would imagine that he is." No telling what kind of *men* this child had known in her brief life. More like monsters, in Kathryn's opinion. Jacob had been so gentle with Sadie last night, so compassionate.

"The look in his eyes . . . same as yours." Sadie blinked again, as though struggling to stay awake.

Kathryn hesitated, certain she'd misunderstood. "You . . . you saw Jacob's eyes?"

"Yes. But he did not want to show me at first."

Kathryn couldn't explain the twinge of hurt that pricked her. Why should it bother her that Jacob had shared this part of himself with Sadie? But she knew why. Because she wanted him to share more of himself with her—she wanted to see into him as Sadie apparently had.

"Sadie, you'd better get some rest now." Annabelle stood in the doorway, her arms folded across her chest, her voice bearing that same disturbing edge. "Doc Hadley's orders, remember?"

"I'll be back to visit soon." Kathryn

brushed a kiss to Sadie's forehead. *Lord, let her feel your presence. Touch her with your healing hand.*

Then she watched, moved by Gabe's tenderness as he bent down and silently, lovingly, laid his large hand atop Sadie's small one on the bedcovers. But Sadie didn't respond; she'd already slipped back into sleep.

"Annabelle, are you sure everything's all right?" Kathryn asked, following her onto the back porch. The evening air, cool and clean with a hint of coming fall, felt rejuvenating after being inside.

"I'll wait in the wagon," Gabe offered. "Good to see you again, Miss Annabelle."

"Yeah, you too, Gabe," Annabelle answered after a moment, barely glancing at him. Her hands gripped the porch railing.

Kathryn joined her, now certain something was wrong. "Annabelle, what is it? I can tell something's not right."

Annabelle stared off at some point in the distance. "Tell me something, Kathryn. Do you still miss your husband? I mean, like you used to?"

Not following her, Kathryn frowned. "Annabelle, you're acting very strangely."

"Just answer my question." Her voice grew softer. "Please."

"Well, yes. Of course I still miss Larson." Kathryn searched for the right words. "I always thought you considered me foolish for saying this, but even after all this time, I still feel him with me. I'm coming to realize, however, that this *presence* I feel is simply my memory of him—the memories of our life together. They're a gift from God, and they've helped me through some very lonely days." She shrugged and looked down at her hands covering her baby. "Perhaps it's God's way of giving me time to grieve and move on with my life. After all, Larson *is* dead," she said slowly, letting the words hang in the air. There, she'd finally said it aloud. "And I'll soon give birth to our child."

"Did you love him? I mean . . . really love him?"

Wondering at this line of questioning, Kathryn nodded. "Yes, I loved Larson. Our marriage wasn't ideal, but I did love my husband, very much. There's something I've never told anyone else, and I hesitate to share it with you now. . . ." She wanted to share with her friend how much of Larson's heart God had chosen to reveal to her through having stayed here briefly, through knowing her and Sadie. "Larson had a difficult time trusting people, and trusting me specifically. Whenever we came into town, he was right by my side. Ranch hands were never allowed to come by the cabin." Kathryn closed her eyes, remembering. "The day before Larson left last December, a young man came to see me. We were friends. That's all. But Larson's view of life was often distorted because of his upbringing."

Annabelle's expression was patient, taking everything in.

Kathryn wondered if she was doing the right thing in telling Annabelle this, but something within urged her to continue. "My husband was raised in a brothel, Annabelle. His mother was . . . a . . ."

"A whore," Annabelle supplied in the barest of whispers, and seeing Kathryn's nod, Annabelle looked away.

"Yes. I never knew his mother. She died when Larson was sixteen. I share this with you to say that staying here, seeing this place, seeing this *life,*" she added gently, "has revealed a part of my husband's heart that I'd never glimpsed before. That he never would let me see. And with good reason." Kathryn shook her head, trying to make some sense of it all. "I don't know if things would've ever changed for me and Larson or if he could've ever learned to trust me completely. Marriage takes trust, pure and simple. Trust is something that's difficult to earn in a relationship, and once broken . . . it's even harder to regain." She let out a breath as tears rose to her eyes. "But the time has come for me to stop looking back on what my life was and to start looking forward to what it will be."

Annabelle seemed to weigh this for a moment, then nodded.

Kathryn briefly considered whether she should share her next thought or not. "There is a man I've met who I've grown to care for very deeply. I'm not sure how he f—"

"Is it Jacob?" Annabelle asked, her voice sounding tight again.

"Yes," Kathryn answered after a moment, wondering how Annabelle knew. "Don't get me wrong. Jacob's never given me any indication that we're anything more than friends to him. Truth be told, I'm actually surprised by my feelings."

"Have you told him?"

Kathryn's eyes widened. "Of course not, and I won't. It wouldn't be proper."

Annabelle stared at her for a moment. "What about Matthew Taylor?"

Kathryn couldn't help but smile. "You're so full of questions today, Annabelle. It's not like you." When Annabelle didn't say anything further, Kathryn shrugged her shoulders at the question. "Matthew Taylor is a very nice man, and he's been so kind to me during all of this. I know he has feelings for me—he's made that clear. I do care for him. . . ."

"But do you love him?"

Kathryn started to answer, then stopped herself. Did she love Matthew Taylor? She certainly felt affection for him, she was grateful for his help and the way he desired to care for her, but *love* him . . .

"No, Annabelle. I don't love Matthew Taylor. My affections for him don't extend that far. Matthew is an honorable man and will make a fine husband. No doubt, God is already preparing a special lady to be his wife someday."

A wounded look slipped into Annabelle's gaze before she turned away, and if Kathryn hadn't known better she might have guessed that something she'd said had hurt her. Then a picture flashed in her mind—the night Matthew Taylor had been at the haberdashery with the news of Larson's body being found. Annabelle had been there and had commented on how attractive Matthew was. Kathryn thought she remembered a spark of interest on Annabelle's part. But as she recalled, and understood to a certain degree, Matthew's reaction to Annabelle had been far less enthusiastic. Outwardly cordial, but with an unexpected coolness that surprised her, and that spoke to something much deeper than a moment of social unease for Matthew. The following morning, right in front of Annabelle, he'd insisted she not accompany them to the undertaker's office, advising that Kathryn shouldn't be seen with a woman like her.

Not knowing what to say, what else to do, Kathryn reached over and drew Annabelle to her. Surprisingly, Annabelle fully returned her embrace. *Lord, would you redeem Annabelle's life from the pit, like you've redeemed mine? Help her to surrender her heart to you. And would you bring a man into her life who would love her like you love your church? A man after your own heart who would gladly give his life for hers and cherish her beyond words. Who will forgive her debt because of the great debt he's been forgiven.*

Conviction suddenly pricked Kathryn's heart as she realized she was describing a man just . . . like . . . Jacob.

———

By the time Larson neared the edge of town, his breath came heavy and the bay mare's coat was slick with lather. Miss Maudie's words kept playing through his mind. *"Kathryn's gone into town to visit a friend."*

The look Annabelle had given him that morning still pierced him. He couldn't get it out of his head. Reaching town, he reined in the mount and prayed he wasn't too late.

After leaving the brothel earlier that day, he'd taken the opportunity to buy supplies, but in reality he'd needed time to try to figure out what to do next. On his way back to Casaroja, ranch hands had enlisted his help in rounding up some strays, and by the time he arrived back, Kathryn was gone.

The brothel came into view, and Larson rode around to the back. When he saw them together on the back porch, and Gabe waiting by the wagon, time slowed to a crawl.

Both women looked up at the same time. Annabelle's expression was as he remembered—disapproving and defensive—and Larson knew in that moment that he was too late. She'd already told Kathryn everything.

He dismounted, barely able to hold a thought in his head, much less try and piece together an explanation for Kathryn. His legs felt as though they might buckle at any moment.

"Jacob!"

Hearing the name, seeing Kathryn's smile, Larson's heart started beating again. *She called me Jacob.* The enthusiasm in his wife's voice, the joy in her expression at seeing him, acted like a balm. He turned his head slightly, hoping Annabelle would know he was looking at her. The woman's expression was a mask, with her emotions safely tucked behind it. He nodded to her, but her eyes revealed nothing. She hugged Kathryn, then walked back inside and closed the door.

Holding onto the railing, Kathryn carefully descended the steps. "What brings you back to town so soon?"

"I came to check on Sadie." Kathryn nodded, but her transparency at being so happy to see him forced Larson's honesty. "Actually, Miss Maudie told me you'd come into town and I figured I'd find you here."

Her eyes sparkled at the admission, and Larson wished he'd been truthful from the start. He wished he'd been truthful about so many things, but it was too late for that now.

"So what did you come to see me about?"

He opened his mouth with a ready reply—one born from months of practiced deception—but then he caught himself. Both coveting and loathing the anonymity he'd worked so hard to create, he looked into Kathryn's face, her sepia-brown eyes so full of life and hope. Her lips, partially open, a smile teasing their full curves. "I came to see you, Kathryn. I just came to see you."

A blush swept her face, and Larson wondered again how, in all the years of living with this woman, he could have missed so much about who she was.

"Thank you again for last night, Jacob. It was the best birthday I've ever had."

He nodded, remembering that she'd said that to him last night but this time experiencing a keen mixture of pleasure, and pain, at her statement.

He helped her into the wagon, where Gabe was now seated, and then swung up onto his mount. As Gabe maneuvered the wagon down the alley, movement from a second-story window drew Larson's attention. Annabelle was staring down.

He hesitated, then raised a hand.

She didn't move. He prodded his horse to follow the wagon's path and looked back before they rounded the corner. Annabelle's palm was pressed flat against the window-pane in silent answer.

He didn't know what had compelled Annabelle to keep his secret, but Larson thanked God for her and for her love for Kathryn. Annabelle knew what was best in the situation, just as he did.

Now if he could only love his wife enough to let her go.

CHAPTER TWENTY-FOUR

Larson urged the team to a faster trot as he turned on the road toward Casaroja. Snowy peaks to the west gleamed deep amethyst against a sunset of crimson, and golden rays shot straight up into the sky. He removed his glasses to better appreciate the colors. August's last sunset was a beauty.

He could easily imagine the clouds above rolling back to reveal a mighty warrior on a white horse, like he'd read about in Revelation the night before. Sometimes the heart of heaven beat so strongly inside of him that this life seemed more like a shadow now than his home. He sighed, knowing this perspective was influenced by his deepening relationship with God, but also by his having to give up Kathryn.

Larson tugged on the reins and brought the wagon loaded with supplies to a halt in front of the stable. He glanced toward the main house. He'd already missed dinner but wondered if Miss Maudie might've saved him a plate. He spotted a distinct silhouette pass by the kitchen window, and a smile tipped his mouth. Over the past two weeks, he'd seen Kathryn on occasion. They'd even shared a few evening walks together, but he welcomed another opportunity to be with her. Larson put his glasses back on, set the brake, and climbed down.

Knocking on the back door, he hoped Kathryn would answer. The door opened.

"Well, Jacob, it's good to see you." Miss Maudie pulled the door open wide. "I've kept your plate warming on the stove. Why don't you come in and keep an old woman company for a spell?"

Larson stepped inside and looked around. "Thank you for keeping dinner for me. I'd appreciate a chance to visit." A twinge of guilt chided him at that not being his first priority.

"Here. The plate's hot." Using a towel,

she set it on the table before him. "Be careful not to burn your hands—" She stilled, and Larson watched discomfort slip into her smile.

Before she could apologize, he covered her hand resting on his shoulder. "Roast beef, my favorite. And an extra portion at that. You're always generous with me, Miss Maudie, and I appreciate it."

Gratitude quickly replaced her remorse as she took a seat beside him. "Kathryn made another pie today. Peach," she said, pulling a covered tin toward her. "I'll slice us each a piece."

"Thank you, ma'am. Is Kathryn around tonight? So I can thank her?" He watched to see if Miss Maudie reacted to the question.

"Yes, she's here." She cut the pie and scooped out two pieces. "She's meeting with Mr. MacGregor in his office right now. People often meet with him for advice. He's quite business savvy, but surely you know that by now."

Larson concentrated on chewing. *Savvy* wasn't exactly a word he'd attribute to Mac-Gregor, but he nodded. The pride in Miss Maudie's voice was unmistakable, and puzzling. "Have you been with Mr. MacGregor long, ma'am?"

"Oh my, yes, I've known him since he was a boy." Her voice took on a doting quality. "My youngest sister, God rest her soul, died when her son was only five, shortly following her husband in death. So I took Donlyn in . . . Mr. MacGregor," she amended, "and raised him myself. My sister would be quite proud of the man her son grew to be. He's had his share of hardships though. Lost his wife and only child in childbirth years ago. He's not been the same since."

Suddenly, the older woman became clearer to him. While Larson didn't share her opinion about his employer, it gave him valuable insight into her perspective. He wondered what advice Kathryn could possibly be seeking from MacGregor. Their land was scheduled to go to auction soon; he'd seen the notice in the paper himself a while back. There was no practical way she could pay off the loan, and no doubt, MacGregor would be first in line to bid for the land.

Losing the land stung, but Larson had come to grips with it. It didn't consume him like it once had. Land could be bought and sold . . . and lost. Isaiah had taught him that. Larson was concerned over losing something far more precious—something that could never be replaced.

Miss Maudie picked up the empty plates and took them to the sideboard. She moved to lift the wash bucket.

"Here, let me get that." Larson grabbed the pail and primed the pump until the water gushed and his shoulder burned.

"You're wincing, Jacob. Is your shoulder paining you?"

He waved off her concern. "On occasion it does. I overdid it today, that's all."

"I have a liniment for soreness and discomfort. I could rub some into your shoulders tonight and see if it makes a difference. I'm sure it would help."

Miss Maudie's concern touched him. "Kathryn told me you were good at mixing liniments. And yes, ma'am, I'd like to try it, but I can rub it in myself." Other than Isaiah and Abby, no one had seen the scarring on his chest, back, and arms. He hadn't even seen his back since the fire. Looking in a mirror wasn't something he'd been eager to do.

"Nonsense. How are you going to reach those muscles? Now you go on in the back room there and take off your shirt. I'll rub it in for you."

"Really, Miss Maudie, I—"

"Jacob." She spoke his name like an austere schoolmarm. "I've seen many horrible things in my sixty years, but the man standing before me now could never be one of them." She smiled and waved her arm at the door behind him. "Go on now. I'll get the liniment."

Miss Maudie's touch was every bit as firm as Abby's, if not more so, and Larson winced as she worked the salve into his shoulders and back. By the time she was done, his muscles ached, but in a good way. Reaching for his shirt, he started to stand, but Maudie pressed him back down.

"Sit here for a minute and let the salve work itself in. I'm going to wash this off my hands. I'll be back shortly."

Larson straddled the wooden chair again and propped his arms across the back. The woman hadn't said anything about his scars. Even when he could see her expression, she'd shown no shock, no pity. She was a good woman, however misguided on MacGregor's character. Love often had a way of blinding a person to someone's true side.

He took off his glasses and rubbed his eyes, then slipped the glasses back on. The door opened and his head shot up.

Kathryn's eyes went wide. "Oh, Jacob, I'm sorry. I didn't realize you were in here." She glanced down at his body, then quickly looked away.

Larson stood and grabbed his shirt from the table beside him. He tried to pull it on, watching to see if she was looking, but the cotton material stuck to the moist liniment still covering his skin. Embarrassment scorched him and he swore softly.

She kept her gaze down. "You finally came to see Miss Maudie about the liniment."

"That's rather obvious, isn't it," he said too harshly. Despite having known Kathryn intimately before, he'd never felt so naked in front of her. Managing to tug his shirt on, Larson held the front of it closed.

"Well . . . I . . . hope it helps you." Head still bent, she turned to leave.

"Kathryn, I'm sorry," he offered, but his voice came out calloused and hard. "I didn't mean to speak to you that way."

Her back was to him, her hand on the open door.

Struck by a reckless impulse, Larson

suddenly wanted to cross the room, take his wife's face in his hands, and let her see who he was. The man he was now. But the possible outcome of that decision made him go weak inside. Even if he could some- how find a way to give Kathryn all that her heart desired, all that she deserved, would her eyes ever hold the love they once had?

In bed at night, she used to trail a finger along his jaw and study him in the shadows, as though trying to set his features to mem- ory. Would she trace the jagged curves of his disfigured face and set them to memory now? Larson looked down and squeezed his eyes tight. The ache in his chest wove its way up to his throat.

"Kathryn," he whispered hoarsely. "Look at me."

She shook her head. "I'm sorry, Jacob. I shouldn't have come in."

"Please, just turn around."

She turned in his direction, her focus still pinned to the floor.

Oh, God, she is so beautiful. And she is my wife. My wife, Lord! Why did you take her from me? His memory allowed him clearer vision than did his eyes, and he saw her body— every curve and arch, beautifully fashioned, glowing with life, once having fit his perfectly. He remembered what it was like to be with her as her husband, and he clenched his eyes tight to quell the power of the memory.

A silent directive from within demanded that he look at her again.

Larson slowly opened his eyes. The first thing he noticed was her hands, small and feminine, clasped protectively over her child. They trembled, and she gripped them tighter. The tremble seemed to travel up her arms until her whole body shuddered. She seemed frightened. But of what? Of him? Why would she be afraid of him? He looked closer. Or was it something else? He saw the quick rise and fall of her chest. Her eyes flitted to his, then away again.

Did he dare hope . . .

Larson crossed the room, and though Kathryn didn't look up, he sensed her tension build with each step he took. Standing before her, his hands were shaking as badly as hers. *Is there a chance she could care for a man who looks the way I do? Who can offer her so little?* There was only one way to find out. And again, that same fervent plea inhabited everything he was.

God, let her still want me.

Standing inches from her, their faces so close, watching her tremble, he reached up to take off his glasses.

"No, Jacob." She turned away, shielding her lips with her hand.

Larson felt the air being sucked from his lungs. She'd thought he was going to kiss her? He took a step back, stunned.

"I'm sorry, Jacob. I . . . I thought I could, but I just can't," she whispered, finally lifting her gaze.

Larson saw the certainty of her desire—or lack of it—confirmed in her eyes. She found his touch loathsome. At least his glasses hid the raw pain of her rejection. The truth of it had been there all along. He'd only hoped for more. While he could be Kathryn's *friend,* he would never again be her husband, her lover.

The latch tumbled into place as Kathryn closed the door behind her.

Minutes later Larson walked back to the stable, to the farthest corner, fell to his knees in the dark, and wept.

———

The next morning, Kathryn stood in front of the Willow Springs Bank. A brisk wind whipped around the corner, and as she took in the breadth and width of the building, she couldn't help but feel as though she were reliving a moment from the past. Last March seemed like a lifetime ago.

"I'll pull on down the street, Miss Kathryn," Gabe called from the wagon. "You just wait here for me when you come out. I'll watch for you."

Kathryn looked back and nodded her thanks. But as Gabe maneuvered the wagon through the traffic, she found she wasn't ready to face Harold Kohlman yet. She sat on a nearby bench and watched the crowds of people passing her without notice.

She hadn't dared ask Jacob to bring her into town this morning, not after what had happened between them last night. She'd seen him outside the stable earlier that morning. He'd acknowledged her but hadn't spoken. Clearly she'd hurt him, and that had never been her intention. It's just that when he'd come so close to her, when he'd started to kiss her, she'd felt traitorous to Larson's memory. Kathryn brushed her fingertips over her lips. Still . . . she couldn't help but wonder what it would've been like to taste Jacob's kiss.

She closed her eyes as heartrending images of his scarred flesh rose in her mind.
White-furrowed slashes that ran deep
across his chest and abdomen as though
the fire had clawed him raw. Compassion
welled inside her, and her eyes burned. She
couldn't imagine what pain he must have
suffered. No wonder Jacob feared the
flame. Any man would.

*Lord, continue to heal Jacob, inside and
out. I find myself attracted to him in a way
that doesn't even make sense to me.* It
frightened her because, in some ways, what
she felt for Jacob surpassed what she had
ever felt for Larson. But it was different.
With Larson, she had first longed for his
touch, then desired his heart. With Jacob,
she'd delighted in discovering who he was
before wanting more from him. And she did
want more, that was clear to her.

Kathryn stood, forcing her thoughts to
the task at hand. She entered the bank
building and crossed the crowded lobby to
where Mr. Kohlman's personal secretary
was seated behind her desk. Kathryn knew
her visit was probably unwarranted, but
since meeting with MacGregor last night,

she couldn't seem to shake the persistent doubt in the back of her mind.

Desperately hoping the answer to her question would be no, she interrupted the woman's work. "Good morning, Miss Stacey. Is Mr. Kohlman in? I need to speak with him about my loan."

The attractive brunette shook her head. "I'm sorry, Mrs. Jennings, but he's in Denver on business today. He'll be back in the office first thing in the morning." Her gaze lowered. "Do you have long before the baby's set to arrive?"

She smoothed a hand over the full swell beneath her dress, certain her excitement showed in her face. "The doctor says I probably have at least two more weeks. He told me to continue with my normal activities as much as I can, but the sooner this baby arrives, the better, as far as I'm concerned."

"Two more weeks? You certainly don't look that far along. I understand the last weeks can be very uncomfortable." Miss Stacey's smile turned sympathetic. "Perhaps there's something I can help you with in Mr. Kohlman's absence?"

Relieved at not having to deal with the

banker, Kathryn forged ahead. "This is simply a formality, but I need to confirm that the funds I was loaned for my property have been appropriately credited to my account. When I last came in about a month ago, the transfer had been approved, but the actual payoff of the loan was still pending." That particular meeting with Mr. Kohlman had left Kathryn with a sense of disquiet. She much preferred having the information confirmed with someone other than him.

"Oh, well, I'm certain they've come through by now." Mr. Kohlman's secretary rose from behind her desk. "Just give me a minute to pull your file and I'll check the balance for you." She walked to a side door and into another office.

After several minutes, she reappeared with a puzzled look. "Mrs. Jennings, I'm sorry, but I can't seem to locate your file. If you have a moment to wait, I'll check Mr. Kohlman's office." She returned seconds later, file in hand and triumph written in her expression. "It was on Mr. Kohlman's desk. He must be handling your transaction personally."

Her raised brow told Kathryn that she considered Kohlman's personal attention something to be coveted. Unfortunately, Kathryn didn't hold that same view, but sharing her opinion would gain nothing. "I appreciate your help finding it. Like I said, I'm sure everything's been taken care of by now, but I want to be certain."

"That's understandable. It's always wise to double-check these things." Miss Stacey opened the file and flipped through the papers from front to back, then shuffled through them again. Her frown didn't bolster Kathryn's confidence.

"Is there a problem?"

"Mrs. Jennings, are you certain you arranged for your loan to be paid off?"

Kathryn stepped closer. "Yes, I'm completely certain. Mr. Kohlman assured me the funds would be transferred a month ago. Are you telling me they haven't been?" She leaned forward in an effort to read the papers on top.

The young woman snapped the file shut. "If you'll come back tomorrow, I'm confident Mr. Kohlman can clear everything up for you. Perhaps he simply hasn't added the appropriate paper work to your file."

Kathryn sensed she knew more. "Miss

Stacey, I need to know whether my loan has been paid off or not."

The woman laid a hand on the file atop her desk. "I'm sorry, but I can't say for sure."

Frustration sliced through Kathryn's patience. "But you can at least tell me what the file says."

As though weighing that thought, Miss Stacey leaned to the side and glanced past Kathryn toward the main lobby. "Mrs. Jennings," she said, her voice lowering. "Technically the files are the property of the bank and are considered private, not to be shared with clients." She hesitated. "This could have been left in your file from before, but . . . the file states that your land is scheduled for auction day after tomorrow at noon on the steps of the Denver courthouse."

CHAPTER TWENTY-FIVE

"Did you or did you not pay off my loan as we agreed, Mr. MacGregor?" Kathryn's anger at discovering his possible deception had steadily mounted through the day, and when he arrived home late that evening, she struggled to keep her voice even.

MacGregor took off his coat and tossed it over a chair. A look of annoyance flashed in his eyes before he smiled. "Kathryn, how wonderful to see you this evening. I wish I could be sayin' you look well, lass, but I'm afraid you appear a bit agitated. And that'll hardly do for someone in your condition."

His blatant patronizing only incensed Kathryn further. A servant passed through the foyer and into the study. "Just answer my question," she insisted, not caring at the moment who heard or that he was her employer. If MacGregor's actions matched her speculations, she wouldn't be working here much longer anyway. "Did you or did you not—"

MacGregor took hold of her arm and guided her to the stairs. "Let's discuss this in my office, shall we? I'd prefer we not have an audience, my dear." Kathryn preceded him upstairs, and he quietly closed the office door behind them. "I don't know what's happened to upset you, Kathryn, but I assure you everything is in order as we agreed."

"That's not what Miss Stacey said when I visited the bank this morning."

He came to stand before her in front of the desk.

"There is no notice of payment in my file. No record listing the transfer of funds. Nothing!" A sharp stitch in her midsection brought a gasp. She put a hand on the desk for support.

"You'd best be calmin' yourself, lass. Like I said, it won't do for you to be gettin' yourself upset over nothin'. Perhaps the notice simply hasn't been put in your file yet."

"You gave me your word that the deed to

my property would be put in my file." She pressed a hand to her abdomen as the pain subsided. "The last thing put in my file was an auction notice for my land to be sold the day after tomorrow. If you can't produce the deed to my land, Mr. MacGregor, I'll be forced to take my copy of the contract to an attorney in town first thing tomorrow morning."

All civility vanished from his expression. "You go see whomever you like in the mornin', dear. I'll drive you there myself." He laughed and shook his head. "And were you referrin' to the copy that you kept in your trunk, by chance? The trunk in the corner of your bedroom? Come now, Mrs. Jennings, did you really think I would loan you that kind of money? I told you the night we had dinner what a risk you were."

A chill snaked through her. "You lied to me? The entire time?"

His mouth tipped in a smirk. "Hard to believe, isn't it, Mrs. Jennings? And me bein' such a fine gentleman and all."

Kathryn felt like the fool she'd been. But her injured pride lashed out. "Perhaps I'll contact an attorney I know and ask him to investigate this for me. Maybe suggest that he inquire about Berklyn Stockholders."

MacGregor's eyes went dark. "You may contact whomever you like. I told you ranching was no business for a woman. I hope you've learned your lesson." He jerked his chin toward the door. "You can show yourself out now. I'll give you till tomorrow afternoon to have your things removed from Casaroja, or I'll have them removed for you."

Numb, Kathryn closed the office door behind her. What a fool she'd been. Matthew Taylor's suspicions had proven right—she never should have trusted MacGregor. She felt her way down the darkened staircase, and even though the pains had receded, she still had trouble catching her breath. Her throat ached with emotion and her cheeks were damp with tears. All she could see was Larson's face. His dream was ruined, and it had been her doing. *I'm so sorry, Larson. Please forgive me.*

Wanting to avoid any servants who might still be awake, she left by way of the front entrance. The cool night air hit her face, and she gulped big breaths of it. Her first instinct was to go to the stable, but it was late—even the bunkhouses were dark.

Besides, Jacob wouldn't welcome her anyway. Not after last night.

Kathryn locked the door to her cottage, wedged a kitchen chair beneath the doorknob, and crossed to the bedroom. She noticed the trunk in the corner and, on impulse, bent and began rummaging through the clothing, searching. If only she could remember, if only she could . . .

Growing frantic, she shoved the top layers of clothing aside. Then she felt it. She held the shirt to her face and breathed in. Her throat constricted. Only the smell of cedar. Nothing else. She pulled another of Larson's shirts from the trunk, and another. But his scent was gone.

Kathryn crawled into bed fully clothed. She took the music box from her pocket, turned the key, and lifted the lid. As the Christmas tune played, random images filled her mind. The cabin draped in each of the four seasons, the towering blue spruce standing sentinel outside the kitchen window. She pictured Larson returning from having bathed in the stream, his damp hair reaching to his shoulders, droplets of water clinging to his muscled chest. She saw her mother's smile and could almost remember the sound of her laughter. Almost . . .

The images faded, and another face

came into view. One with a timid, misshapen smile that communicated a tenderness words never could. She closed her eyes and could almost feel her hand being covered by his smooth, scarred one.

The land was lost to her now, but strangely that wasn't what hurt her most. This pain went far deeper. Somehow, it felt as though she were losing Larson all over again. The music box fell silent on the bed beside her, its last notes sounding appropriately hollow and desolate in the silence. Kathryn turned onto her side and pulled a pillow close to her chest, weary for sleep but needing even more to escape.

A pounding on the door brought her fully awake. She blinked to clear the fuzz from her mind and ran a hand over her eyes. Sunshine streamed in through the bedroom window. It must be morning, but it felt as though she'd only drifted off moments ago. She pushed herself up off the bed and made her way to the door.

More pounding. "Kathryn, are you all right?"

Jacob. Hearing his voice triggered relief. Kathryn removed the wedged chair and opened the door to see Jacob and Miss Maudie standing on her doorstep. Worry clouded Miss Maudie's expression. Jacob simply looked her up and down.

"Are you all right?" he repeated. The gentleness in his voice gave Kathryn hope that perhaps their friendship might be repairable after all. It was surprising how deep the hope of that bond ran through her. "Miss Maudie came to get me when you didn't show up this morning."

"I'm fine, Jacob. Miss Maudie," she added, nodding. If Maudie hadn't been there, Kathryn might have been tempted to walk straight into Jacob's arms.

Miss Maudie held out an envelope. "This just came for you, dear. The clerk said it was urgent."

Kathryn took it. *Willow Springs Bank* was stamped on the outside. She ripped it open, already anticipating the contents. As she'd suspected, Mr. Kohlman was requesting a meeting with her. *Urgent*, the note said. How urgent could the meeting be when she'd already lost her property? *Nothing can snatch me out of your hands, Father,* she reminded herself. *I'm trusting in that.*

Jacob stepped closer. "What does it say?"

"It's a request from Mr. Kohlman to meet him at the bank this morning as soon as possible."

"I'll get a wagon from the lower stable and be back shortly."

As Jacob hurried away, Miss Maudie laid a hand to her arm. "Kathryn dear, perhaps you need to leave this business for later and get some rest for you and your baby."

Kathryn ran a hand through her hair. A tempting thought, yet Kohlman's request sounded pressing. Besides, the pains she'd experienced had stopped, and if the baby came while in town, Doc Hadley would be there to help. Kathryn searched Miss Maudie's face, deciding that MacGregor hadn't told the woman about his ordering her to leave Casaroja. Kathryn debated whether to get the dear woman involved, but what could Miss Maudie do? Besides, it would only create tension between them, and Maudie had been nothing but kind.

Kathryn forced a smile. "I'll head into town and see what Mr. Kohlman wants first. Then I'll come back. I don't think I could go back to sleep right now anyway."

Miss Maudie's eyes lit. "Have you had any signs of the baby's comin' yet?"

"Just a few pains last night."

"If you feel up to it, you and Jacob should stop by the harvest festival in town later today. The whole town turns out for it. Mr. MacGregor hosts a barbecue, and I'll be helpin' with that most of the day." She patted Kathryn's arm one last time. "If you need anything, send Jacob for me."

Thanking her, Kathryn spotted Jacob leading a team of horses from the stable. She quickly changed into a fresh dress, ran a brush through her hair and, for the baby's sake, ate a piece of bread slathered with butter. A heaviness weighted her chest as she thought of the day ahead and of having to face Kohlman again, but the thought of having Jacob by her side made it bearable.

She'd done her best to keep the land, but her best wasn't good enough in the end, and she knew she had to let it go. Nothing she could say to Kohlman this morning would change that.

———

Wagons already cluttered the field behind the church and choked the streets of town, even though the festival supposedly didn't start until noon. Miss Maudie had been right—it looked as though everyone in the surrounding area would be in attendance, along with every cowboy in the territory.

Kathryn glanced at Jacob sitting on the wagon bench beside her, glad he was there. "I see it fits well enough."

He reached up and touched the cap she'd knitted for him. "Like a glove," he answered, laughing softly. "I've been wearing it."

"I've been noticing."

He shot her a quick look. "And I've been thanking God for its maker."

Kathryn sat speechless even after he'd turned around, wondering exactly when this gentle man had stolen so quietly into her life and captured her heart. Looking down, she twisted the gold band still adorning her left hand. How could she love two such different men with such unquestionable certainty?

"This is about as close as we're going to get to the bank." Jacob set the brake and climbed down. "They have the road roped off ahead."

He offered Kathryn his hand and steadied her full frame as he lifted her down. Unlike that day at church, his hands didn't linger about her waist this time. *As though I still have a waist,* she thought with brittle humor.

"Would you like me to go in with you? Or . . . I can wait outside."

Looking up at him, Kathryn caught her faint reflection in his glasses and couldn't help but think of Sadie. Sadie had seen a part of Jacob that remained hidden to her. "I'd love for you to come with me, if you don't mind," she said, taking his proffered arm. Warmth spread through her as he drew her close and maneuvered a path through the crowded streets.

When they entered the bank, they found the lobby unusually quiet. Kathryn counted five employees and even fewer customers. She spotted Miss Stacey, Kohlman's secretary, across the lobby.

Miss Stacey rose as they approached. "Good morning, Mrs. Jennings."

Kathryn greeted her, keenly aware of the moment the woman looked at Jacob, because a frown replaced her smile before she hastily looked away.

"I'll let Mr. Kohlman know that you're here."

"Thank you, Miss Stacey," Kathryn answered, then turned to Jacob.

He smiled.

Clearly he'd grown accustomed to this reaction from people. Kathryn regretted, again, her first response at having seen his face. But as she looked at him now, admiration for him filled her, and she wanted only one thing. She'd already seen past his scars to the heart of the godly man within; now all she wanted was to look into Jacob's eyes.

Harold Kohlman rose from his desk, his brow creasing in obvious disapproval. "Mrs. Jennings, this meeting is of a most personal nature. Perhaps this man would prefer to wait outside."

Larson bristled at Kohlman's tone. "The name is Jacob Brantley, and Mrs. Jennings prefers me to stay."

He hadn't expected such a strong physical reaction toward Kohlman, especially since so much time had passed. Larson knew the man's first concern was managing his bank, but for some reason, a resentment rose inside Larson when he thought of Kohlman foreclosing on his land. He glanced at the clock on the office wall. Tomorrow at this time, the land he and Kathryn had worked for the past ten years was going up for auction to the highest bidder. And somewhere along the way, Kohlman had signed the papers enabling that to happen.

Larson led Kathryn to one of two chairs situated before Kohlman's desk. Kathryn turned, and he followed her gaze to a man looking out the window. Dressed in a tailored gray suit, the gentleman reminded Larson, from the back anyway, of businessmen he'd seen back East years ago.

"Very well. Let's get started," Kohlman huffed, clearly displeased. "Mrs. Jennings, if you'll be seated. Mr. Childers, if you'll join us, please."

The man at the window turned, and Kathryn let out a soft gasp. "Mr. Childers!"

She rose and went to him. He embraced her as he might have a daughter. Larson stared, not knowing what to make of it. He didn't remember ever having met the man, but looking more closely at Childers, he couldn't help but be reminded of William Cummings, Kathryn's father.

"Kathryn, child." Mr. Childers' smile came softly. "Well, hardly a child anymore, I see."

Kathryn hugged him again, then drew

back. "What's brought you all the way from Boston?"

"You, my dear. You are what's brought me here." His smile dimmed, and sadness accentuated the fine wrinkles lining his face. "Your father sent me."

Kathryn's expression simultaneously showed joy and shock. Larson took a step forward, unable to fathom that Cummings had finally decided to pursue a relationship with his daughter. After all these years . . .

Quick introductions were exchanged. Larson shook Childers' hand, and then Childers led Kathryn back to the chair and sat in the one opposite hers.

"How is Father? I wrote to him a month ago, thinking that perhaps he might want to see me again now that . . ."

Larson's throat tightened as Kathryn let her sentence trail off. *Now that she's alone and with child, and that her husband he never approved of is dead.* She'd paid a high price in so many ways for marrying him. She'd left so much behind to follow his dream—a dream that now lay in ruins.

"Actually, your missive to your father is what prompted my visit." Childers sighed deeply. "When we received your letter, I immediately contacted the bank here in Willow Springs, and an employee was kind enough to confirm that you did indeed still live here. I arrived by stage this morning and came directly here to the bank, where Mr. Kohlman graciously offered to send for you."

Childers looked to Kohlman, who sat behind his desk, hands clasped over his thick middle. "Thank you for the use of your private office, Mr. Kohlman. As you mentioned earlier, this meeting is of a most confidential nature, and I appreciate your keeping knowledge of this conversation restricted to the parties present." He turned back to Kathryn. "Your father wrote a letter to you, Kathryn. I know he would have liked to have delivered it himself."

"Is Father still in Boston? Is he well?"

Childers carefully gathered Kathryn's hands in his and shook his head. In that moment, Larson knew the purpose of Childers' visit.

"Your father died this past December, Kathryn. A poor heart is what the physicians said. It wasn't a lengthy illness."

Larson saw the shock ripple through Kathryn's body, and he went to stand beside her.

"My father is . . . gone?" she whispered.

"Yes, child, I'm so sorry." Childers pulled an envelope from his pocket. "He wrote this letter for you. I believe a portion of this was intended for your husband, although I was saddened to learn from your letter that your husband, too, has passed on. You have my deepest condolences, Kathryn."

She nodded as silent tears fell. Guilt needled Larson at seeing them, and Annabelle's voice replayed in his mind. *"Kathryn always told me you weren't dead. She said she felt it—in here. Do you have any idea what she's been through?"* But he had only to remind himself that what he was doing was best for Kathryn in order to silence the voice.

Then a thought struck him, and he wondered how it had slipped by him. William Cummings had been quite well-to-do, and though he'd been an estranged father at best, caring far more about his investments than his family, no doubt the man would've been compelled to leave his inheritance to his only child.

"Kathryn, as you know, your father was a very wealthy man," Childers continued quietly, as though responding to Larson's thoughts. "He wanted you to have the best of everything and he spent his life working to that end, making sure you and your mother had every comfort. Not long after your mother died, your father invested in the mining industry. Silver, specifically, and within months the investment had exceeded even his highest expectations. Within a couple of years your father finally achieved the wealth he'd always sought after, however . . ." A sigh escaped Childers, both heavy and troubled. He took Kathryn's hand. "He had no one to share it with. Which leads to the reason I'm here today, to talk to you about your father's estate and the inheritance he left you."

Kohlman's chair creaked, and Larson turned to see the man standing behind his desk, his ruddy complexion now gone ashen.

"My inheritance?" Kathryn gently shook her head, and Larson read the question in her eyes. Though never having stated it outright, William Cummings had, by his lack of interest and communication, severed all ties with his daughter years ago, after Kathryn had married.

Kohlman made a noise in his throat, at which they all turned. "If you'll excuse me, Mrs. Jennings, Mr. Childers, I can see this is a . . . most delicate moment, so I'll leave you to finish this meeting in private. But please, use my office as long as you like."

Kohlman's hasty exit didn't bother Larson—it was the look of urgency in the man's eyes as he closed the door that roused suspicion.

Childers reached into a satchel by the desk and withdrew a document. "Before I disclose the contents of your father's last will and testament, Kathryn, I feel a need to remind you that I've been your father's business partner since you were a child. I've seen your father through many stages of his life, and his career, so what I'm about to tell you is trustworthy. I was frequently at William's bedside during his last days, and despite what I'm about to tell you, he was not at all a bitter or unhappy man in the end."

Kathryn swallowed convulsively, her attention riveted on what Childers would say next.

"As I said, the mining investment made your father a wealthy man. However, his other businesses were suffering, and several of his newer ventures did not yield to his advantage. Then the mine went bust last year. Almost overnight. All the money, the investments, the houses . . . everything, was gone."

Larson cleared his throat and dared ask the question. "But you said Kathryn's father left her an inheritance?"

Childers smiled. "And that he did. It's just not the one that he'd originally intended."

None of them spoke for a moment, and finally Kathryn lifted her head. "Did my father say anything about me to you before he died? Did he give any reason why he never contacted me?"

"Though very intelligent, your father was a misguided man most of his life, Kathryn, and that by his own admission. Toward the end he told me you'd written him after your mother's passing. Once or twice, is what he recalled."

Childers paused, and from the look on the man's face, Larson found a well of protectiveness rising within him for Kathryn.

"Your father confided to me one night that he'd always intended to find those letters again and read them."

"You mean . . . he never read them?" Kathryn's voice came out small and breathy, like a girl's.

Childers shook his head, then lifted his shoulders and let them fall. "When the time came and he realized all that he'd missed in his life, when faced with the grave mistakes he'd made, it was too late. He was very ill by that time, near penniless. The houses and furniture had all been sold, along with his personal belongings. Your letters were lost to him forever, just as he thought you were.

"I hired someone to try to locate you last winter. All your father knew was that you were in the Colorado Territory, but our search turned up nothing." The seriousness in his countenance slowly lessened. "Then when your latest letter arrived, I finally knew where you were. Your father's greatest regret, Kathryn, was that he was not the father you deserved, nor the husband he wished he'd been to your mother."

Childers started to say more, then apparently thought better of it. He pointed to the envelope in her hand. "But lest I paint too bleak a picture for you, child, again, your father did not die a bitter man, and his prayer was that you would not be so toward him. In truth, he did indeed leave you something of great importance." He rose. "I'll be in town for a few days. Take time to read the letter, and we'll meet to discuss the details later. I'll be staying at the hotel. Contact me when you're ready."

Kathryn stood with him. "Thank you for coming all this way to tell me."

Childers took a moment to study her face. "I didn't want you hearing the news by telegram or post. Plus, selfishly, I wanted to see you again. You've grown into a beautiful woman, Kathryn. When you first walked into the office, I thought I was looking at your mother. If I may be so bold," he said, his tone hesitant, "what is the expected date of your child's arrival? A Thanksgiving baby? Or Christmas perhaps?"

She smiled softly. "Actually it's within the month."

Larson read the surprise in Childers' expression, but it in no way matched the bolt of shock slicing through him. Surely she couldn't be that far along. She wasn't large enough. He looked down at his wife's body, his own tensing with a flood of disbelief. He thought back to last Christmas, then rapidly sped forward through the months, counting. *Could it be that . . .*

"After all these years, God has seen fit to bless me with a child," she told him. "I only wish that Larson were still here to see the birth of his son or daughter."

Larson stifled a quick intake of breath

and gripped the back of the chair beside him. *Could it be true? God, is this what you were trying to get me to see? But Kathryn's still so small.* He thought of the brothel, of Matthew Taylor. He'd seen her there, he'd seen her with Matthew Taylor, overhead their conversations. He'd thought that . . .

Larson looked into his wife's face, into her eyes, and saw a purity there that he wanted to believe in. That he wanted to believe in with all his heart.

"I promised William something," Childers said, dragging Larson's attention back. The older gentleman tipped Kathryn's chin upward with his forefinger as though she were a little girl. "I promised him that I would find you and deliver his letter, and that when I did, I would give you a token of his love." Childers framed Kathryn's face between his hands and gently kissed her forehead. Once, twice.

"My father's last gift, and his best," Kathryn whispered.

As Jacob guided the wagon down the road to Casaroja, Kathryn couldn't help but see the place through different eyes. While grand in its own right, Casaroja didn't begin to compare with the modest cabin that Larson had built. MacGregor had built Casaroja on greed and deception. Larson's foundation had been love and years of honest hard work.

She ran a hand over her belly. Larson's child wouldn't inherit his father's land. He would inherit something far better, something Larson had always wanted, and had always possessed in Kathryn's eyes—an honest name.

Jacob pulled the wagon in front of the cottage. He'd been unusually quiet on the ride back, and she'd caught him staring at her several times.

"Are you sure you want to leave this afternoon, Kathryn? Maybe you should wait until Miss Maudie comes back so you can tell her good-bye."

"No, I want to leave now, today." She wanted—needed—to be gone before MacGregor returned and found her still there.

Jacob considered her for a moment, then climbed from the wagon and came around. He offered her his hand and helped her down and then stood close, his hand still holding hers. Kathryn stared up at him, her pulse quickening.

He let go and nodded toward the harnessed team. "One of the horses is limping. I'll hitch up a fresh team from the lower stable and be back up to help you shortly. Wait for me, though. Don't try to carry anything out yourself." He walked her as far as the porch.

Kathryn shaded her eyes in the afternoon sun so she could see his face. A cool breeze rippled the cottonwood branches overhead.

"Jacob, do you think we could have some time to talk later tonight, once we're back in town? I'd like to explain some things, if I can put my thoughts into words."

Though his eyes were hidden, his smile led her to believe he understood.

She watched him pull away, then looked at the letter in her hand, still unopened. Her father had loved her after all. That meant more to her than anything else.

The inheritance he might have left her, if his businesses hadn't failed, would have seemed like a godsend a few months ago. It would have allowed her to keep the cabin, the ranch, Larson's dream. Yet it could never have replaced the relationships she'd lost or the years she'd forfeited. Years lost with her father through his pursuit to give her everything, when all she'd wanted was him. And years forfeited with Larson by looking past the man he was to some nonsensical dream of the man she wanted him to be.

Kathryn tucked the letter into her coat pocket. She'd waited years for this word from her father and wanted to be able to savor it unhurried. She could wait a little while longer. Right now she wanted to get off this land and to be far away from Donlyn Mac-Gregor.

CHAPTER TWENTY-SIX

In her bedroom, Kathryn made a halfhearted attempt to fold her clothes along with the baby's blankets before stuffing them into the trunk. She grabbed her Bible from the nightstand and laid it on top. Seconds later, she heard the front door open and close. Funny, she thought she'd locked it.

"I'm back here, Jacob. I'm almost ready."

The determined stride of boot steps against hardwood floor made her hands go still. That didn't sound like Jacob's labored stride.

"Nice to be seein' you again, Mrs. Jennings."

The voice sent a thousand skitters up her

spine. Placing it even before she turned, Kathryn instinctively stepped back.

The menacing scar that jagged along his lower right jaw puckered as his smirk deepened. He leaned against the doorframe, one leg crossed over the other. "MacGregor said I was to come and help you pack, ma'am. See you safely off Casaroja." He crossed to the bed, picked up an undergarment, and rubbed the material between his thumb and forefinger. "I told him I was happy to do it. Told him you and me was already good friends, or would be soon enough."

He laughed and the high-pitched shrill made Kathryn's flesh crawl.

Of slight build, not too tall, and more wiry-looking than muscled, the ranch hand gave off a sinister aura. Same as the first day she'd seen him ride up with Matthew Taylor at the ranch, shortly after Larson disappeared. And his voice—maybe it was his twang, from the Deep South if she had to guess—coupled with the manner in which he spoke, rippled with foreboding. He spoke as if they were the best of friends about to take a summer stroll.

Summoning courage, Kathryn took the undergarment and stuffed it in the trunk. "I can pack myself, thank you. And I'm leaving today, just as Mr. MacGregor requested." She glanced out the window for a sign of Jacob.

He reached behind him and closed the bedroom door. "Don't worry, Mrs. Jennings, or can I call you Kathryn?" His expression told her that her answer mattered little. "We're all by ourselves, just you and me. Everyone else is gone to town. You know, the first time I seen you, the way you smiled"—he took a step closer—"I could tell you were a lady. And I ain't been close with too many of them in my life."

Somehow Kathryn didn't find that hard to believe. He blocked the only way to the door, so she had no choice but to stand her ground. The sickening mingle of days-old sweat and liquor drifted toward her.

"I thought maybe we could be good friends, but"—his gaze dropped to her unborn child. "I see another man got friendly with you before I could, and so soon after that husband of yours went and got hisself killed." He laughed again and shook his head, then made a tsking noise with his tongue. "That was a wicked storm Christmas Day, wasn't it? Storms like that can make a man lose his sense of direction." He twirled his left index finger by his head, mimicking the sound of wind. "Turn you round where you don't know where you are or where you been."

Kathryn could only stare at him, then felt her knees buckling beneath her. She sat down hard on the bed. Jumbled pieces of conversations piled one atop the other in her mind, and she strained to make sense of them. *"Storms like that can make a man lose his sense of direction. . . ." "This man here didn't die from the elements, leastwise not that alone. . . . Your husband was shot before he died, square in the chest."*

She looked back, willing her voice to hold. "What are you saying?" The question came out weak, fearful.

He leaned in, his warm breath soured with whiskey. "I'm not sayin' anything, ma'am. Just that accidents sometimes have a way of happenin' to people, that's all."

But reading the look on his face, the ever so slight curl of his mouth, Kathryn caught the silent acknowledgment. Part of her raged and wanted to strike him, while another part wanted to lie down and die in defeat. She searched the eyes of her husband's killer, wanting to know why, but the coldness there repelled her. Larson had no enemies, no reason for anyone to—

Her eyes caught on the Bible she'd laid in the trunk. *Berklyn Stockholders.* Larson's letter from that company peeked at her from between the pages—identical to the stationery she'd seen in MacGregor's office that day. She'd meant to ask Miss Stacey about the company on her visit to the bank yesterday but had forgotten.

One of the jumbled pieces suddenly slid into place. "Does Mr. MacGregor own a company by the name of Berklyn Stockholders?"

His cold eyes grew appraising. "Very good, Mrs. Jennings. I told MacGregor he didn't have a reason to worry about you, but I guess he was right after all." He pulled her up from the bed. "We're gonna take a walk. Not far, just a ways over the bluff out back. It ain't safe for a woman in your condition to be out by herself, you know. But you're a headstrong woman, Kathryn. Everyone around here will say so. You just wouldn't listen to reason, that's what they'll say. You went off on a walk by yourself, and . . . well, accidents happen."

He shoved her toward the door and Kathryn lost her balance.

She tried to turn enough to absorb the fall with her shoulder, but her abdomen took the brunt of the blow. She gasped, hunched over on the floor. A spasm arched across her belly, throbbing low and steady. *Oh, Jesus . . . not my baby, not my baby.*

"Please," she panted, face down. "Tell MacGregor he can have the land, the water, everything. I won't contest it."

He knelt down beside her and slipped his hands around her throat, gently at first. He tipped her chin with his thumb, forcing Kathryn to look at him. "It's a bit late for that, ma'am. Maybe if you'd been more agreeable on the front end." His grip tightened around her windpipe, his thumbs pressing in, cutting off her air. Then, with his hands still encircling her throat, he drew her up and held her against the wall.

Choking, Kathryn tried to fight him, but it did little good. His strength far outmatched hers. She watched him gleam with pleasure just as his face started to fade. . . .

In the instant before she blacked out, he let go and she slumped back to the floor. Her lungs burned as she dragged air in. She coughed and cradled her throat with her hands, swallowing convulsively. She pictured Sadie lying in bed that night, her body limp and pulse erratic, the faint outline of fingerprints spanning her slender neck.

"Time to go, Mrs. Jennings."

Kathryn heard the bedroom door open, then felt a vicelike grip on her arms. He pulled her along with him into the next room, but her foot caught on a table and she went down again. Something crashed beside her head and the scent of lamp oil layered the air. She felt the dampness in her hair.

She curled on her side as the spasm in her belly heightened. Pain ripped through her body, and her breath came in short gasps. Sudden warmth gushed from between her legs, and Kathryn heard a low moan, only to realize seconds later that it was coming from her.

He stood over her, and she instinctively shielded her abdomen with her arms. He searched his pockets, then cursed and strode into the kitchen.

As quickly as it came, the pain subsided.

Kathryn tried to push herself up and stood successfully on the second attempt.

She'd never make it to the front door, and certainly wouldn't be able to outrun him in her condition. She crept toward the kitchen and watched him pull open a cupboard drawer, curse again, and throw it on the floor. Silverware scattered over the hardwood floor as he jerked open another.

Then he stilled, with something in his grip.

Kathryn looked around and grabbed the first thing she saw—a brass candlestick. The solid metal was cool to the touch, and the weight of it gave her courage. She crept up behind him and swung just as he turned. The crack of the candlestick against his temple made a dull, sickening thud.

His eyes went black with rage. He lunged for her, then fell to the floor, motionless. Kathryn dropped the candlestick and ran.

"Jacob!" She moved as fast as she could away from the cottage and toward the stable. The corrals were empty, the doors closed. Though the stable was not far from the cottage, she tired quickly and slowed her pace, glancing behind her every few steps to see if she was being followed.

The fall air combined with the dampness between her legs and chilled her. The cold seemed to seep deep inside her bones, and her body started shaking. She rubbed her arms for circulation, but the tremors seemed to start from somewhere deep inside her. Kathryn reached to open the stable door just as another spasm hit. She went to her knees.

Scarcely able to breathe, she checked behind her. No sign of Jacob, nor anyone else.

Minutes passed.

Finally managing to lift the bar, she pulled the door open and stepped inside, certain she'd find Jacob there. Thinking twice, she turned back and closed the door behind her. Most likely the man would check the main house first. He wouldn't think to look in here. For a time, she was safe.

She quietly called Jacob's name while searching the empty stalls. Then she stopped, remembering something Jacob had said about having to visit the lower stable. Alarm shot through her even as an overpowering sensation began building deep within.

It started low and hard in her pelvic region, then moved downward. Her legs went weak. Wide-eyed, she looked down at her body, partly in awe of the miracle secreted inside her womb, but mostly terrified that the child had chosen now to make its way into the world!

She spotted a blanket on a bed of hay and sank down on top of it. Her legs shook uncontrollably, and a shudder swept through her. Leaning back against the roughhewn wall, she drew her legs up, trying to get warm.

The creak of a door brought her head up. She kept perfectly still.

"I know you're in here, Kathryn."

Stifling a cry, Kathryn scooted to the farthest corner of the stable and hid between bales of hay. She pulled the blanket over her head and prayed God would make her invisible.

"You know I'm kinda proud of you in a way, ma'am. I had no idea you had such mettle." The stall doors creaked open, one by one, before banging shut. His voice came closer. "You're puttin' up a much bigger fight than your husband did."

Kathryn imagined Larson being ambushed by this man in the storm that night. Did Larson hear anything before the bullet struck him? Did he see the gun or feel pain for long? Closing her eyes, she hoped again that he'd died quickly, without suffering. And she took odd comfort in knowing that, if death *did* come for her and her child today, they would be united with Larson. But right now, in this moment, all Kathryn wanted was *life.* Life for herself and her child.

Making herself as small as she could, she pressed back between the bales. The air beneath the blanket grew warm and stale. Another spasm ripped across her abdomen, and she bit her lower lip to keep from crying out. Her body broke out in a sweat as the metallic taste of blood reached her tongue.

"Why, there you are, Mrs. Jennings." He ripped off the blanket. The right side of his face was streaked with blood, his mouth twisted. "I think we're gonna have to call off that walk though. I'm just not in the mood for it anymore. But I've got something else in mind."

The disturbing calm of his voice, coupled with the crazed look in his eyes, sent a shudder through her.

He walked to the side door and picked up an ax. Kathryn tried to stand up, but weakness pinned her down. He secured the bar against the back door, took the ax, and sank it deep into the wood, effectively wedging the bar into place. Then he grabbed a coil of rope from the workbench.

Kneeling in front of her, he grabbed her ankles, jerked her flat onto her back, and looped the rope around her legs several times, pulling it taut.

"Please don't do this," she cried. *Where is Jacob?* She screamed his name.

"Yell all you like, ma'am. I told you no one else is here." He bound her wrists behind her back, then walked to the workbench and picked up a lamp. "You've surprised MacGregor once too often, Kathryn. And me too." He touched his temple and pulled away bloody fingers. "You won't be doin' that again."

Lighting the wick, he came to stand beside her and began swinging the lamp in slow, lazy arches over her legs. "If it makes you feel any better, you'll be joining your husband real soon. That should at least be some . . ."

As he spoke and she realized his intention, Kathryn couldn't help but think of Jacob. She screamed for him again, over and over, thinking of the scars that covered his face, chest, and arms. Her eyes followed the flame arching over her—back and forth, back and forth—and she could almost feel the fire licking at her skin. Remembering Jacob's fear of the flame, her breath came harder.

"Please don't do this, please . . ." In broken sobs, she begged for her life, for the life of her baby.

"It won't hurt for long, or so I'm told. . . ." He talked over her as though not hearing.

She wriggled her arms and legs, trying to scoot away, her eyes never leaving the flame. "I'll give you whatever you want. Tell me what it is you want."

He knelt down and brought the lamp close to her face. She turned away, clenching her eyes shut. "It just hit me, there's something . . . What's that word . . . ?" He paused. "Oh yeah, *poetic* about this. Don't you think? You're dyin' the same way your husband did."

He made an exploding noise, and Kathryn went absolutely still inside.

She opened her eyes in time to see him heave the lamp against the stable wall behind her.

CHAPTER TWENTY-SEVEN

Kathryn heard the crash of glass, then smelled the acrid scent of burning hay and wood. When she looked back, the man was gone and flames were creeping up the wall toward the loft. Feeding on the aged lumber, the fire kindled and sent sparks shooting into the dry hay around her.

"You're dyin' the same way your husband did."

She tried to scoot away, but the small distance her efforts gained drained her energy. Her arms ached from being wrenched behind her. The rope cut into her wrists, but she continued to work her arms up and down, praying the knot would give. Smoke layered the air, taking oxygen with it.

"You're dyin' the same way your husband did."

What had he meant by that? Larson had died by a gunshot wound to the chest. But the man who claimed to have killed her husband said she was dying the same way he did. Crying, choking, her lungs clawing for air, Kathryn felt her chest growing heavy and tight. The ceiling above her rained down sparks, writhing and dancing like a living thing.

She tried to form a prayer in her heart but couldn't. Only one name came to mind, and as the smoke thickened, shrouding her and her child in a suffocating blanket of gray, she whispered the name over and over and over again.

Jesus . . . Jesus . . . Jesus . . .

Larson finished hitching the fresh pair of sorrel mares to the wagon, still unable to comprehend what had just been revealed to him. Kathryn was carrying *his* child, a child they'd made together. Remembering the look in her eyes as she'd told Childers the news—*truth* was the only word Larson could think of to describe it.

The mares pranced nervously in the harness as Larson closed the gates. He spoke in hushed tones in an effort to soothe them, puzzled at their skittishness.

It was hard to believe that William Cummings was dead, and had died penniless in the end after having spent a lifetime in pursuit of wealth. Climbing into the wagon, Larson caught a glimpse of his scarred hands and knew there was a lesson in there for him, one he had already taken to heart. *God, Kathryn deserves better than me, I know that. But if you give me another chance, with your strength inside me, I'll love her better this time.*

Larson released the brake and the horses pulled forward without command. He reined in to keep control, but the horses only whinnied more and strained at the bit.

The breeze shifted, revealing the faintest hint of smoke.

He scanned the plains stretching west to the mountains. Not a cloud in the sky, no haze on the horizon. The ranch hands he'd run into moments ago had already crested the western bluff and were out of sight, gone to check on the stock. The lower stables blocked his view of the big house and the upper buildings, so he urged the mares forward. When the wagon rounded the corner, he went numb. Panic rushed to fill the void.

Wisps of smoke seeped from the sides of the stable near Kathryn's cottage, spiraling upward. Flames licked the rooftop. Larson could feel them on his skin. Dread poured through him, and for a moment, he was back in that shack, when the world turned to fire.

At his command, the horses surged forward. The wagon jarred and bumped over the rutted road. The cottage was a fair distance from the stable and the wind was minimal. *Plenty of time to get Kathryn.*

He reined in by the cottage and jumped down. The door was open.

"Kat!" he yelled. A lamp lay shattered, and dark stains splattered the hardwood floor. When he didn't find her in the bedroom, he ran back outside and looked toward the stable. *She couldn't be. If she was in the main house, she was fine. If she was in the stable . . .* He ran, ignoring the pain in his leg.

He pulled his bandanna from his back pocket and tied it over his nose and mouth, then shoved his glasses into his coat pocket. As he reached the door, it swung open.

Smoke poured out as a man backed out of the stable. Coughing, the man slammed the door and turned. The right side of his face was covered in blood, but Larson recognized him—a ranch hand he'd seen a couple of times, but only at a distance.

The man's expression registered surprise, then hardened. "Well, what are you waitin' for, man! Help me get some water!"

Larson didn't move. Neither did the other man.

"I said get some water!"

That voice. Something about it—

A cry came from inside the stable. Larson glanced at the door, then back to the man, and panic inside him exploded. He threw the first punch.

The fellow staggered back, looking stunned. Then he cursed and flicked his tongue along the edge of his mouth, meeting blood. His lips twisted in a sneer. "Let's get on with it, mister. You can die slow or long, don't matter to me."

Like an invisible blow, recognition hit him. It wasn't the man's face, but his voice. Larson looked him in the eye, then tugged his bandanna down. "I think you already tried to kill me once. Or don't you remember?"

Confusion clouded the man's smirk. He stared at Larson's face for a second; then his eyes narrowed to slits. Larson braced himself for the charge.

He hit Larson hard, putting his full weight into the assault. Larson staggered back, his right leg buckling until only sky filled his view. He turned to avoid a right-handed punch, but the man's boot connected with his ribcage and expelled the air from his lungs. Larson rolled to his side, struggling to fill them again.

Expecting another blow, he looked around and glimpsed the guy striding back to the stable. The man jerked open the door and smoke poured out. *Oh, God, don't let him hurt her.*

Larson struggled to his feet and followed, pausing inside the door. No sign of the man. Fire engulfed the loft, greedily licking the walls of the stable. Larson's feet felt bolted to where he stood. He remembered the feel of it on his skin, scathing his flesh, and he couldn't move. The acrid scent of its fury filled his nostrils.

Then came another memory, stronger and clearer than the others—the memory of invisible arms rescuing him from a similar fate last December. He pulled the kerchief back up and raced inside.

"Kathryn!" He checked each stall, watching behind him as he went.

Thick smoke hovered in heavy folds, and the farther back Larson went, the less he could distinguish. *God, you are my strength, my shield, my deliverer. Give me eyes to see.* He felt his way along the stable wall to the back, the smoke choking him. He called her name again, but the hungry blaze devoured the sound.

Then he heard it. She was calling out a name, but it wasn't his. Still, it was the sweetest sound Larson had ever heard. Like a candle in the darkness, it led him to her. He found her lying on her back.

As he bent to lift her, a slice of wordless warning shot through him.

He turned and caught the man hard in the gut with his shoulder. The guy staggered back, dropping the ax that had been in his hands. But he didn't go down. Instead, he charged again. Using his opponent's momentum, Larson undercut him and vaulted him onto his back. He landed with a thud. Larson hoped he would stay down—silently willed it—but the man struggled to his feet.

Larson came at him full force, and the ranch hand fell back, groaning. The heavy beams supporting the loft above them groaned in protest, and Larson watched the flames devouring the thick beams like parched kindling.

He crawled back to Kathryn and lifted her. Her body was limp in his arms and his hope followed suit. He carried her outside and gently laid her beside the well. She stirred and coughed, drawing rapid, shallow breaths. He sank down beside her, the muscles in his arms and shoulders aching with fatigue. Larson yanked the bandanna from his face and dragged air into his lungs.

After untying her wrists and ankles, he felt her arms and legs, checking her body for burns. He hesitated, then slowly moved his hands over her unborn child, *his* child. *Lord, please let him be all right.* Faint movement rippled beneath his hands, and he almost laughed for joy.

A deafening crack exploded behind him, and Larson spun.

The walls of the stable surrendered to the fiery onslaught and caved in, taking the loft with it. Flames engulfed the building, sending sparks shooting high into the air. He thought of the man inside but felt no remorse. Kathryn was his only concern.

Larson drew water from the well and drenched his kerchief. "Kathryn," he whispered, smoothing her face with the moist cloth.

Her eyes fluttered open, then clamped shut again. A deep cough rattled her chest. He knew what she must be feeling, like the inside of her lungs were charred. He encouraged slow breaths and checked her face and neck again for burns. Even streaked with a combination of dirt and soot with tears, his wife was still the most beautiful thing he'd ever seen.

She tried again to open her eyes. "My eyes . . . I can't open my eyes." Her voice came out raw.

"It's the smoke. Don't try to open them yet. Give it a few minutes." Larson cradled her face with his hand. "But you're not burned—you're all right." He started to rise. "I'll go soak this cloth again and—"

"No, don't leave me." She clung to him, fisting his shirt in her hands. "That man. Where is that man?"

"He can't hurt you anymore, Kathryn. He's dead. He didn't make it out."

Her face twisted. "He said he . . ." She wept, her words growing indistinguishable.

Not understanding, Larson gently cradled her against his chest, feeling her body shudder against him. Unexpectedly, she reached up to touch his face, and Larson couldn't believe the name she was whispering. It wasn't Matthew Taylor's. It wasn't even Jacob's. It was *his*.

Suddenly Kathryn arched her back and groaned, then wrapped her arms around her middle. "The baby—"

She cried out when Larson lifted her. Her body stiffened in protest as he carried her into the cottage. With one hand, she cradled her abdomen. With the other, she dug her fingers into his shoulder until Larson was certain her nails were drawing blood. He laid her on the bed, and she immediately rolled onto her side, moaning.

He got a cup of water from the pump in

the kitchen, freshened the handkerchief, and returned to the bedroom. As he draped the cool cloth over her closed eyes, he realized his own were exposed and quickly slipped his glasses back on.

"Don't leave me again," she whispered, reaching for him.

Larson caught the unexpected command in her tone and couldn't help but smile. He leaned close and cupped the back of her neck, then lifted the cup to her lips. "I'm not leaving you, Kathryn." *Not ever again.* "But I do need to get ready to deliver this baby."

"Stay with me for a minute first."

Larson sat down on the bed and took her hand. Her grip turned viselike.

After several minutes, the contraction apparently subsided, because Kathryn relaxed, her breathing evened. Larson knew enough about the process to know that there was no telling how long this reprieve might last. It could be minutes, could be hours.

She turned her face in his direction, her eyes still draped with the damp cloth. "Have you ever been married . . . Jacob?"

Larson stared at her for a moment, wondering if he'd imagined the slight inflection she'd given his name. "Yes, I have."

She nodded, her lips absent of the least smile. "May I ask you a question?"

"Anything," he answered, his pulse kicking up a notch. The longer it took her to ask, the more nervous he became. He heard the crack of timbers and looked out the window. The stable still burned, but the fire was contained—the cottage wasn't in danger. Surely someone had seen the smoke by now. Others would soon come.

"Will you tell me about your wife? What she was like? I've talked—" Her voice caught. Larson lifted the cup of water back to her lips, thinking she was thirsty, but she refused. Kathryn drew in a quick breath and briefly pressed her lips together. "I've talked enough in the past months about my husband to you; I'd really like to hear something about your wife."

He decided to take the safe road. "I've enjoyed listening to you talk, Kathryn. I've learned a lot from the things you've told me." He covered their clasped hands with his other one, but Kathryn suddenly drew hers away. The reaction took him by surprise.

"You've learned a lot about me or about my late husband?"

There it was again, that strange trace of . . . hardness in her voice.

"Both," he whispered, while something inside him told him to tread carefully here. It suddenly felt like the tables had been turned and that Kathryn knew something he didn't. It wasn't a comfortable feeling. She frowned, and he shifted uncomfortably, glad he couldn't yet see her eyes. He feared he might crumble beneath their scrutiny.

A distant thought provoked his memory. In reading the Old Testament, he'd learned that God likened himself to a lover, and the people of Israel to His lost love. *Lord, I love this woman with all my heart, and I'm willing to do anything to have her back. But I want to follow your lead. You know all about pursuing something that's lost, don't you, Lord? Would you help me win my wife's heart again?*

He started softly. "My wife was the most beautiful creature I'd ever seen. She was everything I'd always wanted to be, in so many ways. The moment I saw her, I loved her." His throat suddenly felt parched. He took a drink from her cup. "But I didn't love her fully, not in all the ways I should have. I wish I'd taken the time to know who she really was, to know what she wanted before I lost her."

When Kathryn didn't say anything, doubt flooded him. Doubt about his actions since he'd returned to Willow Springs, doubt at how he should proceed now.

"Go on." It wasn't a request as much as a demand.

"I always knew that my wife wanted more from me, but I was afraid. Afraid she wouldn't want me once she saw who I really was. I know it's hard to believe, but I think the first thing she liked about me was the way I looked." He smiled to himself at the irony. "It didn't bother me at the time because I wanted her so badly I would've done anything to make her mine."

With that admission, Larson felt a barrier inside him coming down. To the extent he'd disguised himself from Kathryn before, he now prayed for the strength to lower his mask and let her see him again, let her see the man he'd become.

"Then after we were married, as we got to know each other better, I realized what a special woman she was. She deserved more than I could give her. She deserved a better man, better than I could ever hope to be."

Kathryn removed the cloth from her eyes, blinked a few times, then closed them again and rubbed them gently. "You said you'd lost your wife. Did she leave you in some way, Jacob? Or . . . did you leave her?"

Awareness hit him like a blast of frigid wind. *Oh, God, she knows!* He was sure of it. Heart hammering, Larson kept his head down. His thoughts reeled.

Answering her question unleashed a dam of regret. "I . . . lost my wife many years ago. To my pride, my own selfishness. . . . Trust is something I learned later in life— and something I never learned with her, until it was too late. Something happened to me, and I became a different man. At first I thought I wasn't even a man anymore, but since then I've learned that . . . what a man is on the outside doesn't necessarily reflect who he really is." *God, let her still want me.* "I want to be the man God intended for me to be, and whatever He needs to do to make that happen, I ask Him to do it. He's the Potter; I'm the clay." He studied the palms of his hands, scarred as they were and refashioned by the flame. "I've also learned that God uses fire to refine a man's faith, and sometimes to refine the man."

Kathryn began to cry. Tears slipped down her sooty cheeks. Larson reached over and tentatively touched her hand. *Oh, Kat . . .*

She took his hand and held it against her chest, drawing him closer. Larson could feel the solid beat of her heart, and it gave him strength to let his mask slip ever lower.

"In time, I got a glimpse of who I was becoming on the inside, and I knew God was finally making me into the man He wanted me to be, and the husband my wife always wanted me to be. Only problem was . . . I was certain she wouldn't be able to see past what I had become."

She let out a sob. "But why?"

He didn't understand and leaned closer. "Why what?"

She opened her eyes, blinking as they gradually adjusted to the light, then finally she turned to him. Raw pain filled her eyes. "If your wife was so wonderful to begin with, why did you think she wouldn't be able to see past what the fire had done?"

Larson started to speak but couldn't. He had no answer.

Reaching up, Kathryn slowly traced the jagged lines of his face as though trying to memorize them all over again. Sensations moved through him as her fingers passed over his lips, up his cheek, and then hesitated at his temple.

Larson covered her hand with his and brought it away. This was something *he* needed to do.

"Take them off," she whispered. "Let me see you, please. . . ." All hardness gone, her voice was now beseeching, and bathed in hope.

Slowly, Larson removed the last barrier separating him from his wife.

For a moment Kathryn said nothing, then a stifled cry threaded her lips as she whispered his name. "Everyone said you were dead, but I knew you were alive. I felt it, in here." Taking his scarred hand, she kissed it and laid it over her heart.

With his other hand, Larson cupped her cheek. "Kat . . . I'm sorry. I'm so sorry." His voice would hardly come. "Can you love a man who looks the way I do? Who has so little, again, to offer you?"

She touched his face—gently, reverently—and Larson knew her answer before she even spoke. "How can you not know this already? I desire you more than any man I've ever known. More so now than ever before." She pulled him down beside her on the bed and kissed his mouth, his cheeks, and his eyes before finding his lips again.

Larson cradled her to him. "I've always loved you, Kathryn, but . . . this time I'll love you the way God intended."

She whispered his name against his chest, over and over. Larson couldn't see her face, but he thought he detected a smile in her voice.

"All this time I felt so guilty because I was falling in love with Jacob while my heart still belonged to you. I was so sure—"

Kathryn suddenly let go of his hands and clutched her belly. Her eyes clenched tight, and when Larson heard her groan, fear cut through him.

She curled onto her side, her hands spread across her abdomen. "I think our baby . . . is coming," she panted.

Larson left and returned minutes later with clean cloths, fresh water, a knife, and most of the other things they needed. As he helped Kathryn undress, he heard riders coming up the long road leading to Casaroja but knew their efforts to save the stable would be too little, too late. He only hoped Miss Maudie was on one of the first wagons, and that Donlyn MacGregor wasn't.

Turning back to his wife, he promptly forgot whatever it was he thought he knew about this process. His wife's body was nothing short of a miracle, and the life inside her—the life they had made together—was determinedly making its way into the world.

CHAPTER TWENTY-EIGHT

Kathryn laid a hand to Larson's arm as he cradled their son against his chest. God had answered her prayers beyond anything she could have ever asked for or imagined. The love in her husband's eyes made her breath catch. It always had, always would.

She listened as he told her about the night he'd been ambushed, the stranger at the fire, and then the explosion. He talked of Isaiah and Abby and promised to take her to meet them one day. She had so much to share with him too. So much to tell this man whom she'd loved for so long and with whom she had found love with again, however unexpected.

What a gift God had given her—the chance to meet and choose her husband for a second time.

Kathryn smiled when thinking of the senseless guilt she'd endured over desiring the gentle man named Jacob, only to discover that her desire was finally centered where it always should have been—in the true *heart* of her husband.

"There's something in the pocket of my skirt I want you to see." She touched Larson's arm again, simply because she could. "Would you get it for me, please?"

He laid their child in her arms and picked the skirt up off the floor. He sat on the bedside and felt through the folds until he located the pocket opening. Kathryn's anticipation grew as he reached inside.

He looked over at her, then back at the music box in his palm.

"My husband gave me that for Christmas last year."

He ran his fingers over the top and shook his head. A wry smile tipped the left side of his mouth. "Doesn't look like it cost him very much."

Kathryn laughed softly. "It's the most precious gift I've ever received. And the most costly."

Her pulse quickened as her husband—always her mate, and now her lover and partner in every sense—leaned close. His eyes shone with a tenderness she was certain she'd never seen from Larson before. But she *had* felt that tenderness there when she knew him as Jacob.

He brushed his scarred fingertips across her skin and kissed her mouth with a delicate, slow intensity that aroused a passion too long latent, making her feel cherished and desired. When he finally drew back, Kathryn found it difficult to breathe, and from the look in his eyes, he was pleased by her reaction.

She nodded toward the box in his hand. "When did you buy that for me?"

"I bought it from an old peddler on my way to Denver that day." He recounted the story, then lifted the lid and gave the key on the side a twist. He waited. After several seconds, when no music played, he looked back and smiled. "See, I told you it was cheap."

Loving the sound of laughter from this man God had fashioned just for her, Kathryn laughed along with him. Sorry as she was about the music box having broken, she didn't need to hear the music to make her feel close to him anymore.

Larson gathered the baby from her arms and placed a kiss on his forehead. "Isn't it time you read that?" He pointed to the letter on the nightstand beside her.

Hesitating, Kathryn picked up the envelope and stared at her name on the front. The scrawl didn't even resemble what she remembered of her father's crisp handwriting. Taking a deep breath, she opened it and slid the letter out. The handwriting inside matched that of the front of the envelope, and the length of the letter surprised her. Her father had always prided himself on his economy of words.

My dearest Kathryn,

This letter is long in coming in some ways, and with little time left in others. How often I have wished I could reclaim what I so carelessly neglected. I have been a foolish man most of my life, but my faults as a father far outweigh all my other regrets.

I ask your forgiveness and somehow

know that you will grant it. Not because I am worthy, but because you always were, and no doubt remain, your mother's daughter. I imagine even now that Elizabeth's love and enduring faith live on in your heart. That very thought has sustained me in these last days with a peace that passes understanding.

Childers has vowed to find you and deliver this letter, and I have every confidence that he will succeed. He has been a steadfast friend to me through the years. As he has no doubt told you by now, I have little of earthly wealth left to give you, Kathryn. My next desire, before I die, would be to leave you a legacy of faith. But again, a man cannot bequeath that which he does not possess. My faith in Christ is fragile and new, yet it is the strongest bond I have ever known. If I could leave you anything of lasting worth, I would leave a path for you to follow in His steps. But I trust you are already walking that road.

I pray that the untamed Colorado Territory, which seems an entire world away from Boston, is all that you were dreaming it would be. And I pray you've found a fulfilling life there. Which leads me to another grave failing on my part.

I could tell that day in my study that Larson Jennings was a man of a most determined nature and one not easily swayed. By my standards he was a ruffian and far from the sort of gentleman I had envisioned would form a connection with you, my daughter. I insisted to him that you deserved better, someone of greater wealth and import, who could give you the life you deserved. His answer to me that day, especially in the face of my most severe and personal insult to him, has never left me.

With all solemnity he pledged that he would work to be the man you deserved and that he would give you a name you would be proud to have. I have no doubt, my dearest Kathryn, that Larson has kept true his pledge. Far better than I have done.

I am signing this missive with my own hand and have asked the young man who transcribed it to sign below mine. He has been a strength to me in recent weeks and speaks of heaven in such a way that makes me yearn to see my eternal home. On that count, I do not think I shall have long to wait.

Until I see you again, I will hold you in my heart.

Father

Kathryn brushed her fingers across her father's scrawled signature, then wiped a straggling tear. Reading the name below her father's, her breath caught.

The signature simply read *Gabriel.*

"Our son is finally asleep. Hurry up and come to bed."

Larson looked up to see his wife standing in the bedroom doorway. Soft light from an oil lamp silhouetted her form, and he suddenly found it difficult to swallow. The glow of firelight on her face gave her skin the appearance of fine porcelain. Her freshly brushed hair fell across her shoulders in curtains of gold.

"I'm coming, I promise." Larson's voice lacked the convincing quality he'd hoped for.

Kathryn tossed him a knowing look.

"Don't try to peek at your present. You have to wait till morning."

"I wouldn't dream of peeking." He playfully eyed the tree in the corner of the cabin, loving the smile it drew from her.

"Really, Larson, don't be long. I don't want to spend my wedding night alone."

The desire in her eyes mirrored his own, except that she didn't look the least bit apprehensive. He wished he could say the same about himself. "I was there for the first one, and I'm not about to miss our second."

With a promising look, she turned.

Larson stared at the Bible in his hands and knew he'd never be able to concentrate again after seeing his wife in that gown. Truth be told, he wanted to be in their bedroom with her now, but so much had changed since the last night they had been together.

He fingered the band of gold on his left hand. The ring caught the firelight and reflected it back into his eyes. The wedding had actually been his idea, but Kathryn had loved it from the start. After little William was born, Kathryn had moved in with the Carlsons—at Larson's insistence—and he had taken a room nearby in town, until moving out to the homestead to prepare for Kathryn's return. He'd courted his wife properly this time and marveled every day at the precious son God had made from their love.

He smiled, remembering the wedding that morning. Hannah had played the piano and sung, and Annabelle and Sadie had served as Kathryn's attendants. What an unlikely scene. Gabe had even shown up to give the bride away. It couldn't have been more perfect. But Larson's smile dimmed as he recalled getting into the wagon to make the trip back up the mountain to the cabin. Matthew Taylor had been standing just beyond the churchyard, at the edge of the cemetery. Larson had started to go to him, but the man had turned and walked away. Larson had wronged Matthew by his silence after returning. Larson took full responsibility for that and prayed for the day he could reconcile their friendship.

"Larson," Kathryn called softly from the bedroom.

He stood, laid his Bible on the stone-hewn hearth, and stooped to bank the fire. Warmth radiated around him as he looked at the glowing white-hot embers. He felt only a slight shiver. Each day, his fear was lessening. *Father God, help me to love my wife with a selfless love—the way you love me. To live a life that will see us partnered together, in every way.*

Larson pushed open the door to find Kathryn waiting for him. She was lying on her side, with the covers turned down. Wordless at the sight of her, he stared into her eyes and was amazed, again, that she'd actually chosen him, a second time. He heard their son coo and went to stand by the cradle on her side of their bed. He gazed down at little William.

His son. How could he have ever doubted Kathryn's faithfulness? He'd married a woman who loved God more than she loved him, and for that Larson would be forever grateful.

Kathryn took his hand and pulled him closer to the side of the bed. She began unbuttoning his shirt. Larson touched her face, her hair. He wanted to go further but something stopped him.

How could he want to be with her so strongly and still feel this hesitance? She had yet to see the full extent of his scars, but that wasn't the basis for the anxiety filling him now. This went far deeper.

"Love Kathryn with the same love Christ Jesus showed the church," had been Patrick's counsel as they'd waited for the women to arrive that morning. *"He gave His life to be her Savior, and you ought to love Kathryn as you love your own body."*

Kathryn sat up and rose to her knees to meet his lips. Larson tenderly cradled the back of her neck as he returned her kiss, and she melted against him. A soft noise rose from her throat. She slowly drew back to look at him, then took his hands in hers, a wife's intimate smile curving her mouth.

Bringing her hands to his mouth, he kissed the smooth of her palms. "I love you, Kathryn, and I want to be with you again—you don't know how much."

Before he could say anything else, she kissed him again. "I know," she whispered.

He drew back, shaking his head. "It's not the scars, Kathryn, as difficult as that is. It's that I want to love you like you've always wanted to be loved, the way you deserve."

"Don't you see?" She tilted her head. "You're already loving me that way." She lay back down and lifted his side of the bedcovers.

Larson finished unbuttoning his shirt and

laid it aside, then moved to sit on his side of the bed. He reached over to turn down the lamp.

"Leave it on." Her voice was soft behind him. Her hands moved over his bare back. "Oh, Larson . . ."

Her fragile tone told him that the scars on his back must be hideous. He swallowed hard. "I've . . . I've never looked at my back since the fire. The scars must be horrible. I'm sorry, Kat."

Keenly aware of her pressing close against him from behind, Larson closed his eyes against the mixture of rekindled desire and regret.

Her arms encircled him tighter. "No, beloved. It's not the scars from the fire that I'm looking at." He turned to face her. "It's your scars from before." Her brow lifted with a soft smile. "They're gone."

———

The next morning, after they'd exchanged gifts around the warmth of the hearth, Kathryn set about making breakfast while Larson rocked little William by the fire. Larson noticed his Bible where he'd left it the night before and the music box sitting on top of it. Who would have ever thought that such a simple gift could represent so costly a treasure?

He took down the music box and lifted the lid. Reading the inscription inside, he rewrote it in his heart. *May you be our heart's desire, Lord.*

His thoughts drifted back to the explosion in the shack. The life he'd known had ended that night, and a new one—a better one—had begun. He had no way of knowing whether his life would've taken such a turn without the fire, and even now it was hard to say that he would go back and relive it all again.

But he did know that what he had now—with his wife and son, and with his Lord—he would never trade, for anything.

Harold Kohlman and Donlyn MacGregor had been charged with land fraud and would stand trial in two months. Miss Maudie's face came to Larson's mind, and a wave of compassion swept through him. *God, give that precious woman comfort and peace.* The punishment of Conahan—the ranch hand who'd been hired to kill him—had been swifter than Larson would have preferred, but he left that in God's hands.

With little money and their loan in default, he and Kathryn had filed a late bid for their land but had lost. However, the buyer, desiring to remain nameless, sold Larson a portion of the land back, including the homestead with water rights to Fountain Creek. It was a modest beginning, again, but it was enough.

With little William asleep in his arms, Larson rose and went to stand at the window. A light snow had begun falling during the night, and a shimmer of diamonds sprinkled tree limbs and covered the ground. Kathryn came up behind him and kissed William, then him.

He slipped an arm around her and pulled her close. "Merry Christmas, Kat."

He looked out the window to the spot near the towering blue spruce where he could barely see the tip of the stone marker Kathryn had ordered for his grave months ago. When it finally arrived in late October, Larson had insisted on keeping it and brought it with him when he returned to their homestead, to serve as a constant reminder of his wife's undeserved love, and of life's brevity.

He knew the words carved on the snow-mounded marble stone by heart and vowed, with God's strength and mercy, to live each day of the rest of his life keeping them true.

Just below the dates 1828–1868 was the inscription:

LARSON ROBERT JENNINGS
BELOVED HUSBAND AND FATHER
And desire of my heart

No book is ever written alone, and *Rekindled* is no exception. To the One who rescued me and gives me new life—Jesus, I adore you. To my husband, Joe, for his continual support and encouragement, and for daring me to take a leap of faith that I wouldn't have taken on my own, I love you. To Kelsey and Kurt, our children, for teaching me invaluable lessons about life and love, and for giving me room (and time) to explore "what I want to be when I grow up." I delight in being your mom.

God has blessed me with people who act as encouragers, motivators, and accountability partners. For their support during the writing of *Rekindled*, my heartfelt thanks goes to: Robin Lee Hatcher, for praying God's will for my life and then for encouraging me to follow Him, wherever that may lead. Deborah Raney, for sharing your gift with words while sharpening mine in the process. Deidre Knight, my agent, for sitting on the bench with me at Mount Hermon and showing me that dreams really can come true. Karen Schurrer, for fulfilling this author's idea of the perfect editor. So glad we're partnered together, and here's wishing you endless Biaggi's Potato Croquettes. The wonderful folks at Bethany House—so much goes into seeing a manuscript to final publication, and every step is crucial to its success. Thank you for working so hard on *Rekindled.* Paul Higdon, thanks for the gorgeous final cover! Mr. W. D. Farr, Sr., the pre-eminent expert on Colorado water rights, for the delightful lunch we shared at Potato Brumbaugh's while discussing historical water rights in the Colorado Territory. Special thanks for your offhanded comment, "Some of those gate riders suddenly forgot how to swim." Melinda Shaw, for reading the first 138 pages of the rough draft and then knocking on my door for more! Suzi Buggeln, for showing me what a real hero looks like. Susanne Bjork, for your encouragement, and for bugging me to finish the second book in the series! Kris Hungenberg, for teaching me point of view all those years ago. My fellow writers who read *Rekindled* in varying stages: Kathy Fuller, Beth Goddard, Lisa Harris, Jeanne Leach, Maureen Schmidgall, Jill Smith, and Debbie Vogt. Keep speaking "the truth in love" to me, gals. You make me write deeper and better than I ever could on my own. And to Todd Agnew, for your song entitled *Still Here Waiting*. I listened to it countless times as I wrote, and rewrote, *Rekindled.* Truly, God's love never fails.

———